THE CHILDREN OF HYDESVILLE

by

Jeff C. Stevenson

A HellBound Books Publishing LLC Book
Houston TX

Jeff C. Stevenson

A HellBound Books LLC Publication

Printed in the United States of America

Also by Jeff C. Stevenson

*Fortney Road: Life, Death, and Deception in a
Christian Cult*

THE CHILDREN OF HYDESVILLE is a work of fiction. Where real-life historical figures or events appear, the situations, incidents, and dialogues concerning those persons are for the most part entirely fictional and are not intended to depict actual events. The Fox sisters and their family, however, were very real, as is most—but not all—of what I've included in this story about what occurred in Hydesville in 1848. In many instances, other names, characters, places, and events are products of my imagination, and any resemblance to actual events or places or persons or apparitions, living or dead or otherwise, is entirely coincidental.

Lyrics to "The Hangman, or the Maid Freed From the Gallows" written by [English or European Folk Song] - Traditional.

Reviews for *The Children of Hydesville*

"Rich in character and solid pacing, Jeff C. Stevenson delivers chills and suspense in his erotically charged supernatural thriller, *The Children of Hydesville*."
—Tony Tremblay, author of *The Moore House* and *The Seeds of Nightmares*

"Stevenson brings a modern eye to classic horror in *The Children of Hydesville*. My pulse raced and I wanted to hide beneath the covers but wasn't able to put the book down."
—John C. Foster, author of *Mister White* and *Dead Men*

"Something evil lurks in the village of Hydesville, something far more sinister than the 19-century haunting there which inspired the Spiritualist movement. Master storyteller Jeff C. Stevenson is back with a vengeance. *The Children of Hydesville* is a frightening read."
—Jill Hand, author of the time travel adventures The Blue Horse and Rosina and the Travel Agency

"An unsettling blend of fact and fiction, Hydesville and the Fox family will stay with you long after you close the book."
—Tom Deady, Bram Stoker Award winning author of *Haven* and *Weekend Getaway*

"This book is a special kind of creepy, the kind that crawls into bed with you during your most intimate moments, your most private dreams. I can't help but feel the influence of *The Shining*'s woman in room 237 reaching out from the pages."

—Mark Matthews, author of *Milk-Blood* and *All Smoke Rises*

"Jeff C. Stevenson has done something remarkable with this novel. Using an eerie bit of real Americana as his jumping-off point, he spins a dark yarn that immediately plunges away from the factual and into an uncharted territory of inexplicable, terrifying weirdness. Stevenson mixes history and mystery and a lot of twisted imagination to create a horrific and unforgettable experience for the reader. *The Children of Hydesville* is an intriguing blend of cutting-edge attitude and old-school epic storytelling, and the result is unlike anything you've encountered before. The book does what only the best horror fiction can do. It makes you afraid to keep reading but utterly helpless to stop. Consider yourself warned. Once Jeff C. Stevenson sinks his claws in you, he never lets go."
—Paul F. Olson, 2017 World Fantasy Award Nominee, author of *Whispered Echoes* and *Alexander's Song*

Dedicated to three other powerful women: My sisters Jan Laidlaw and Jill Stevens, and my niece, Kim Buczkowski.

"You'll all be guessing...for the rest of your lives."
—Mina **"Margery" Crandon, renowned trance medium of the 1920s**

"These psychic discoveries by reputable scientists have opened up, literally, a new world."
—**Dr. William Moulton Marston, Duke Parapsychology Laboratory,**
Notes and Comments on Progress in ESP Research, 1941

"Reality is merely an illusion, albeit a very persistent one."
—**Albert Einstein**

"All warfare is based on deception."
—**Sun Tzu, The Art of War**

"Do as I do."
—**Maggie Fox**

"It can see as well as hear."
—**Katie Fox**

"What if you slept? And what if, in your sleep, you dreamed? And what if, in your dream, you went to heaven and there plucked a strange and beautiful flower? And what if, when you awoke, you had the flower in your hand? Ah, what then?"
—**Samuel Taylor Coleridge**

Contents

PROLOGUE:

On the Night of the Disturbance

The cottage caught fire faster than he expected.

He had assumed it would defy him, but he had no trouble lighting the matches—no sudden drafts appeared to extinguish the flames—and the old clothes he had set alight in the second-floor bedrooms had offered no resistance.

"Come down here. We have more to show you."

He glanced at the cellar door. It was a trick; nothing to see down there anymore.

"Do we have to come up there and get you?"

After a moment, a heavy footstep. Then another. Even over the gathering roar of the fire, he could hear the sounds of the girls slowly clumping up the steps. But it was just a distraction; he needed to stay focused.

Smoke from upstairs was now beginning to push its way into the first floor. He could hear the hungry crackle as the teeth of the fire consumed all in its path; he envisioned a lawn mower aflame, the blades greedily chewing up the second floor. He was certain the fire could be seen from outside by now, but there would be no fire trucks to the rescue, no ambulance, no gawking neighbors. No one lived in Hydesville anymore, and even though he stood firmly and solidly on the landing of the Fox house, he wasn't fully persuaded the floorboards—or the town—even existed. Like waking from a dream, too often they had simply evaporated from his mind, from history, from maps, GPS systems…

The noises from the cellar were now a thick and menacing chorus. The children's call to him reverberated through the walls, cut through the flickering snarl of the flames.

"Open up. We have something to show you…"

The basement door handle rattled.

It was like they were on some film loop or were hosting a residual haunting, simply repeating themselves. *I've already heard the joke,* he thought to himself. *I know the punchline.*

"Go away!" he finally shouted, couldn't help himself.

Overhead, a crash followed by a muffled *whoosh*! as the flames found something new to devour. Thick gray clouds were now rapidly billowing down the stairwell like huge tumbleweeds. He was sweating from the stifling heat. The house seemed to be closing in around him. He started coughing. His chest was tight, he began gasping for air. The old property was now an inferno. The kitchen ceiling to his right blasted open as the second story storeroom crashed into it. The tremendous pressure of the fire shattered windows. The place was collapsing around him.

The walls trembled, split…

PART ONE

"It is indeed curious that this movement, which many of us regard as the most important in the history of the world since the Christ episode, has never had a historian from those who were within it..."

—Sir Arthur Conan Doyle, The History of Spiritualism, 1926

I:
The Invitation

Jeff C. Stevenson

CHAPTER 1.

Following one of his spells, Derek David received a letter from the Keilgarden Colony, located about five hours north of Manhattan in the village of Hydesville. He and his wife, Edith, were invited to attend a dinner in appreciation for the series of generous grants the David Foundation had awarded the Colony at its inception in 1948, and continuously throughout the years.

Derek knew very little about the organization other than it was a place for psychically gifted children to be raised and live among their own kind. His great-grandfather, Maxwell David, had bestowed upon the Colony a one million dollar contribution after just one meeting with its founder, the esteemed child psychologist, Dr. Charles Von Keilgarden.

The Colony had always been specific in its intention: Purchase land and establish its facility in the village of Hydesville, New York. Located thirty-five miles east of Rochester, the hamlet was founded by Dr. Henry Hyde in 1815. He built a two-story cottage at 1510 Hydesville Road that he rented out. On December 11, 1847, John and Margaret Fox and their family—including daughters Katie and Maggie—took up residence. Two months later, the ghostly rappings were first heard and Spiritualism, the belief that departed souls can interact with the living, was born.

The money Derek's great-grandfather gifted to the group enabled the organization to not only purchase the Fox cottage—revered as a sacred place to Spiritualists—but also much of the surrounding area which included the Fox Woods.

There was no website for the group and the only online article about the Colony was from a short, archived 1949 profile in *Life* magazine. It revealed that the Colony had been formed under the auspices of Dr. Keilgarden who said it was his desire to form a community for psychically gifted children, those with talents "outside of the norm." His goal was to create a nurturing environment where their extraordinary potential could be fostered and explored without the "restraints and judgments modern society might impose on them." The article went on to state that the "gifts" the children possessed included telepathy, mind communication, clairvoyance, telekinesis, spirit communication, and "several other abilities this reporter won't attempt to explain" the writer of the article had wryly stated.

Regular donations were funneled to the Colony over the decades as part of a trust Maxwell David had set up. Although Derek and his brother, Oswald, made an extremely good living as partners in the David Art Gallery, they always cringed when they saw the monies that were sent to the Colony each year. So, it was a bit of a welcomed surprise when Derek received the invitation from the reclusive, somewhat mysterious facility.

"Why would your great-grandfather want to waste money on this?" Edith had asked, handing the *Life* article printout back to Derek.

"I have no idea. I never knew he had any interest in the occult. But you're game to go, right?"

"Of course! I want to see where millions of your hard-earned money has been going all these years. And I want to visit that creepy old Fox house. How does it feel to know your great-grandfather helped purchase the cottage that is responsible for bringing séances into fashion as well as the use of Ouija boards, the success of the Long Island Medium and all those ghost hunter shows on TV, the Amityville horror, Casper the Friendly Ghost—"

Chuckling, Derek said, "Enough! You married me, it's your legacy, too." He thought it might be nice if they made the trip to Hydesville a starting point for a brief, much needed weeklong vacation. "We've always wanted to visit Canada and go antiquing, so why don't we take a week and do it?"

Edith was thrilled with the idea since Derek rarely took any time off from the gallery.

"Are you sure Ozzie can handle everything?" she had asked.

"Oz can handle anything for a week."

###

Oswald's response was immediate and enthusiastic.

"Yes! You must go, and of course, Manny and I can handle the gallery for a week!"

21

He and Derek were having lunch at the New York Athletic Club following their twice-weekly game of racquetball. "We've always been curious about that money pit that's been sucking on us for decades, so now's your chance to find out what's really going on."

Derek nodded, added, "These people must have had some amazing powers of persuasion because they convinced great-grandpa Maxwell to give them a million dollars to help them get started."

"And back then, a million dollars was a million dollars. That's probably why they are having this dinner, to hit us up for more funds, increase the yearly amount."

Derek said, "Well, if that's the case, they're in for a big no."

Derek hadn't mentioned to Oswald or Edith about the odd, troubling phone conversation he had had with a woman from the Colony when she had returned his call at the gallery.

"Mr. Derek David?" A sharp burst of static white noise interrupted her, immediately subsided. He thought he could hear faint murmuring in the background.

"Yes, this is Derek."

"Hello, Mr. David. I'm Vanya Avery from the Keilgarden Colony, returning your call." There was a slight accent to her voice, a breathless, singsong quality to it. Swedish? Perhaps Asian?

"Oh, yes, yes!" Derek had said, sitting up straight at his desk, almost as if she had actually entered his office. There was something about her voice that drew him like a comforting embrace.

"We are *so* pleased that you and your wife have accepted our invitation."

What was it about her accent? Each word seemed to have a playful lilt to it. He wondered what she looked like.

"Well, thank you. We're...we're more than pleased to accept your invitation," Derek had replied, cringing at his lame response. *Get ahold of yourself!* he thought, as a pleasant flush swept over him. He shifted in his seat, aware of the subtle tingling that had begun at his groin. Why was he getting an erection?

"It can be a little difficult to find the Colony," Vanya continued, "and most GPS units aren't very reliable here. Neither are cell phones, so we usually like to meet guests for lunch at a restaurant, and then you can follow me to the Colony in your car." The white noise crackling returned for a moment, then abruptly faded.

"That sounds...fine," Derek said, now firmly aroused, glad he was seated behind his desk in case anyone walked in. He rubbed his crotch, wondered again what Vanya Avery looked like, couldn't wait to see her in person.

"I can text or email you the directions to the restaurant," she said.

"Email...would be fine," he managed to say. He imagined her hands on the keyboards composing a message to him.

"Great! I'll get that off to you today and we'll see you at the ClearView Restaurant at 1 p.m. We are so looking forward to meeting you and Edith."

He ended the call. Abruptly, something changed in the environment. The surprisingly heightened state of arousal diminished, then departed. He felt a little disappointed; he had not had such an intense hard-on in many, many years.

What was that all about? he wondered.

###

"I am so excited about this trip!" Edith said as Derek guided the Mercedes up I-80 West towards Hydesville. It was just after nine in the morning. "It really will be an adventure, what with the dinner at the mysterious Colony, then antiquing around Canada. And no business phone calls or conference calls, right? Oz is taking care of all of that. Right? Promise?"

Derek nodded. "Promise." Edith continued chatting, Derek smiled, amazed, as always, by his wife's delightful, rhapsodic nature. She would have made a terrific, energetic mother, he thought, then wondered where that had come from. They had decided early on not to have children; as the years had passed, they had both remained content with their decision.

Reading from the email Derek had printed out, Edith said, "We'll merge into that lane."

He had to admit he was as curious about the Keilgarden Colony as she was, but for a different reason. Ever since he had spoken to Vanya Avery, he had developed an unusual fascination for her. For the rest of that day, he had waited impatiently for the ding on his phone alerting him that an email had been received. Each time it wasn't from Vanya, he grew unnaturally frustrated, feeling as if she was intentionally teasing him, edging just out of his reach; a belly dancer who relentlessly gyrated at your table, then moved on, leaving you exasperated and yearning. *What's wrong with you?* he asked himself repeatedly, bothered yet intrigued by his growing obsession with the woman. He had Googled her, but there were no images of her, no social media presence, nothing. That only caused him to fantasize about her more. When the email from her finally did arrive, it contained only the directions to the restaurant (what had he expected?) but he had spent the rest of the day frequently looking at it, rereading it.

While Edith chatted happily, Derek shifted in the car seat, thinking about Vanya.

###

It was quarter to one when Edith read the last of the directions.

"...okay, and a right here. Isn't it beautiful, with all the trees? It's like we're in the middle of a forest! So glad we have a break from the city!"

Glancing about at the thickly wooded area, Derek understood why Vanya had said it was easy to get lost. None of the roads since they had exited the parkway were marked. It seemed that the directions were based on a series of numbered and coded landmarks. Edith kept track, telling him to make a left after they passed the third road on the right, turn left at the split tree, then another right just past the old gasoline sign, and so on.

"...and then a right where the old barrel is. Let's see, is that it? No...there? Yes! Make a right here, then go down this road. It's supposed to lead us right to the ClearView Restaurant."

"'*ClearView*?'" Derek had said good naturedly. "That's a good one. With no road signs and trees lined up next to each other like a fortress wall, there is certainly no *clear view* around here!" He was feeling jovial, a renewed sense of energy after the long, five-hour drive. In just a few short minutes, he was finally going to meet Vanya Avery.

The road curved. Then, in front of them loomed the strangely-out-of-place restaurant. It gave off the unsettling impression that it had only appeared seconds before Derek and Edith had set their eyes upon it. It was a modest brick building that seemed to have been moved from a suburban shopping mall, then placed in the middle of the woods. Neatly landscaped with flowers and shrubs, there were two cleanly marked parking spaces in front of it, one of which was occupied by a brown Toyota. Something about the parking spaces bothered him.

Derek pulled in, killed the motor. The silence was thick when they climbed out of the car, each of them stretching. No parkway traffic could be heard; Derek realized then that he was so turned around from the directions that he had no idea where the thruway was. Although it had been a beautiful morning when they had left Manhattan, he noticed that the sky was now a dead, pale yellow, flat with no illumination, almost hazy. No shadows followed them about; it was as if the sun had lost its full power, could only emit a dim glow.

And so quiet. No wind rustling the trees, no planes droning overhead, no animals racing through the woods rustling the undergrowth, no insects buzzing, no birds scattering across the sky. But it was more than the absence of noise, it was as if sound itself had been swallowed up. *We've lived in the city so long, we've forgotten what it's like to have peace and quiet,* he mused, trying to slough off the unsettling observations.

Edith started toward the restaurant. She turned back to him. "What?"

"Hmm? I didn't say anything."

As Edith spoke, her voice was slurred, the words garbled, as if she was speaking under water.

"What?" he asked. "What are you doing? Why are you talking like that?"

Edith stared at him, tried to speak again. The same muddled result. She put her hand over her mouth. Her composure slid from doubt to confusion. Up until that moment, regardless of the situation, Edith had always managed to maintain an optimistic, practical attitude about things. At just under five feet five, she was a short, stout woman who made up for her limited stature by her boisterous personality and ever-present zeal for whatever was going on about her. Derek thought of her as the classic "dame," firm, no nonsense, steel wrapped in velvet. He had never seen her shaken or uncertain about what was going on about her, she always took control of situations that were unfamiliar to her. To see her so perplexed in front of the ClearView wasn't right.

She hurried back to Derek, whispered, "Something's...wrong here." Her words sounded as if she was speaking in slow motion, the sentence was thick, deep, the tone heavy. She glanced nervously about the area, at the woods, the road that had led them there, the parking lot, the restaurant in front of them. She squinted at the sky. "It's like someone's…watching us. Do you...don't you feel it?" She gripped his arm.

What's wrong with her voice? Derek wondered. *She speaks as if it was a deaf person trying to talk.* "Your voice," he said quietly, "Why are you—"

Edith, her eyes wide with alarm, leaned closer. "I can't understand you—"

"Mr. and Mrs. David? Hello! I'm Vanya Avery. Welcome to the ClearView Restaurant. You're right on time. Please, come in."

CHAPTER 2.

Vanya Avery stood before them on the top step that led into the restaurant. She had not been there an instant—a second—before. Derek was certain of that; at least, he thought so. Edith hadn't seen her because she was speaking to him and her back was to the restaurant. Regardless of how she had gotten there, here she was, he finally saw what she looked like.

Vanya Avery appeared to be in her early 30s with long, waist-length blonde hair. Her narrow face was offset with thick, sensual lips, a wide, strong chin, and a small mole, just above her lip, which added an exotic demeanor to her. Taken as a whole, there was something foreign and distinctive about her; you were almost required to study her, to figure out where she was from. Derek wasn't able to determine her nationality. The shape of her eyes reminded him of women from Greece while her mouth and nose seemed of Italian descent.

She was beautiful, her figure exactly how Derek had hoped it would be. Everything about her was extraordinary. She was lovely.

But it was her peculiarly luminous green eyes that immediately captured and held him. He knew at once by her steady, unyielding gaze that she was not the type of person to ever have anything to hide; it had been her intention for him to see her appear in such a dramatic fashion. *Always one step ahead*, he mused as he smiled at her. *Always in control, never really surprised.*

Edith had released her grasp on Derek's arm, but he could see she was still distressed by whatever had distorted their voices, whatever unseen presence she had thought had been watching them. He supposed it had been Vanya, observing them from inside the restaurant.

"You both look as if you've seen a ghost," Vanya said brightly, stepping easily down the steps toward them. He could understand perfectly what she was saying, the words were not at all garbled or strange sounding. She carried herself with a great deal of confidence, as if there was a joke about to be told and only she knew the punch line. She was gorgeous.

He couldn't look away from her, was immediately, fully aroused. Vanya's eyes flickered down for a moment, noticed the hard tent in his pants. Her smile broadened into—what?— Pleasure? Triumph? He couldn't tell, but it was a private moment between the two of them, over in seconds. He was left feeling he had lost at a game that he wasn't even aware he was playing. She was stunning. He was glad Edith was facing away from him.

"Edith, welcome."

"Hello, Vanya. Pleased to meet you," Edith said, recovering quickly from the awkwardness of the situation, almost back to her old self. Derek was relieved that he could also once again understand what his wife was saying. Whatever strange event had occurred that had distorted their ability to speak, it seemed to have passed.

Vanya put her arm around Edith, escorted her away from Derek. As she brushed passed him, with the briefest of a touch, he climaxed. It surged hot and thick. He gasped quietly. Momentarily shocked and baffled by what had occurred, he leaned against the Mercedes, shaken, wondered *What is happening to me?* He quickly examined himself. His dark blue pants were stained but it wasn't too noticeable due to the color; if he kept his sports jacket on, it would hide some of the evidence. He was glad they were going to sit down to eat since his lap would be hidden.

Still unsettled over what had occurred, he started up the steps after the women. That was when what had troubled him about the parking spaces registered: There were only two of them. Just room for his Mercedes and Vanya's Toyota, as if no one else was ever expected.

The inside of the restaurant was expensively and carefully decorated, almost like a private club. The half dozen tables were covered with white cloths, fresh flowers, crystal vases, fine place settings, all anchored with heavily polished sterling silver. Their footsteps echoed over the dark wooden floors as

Vanya led them to a table that was prepared for them. No other guests were present.

Once they were seated, Derek picked up a fork. It was heavy, a sign that it was expensive. He wondered if the millions of dollars the David Foundation had given to the Colony over the decades had been used to purchase the silverware. He glanced at a painting on the wall next to the table. It was an oil of three unsmiling women from the 19th century. The eldest on the right looked to be in her thirties while the other two were children. All of them wore long, heavy dark gowns with white starched collars. Derek found their intense, scrutinizing expressions distracting; they seemed to pull at his attention while all he wanted to do was engage with Vanya.

"This room is amazing, Vanya," Edith said, her eyes delighted by all she was seeing.

"The Colony owns the ClearView?" Derek asked, turning away from the painting.

Vanya nodded.

"I ask because I thought the Keilgarden Colony was a non-profit organization. I don't remember seeing any business licensing papers for a restaurant in your financial records."

"Oh, you checked up on us, I see," Vanya said, teasing him, her gaze never wavering.

"I tried to," Derek admitted. "But I have to say, it didn't take long since there's virtually nothing available in print or online."

"That one *Life* magazine article is all we could find," Edith added. "Your organization is a bit of a mystery."

"Your great-grandfather had tremendous respect and trust in the work that is done here," Vanya said evenly. "We have lots of people who have given to us over the years, but your family is special. As you know, Maxwell David helped get us established, provided the funds to purchase the Fox cottage and the surrounding land, and that's something we thought was high time to acknowledge and honor."

Derek waited for Vanya to continue, but she simply watched them both. The conversation stalled for a moment. In the stillness, he saw one of the petals in the table's flower display quiver for an instant as if from an invisible breeze.

"Who else is joining us for lunch?" Edith asked as she made a point of looking around at the other prepared tables.

"No one, just you and Derek."

Surprised, Derek said, "What about this evening? I thought this was an appreciation dinner for donors. You have others who have contributed over the years, right?"

Before Vanya could respond, shuffling footsteps on the wooden floor approached. To the left of Derek and Edith, a waiter appeared. Derek watched as the man hesitated near the table. Vanya nodded, giving him the okay to approach.

"Good afternoon," Vanya said warmly to the waiter.

The man only nodded. Derek wondered if he could speak. He must have been in his eighties; what little remaining hair he had was slicked back over his oddly misshapen skull. His bright green eyes were oversized, bulky; Derek thought they resembled swollen fish eyes. When he handed out menus, Derek noticed the arthritic hands were encased in inflamed bumps the size of walnuts.

Sympathetic to the pain that the waiter must be in and not wanting to stare at his deformities, Derek quickly averted his eyes. The man had probably been born that way. Derek thought it was good of the restaurant to employ him, even if business was nonexistent. *Except for us donors*, he reminded himself.

"Would you care for something to drink?" Vanya asked them. They settled on a bottle of white wine. The waiter nodded again, shuffled away. Derek noticed that the man had a hump on his back; his twisted gait suggested that he had a crooked spine.

"That poor man," Edith whispered, leaning toward Vanya. "What happened? Was he in an accident or—?"

"No, he wasn't always that way," Vanya said. "And, he's my father."

"Oh, I'm so sorry," Edith said, embarrassed. She glanced at Derek. He shrugged in support of her gaffe.

Vanya placed her hand lightly on Edith's. "Don't be, there's no need to apologize. Daddy came to the Colony a long time ago, with Dr. Keilgarden. He was involved in some of the earliest experiments, was a true pioneer in psychic research. He was one of Dr. Keilgarden's success stories due to his advanced ability with telekinesis. In the early days of the Colony, a great deal of attention was focused on telepathy and telekinesis, the ability to move objects with your mind. That's what Daddy was so gifted at. However, over the years, the strain of it began to have an effect on him…"

Derek and Edith waited for her to continue. After a moment, Vanya said, "That's really all there is to tell. The experiments were tremendously taxing, as you can imagine, and the stress on the brain and other organs was enormous. But it's all worth it," she finished passionately, obviously proud of her father's contributions. "And that's why we turned the focus to children and young adults; they were able to withstand the stress of the experiments with little to no impact on their bodies. That wasn't the case for those we call the Elders."

Derek noticed how thick, full of body her long hair was. It brushed back and forth over her breasts as she moved her head. He found himself roused again by her presence, was glad he was seated. She was breathtaking.

"Is your mother alive?" Edith asked.

Vanya shook her head. "No, my mother died a long time ago. To be honest, I don't really remember her. As far as I'm concerned, it's always been just Daddy and me."

"You both live at the Colony?" Derek guessed.

"Yes. In fact, I was born there. This area—Hydesville—is the only home I've ever known."

Edith abruptly shifted in her seat as if startled by something. She quickly said, "You know, we really don't know much of anything about the Colony. As we said, there's just that one article. I'd hate to sound foolish or uninformed when we meet the staff and residents later at the dinner..."

Derek noticed that she continued to be distracted by something. She squirmed about in her seat a bit, then glanced at him but he couldn't read her expression. Why was she suddenly so fidgety?

"The Colony has always been at the forefront of paranormal and occult research, but we've always kept a very low profile," Vanya explained. "We've picked up and followed the lead of other well-known pioneers in this field. Psychic abilities such as psychokinesis, or PK as it's known, have been studied very extensively in this country. In the 1930s, J. B. Rhine and his associates at North Carolina's Duke University began their groundbreaking work in parapsychology. Rhine started his experiments in PK and ESP, evaluated them statistically, and then published his findings."

"What were the results?" Edith asked. Derek could see she was still distracted about something.

"Unfortunately, at first his papers were not well received. Psychical researchers and scientists tried to demolish and discredit Rhine's scientific reputation. But they were more or less silenced in 1937 when the president of the American Institute for Mathematical Statistics released an endorsement of Rhine's methods."

"So, Rhine proved there was such a thing as ESP and PK?" Edith said.

Vanya nodded. "Oh yes, he proved that, plus much more. But his records were sealed and the nature of some of his experiments were kept secret."

"Why was that?" Derek asked, intrigued by the information but still bewildered as to why his great-grandfather would ever have gotten involved with such an organization as the Colony, much less donate millions of dollars to their experiments.

"Some people are afraid of learning too much, I suppose," Vanya said dismissively. "That's one reason that the work of the Colony has been so invaluable over the years. We picked up where others left off, expanded and pushed forward their research. There's no place else like it on earth, you know. That's why we've invited you here, why we are so grateful for the support the David Foundation initially made so long ago, and continues to."

"But I still don't really understand. What exactly *is* the Colony?" Edith asked. "What work do you do there? I know it's with gifted children, but—"

"You'll see," Vanya said pleasantly enough, but it was clear she was not going to answer Edith's questions. "Perhaps we should look over the menu now. We need to be on our way soon."

###

Derek found the conversation during lunch maddening in its evasiveness. He was a man who was used to having questions answered immediately and thoroughly. But it was obvious that Vanya was going to politely dodge their specific inquiries about the Colony; she would go only so far and no further.

Edith kept the conversation going, talking about everything but the Colony once she realized Vanya was closed mouth on the subject; Derek listened half-heartedly. He was content to simply look at Vanya, to be in her proximity, to hear her voice. Several times during the meal he found he was drawn again to the odd painting of the three women on the wall. He found their austere gaze troubling, as if the women were looking directly at him.

They finished lunch. Over coffee and fruit, Vanya explained to them what was to happen next. "You'll follow me in your car. The roads are not marked. That's intentional. After the *Life* magazine article, we were flooded with curiosity seekers, it spoiled the temperament and privacy of the Colony. We removed the road signs, we've allowed the surrounding forest to become overgrown, to run wild. The town of Hydesville isn't very large, and the Colony is well hidden in the Fox Woods that surround the village." She smiled at something, said, "Without me, you'd be lost."

Vanya's father entered the room, his footfalls lazy, uncertain against the floor. He hesitated before Vanya, then said, "You have a call." Derek noticed that the old man seemed somewhat in awe of his daughter. Derek watched as Vanya left the room, her hips swaying pleasantly.

Once they were alone, Edith leaned over. "That woman was groping my leg through most of lunch!"

"What?!" Derek almost spat out his coffee in astonishment.

"I'm not kidding! Almost as soon as I sat down, she put her hand on my knee, gave it a little squeeze!"

Edith stared at Derek, waiting for his response. After a moment, they both started chuckling; it took them a moment to compose themselves.

"I could tell you were a little upset and distracted over something," Derek said, "but I had no idea. Are you going to say something or want me to?"

"No, of course not!" Edith said, dabbing her eyes with a Kleenex fished from her purse. "I moved as far away from her as I could. I think I made it clear I wasn't interested, but my God, Derek! I've never had that happen to me before!"

"I suppose we really should get out more," Derek teased, and they both laughed again.

"I can't wait to tell Oz about this!" Edith said.

When Vanya returned, Edith excused herself to use the ladies' room, touching Derek's shoulder as she left. He found it intriguing that Vanya was interested in Edith; she certainly had a healthy libidinous nature about her. Her perfume lingered about the table. It was light and spicy; there was a friendly, familiar and teasing pull to it. Even now as she sat across from him, finishing her coffee, he felt an erotic pull that his body responded to. He felt like a horny teenager in her presence.

God, she is so sexy, he thought.

Vanya glanced up at him, smiled. Almost as if she was reading his mind.

Outside, the weather had changed drastically. It was almost as if it had shifted seasons, from early August to late fall. It had dropped twenty degrees; the sky had paled to flat slate.

"It's so cold!" Edith cried, surprised. She wrapped her arms around herself, shivering.

"Temperatures tend to change drastically around here, so I always keep a sweater in the car," Vanya said. "All set?" She hurried to her Toyota, started the engine, backed out.

"Come on," Derek said. "We'd better hurry." They climbed into the Mercedes.

Edith fumbled with the heater.

"I can't believe how cold it got!" she said. "Look, the thermometer reads 55 degrees out! And it was almost eighty when we left this morning."

Derek was barely listening. Following Vanya was a challenge since she seemed intent on losing them. She was averaging fifty miles an hour and the roads, as promised, were an overgrown mess, as well as being badly paved, littered with broken branches.

There were no curved inclines, so the Mercedes' tires squealed and skidded painfully around each sharp corner.

"What is her *rush*?" Derek said between clenched teeth. He also felt a hollow sense of loss to no longer be near her. *Get a grip,* he chided himself.

Within seconds, he had lost sight of the Toyota. He could only follow the trail of dust her speeding car had left in its wake. The road narrowed. Bulky wild weeds brushed and scratched past the racing Mercedes. He glanced down at the speedometer: sixty miles an hour. Edith sat silent, twisting her hands nervously, trying to calm herself. Derek was a skilled driver, but the cramped road was difficult to maneuver, especially at such a high speed. The landscape rushed madly past the car, blurs of green trees, dark shadows.

Ahead of them, the lane split into a Y formation. Derek went left where a trace of disturbed dust seemed to indicate that the Toyota had been there a moment before. A half mile later, another fork in the road. This time, there was no clue as to which way to go, left or right.

"Well, the Lady or the Tiger?" Derek said, irritated. He so wanted to be with Vanya, but she seemed intent on losing him, leaving him behind. She was enchanting.

"I think…left?" Edith said uncertainly. "It looks to be a little more travelled, don't you think?"

"Maybe," Derek said. "We'll see." He turned the steering wheel left.

CHAPTER 3.

Five minutes later, Derek pulled the car over to the side of the road. "This is crazy," he said. "We've lost her. I have no idea where the hell we are! What was she thinking, to take off like that? It was like she was trying to intentionally lose us! Why would she do that?"

"Honey, relax. Calm down. Don't take it so personally," Edith said, surprised at Derek's reaction.

Trees and overgrown shrubs surrounded them. The road ahead vanished into the gloom of the forest. The sun was shrouded behind a bank of clouds. Glancing around, they were both acutely aware of the desolate location they found themselves in. No cars would be passing by, no one to flag down and ask directions from. He tried the car's GPS but was unable to access it. For several seconds, Edith watched him put in destinations, get no response.

He gave up. "Try your phone GPS."

No connections for either of them. Derek sighed again. "Any bars on your cell?"

Edith shook her head. "What should we do?"

"We can try to find the town of Hydesville and the Colony on our own or get the hell out of here."

"Let's get away from here," Edith said immediately, her voice tight with anxiety.

Derek couldn't help smiling. "And you were so intent on seeing the Colony. And all the adventure-"

"What I've seen of the Colony's residents— Vanya and her father—I don't particularly like. There's something odd about them, and this whole area. Why don't we get back on the parkway, continue north, get up to Canada like we planned, pretend we never ever stopped here? Then we—"

The Mercedes shuddered, died. Derek turned the key. The engine only groaned for moment.

"What is it?" Edith asked anxiously, staring at his hand, still wrapped around the ignition key.

"Don't know."

The third try brought no response, only a sharp click. He got out, opened the hood. He was no mechanic but reasoned that it couldn't be too serious since only a moment before the car had been fine. Perhaps something with the engine would simply look out of place or disconnected. He kept the car well cared for, regularly serviced, so the parts were all clean, the chrome plate coverings free of grime. He tugged at the connections and belts, looked around. Everything appeared to be secure and in place.

He closed the hood. It clanked shut like a rifle being cocked. He glanced around.

It was a bleak, dreary landscape. Hemlock, poplar, birch, ash and cherry trees mingled closely together, their branches rustling and nudging one another even though he didn't feel any breeze. The Catskill Mountains loomed over and around the forest. The strange region was embraced in a powerful hush. He cupped his hands over his nose, exhaled sharply to warm himself. The cold air tingled, stung his face.

"Anything?" Edith asked once he was back in the car.

Derek shook his head, tried his cell phone again. Edith did, too. Neither had a signal. "I doubt if any cars are going to come by," he said. "I suppose we can walk up the road a way, see if we can find the village or a farmhouse or something." He hesitated as a shivering spasm pounced. "Plus, it would get us moving so maybe we wouldn't be so damn cold!"

Once outside, he opened the trunk. Their hands were shaking from the chill as they rummaged through their suitcases. They each pulled on a lightweight jacket, all they had expected to need during a trip in August.

"Lock it up," she said after Derek closed the trunk. "I don't want anyone to steal it." They glanced around the deserted area; she shrugged. "Not that anyone looks to be coming this way…"

They joined hands, started walking. The dirt road was uneven, with rocks and sticks embedded in it, almost like a rough patch of cobblestone. Derek wondered how far any car could have made it without having the shocks destroyed, the underside scratched raw.

"I wasn't expecting this, or I would have worn sensible shoes," Edith said lightly, trying to joke, her tone weak. Their footsteps made a crunching sound, like chewing cereal. It was loud in their heads. Their feet were now trampling over crisp, dead leaves, leaves that couldn't have—shouldn't have—already been dried up and dead in August.

"I'm *so* cold!" Edith cried. Even zipped closed, their summer jackets provided little warmth. He put his arm around her as they walked, kissed her head. She leaned into him for support, protection against the frigid air. It wasn't as if a wind was blowing, it was more like they were being embraced by an icy presence, an unseen escort who insisted on hovering too close to them.

They rounded the curve in the road. Before them was a clearing. At the far end was a gatehouse, which appeared to be some sort of security checkpoint.

"Why would there be—" Edith started to ask.

"I have no idea. Maybe the guard can answer some questions for us, show us the way out of here or has a phone we can use."

Although the small wooden shed was battered by years of abrasive winters, was in need of paint and repairs, it was still in use. Inside, a man sat on a stool, watched them.

"Hello," Derek said, trying to sound as if he was greeting a neighbor during an afternoon stroll. "We seem to be lost. I'm Derek David, this is my wife, Edith."

The man climbed stiffly off the stool, slowly approached the front of the booth.

Edith stiffened next to Derek, squeezed his hand.

The guard was ancient; he looked to be in his nineties, but it wasn't only his age that was startling. Two prominent, engorged veins pulsated down the sides of his face like deformed side burns. His watery olive eyes were greatly enlarged, as if he had been savagely choked at one point and the expression had remained etched on his face. He stared at them as if hypnotized, as amazed at seeing them as they were of encountering him.

When the man didn't respond, Derek continued. "We were following a woman, Vanya Avery, to the Keilgarden Colony? In Hydesville? We're going to a dinner there tonight, but right now…I guess we're lost…"

The guard finally said, "If Vanya brought you this far, you're not lost. Just follow along through here. Look for 1510 Hydesville Road, just before Parker Street. That's the Fox cottage, the first one on the left. Everyone stays there, it's the hospitality house. They're expecting you, they'll settle you in." His voice was thick with age, a heavy baritone that resounded with facts, information, similar to an indifferent tour guide.

"Our car—" Derek started to say.

"Vanya will see to it." Finished with them, the guard backed carefully away, resumed his seat on the stool as if he had never moved. Derek had a sense that the man had simply repeated some lines like an actor; now his scene was over. Feeling dismissed, he and Edith started down the path past the gatehouse.

Once they were out of earshot of the man, Edith asked, "Why is everyone so old around here? I thought this was a place for children?"

"He must be one of the Elders Vanya mention. You can see how those early experiments really must have done a number on them. Their heads are all messed up, like they've been put in some kind of pressure cooker."

"Exactly!" Edith agreed. "Just imagine how the children look! I can't believe that the experiments would have no impact on young kids."

"It's kind of bothersome that Vanya is allowing it to continue. She's clearly in charge," Derek said. He no longer had the lingering desire for her. It was almost like out of sight, out of mind. *But that's good,* he thought. *It's not like me to be so attracted to another woman.*

He said, "Notice how everyone seems to be at her beck and call."

"Especially her father. That was weird, the way he almost bowed to her at times."

"Like he was in awe of her, or in fear of her."

"And didn't he seem terribly *old* to be her father? More like a grandfather."

Overhead, a bolt of lightning cracked thin, white-yellow lines across the sky. They waited, but no sound of thunder chased after it. Storm clouds suddenly began piling up.

"Oh, great," Edith said. "Where did *they* come from?" Then: "This will sound strange, but do you get the feeling that we're being…pushed along, *led* somewhere?"

"Maybe," he said, not admitting that ever since they had left the car, he had felt the need to *get* somewhere, but he had no idea what the destination was. He didn't want to spook Edith.

The wind picked up; they had to almost shout at one another to be heard.

Edith said, "See what I mean? This storm is hurrying us along, just like the guard told us, moving us toward Hydesville. Then we'll have to find shelter in that Fox house. Even though we'd rather get out of here, it's moving us in a different direction."

"Not sure what you mean by 'it,' but honey, we *were* supposed to go to Hydesville and the Colony in the first place, remember?"

"Oh, yes, for the special dinner party in which we're the only guests."

Lightning flashed; in the split second of illumination, Derek stiffened, thought he saw an oddly shaped silhouette, something with three peaks hidden in the trees along the road. Whatever it was, it appeared to be observing them. A disturbing idea was forming but he lost it when heavy drops of rain began pelting down. There was an unnatural, oily heaviness to them; the moisture clung to his face for a moment, a living thing that desired to caress him. It touched his brow, explored the folds and ridges of his features, then it dripped and slid reluctantly off his chin, only to be immediately replaced with the next raindrop, or whatever it was that was dive bombing them from the sky. There was a slow, lazy seduction to it, the way it lingered on his body. He thought of Vanya. She was so sexy.

He would have remained there enjoying the sensation if Edith hadn't pulled him out of his stupor. "Come on! Whatever is going on, 'it' clearly wants us to go to Hydesville, so let's hurry and get there before we're soaked through!"

CHAPTER 4.

Hydesville resembled a ghost town, especially in the deepening twilight. Once Derek and Edith had set foot in the township, the rain had abruptly eased back, becoming a thin mist that soon ceased all together, as did the wind and lightning. It was as if the storm had been reined in once they arrived in the village. The same unnatural silence they had first encountered at the ClearView returned. They entered the desolate town as stealthily as two cats stalking a bird.

There were no cars parked on the main avenue. Each small, dreary home resembled the one next to it. No one had made the slightest effort at landscaping any of the properties: no flowers had been planted to splash color about, no shrubs were in evidence to provide texture to offset the somber tone of the region. The village consisted of a cluster of scattered, tumbledown clapboard and brick houses, a Methodist Episcopal church with a graveyard, a red brick schoolhouse, a general store, a few shops, and a myriad of dead end streets. The secluded hamlet was surround by dense woodlands, high rolling pastures, wide fields.

And a stern, unyielding quiet.

They stopped in front of the first house on the left, the one the guard had mentioned. "1510 Hydesville Road," Edith said. "This is the Fox cottage."

The decrepit, two-story home was not at all inviting; Derek would never have considered it a place of hospitality as the old man had stated. The small framed homestead faced south, was separated from the road by a wood rail fence. Horizontal wood slats framed the property. Two twelve-paned windows faced them on either side of the front door. It was a dirty brown, dreary home that slouched to the right as if fatigued by the history it had been forced to bear. The roof peaked with a circular attic window that appeared like an unblinking eye, glaring balefully down at the street. The entire place seemed to be shrouded in shadows; the windows were so dark, they looked to Derek as if they had been painted black.

If the Fox house had ever been painted, the color had been violently scraped off years earlier by the elements. What remained was filthy gray with a rust residue, the shade of an old scab. Derek and Edith stood in front of the ominous residence as dusk closed in. Edith said, "It's monstrous! Why would they use *this* as a place to welcome visitors? To welcome *us*. What was Vanya thinking?"

Before Derek could respond, the front door opened. An elderly woman called out gruffly, "Your room is all prepared." He and Edith looked at one another, then hurried into the house.

Derek introduced himself and Edith. Up close, the woman appeared to be another Elder, only a few years younger than the guard. Her white hair, done up in a severe bun, was thinning; Derek could see her enlarged, misshapen skull was riddled with what appeared to be tumors, some of which were oozing a yellow-white, jelly-like substance. He was surprised she didn't wear something to cover the repulsive condition, but she seemed unconcerned with her appearance. He discovered why when he looked her full in the face, saw that both her eyes were clouded with cataracts. She was blind.

Obviously familiar with the layout of the small cottage, she quickly settled them in the cramped parlor where a fire with a peculiar, bluish hue was burning. "Fresh linens are laid out on your bed upstairs. The bedroom down here has a ceiling that leaks. We haven't had a chance to fix it yet. There is a stew simmering on the stove, bread warming in the oven," she said, staring past them. "An apple pie is cooling on the table in the kitchen."

"Thank you so much," Edith managed to say, wondering, *How'd she know we were outside if she is blind?*

Once the woman had scurried out of the room, they moved toward the fireplace, stretched out their hands against the indigo-tinged flames. Outside, they heard the wind bustle about, then the rain returned, lashing out against the house as if it was a living thing eager to gain entrance. The front door rattled, the beams groaned against the intensity of the storm.

"No surprise that the weather is bad again. Just like we suspected, it's here to make sure we stay inside," Edith said as they stood in front of the blazing fireplace.

"Don't get paranoid," Derek said.

"Too late."

After a moment, they moved nearer to the fire. Then, closer.

"Strange," Derek murmured.

"It's not giving off enough heat, at least for the size of the fire," Edith said. "It's like a heater that's turned on too low to do any good."

"And the color of the flames. What's with that strange blue tint? Never seen anything like it." Derek added logs, poked at the wood, watched as the purple sparks jumped up in response. The timber cracked, popped dully, apparently disinterested in the violet-colored flames that enfolded it. The warmth didn't increase. "...as if the fire isn't real," he mumbled, puzzled, even as a thought formed then drifted away.

With a disappointed sigh, Edith turned away, looked around the room. The blue, flickering glow revealed little: a bookshelf, some paintings on the wall, a rocking chair, a tattered sofa. A very humble dwelling, not at all welcoming, no effort made to spruce it up. "*This* is the place where spooks had their coming-out party? Derek, I can't believe after all these years and all the money your great-grandfather has given them that they haven't spent a dime on this place."

"I agree. It seems to be untouched. I guess they wanted to keep it this way, sort of a shrine to the Spiritualist movement."

The storm suddenly increased, its volume turned up; the wind and rain smashed into the parlor. The front door opened, then slammed shut.

"Hello?" Derek called out. He and Edith hurried to the window, saw the old woman totter quickly down the front path, disappear into the darkness. The rain pattered down hard against the house. "What the hell?" Derek said, peering into the front yard. "She just ups and leaves?"

"Gracious host," Edith agreed. They watched the rainstorm for a few seconds.

There were no streetlights, so they couldn't see very far but the sounds told them there was a furious battle being waged. Another bolt of lightning. For an instant, Derek again thought he saw something in the darkness, the same three-peaked presence he had seen earlier in the forest.

"I suppose we should eat," Edith said, distracting Derek from his effort to discern shapes in the night.

In the tiny kitchen, a candle flickered on the ancient wood-burning stove. Edith grabbed it, inspected the small area, discovered no outlets. "I suppose this confirms there's no electricity," she said, annoyed. "I really don't understand why they haven't renovated this place."

"Maybe they just want to keep it the way it was back when the Fox family lived here," Derek suggested. "You know, 'experience it as they did.'"

"Is there even an indoor toilet or running water?" Edith asked, continuing her litany of complaints.

"—liked the purity of the place, wanted to keep it like a museum piece, untouched, true to its era and the events that happened here—"

"No, thank you very much, not with the millions your great-grandfather has given them over the years. They should wire this for electricity, remodel the kitchen..."

"Maybe Oswald was right. They really just invited us here to hit us up for some more money, maybe do what you're suggesting, fix up this place," Derek said.

"What have they been doing with all the money coming from the trust?" Edith asked as she stirred the stew, gazing into the large pot. "That ClearView Restaurant was nice enough. They should send that decorator here to fix up the Fox house, make it into a little B and B like the owners of the Lizzie Borden house did."

Derek smiled at Edith's suggestions. They both knew the Colony abhorred publicity, would never want to be considered a tourist destination. He found a knife in the drawer of silverware. He sliced the still-warm bread as Edith set out bowls of stew. An opened bottle of red wine was on the counter, he poured them each a glass. It was the ideal meal choice after the confusing day and the terrible storm outside, the perfect comfort food. He was prepared to forgive much of the disastrous day, put the events behind them with a good, fulfilling meal.

"Ugh," Edith said, pushed away her bowl after a couple spoonful's. "It *looks* good, like the fire looks like it should provide warmth, but there's no flavor to it." She tried the bread, set it aside. "There's nothing that smells as good as fresh baked bread, but did you notice? It has no aroma, tastes like…like baked paste."

Derek tried the wine. Watered down, somewhat flat. But they hadn't eaten anything since their lunch that afternoon at the ClearView, and the bland, tasteless food was at least quieting the hunger in their stomachs.

When the meal was finished, Derek reached for his phone which he always carried in his pocket, realized he had left it in the Mercedes. "Any chance your phone is with you?"

"Oh, no," she said. "We left them in the car, didn't we?"

They sat there in the near darkness. Outside, the wind lashed against the house, the wood paneling creaked as it held against the storm. Edith yawned.

"That's a good idea," Derek said. "Let's put an end to this bizarre day and go to bed." He held the candle in front of them as they stood up.

"This is all so strange, maybe it is a dream," Edith said hopefully, her voice sounding small and lost.

"Wouldn't that be nice," he said, "but I don't think so."

They started up the narrow stairway, their footsteps muffled in the tight space. On the small landing half-way up, attached to the wall was an oval-framed photograph of three girls from the mid-1800s. "I think that's the same painting I saw in the restaurant," Derek said. It was difficult to make out the figures in the dim light. They glanced at it for a moment, then continued up the section of steps that led to the second floor. They walked the short hallway, found a tiny storeroom and two bedrooms, one with twin beds, the other with a connecting washroom but no working plumbing.

"Lovely," Edith said.

Derek put the candle down on a battered chest of drawers in the larger of the two rooms. "This must be the master bedroom," he said dryly.

"Charming," she said. "Furnished in early Goodwill." Then she chuckled, lifted a long linen nightdress off the bed. A matching nightshirt for Derek was laid out next to it. "I guess they *were* expecting us. They've provided pajamas. Welcome to the 1800s!"

Fifteen minutes later, they lay in the darkness, exhausted by the days' events, all questions, no answers. Although the lightning and thunder had departed to disrupt another part of the county, the rain continued to drip heavily on the roof, never increasing or decreasing in its intensity. It was like the steady beat of a far-off drum; it lulled them into a drowsy state.

They fell asleep, neglecting to kiss one another goodnight, something they had done every evening since they were first married.

CHAPTER 5.

Tap. Tap. Tap.
From deep sleep, Edith stirred, reached over to turn on her bedside lamp, discover what the annoying noise was, how to stop it. She fumbled about. The switch wasn't there. It took a moment to realize where she was: The Fox house in Hydesville. All of the uncanny events of the previous day rose up before her, a silent howl. Wearily, she thought, *Derek was right, this isn't some terrible dream.*

She checked on him beside her. The bedsprings squealed as she moved. He was sleeping soundly. She wondered why she awoke in the first place. Listened. After several seconds, she heard a light tapping. Was that what had disturbed her sleep? The persistent sound resembled someone's sharpened fingernail tapping against wood, the type of noise you would make to get someone's attention.

Where was it coming from? She waited. Held her breath. Listened.

It seemed to be originating from the foot of the bed.

She glanced warily through the darkness to the bedpost, hoping she'd see nothing there. She peered into the gloom, her ears straining through the thickening hush.

Tap, tap, tap.

Fully awake and alert, Edith swallowed nervously. Whatever it was, it sounded louder or nearer then when she had first heard it. Maybe it wasn't at the foot of the bed. Perhaps it was at the far wall, near the window?

She tilted her head as if that would help to discern its origin. Maybe it was simply rainwater dripping from the roof onto the porch below? She grabbed hold of that solution. In the seconds of silence that followed, relief settled gently over her. *Yes, that's what it was,* she thought, relieved. She exhaled slowly, glad she hadn't disturbed Derek. With all the strange things that had already gone on, she needed to keep her wits about her, no need to waken him because she thought she heard something. Satisfied, she settled back on the bed, closed her eyes.

All was restful silence. She could feel herself teetering on the edge of sleep, just slipping over.

"Edith?

From downstairs, a male voice had softly called her name.

Her eyes snapped open, she elbowed her way up on the mattress. *I'm hearing things,* she thought frantically. First the tapping, now the voice. Her heart was pounding hard. *I must have dozed off for a moment,* she told herself, *it was just a dream.*

"Edith? Come down here. Now."

The voice was insistent, had quickly lost patience. It seemed louder, too. Closer.

She whimpered, couldn't help herself, put her hand over her mouth like a child, started to tremble. Was she awake? Was this happening?

Tap, tap, tap.

This time, the noise was just over her head, near the ceiling, certainly inside the house, not rain pattering on the roof or porch, not a loose shutter or any other reasonable explanation she was anxiously sifting through. It was somewhere in the bedroom.

I am awake, she assured herself, pinched her arm. *This is really happening. It's not a dream.* She was breathing heavily, almost panting. Her heart was battering hard against her chest. She shook Derek, grabbed hold of him, dug her nails into his arm, certain it would awaken him. He murmured something, slumbered on.

Frustrated with her fear and uncertainty, she sat up straighter in bed, the better to hear. She concentrated on the room, the house, heard nothing. Waited. Strained to hear through the hush that had seemed to fill the space around her. Only the quietness of late night. Gradually, her heartbeat settled down, the blood rushing through her head went from a dull roar to not even noticeable. Finally, sleep began to once again beckon her. She scrunched back down, tried to match Derek's even, sleepy breathing pattern, serenely inhaling and exhaling as he did. Relax, relax, relax...

"Edith?"

Her eyes sprang open, but she didn't change her position, only listened, heard:

"Are you coming down here? Or do I have to come up there to get you?"

The slow squeak downstairs of pressure being put on the first step. Someone was in the house, beginning to softly climb the stairs so as not to disturb them, sneaking up on them. Down at the end of the short hallway, a cold, hollow tone, like a hammer being gently tapped on the floor. Once, twice, three times: *Bang, bang, bang.*

From the bottom of the stairs, another squeal, weight upon a step.

The dull thuds and approaching footfalls continued in even, measured tones. Both were steadily getting nearer to their room. After one muffled series of bangs ended, there would be a few moments of stillness, then the hesitant squeak of someone stealthily ascending the steps.

Panicky thoughts rushed at her: *Had they closed the door when they went to bed? Had Derek locked the door while she was in the washroom? Was there even a lock on the door?*

Another step on the stairs. A gathering silence. Then, a muffled bang on the floor.

Derek continued to slumber next to her. She hissed his name several times, continued to grip his arm, shake him. Her heartbeat had started up its terrified drubbing again, the blood in her head was like frantic river rapids. *Do I scream now?* she wondered. *If that's the only way to wake Derek and end this, is that what I do?*

Everything stopped for the moment.

Somehow, she knew that whatever was happening, it wasn't over yet. The quiet was coiled, tense. It wasn't the silence of an end to something, it was the beat taken before the next part began, just a pause before the show goes into overdrive.

Out of the noiseless vacuum, she heard something new, a scratching, a rustling noise, the amplified sound of calloused fingertips rubbing against one another. But it wasn't coming from the bottom of the stairs or at the end of the hallway where the other sounds were heard; it seemed to be coming from the other bedroom.

Had someone reached the second floor?

Desperately, she shook Derek again, but he was unresponsive, lost to sleep.

The odd noise began again, the brittle rustle like calloused old flesh rubbing together. *Old* reminded her of Vanya's elderly father, the ancient guard at the gate, the aged blind woman who had prepared the house for them. The Elders. Were one of them in the house, causing all the sounds, attempting to terrify her? The clamor of the strange thuds and the creeping footsteps and the tap, tap, tap and the voice all filled her mind like the buzz of a gathering swarm, and then, at their crescendo, they all abruptly ceased, slipping away as easily as she would slink off her nightdress.

After the quiet had continued for several seconds, as if it had never been disturbed, she was able to wonder, again, if it had all been in her head. Nervous, apprehensive that it would begin again but sensing it really *was* over this time, Edith kept watch over the room. Keyed up, anxious for any sound, she continued to grip her husband's arm as her eyes darted about the darkness. Gradually, her breathing and heart rates calmed. By the faint moonlight, she tried to determine if the bedroom door was open or not. She couldn't tell, was now too exhausted, too frightened to get out of bed to check.

Still uncertain over what had occurred, she exhaled, swallowed, her throat tight. She would have loved a glass of water, the chance to pee, but she was not leaving the bed.

Within minutes, she joined Derek in a deep, dreamless sleep.

CHAPTER 6.

Derek woke first, immediately knew where he was: The old Fox house in Hydesville. *So, everything that had happened had been real, it was no dream,* was his first thought. *Shit.*

Next to him, Edith was sleeping peacefully. He had to hand it to her: She had held up well with what were the strangest experiences of their lives. He was grateful they had both had an undisturbed night of rest since they would need to be energized and alert for the day ahead. *Today, we will get out of here,* he silently promised himself. *We won't spend another night in this house, in this village.* He had a fleeting image of the property engulfed in flames and a sudden, bad taste in his mouth. *Where had that come from?* he wondered, wishing he had a toothbrush.

Edith stirred, murmured something. He reached over, smoothed the matted hair from her face. "Wake up."

"I won't go downstairs," she mumbled, still half asleep.

"What?"

She shook her head like an adamant child. "No! I won't!"

"Edith, honey, wake up." Derek touched her shoulder gently, wanting to take her away from whatever bad dream was haunting her. She opened her eyes, focused on him, sighed. "Oh, so this is real. We are still here."

"I thought the same thing myself, but the good news is, we're going to get out of here today. The sooner you get up, the faster we can leave."

Edith climbed eagerly out of the bed. "And just how are you planning to get us out of here?"

Derek was staring out the bedroom window. "We'll drive."

"If we can find the car," she said, fluffing her matted hair, "and if it starts up."

"It's in front of the house."

Edith hurried over, stood next to him.

"How—"

"No idea," Derek said at the same time. "Picking up on your theory of some 'thing' moving us about, maybe the whole point was to get us to spend the night here in the Fox cottage? And now that we have, we can leave."

After they had dressed, collected their few belongings, they hurried downstairs, were surprised to see that the kitchen table was set for two. The stove had a small, crackling fire with flickering blue flames. They both stared at the oddity for a few seconds.

"Let's get out of here," Edith said, pulling at Derek. "That fire just isn't right."

A pot of hot coffee was prepared for them, Edith found several bagels wrapped in cloth sitting near the stove, keeping them warm. On the table was a ceramic container of honey, an assortment of jams, a slab of butter.

Derek said, "Looks like we had a busy early morning visitor. I *am* hungry, aren't you?"

"Then hurry, let's eat and run," Edith said nervously, recalling the nightmare she had had, the sounds and voice asking her to come downstairs. But seeing the prepared breakfast, she wondered: What if it hadn't been a dream; had someone—or several people?—actually been *in* the house all night, hiding from them while they slept, then leaving the meal laid out for them? Who'd do that and why? She remembered that at some point during the events, she had had the wild notion that if it *was* real, maybe they were ghosts or spirits she was encountering— after all, it *was* the Fox cottage they were in—but she found it even more terrifying that actual people may have been with them, sneaking around.

She set aside all her crazy musings, sniffed the coffee but there was no rich aroma. She broke open one of the warm bagels. No pleasant scent escaped. It was as if everything was a prop, just staging for a show. They ate quickly, knowing the food was providing no nutrition, only quieting their hunger.

Minutes later, when Edith stood to refill their cups for the last time as they prepared to leave, she saw an old book next to the coffee pot. "This wasn't here a minute ago." She thumbed through it. The yellowed, dried pages were covered with neatly composed handwriting. "It's the diary of Margaret Fox."

"Mother of the Fox sisters?"

Edith nodded, started to read to herself, stopped. Derek watched his wife's face light up with excitement as her eyes darted across the pages.

"What is it?"

"Whoa, listen to this. This is *it!* It's dated March 31, 1848."

On the night of the first disturbance we all got up, lighted a candle. The flames burned blue and yellow, an oddity we noticed yet had no explanation for. We searched the entire house, the noises continuing during the time, and being heard near the same place. Sometimes we heard a mere knocking; at other times, loud bangings and sometimes it sounded as if heavy pieces of furniture were being thrown about.

The children, who slept in the other bedroom, heard the rapping, and tried to make similar sounds by snapping their fingers. Maggie said, "Do as I do," and then she clapped her hands twice. The sound instantly followed her with the same number of raps. Then she said, in sport I believe, "Now, do just as I do. Count one, two, three, four," and she clapped one hand against the other at the same time; and the raps came as before.

Katie then held up two fingers, didn't say a word. After a moment, the spirit rapped twice. Shocked, Katie said, "It can see as well as hear."

My husband and I have heard footsteps on the second floor when we have all been together on the first, and at other times, footfalls walking up and down the stairs. Sometimes voices call out from empty rooms.

The girls now sleep with us; they say their room is too noisy to sleep in. We keep their door closed and at times I hear movement in there, yet to this time have been hesitant to open the door. We have no other place to live and if the presence must have its own place to inhabit, I willingly give it that one room.

If only it will leave us alone.

Edith closed the book. "I have to tell you about what happened to me last night."

"Please don't tell me you heard rappings and bangings and voices."

Edith nodded weakly. "I thought it was just a bad dream, but after reading this..." When she finished telling him what had occurred, Derek asked, "Why didn't you wake me?"

"I tried but wasn't able." She shivered, glanced around warily. "It's weird to think this is the very house Maggie and Katie Fox heard the rappings that started the whole Spiritualist movement."

"And thanks to funding from my great-grandpa, the Colony had the money to purchase the Fox Woods along with this luxurious, palatial property, which was featured last month in *House Beautiful*," Derek said, arms spread out as if he was presenting a valuable asset. Edith wasn't responding to his jokey comments. "Hey, it was just a horrible nightmare, okay?"

She shook her heard. "No, it really happened, Derek. It was the same sounds the Fox family heard. It was creepy, and someone was calling *my* name."

"You're saying this place is haunted, just like they did back whenever that was written."

"1848. I'm saying whatever happened last night wasn't a dream. Maybe it was ghosts...or something. I don't know what you call it. The voice, that was the most upsetting part. It said my name...." She shuddered. "Please, let's just leave."

From upstairs, a loud thud startled them. It was immediately followed by the scraping sound of a heavy piece of furniture being dragged violently back and forth.

Edith looked up, whispered, "It *wants* us to go upstairs, to see what is going on."

A bed or chair scrapping across the wooden floor grew louder, more aggressive.

"That's not going to happen," Derek said as he started toward the front door, pulling her quickly along behind him.

A gruff voice from behind the cellar door, muffled but urgent, called out clearly:

"Edith? Come down here. I have something for you."

Startled, Edith turned away from the front door. "You heard that, right?"

Derek nodded, put his finger to his lips, wanted to listen. He was blocking the front door, his hand tight on the handle but he was frozen in place.

Terrified, desperate to get out of the house, Edith struggled against him. "Derek!" she yelled, wanting him out of the way, pushing him. He stumbled to the side. He seemed to be in a stupor, half-asleep on his feet. She twisted the doorknob. Upstairs, something was banging against the wall with such force that the stair bannister quivered.

Who was calling for Edith? Derek wondered. He could hear a gentle humming, a mother calming a baby. *Why did it call for her and not me? Why had Edith resisted going down into the basement? I would have. If it would only invite me to the cellar, I would accept the invitation.*

"Derek! Help me!"

He felt a vile surge of irritation as he watched Edith laboring to open the front door. *Why does she want to leave? We just got here.*

"Derek, for God's sake, what's wrong with you?" Then she hesitated, looked closer at him. After a few seconds, her voice changed, she forced her tone to become softer, gentler. Concern replaced the panic. "Honey?"

Her familiar voice finally broke through the soothing hum, stopped it. He blinked, surprised to see Edith right in his face, staring at him. He knew immediately what had happened. He had blanked out for a moment, like he always did when he had one of his spells.

Since he was eight years old, Derek had had what the doctors had simply come to call spells or "time lapses" in which he would blank for several moments, yet his eyes would remain open, he would not lose consciousness. It was similar to a fugue state a person with epilepsy would experience.

To those around him, Derek would appear to drop off into his own world, his eyes would take on an unblinking, glassy appearance as if he was staring at some sight so incredible that it was impossible to look away. According to those who were with him when the events happened, the spells usually only lasted ten or fifteen seconds; Derek would come out of them abruptly, blinking quickly, fully conscious, as if he was waking from a deep sleep. When he was in the spell state, he had no recollection of what was going on around him even though his eyes remained opened. And when he came out of it, he had no remembrance of what the experience was like.

"It's just a blank spot," he'd tried to explain to the doctors, his parents, Edith, and friends over the years. "It's like when you fall asleep and then wake up; it seems that an instant after you close your eyes, it's morning, time to get up. No memory in between. Just a blank spot..."

Neurologists had ruled out epilepsy and other common brain disorders. CAT scans had not revealed abnormalities in any sections of the brain; the temporal lobes, where memory and conscious thought originate from, had tested normally.

The spells were just a blank spot.

###

Edith was pulling at him, her nails digging into his arm.

"Derek? Derek, are you okay?" Her tone was calm, but her eyes were wide, terrified. He looked at her, recognized her, heard her, felt her touching him. He was vaguely aware of some unpleasant thoughts that had crossed his mind about her...but now he was back from wherever he had gone.

"You're okay?" she asked, holding his face between her hands, looking closely at him. He nodded, drew her close. "You were just standing there, staring off into space," Edith murmured into his shoulder. "I realized you had fallen into a spell. I was so scared..." They released one another. The sounds upstairs had stopped. The voice had not spoken again. Edith reached for the doorknob. This time, the handle turned.

Vanya Avery was standing on the porch, her arm upraised, preparing to knock.

"Oh, hello! Good morning," she said brightly. "I wasn't certain if you'd be up yet." Derek and Edith stared at her for a moment, uncertain how to respond. She smiled at Derek, her eyes gently luring him. His pants tightened, he felt as if she had reached down and begun to stroke him. She was beautiful. When he blinked, the sensation subsided.

"You both sleep well?" Vanya continued pleasantly.

"What's going on?" Edith demanded

"Going on? I don't follow..."

Derek broke in. "Why did you drive so fast, lose us on the road? We were *lost*, Vanya, lucky to find our way here last night in that storm!" She was striking.

"You never even bothered to come look for us," Edith added.

"Because you were never lost," Vanya said easily. "This is the Fox cottage and it's exactly where you should be." She studied Edith for a moment, then reached out, touched her cheek with the back of her hand, stroking the skin. Fascinated by the gesture, Derek watched his wife tremble under Vanya's unexpected caress, but she didn't resist, didn't step away. There was a familiarity about the exchange, as if they had known one another for a long, long time.

Edith swallowed, composed herself, turned from Vanya. "Let's get out of here," she said weakly to Derek, almost pleading.

He heard his wife but couldn't help staying fixed on Vanya. She returned his gaze, her deep green eyes dragging him under so that his only desire was to leave his wife there on the porch, enter the house with Vanya. Surely there was a comfortable place in the cellar set aside for them? Once they were alone, he would stroke her hair, her face, explore the curve of her neck, her breasts, bury his face between her legs, pleasure her—

Derek felt the pressure of Edith squeezing his hand. He cringed, the licentious images vanished. Edith led him quickly past Vanya. Once they were inside the Mercedes, he locked the doors, fished the keys out of his pocket with trembling hands. He was ashamed of the thoughts he kept having about Vanya. He had never been unfaithful to Edith, he loved her, would never, ever consider being with another woman, rarely fantasized about them, but ever since he had first encountered Vanya Avery, he couldn't seem to get her out of his mind.

He prayed the Mercedes would start, was relieved when the engine immediately roared to life. Then, a feeling fluttered about his shoulders, across the back of his neck. He was being watched, was certain of it, knew he *had* to turn around, to see whatever it was that was looking at him.

"Derek?" Edith said. "What are you waiting for? Let's go!"

He put his hand up to quiet her for a moment. Then he turned around in his seat.

Two young, despondent girls stood on the porch. Their eyes had a strange, luminous quality, almost hypnotic in its bleak intensity. They were identically outfitted in clothes from the 19th century, adorned in long black dresses with white starched collars sternly surrounding their necks. Each child had her raven hair parted down the middle, tied back in a severe bun. Their hands were clasped tightly in front of them, fingers intertwined, as if they were praying or begging for help, imploring someone to meet a need. Even from the distance of the car, Derek detected a pleading intensity from the two of them, a desperation that was inching its way toward him and Edith. The girls weren't just watching him, they were beseeching him for something.

"Do you…see them?" he asked Edith. It was two of the three figures he'd seen in the painting at the ClearView Restaurant.

From some far-off place, he heard his wife asking him what was wrong, what was he looking at?

Who are these forlorn children who are so anxious for my assistance? he asked himself, wondering what they wanted, how he could help.

"Derek!" Edith cried, her voice blasting at him, shaking his arm.

Startled, he blinked. The children vanished. The porch was empty.

"Are you okay?"

He nodded, gunned the engine, the Mercedes raced down the road. Derek grimaced as the car rocked and rolled over the potholes, wondering how bad the damage would be, not willing to slow down. Soon they approached what appeared to be a gatehouse. Derek glanced inside as they sped pass. It was empty; only a stool occupied the small shed. A thought tried to form—something about an Elder— but whoosh! it vanished. Words came out anyway. Derek asked, "Wonder where that old fellow went?" *What had he meant by that?*

"Hmmm? What old fellow? And slow down!" Edith said. "What's the rush?"

Derek tapped the brakes; why *was* he in such a hurry?

"Have you decided which pictures you like best?" he asked. They would sort through the digital images she had taken from their trip, he'd indicate some of his favorites, but she always had final say. It was photographer's choice. She'd have them enlarged and framed to decorate their apartment.

But even as he asked the question and she turned to look at him curiously, he realized he couldn't remember her taking any pictures. He couldn't land on a thought or conjure up what they had done the previous week, what the hotel room looked like, where they had eaten or where they had gone during the day. His mind had turned shadowy, slippery.

"What?" Edith asked. "What did you say?"

Derek cast about but wasn't able to get a hook in anything. It was like he couldn't quite see what he was thinking about. It was the strangest feeling, like déjà vu but without the wonder, only the unsettling murkiness. Absolutely nothing came to mind about where they had spent the past few days. He recalled their preparation for the trip but had no idea of the destination or purpose.

"Nothing," he answered, tried to give her a reassuring smile. She nodded, glanced out the window.

He turned the Mercedes onto I-90 East. *It's a blank space,* he thought, *but never like this. I've never just forgotten days of my life.* He had to ask Edith where they had been, what they had been doing for the past week. His heart was knocking about nervously, his hands were perspiring as he gripped the leather steering wheel.

They continued to speed down the interstate. He kept hoping the missing days would reappear, but they remained out of reach. What if he was sick, a brain tumor or something? Minutes clicked by. Nothing. Edith had fallen silent, watched the other cars. He cleared his throat. "Honey, it's the craziest thing. I…can't seem to remember how we spent the past few days. What we did on this trip, how long we've been gone. I know how to get us home, where we live, our life together, the *past*, but I don't know…I don't remember anything about what happened yesterday or the day before…"

He glanced over. She was crying. "Me neither. I can't remember *anything*."

Derek felt mildly relieved. It didn't make any sense, this sudden onset of amnesia, like a blinding light they couldn't see through or past, but he was grateful he wasn't alone, it wasn't just him.

Edith said, "All I can recall is driving north on the parkway and…and now we're driving home. There's…*nothing* in between. Derek. Nothing. What happened to us?"

"I don't know." He realized he was scared once he heard how frightened his wife sounded. "I don't know."

He looked over. She was hugging herself, was trembling. "Why'd we forget the last few days of our lives?"

CHAPTER 7.

Still anxious and confused over the memory lapse they had experienced, Derek and Edith arrived home exhausted. The rest of their ride had done nothing to help restore their recollections; the absence of memories, a white hole in a white wall, was still firmly lodged in place. Any attempt to recall an event from the previous week was rejected.

They settled in the living room to relax; Edith flipped through *People* and *Architectural Digest* while Derek sorted through the mail. His phone rang. "It's Oswald."

"Oh, let me talk to him really quick," Edith said, grabbing the iPhone. "Hey, Ozzie! How are you doing, sweetie? Oh, we had a great time, very relaxing, a lot of fun." She glanced at Derek, shrugged. What else was she supposed to say? We have no idea how we spent the past few days? After a few moments, she said, "Oh, really?" She whispered to Derek, "He's met someone!"

Derek watched with a growing sense that something wasn't quite right with the phone conversation. Edith didn't speak, her face expressionless. From what Derek could see, it didn't appear to be bad news. However, whatever Oswald was telling Edith was certainly causing her to remain silent, a rare state for her since she and his brother were very close, could almost finish one another's sentences. Edith looked at Derek, raised her eyebrows, smiled uncertainly, nodded several times, finally said, "Yes, I do understand, you're absolutely right: falling in love does amazing things to people, but you have to understand, Ozzie, that this is really a lot to take in."

Edith asked, "What do your friends say?" Derek's curiosity was rising. More nodding from his wife. "Well, it's a lot to digest but as long as you're happy, that's what's important. I'll put Derek on, he's desperate to hear what we've been talking about." She handed the phone to Derek. "You'd better sit down. Oswald has news."

"Oz? What's going on?"

"Love! I'm in love!"

Oswald's ecstasy was surprising to hear. He was usually very quiet about any relationship he was involved in, few lasted longer than a season. Derek had met a few of his brother's boyfriends over the years, but he had never known Oswald to be so forthright in declaring his affection for someone, let alone using the L word.

"Who is—"

"It's a woman."

Derek glanced at Edith who was watching, waiting for his reaction. She shrugged.

"I know! I know! It sounds crazy. Even to me. But once I met Vanya, everything changed!"

"Who's Vanya?" The name meant nothing to Derek.

"Vanya Avery."

Edith was smiling now as Derek looked to her for help. She sipped her drink, mimed for Derek to do the same. He finished his off in one gulp as he listened to his brother.

"She came into the gallery last week. We hit it off immediately. She had brought in a turn-of-the-century portrait she wanted appraised. We just got to talking and talking and talking and the next thing you know, I was having lunch with her, then dinner that night and the next thing you know…"

Oswald continued to pour out a rush of words. Derek listened, fascinated yet bewildered by his brother's passionate desire for this woman. Whoever Vanya Avery was, she had turned Oswald's life around 180 degrees, in more ways than one. He put the phone on speaker so Edith could listen to the details, share in Oswald's joy. After ten minutes, he finally managed to interrupt the conversation. "You're going to give Edith and me an ear ache and yourself a sore throat if you don't shut up for a minute. When can we meet this extraordinary woman?" He asked Edith if they were free for dinner the following evening, she said yes, he suggested the idea to Oswald.

"Perfect! Okay if we come over there? A nice, home cooked meal would be terrific after all of our meals out."

"That would be fine," Edith spoke up. "Why don't you come over around 7:30 and we'll have drinks on the terrace."

"All right, all right," Derek interrupted, "now that that is settled, can we talk a little about the gallery?"

"Of course," Oswald said through the speaker. "But first tell me about your dinner at the Keilgarden Colony. Your other half just glossed over it."

Derek heard the question, but his mind was a blank. Before he could think about what he was going to say, he blurted out, "The dinner never happened. Seems there was some sort of mix up, they canceled on us." He had no idea what he was saying, the words came out as if he were speaking a foreign language, but it seemed to answer his brother's questions. Edith's expression didn't change.

"Too bad," Oswald said dismissively. "Okay, back to business then."

###

It wasn't until they were in bed with the lights out, drifting toward sleep, that Derek brought up their amnesia again. "I take some comfort that at least this memory lapse or blockage has happened to both of us."

"Why do you say that?"

"Because if it only happened to me, it would be easy to conclude that I had just had a particularly bad spell. Or that I had brain tumor…or something worse."

"Think we should see the doctor?" she asked. "That's what I keep asking myself."

"Can't see why. I mean, we both feel fine, right? I guess I'm figuring that since it's happened to both of us, we can't *both* be sick or crazy, can we?"

Edith didn't respond. Derek said again, "I said we can't *both* be crazy, can we?"

"I'm thinking, I'm thinking," she said before she started to laugh. They kissed good night. Within minutes they fell asleep, nestled in one another's arms.

"Derek!"

From the depths of sleep, he heard her, couldn't muster the strength to respond.

"Derek! Wake *up*!"

Now he was being shaken, had no choice but to leave the land of nod; he surfaced from slumber. When he opened his eyes, the room was shadowy, but he saw Edith's face was right there; it was tense, her eyes wide with uncertainty.

"What?" he asked, elbowing up off the bed.

"We're back," she said, her voice catching on itself, breaking into a sob.

He blinked, rubbed his eyes, finally woke up.

They were not in their Park Avenue apartment. Even in the dim, pre-dawn light, he was able to identify their location with terrifying clarity: They were back in the Fox cottage in Hydesville. They held each other, both staring out the small, dirty window, watching as thin wisps of clouds drifted by the moon.

He asked, "What's the last thing you remember?"

"Going to sleep at home, in our own bed."

"Same here." Then, almost to himself, he said, "Was everything that happened with Ozzie something I dreamed—"

"—him falling in love with Vanya Avery?" Edith asked immediately.

Derek nodded. "You had the same dream."

"God, I wish *this* was a dream," she said, glancing around.

Tap, tap, tap.

They both stiffened. Edith grabbed his arm, squeezed. He winced. "That's the noise I heard when we were last here," she whispered.

From the foot of the bed: *Tap, tap, tap.*

The old bedsprings rocked and squeaked as they crept to that spot. Then, as if it was teasing them, trying to disorient them, the rapping bounced from the foot of the bed to behind them, echoing back and forth. After several seconds, there was a break in the racket, a hesitation. During that silent gap, the bedroom door shut, the ancient latch clanking into place.

A flurry of icy, wickedly cold air filled the room as if hundreds of frigid butterflies were desperately seeking massive amounts of flower nectar. By the faint moonlight that streamed into the window, Derek could see his breath burst forth in wild, white gusts. He pulled the blankets around them as the temperature in the bedroom bottomed out. Something about the experience registered with him. *Ghosts,* he thought. *Isn't this the cliché movie-version of how spirits manifest, the room temperature drops? Always thought that was made up nonsense.*

Edith shivered, Derek held her, the hair on the back of his neck prickling about as if an insect was stroking him. At the sound of sharp knocks from the ceiling, knuckles on a hollow wood plank, Edith gasped. It seemed to be directly overhead. Derek stared at the spot on the ceiling, speculating that someone was probably in the attic above them, pounding a stick down on the floor, causing the noise, trying to frighten them. *This is just a reenactment of what Edith read in that Margaret Fox diary*, he thought. He was just getting ready to tell her it was a hoax when, from downstairs, a garbled voice called out, sounding as if it was speaking underwater.

"Edith...?"

Even with the bedroom door closed, the sound carried clearly into the room. A male voice, commanding, insistent, not to be ignored.

Edith stiffened next to Derek, hugged him tighter, whimpered into his chest.

"Edith? Come down here. I have something to show you..."

It's like we're encased in ice, Derek thought wildly, trying to determine where the cold air was coming from. *Spooks?* He didn't want to accept the idea, didn't believe in ghosts. The chill had arrived out of nowhere; the window and door were closed but it seemed to be getting worse, like it was being pumped into the room from some hidden air duct. His feet and hands ached; the frozen air burned his skin like frostbite.

They must have refurbished this house with some kind of massive forced air conditioning unit to achieve this effect, he reasoned. *But why would they want to try to scare one of their most generous benefactors?*

Above them, the rapping continued its steady, uncertain yet ongoing pace, while an occasional *tap, tap, tap* could still be heard from either end of the bed.

From downstairs:

"Edith?"

"Maybe you should go," Derek heard himself say, immediately appalled at what he said, wished he could take the words back. He had no intention of releasing Edith to whatever was calling her. Why would he say such a thing? He tried to correct himself, but found he was unable to form a sentence. Edith clung tighter to him, whimpering, shocked at his suggestion. He hissed in pain from the pressure of her frantic embrace.

"Edith? Am I going to have to come up there to get you?"

"You'd better go," Derek said. He needed some relief from her clinging to him. He grunted as he started to untangle himself from her. Like a drowning woman, she locked herself around him. He pushed her away as if he was shedding clothes; she refastened herself around his waist, crying and protesting.

"Edith?"

Derek pushed her shoulders down, away from him.

Rap...rap...rap...

She grasped his legs, whimpering.

"You really have to see this..."

Tap, tap, tap...

"Edith?"

She was now covered over by the blankets, her arms wrapped around his legs.

Tap, tap, tap...

They were both panting from the exertion, he from pushing her away, she from clinging to him. All the while, Derek's mind was fuzzy, blotchy with musing on how their unseen tormentors were manifesting the effects, knowing it wasn't really supernatural manifestations, couldn't be, he didn't believe in that nonsense.

Rap...rap...rap...

"Edith..."

Then, the pounding, the voice ceased, as if a switch had been turned off. The room temperature returned to normal; he could feel the icy cold exit the space as completely as it had entered. Derek relaxed. Edith still clung to him, but she loosened her grip. Her hands began to move lightly, slowly, up and down his legs. She began stroking him; immediately, she summoned an erection. Her breasts covered him, the fullness of their weight in proximity to him increased his excitement. She repositioned herself, slipped her mouth around him, began sucking greedily. He moaned in pleasure but was also taken aback that this was what she chose to do after the bizarre experience they had just been through.

Her head bobbed up and down under the blanket while her fingers found his nipples, twisted and flicked them just as he liked. He lost all track of time and himself as the pleasurable sensations washed over him. She abruptly repositioned herself, moved her hips and buttocks about beneath the blanket. A fierce desire to fuck her rose up. He acted on it immediately, grabbed her head and with an aggressive force of strength he had never before exhibited with her, managed to wrest her over onto her back. He mounted her, she swung her legs around him, pulled him in deeper. He groaned as he thrust, heard her cry out in pleasure. He kissed her deeply, devouring her with every portion of his body. The mattress rocked, shook, twisted about as it supported their violent movements. The bed post banged against the wall repeatedly. At some point, a rush of cool air brushed over his back. Derek shivered. He sensed that the bedroom door had opened. He glanced over his shoulder quickly. Two shadowy figures were creeping into the room; when he looked closer, he wasn't sure if they were there or not. He didn't care; he resumed his focus on his wife.

Edith dug her nails into his back, tightened her legs around him, both movements urging him on even wilder as he rutted into her, increased the excitement, made him abandon whatever restraint he had ever shown his wife. *It had never been this way before,* he realized as the sweat streamed off his body. *We've never been this hot for one another.* His thoughts became animal-like; he could only grunt as he dug in deeper. He saw red, he saw black. She rubbed her hands over his back, down his arms, crying out as they rocked together. When Derek opened his eyes to witness Edith's pleasure for himself, he was looking into the ecstatic face of Vanya Avery.

He reared back in horror and disgust, astonished, confused. He pushed himself away. "Where's Edith?!"

"Edith is fine," Vanya said. "She went downstairs, to the cellar. She's needed there now."

"What do you mean? What's down there?"

From behind Derek, voices: "*Justice…*"

Startled, Derek turned. In the gloom, he was able to discern two young girls in long black dresses, their eyes glowing green in the shadows, the same children he'd seen on the porch of the Fox cottage with Vanya. He scrambled off the bed in one fluid motion, put distance between himself and Vanya. Shivering, he stammered out, "Who …are they?"

"The Fox sisters, Katie and Maggie," Vanya said calmly. "They live here, they always have."

The girls raised their arms toward him in supplication. "*Justice*," they said as one, their voices weary, carrying the weight of centuries in the one word.

"My Father called Edith," Vanya said. "She responded; in fact, she's responding to him right *now*. Me, I just wanted to sample you, in case I need you later."

Derek backed out of the bedroom, hurried down the stairs. He wished he had put his shoes on as protection against the frigid, rough wood floorboards but realized that it would have made no difference: That all-encompassing, bone-freezing chill had returned, and it tightly contained the house; there was no possible way to secure warmth. He saw the basement door off the main hallway was open. He hurried to the doorway, looked down into the darkness.

"Edith?" He took a hesitant step onto the descending staircase. The ancient planks felt spongy under his weight, as if termites had chewed them into the consistency of basal wood. A movement from the darkness below, a stirring; he thought he heard her voice, a sigh or murmur.

He started down slowly, the steps creaking in pain. There was an odor all around him, a musty, dank smell, the quality of something that was about to go bad. A faint glow appeared below him, an illumination that allowed him to see a bit through the murkiness. He reached the basement floor, cool packed dirt under his feet. A thick, wide support beam rested solidly on a cement base directly in front of him. The stench about him now was heavier, as if a greater mass of it was now contained in a smaller area. He managed to make his way in the dimness toward the hazy light that was off to his left, his footsteps muffled on the thick earth.

"Edith?" he whispered into the darkness. He banged his knee into a solid, stone-like object, winced in pain. A panting sound, followed by a moan. He thought it might be Edith. Was she injured? The shimmering at the rear of the cellar suddenly brightened.

He saw her.

She was standing with her back against the far cement wall. Both of her arms were extended over her head, held in place by an elderly man, whose back was to Derek. His long, emaciated left arm was ghastly in appearance, resembling something more insect than human. It had secured Edith's arms over her head. With his right hand, he stroked her breasts. Derek was able to see that the man's hands were covered in swollen bumps.

"Edith!"

The man turned. Below his waist, an enormous, misshapen erection rested against her thighs. His eyes glowed bright, white-green. He flashed Derek a hideous grin of pleasure. It was the waiter from the ClearView Restaurant, Vanya Avery's father.

Mute, frozen in place by the nightmare he was seeing, Derek wasn't sure if what he was witnessing was even real. For seconds, he could only watch as the man kissed Edith; she murmured with pleasure. Then Vanya's father shifted until he was able to maneuver himself into Edith.

This can't be happening, Derek thought, *it must be a horrible dream.* Nevertheless, he shouted, "Edith! Edith, oh, my God, no! *No!*"

In the dark glow, Edith turned to him, smiled as the Elder began thrusting.

Vanya's father faced Derek fully, his emerald fish eyes huge in the shadowy cellar. He grinned lasciviously. "Maybe one day you will do as I do if it's what She desires."

As the intensity of their movements increased, a pearl-white shimmer began to glow and encompass the man and Edith while Derek stood, horrified, unable to move. Vanya's father opened his mouth wide, engulfed Edith in a kiss, which she returned with equal abandon, then he cried out, "This...is... finally... our...day!"

He finished off with one final thrust, his legs quivering in ecstasy. After a moment, he stepped back, gasping as his chest rose and fell in huge movements. Spent, Edith slid to the floor. The white light glistened over her entire body for a moment, then it gradually diminished, until all that remained was a small portion over her stomach.

Only when it had finally flickered, then faded from sight was Derek able to move.

In the darkness of the cellar, he rushed to Edith's still figure on the floor, gathered her in his arms, cried out, "Edith! Oh my, God! Oh my, God!"

CHAPTER 8.

Edith! Edith!"

Derek was having difficulty breathing. His wife's name caught in his throat. Thrashing about in some strange, half-alive state, he felt restrained, bound. All he could manage was to call for her repeatedly, his heart beating rapidly in terror.

"—Yes, Derek, I'm here, I'm here, I'm all right. Wake up, honey, you're having a bad dream."

Edith's face. Her eyes were alert with concern, her hair disarrayed, matched the rumpled nature of the sheets, which he had twisted around himself during his frightening dream, confining his movements. His heart was still racing as he untangled himself. Edith handed him a glass of water from her nightstand.

"Here, drink this."

The water relieved his throat; he realized it felt strained, the way it did after he attended a hockey game, yelling and cheering on the team. Had he been screaming in his sleep?

"I…had a nightmare."

"No kidding."

He looked around. Heavenly, early morning light spilled in through the windows of their Park Avenue apartment. There was a warm, comforting glow about the room. It was a familiar place, everything about the bedroom was as it should be since they had slept there for more than a decade. The stack of paperbacks on her bedside table; the magazines on his. The photos she had blown up and framed from their trips together. The pictures of he and Oswald as boys. He took Edith's hand into his own; at once, portions of the dream returned.

"I dreamt we were back at the Fox house." Then he stopped before he mentioned his bizarre sexual encounter with Vanya and hers with Vanya's father. Edith waited for him to continue. "There were these rapping noises, a voice, banging sounds. And the room was so cold, but it was *alive* with its coldness. It seemed to move around you, embrace you, touch you. It's hard to explain…" He paused again. He had never kept anything from Edith in all their years of marriage; there was never a need to, yet the lustful intensity of the dream was so extreme that he was embarrassed to tell her about it. Even though it was only a dream, it would be hurtful for her to hear about it, disgusting for her if he described her encounter with Vanya's father.

He pulled her close. "Never mind, it was just a terrible, bad dream, but it's over now."

"Is it?" she murmured into his chest. "Or are we going to go back to Hydesville and that awful house every time we fall asleep? What will be real to us, what will be a dream? What will we remember when we wake...or when we sleep?" Edith's voice trailed off.

All at once it dawned on him. He released her, said excitedly, "We remembered what happened!"

Her eyes wide, she nodded once she realized what he was saying. "Yes! Just now, when you mentioned the Fox house, it all came back to me! I *do* remember our trip to Hydesville, the ClearView Restaurant, meeting Vanya..."

Yet even as they spoke the words, the images, the memories, began to fade, dry up, blow away. They had been given a brief, tantalizing peek at something, but a door was swinging stubbornly closed, obscuring what they wanted to see. Derek could almost hear a lock snapping shut over their shared recollections. The last wisps of something was trailing away, now dissipating into forgetfulness. The connection between them of a shared event dimmed, fizzled out. Vanished.

Edith was speaking to him. "We should get up. This is a big day. Dinner tonight with Oz and Vanya, the love of his life!"

"Ozzie!" Edith said, standing to embrace her brother-in-law as he stepped out on the terrace where she and Derek were having drinks.

"I'd like you to meet Vanya Avery," Oz said, positioning the attractive, thirtyish woman in front of them. He rested his hands on either side of her waist, which Derek found peculiarly possessive, strangely sexual. He still could not get over that his brother was dating a woman. Her perfume was light and spicy; there was a friendly, familiar, teasing pull to it. They exchanged greetings, pleasantries, settled out on the terrace.

"So, do I pass inspection?" Vanya asked, smiling brilliantly into the gently setting sun. "I know this must be a shock to both of you."

Hesitating only a moment, Derek said, "To put it mildly, yes. I never knew my brother to take a second glance at a woman."

"Or a first glance," Edith added, smiling at Ozzie. He was beaming; she didn't think she had ever seen him so happy or relaxed. He always appeared to be ready to leave a room as soon as he entered, forever on edge, constantly had somewhere else to be. But now he seemed calm, almost serene. Oswald put his left hand on Vanya's tanned leg, gave it a little squeeze. Vanya sipped her drink. Ozzie started talking, something about the Hampton Classic, but Derek was captured by Vanya's gaze. She was beautiful.

When I ask to have a tour of the apartment, offer to show me around. Alone, her voice whispered. Edith and Oz continued chatting as if they hadn't heard. Mesmerized, Derek could only stare at her. She was exquisite. He managed to sip his drink, a familiar, automatic movement. He needed something ordinary to do. *Had she really just spoken directly to my mind?* he wondered. He looked over at Edith. She and Ozzie were deep in animated conversation, laughing, gesturing, caught in their own world as if he and Vanya had left the terrace.

"Excuse me," Vanya said, her hand on Ozzie's arm. "While you two catch up, would you mind if Derek showed me the apartment? It looks beautiful. I'd love a little tour."

###

Fifteen minutes later, the sun had finally set, leaving behind a cooling, red glow. Matilda, the cook and housekeeper, had called them to dinner twice. By 8:30, she was pleading with Ozzie to "gather everyone before the meal is ruined."

Derek was in his study, alone with Vanya, the apartment tour finished, the silence between them like a ticking clock that was about to stop. He could barely distinguish her in the dark room, but what he saw was perfection. The lamp he had turned on when they entered had flickered, dimmed, then clicked off. He didn't bother with it. He was enthralled by her presence. To stand there perfectly still with her so close was intoxicating.

"Who are you?" Derek finally asked. She was dazzling.

Vanya stepped closer. He felt his heart begin to race, his breathing shortened into little puffs of anticipation. Her green eyes were rounder now, shifting in size as she moved nearer. How he wanted to touch her.

Her face, now only inches from his.

Her eyes…

He stammered, "Please, let me touch you."

"Maybe," she teased him. "Oswald first. You seem so loyal to Edith, but your brother isn't attached to anyone. It should be easy to take what I want. I probably won't need you."

She doesn't know, Derek realized, puzzled, assuming she was referring to a sexual encounter. Was that what it was that she was after? He started to tell her about his brother when, from the other room, Ozzie called out for them. Derek blinked. The lamp was on. Vanya was across the room, admiring a painting. Disoriented, Derek was saying, "...in Italy when we were there last spring." *God, have I had another spell?* he thought uneasily. *What just happened? Something happened.*

"Really? It's beautiful," Vanya said, her voice relaxed, as if she had been discussing the canvas for several minutes.

"Here you are! Didn't you hear me calling?" Ozzie asked, swooping in on Vanya, embracing her. She giggled as he swung her around.

"Sorry, Derek was giving me a lesson," she said, "in art history."

Ozzie glanced down at Derek's stiff crotch. "I'll bet he was."

The next morning, with only a few hours of sleep behind him, Derek arrived at the Regency Hotel dining room at 7:00. Just as Oz had left the night before, furious with his brother's behavior, he had hissed into his ear to meet him alone for breakfast. Derek, knowing Oswald would be there promptly at 7:30, arrived early so he could settle in with a cup of coffee, review the notes he had brought with him, and mentally prepare for the unsettling information he was going to share with his brother.

Derek and Edith's locked away memories had suddenly been freed the night before. They now knew who Vanya Avery was.

Soon after Oz had left their apartment, the spotty memory lapses they had experienced about Hydesville reappeared, rapidly fused together into coherent bits and pieces. They spent most the night writing down what they remembered when their thoughts were clear. Then, exhausted by the effort, they would fall asleep, dream up new recollections, then awaken with fresh details, using what they had already written as a prompt to continue discovering what had occurred. Before dawn, they guessed they had regained and recaptured maybe seventy percent of what had been hidden from them. Whatever it was—and they could only refer to it as an "it"—that had taken their memories, it seemed that it was now reluctantly returning them.

"Maybe it's only able to give us that amnesia for a short period of time," Edith suggested, "and then it loses its strength, so the memories are returned to us."

Derek nodded, jotted down the idea, then reread all the information to her. It was a bizarre, disjointed story but with their notes, they were able to recreate most of what had happened to them when they were in Hydesville. He only hoped he could communicate it to his brother in a fashion that would make sense.

The waiter refilled Derek's coffee just as Oswald seated himself. He didn't waste any time. "I want to know what happened between you and Vanya last night in the study. What were you thinking, your dick almost out of your pants! It was *disgusting*."

"Nothing happened and keep your voice down."

The waiter returned, took their orders. Oswald glared at his brother, waited for an answer. Derek sipped his coffee, giving himself time to think of how to best begin to tell the story. His hand trembled when he returned the cup to the saucer. The dark liquid reflected the ceiling lights, distorted flashes dancing about. Derek waited until they settled before he looked at his brother. "To be honest, I don't know what happened, or what *is* happening, but something...really strange is going on. You probably are not even aware of it."

Oswald said, "I know what this is about, I know it's 'strange' that I'm in love with Vanya. I know that sounds impossible that I could love a woman, hard for you to wrap your head around, but it's true. That's why it sickens me, the idea of you last night in the study, standing there like that, lusting after the woman I love—"

Derek blurted out, "There's something about Vanya you should know."

"What? You just met the woman last night and now you're going to tell *me* something about her?"

Derek leaned across the table. He looked into the eyes of his older brother. "I have to start at the beginning, tell you what has been going on with Edith and me." He pulled out the folded pieces of paper where he and Edith had written down all they could remember about their time in Hydesville.

For the next thirty minutes, Derek told Oswald about his and Edith's strange, half-remembered experiences in the Fox house, the role Vanya Avery played in it all, Derek's sensual encounter with her which he had still never mentioned to Edith, as well as when he had found Edith in the cellar in the arms of Vanya's ancient father. Derek finished by admitting how aroused he had been with Vanya in the study, that it was something that had happened before at the ClearView Restaurant and on the phone, and how he had no control over it.

"I don't get it, Oz, I have no idea why it happens, I love Edith, you know that. I would never…"

Derek heard himself, knew that what he was telling his brother sounded like the rants of an insane, paranoid man but he was unable to stop; it felt like a cleansing, getting scrubbed clean of some seriously bad filth. Plus, it seemed that the longer he went on relating what he and Edith recalled, the more information came to him, insights that he added to the notes to tell Edith when he returned home. When he finished, both of their omelets had cooled. Neither had been able to eat during the tale: Derek, because he was busy telling the story, and Oswald, because he had lost his appetite as the strange events had been revealed to him.

When he finished, Derek shifted in his chair. "So? Say something. What do you think?"

"I think you need to see a doctor. Immediately. I think your spells have taken a turn for the worse, that's why you briefly lost your memory."

"But it happened to Edith, too, she experienced the same things I did, the same amnesia, everything, so it isn't just me or my imagination or a spell I'm having. Something weird really *is* going on, and Vanya is part of it."

"Listen to yourself talk, Derek. If Vanya was this weird, erotic, mind reading, dream invading, mysterious…*thing*, I'd know it, too. Right? And if she's so scary, why would you ever let her into your home? Or let me date her?"

"That's just it! The awareness of all of this comes and goes. It's like a switch that turns on or off. Sometimes Edith and I will be in the middle of discussing it, then our train of thought will just jump track, we'll forget about it. Like it never happened! At times, Vanya Avery is a familiar, strange presence, other times…she's just a woman that you are dating. We didn't recall any of this until after you had both left last night."

He held up the sheaf of papers, rattled them at his brother. "It took us most of the night to gather this information! It's the only way we can remember it, to write it down, and then refer back to it to recall what we wrote. It's like whatever happened to us wants to keep slithering away, so we have to constantly jot down the events, read them over and over and over again, hammer the memories to pieces of paper."

Oswald was shaking his head. "One thing you're forgetting is that I met her *here*, in Manhattan, at the same time you said you were with her in Hydesville. She can't be in two places at one time. Right? It's impossible. This whole story is just unbelievable…"

"Unbelievable? You want to talk about unbelievable, what about *you*? Why would you suddenly start dating a *woman*? Don't you think *that's* a little unbelievable? If you think our story is so farfetched, how do you think we feel about yours?!"

Derek waited but Oswald didn't respond, only signaled for the check. They stood up, made their way out of the nearly empty restaurant, neither speaking. Once outside, they headed down Park Avenue.

"I want to talk with Edith about all this," Oswald finally announced once they were standing in the shadow of Derek's building. The doorman nodded at them, his hand on the double doors.

"It's upsetting for her," Derek said protectively.

"It's upsetting for *me* to hear the things you both think about the woman I love!" Oswald said angrily. "Besides, I want to know what Edith thinks about you."

"Me?"

"Yes, I want to see if she agrees with me that you're going bat-shit crazy."

"Ozzie!" Edith said, planting a kiss on her brother-in-law's cheek. "I was just on the phone with your lady friend. She was calling to thank us for a lovely evening. She really is delightful, you know. But I have to admit, I am still not quite over the fact that—"

"—that I brought a female to dinner, right?" Oswald said, smiling broadly, throwing a smug look at his brother that seemed to say, *See, your wife isn't freaked out over Vanya.*

Edith nodded. "Yes, a bit of a shock, but as long as you're happy. So, what brings you both home? I thought you'd be at the gallery. Some scandal at the Regency you just had to tell me about?"

"Actually," Derek said, taking Edith by the arm, guiding her to the couch, "remember how we spent most of last night?" She looked at him blankly.

"Derek said you were writing down your memories from your vacation," Oswald said.

Edith looked at both men, confused. Derek pulled out the notes, started to read aloud. He and Oswald glanced at Edith until they saw recognition appear in her expression.

"Yes, now I remember," she said wearily, touched her hand to her head as if in pain. "Oz, it's *awful*, like our recollections are submerged, can't be accessed. Derek calls them slippery, which is how it feels, like we can't hold on to them. Thank God we thought to write down what happened, or it would be lost forever."

For the next few minutes, she collaborated all that Derek had told Oswald during breakfast. Relieved, Derek pulled her close. She rested her head on his shoulder.

"I wanted to assure Oswald that it wasn't just me."

"Wasn't just you? What do you mean?" Edith asked.

"That it wasn't just Derek who was nuts," Oswald said, no humor in his voice. He, too, had been visibly shaken to see Edith respond to the notes, to watch her memory return. He leaned forward, his face serious, all anger and doubt gone. "Look, I'm sorry. You're right, something *is* going on, but it's all happening so fast that I can't seem to catch up with it, to stop and think. Even now, right at this moment, I have the creepiest feeling, like something is…tugging at my mind…"

Derek and Edith nodded; they had felt the same thing.

"…making me think things I don't want to. Right *now*, here with you, I have no interest in Vanya, or women at all. None. Never had. It's the craziest thing for me to even consider it."

He hesitated, then said, "Look, I know this is TMI, but we even tried to have sex several times. I wasn't able to. Why would I, right? I have no interest in women. But she insisted—demanded actually—that I keep trying. It was weird, it seemed so important to her. It didn't matter how embarrassed and frustrated it made me feel. She just kept wanting me to try."

Something Vanya had said flashed through Derek's mind: *"Oswald first. It should be easy to take what I want. I probably won't need you."*

CHAPTER 9.

Neither Derek nor Oswald made it to the gallery that day,
Oswald spent the rest of the morning talking with Edith and Derek, relating his encounters with Vanya, hearing in greater detail what occurred while they were at the Fox house. Derek kept careful notes. They moved out on the terrace for lunch; at two o'clock, they moved back inside, fatigued by the sun and having finished two bottles of wine. Derek excused himself to return some business calls in the study. Oswald used his cell phone in the library to check in with the gallery. Edith took the mail into the living room, glanced through the latest *Vanity Fair*. Drowsy from the wine and sun, she settled herself back on the couch, slipped quickly into a deep sleep...

###

In the study, Derek finished his calls, yawned, rubbed his eyes. He pushed away from the desk, banged his knee on an open drawer, slammed it closed. He settled himself in the recliner, his "thinking chair," quickly lost consciousness…

Oswald, satisfied that the manager of the gallery had accurately finished the monthly inventory report, stretched, sighed contentedly, called out to Edith in the living room. "I'm taking advantage of your unoffered hospitality and taking a little nap, all right?" He stretched out on the plush sofa, was slumbering in seconds...

With the apartment asleep around her, Matilda finished her cleaning as quietly as she could. Derek and Edith's houseman and driver, Warren Adler, had slipped out to do some errands for her and she was preparing to take a break herself when she remembered Edith was resting in the living room.

Matilda checked on her, found her breathing low, soft and regular. *Vanity Fair* laid open on her chest. Matilda carefully removed it, set it on the coffee table.

Derek tried to roll on his side but wasn't able to. Thinking he was in bed, he opened his eyes to see what was restraining him, was surprised to find himself in the recliner, unable to turn due to the thick arms on the chair. He yawned, rubbed his eyes, stretched. It wasn't like him to fall asleep in the afternoon; he felt groggy, his thoughts musty and slow. He glanced at his watch: 4:40 p.m. How long had he been out? He pushed through a fog of weighty, residual slumber. He remembered the lunch on the terrace with Edith and Oswald, then they had all gone inside, he had made some calls. Then what, taken a nap?

He used the study bathroom to splash cold water on his face, trying to remove the slumbering haze that still clung to him. *I must be a little hung over*, he thought, sun-tired from eating outside. He'd put up the umbrella next time they ate on the terrace. One of the desk drawers was extended again, something that had been happening frequently. He wondered if something was wrong with the ball bearings or if the desk was no longer level. He pushed it closed, made a mental note to have Warren look at it; he was good with that sort of thing.

He found Edith asleep on the couch in the living room, her breathing slow, even, barely perceptible, almost as if she were hibernating. It was difficult to keep his eyes open; the thought of returning to his thinking chair beckoned.

Derek worked his way down the hallway to Matilda's room where he was surprised to find her asleep on her bed, her face lightly perspiring. Curious, he headed toward Warren's living quarters. He found the elderly man prone on his bed, snoring softly, his mouth slack. Derek watched him for a moment, distressed by what he was seeing. He and Edith treated Warren and Matilda like an elderly aunt and uncle—they had worked for Derek's father, he had grown up with them—and they all called one another by their first names. It was family, not formality. He had known them a long time. It was so out of character for all of them to have fallen asleep in the afternoon.

Where was Oswald? Had he left after lunch?

Derek wandered back into the main part of the apartment. The silence thickened about him as he stood there. For some reason, all at once he was apprehensive, tense, as if the stillness was coiling, preparing to strike. *Get a hold of yourself,* he thought. The insistent, steady ticking of the grandfather clock—something he rarely if ever noticed—seemed louder than usual. So was the white-noise swish from the air conditioners, the dry rustle as he inhaled, the blood pulsating through his veins, the rumbling beat of his heart. He was very aware of himself, the atmosphere in the room, still felt a bit on edge as if… as if… *As if what?* he asked himself impatiently. *You feel like you're not alone, as if you're being watched. Admit it.*

"Justice."

Startled, he turned. Reflected in the large hallway mirror were the Fox sisters, motionless, staring at him, hands open, silent pleas. Their bright green eyes were the only sign of color in their otherwise drab, murky appearance. They seemed tenuous, uncertain in their ability to manifest themselves; if he blinked, would they vanish?

"Derek?"

He flinched, quickly turned away from the mirror.

It was Oswald. His hair was disheveled, his face creased, flushed from his nap, his eyes moist with fatigue, clothes wrinkled. "God, I feel like shit, like I'm hung over, or something." He finger-combed his hair. "You don't look so well yourself. What's wrong? What were you looking at?"

Derek glanced back at the mirror. Only his reflection. He turned to Oswald. "Nothing. Thought I saw something. I don't feel so great, either. I dozed off, when I woke up, it was so quiet around here. It was strange. I was just looking for you."

"I fell asleep, too, must have gone out like a light after I phoned the gallery. Really bad, scratchy connection by the way. I had to dial back twice; the call kept getting dropped."

"Warren and Matilda are snoozing, too," Derek said.

"You're kidding. I didn't think they *ever* slept. They've got more energy than people half their age, always have."

"Edith's napping in the living room," Derek said. He couldn't help stealing another glance at the mirror again. Nothing.

He and Oswald spent a few uncomfortable seconds looking at one another. Something bad had transpired, the brothers were not in a good place. Derek tried to form a thought, begin a sentence, create a bridge, but nothing happened. *What was wrong? What did I say or what did he say?* Derek asked himself, an ominous pit in his stomach.

What happened between us?

"...leaving," Oz said.

"Huh?"

"Said I should be leaving," Oswald replied. "I'm taking Vanya out tonight. We're meeting early for drinks."

"Vanya," Derek said, still feeling dazed, half deaf, dumb and blind. Everything was so fuzzy. Where had he heard that name? Before he could ask, the thought came to him hard and fast: *It's all right. Let it be. Vanya is Oswald's girlfriend. It's all right.*

After Oswald had left, Derek went to the living room to wake Edith. Normally, he would have let her sleep, but the apartment was still too quiet, he was too jumpy now with Oswald gone, he needed company, needed people around to talk with, make noise.

"Honey? Wake up." He stroked her arm until her eyes opened. She smiled, her face enraptured when she saw him, delighted by his presence. She reached up and caressed his face.

"I was having the nicest dream..."

"What about?"

"We were having a picnic, I had a baby...a boy," Edith stopped stroking his face.

Her eyes were troubled for a moment. She looked around the room, said sadly, "It was so real. Oh, Derek. He was so real..." She sat up.

He saw such grief and longing in her eyes. "Honey, who are you talking about?"

"We were so happy, Derek. He was such a bright, charming little boy, a little angel! We were having a picnic, he was playing with a toy. A ball, but it was...strange. The ball was glowing. It was so odd, that part. Oh, Oswald was there, too!" She smiled sadly, closed her eyes to better see what she was describing. "Oz was married. Yes. That's right. There was a woman with him, they had a child, too, a daughter. She had one of those odd balls, too. It was such a beautiful day..."

Edith rarely remembered her dreams, never with this type of detail. Derek was surprised at what she described, but also bothered by it. "My *brother* was married, to a woman? They had a daughter?"

She nodded, continued to relate all she was seeing behind closed eyes. The more she spoke, the more uneasy Derek became. For some reason, he felt as if she was telling a story that was going to have a disturbing conclusion; he needed to stop her before she got to that point.

"Hey, come on, let's go for a walk," he said abruptly, squeezing her hand. She opened her eyes. For an instant, he could see she was still caught up in the peculiar bliss of her dream, was annoyed he had interrupted what she had been saying. "We should be outside, it's a perfect day. Forget your dream."

Under the radiant early evening sunlight, he and Edith held hands as they wandered west to Central Park.

"This was a great idea," Edith said as they strolled under the trees. She pulled him over to the ice cream stand, bought them each an Eskimo Pie. They munched on the ice cream as they meandered through the pathways of the park, stopping to watch a puppet show of crows singing old Motown hits. Further on, they examined the wares of a talented ceramic artist, finally settled for cocktails at the Outside Bar.

They sipped their drinks, relaxed, nibbled on pretzels, stared at the lake where adults and kids paddled about on rented rowboats and tossed breadcrumbs to the ducks, watched the crowd about them enjoy the pleasant weather. A couple nearby each balanced a child on their laps, helping the youngsters sip their sodas while the adults managed occasional swigs from their bottles of beer. Derek noticed Edith was paying close attention to the children, didn't take her eyes from them. "The little boy is so sweet, almost like the one in my dream."

Derek ordered them each another drink. He was troubled that she kept returning to her dream, wished she'd forget about it. Ten minutes later, the family vacated their table. Edith waved at the children as they were carried away over their parent's shoulders. At first, they waved solemnly back at Edith, but then they each broke into such brilliant smiles that Derek saw it just about broke Edith's heart. Her eyes glistened when she turned to him.

"Silly, isn't it?" she said, dabbing her eyes. "One little dream about a child and I get all emotional."

He reached across the small, round wood table, took her hand, didn't know what to say, wanted to change the subject.

"It's so odd, a dream I actually remember," she said thoughtfully. "And then to get all mushy seeing children."

Derek shrugged, wanted her to stop talking about her dream.

"In my dream," Edith started to say, then stopped, shaking her head. "I'm sort of babbling, aren't I?"

He watched, waited.

"In my dream, with this child, this baby boy, I had such a sense of completeness …or destiny, maybe. Like I had found my purpose or something. It was terribly important to care for him, look after him. I had *finally* found something I had wanted all my life, something I had been searching for. It was the most marvelous feeling, complete fulfillment, to have this child."

She sipped her drink, sat back in her chair, restless yet jubilant by what she was telling Derek. "Having him was so…vitalizing. I mean, you saw me when I woke up; didn't I look...excited? Happy? Elated?"

"I thought you were just glad to see me."

Edith laughed, her voice light, carefree. Derek leaned across the small table, pulled her close to him, kissed her quickly. Then it dawned on him why he found all her talk about having a baby so unsettling: In her dream, she had only referred to the child as her baby, never their baby.

Just as they arrived home, Derek's phone rang. It was Oswald. For some reason, a seed of apprehension suddenly lodging in his stomach, began to grow, then it bloomed.

"Hey, what's up?" Derek asked.

Derek almost dropped the phone when Oswald told him his news.

"What?" Edith asked after Derek ended the call, quiet alarm in her voice. "What did Oswald say? What happened?"

"Oswald called to say…he had good news." Derek's voice was robotic, reciting lines.

"Derek? What—"

"Oswald said...he told me that...he's asked Vanya to marry him. And she said yes."

CHAPTER 10.

Oswald's friends expressed shock and disbelief at his decision to marry.

"Is this some kind of a joke?"

"Now that Oswald can legally marry a man, he's choosing to marry a *woman*?"

"Who is this Vanya Avery? Nobody's ever heard of her! Nothing on Google!"

That was the issue that drew the most attention, and was the featured angle in a *New York Post* item: Who was this mysterious Vanya Avery, the woman with absolutely no internet presence? Where had she come from and why would she—and how did she—snag Oswald David? Speculation went in every direction, but it was Oswald himself who issued the statement that shut down all the inquiries:

"Yes, it's true that I plan to marry Vanya Avery this fall. We met a few weeks ago, have fallen in love and want to spend the rest of our lives together. It's that simple."

The media tried in vain to get some significant background on Vanya Avery, but all they were able to discover was that she was born and raised in the small upstate hamlet of Hydesville, had never married, lived with her father at the infamous Keilgarden Colony. The few reporters who attempted to locate the Colony became hopelessly lost in the Fox Woods and twisted back roads of the area. "There's no story here," one frustrated correspondent wearily stated.

Each year, Derek and Edith spent the last two weeks of August at a close friend's home in East Hampton. Everywhere they went, people were hoping Oswald and Vanya would be with them or that Derek and Edith would comment about the upcoming wedding, but they were mum on the subject. They didn't know anything, so they had nothing to say. Oswald and his bride-to-be kept a low profile, preferring to spend all their time upstate in Hydesville.

Derek and Edith had not seen Vanya since their luncheon two weeks earlier, and Derek had only breakfasted with Oswald twice before he departed to stay with Vanya. Oz had been pleasant but terribly distracted at both meals. Once he left the city, he hadn't returned any calls, which angered Derek since he had questions about the gallery he needed help with. Once Derek and Edith had moved to the island for the remainder of August, they had given up hearing from Oswald, assumed he was fully occupied planning the wedding.

One evening, Derek had been thrilled to see Oswald's name and number light up his phone. His and Edith's notebook, unread, lay on a stack of *American Art Collector, ArtNews,* and other magazines he was planning to catch up on. He had tossed the binder into his knapsack at the last minute; it kept nagging at him, the need to read whatever he and Edith had written in it. Maybe he'd have a chance while in East Hampton. He was just planning to look over the notes he had written when the call came through.

"It's so great to hear your voice, Oz! We've missed you." No response. "What have you been doing?"

"Spending time getting to know one another," Oswald had said vaguely. "There's so much to do and see here. I'm trying so hard to please her…"

"People are asking about you, wondering where you are, *how* you are. Including me."

"I'm fine. Don't worry about me." His voice sounded like it was floating away, disinterested, aimless.

Derek waited, then forged ahead. "What about the gallery? You haven't checked in, Manny says you haven't returned his calls. When will you return?"

Silence.

"I mean, thank God for Manny," Derek said, referring to the gallery manager who had been with them for more than five years, "but they do need you there, especially for the private clients and the auctions; Manny can't do everything."

An angry static buzzed the phone. Derek held it back from his ear until it ceased. "You still there?"

"Yes."

"You are going to Europe this fall, right? Those estate sales look very promising."

"I'm getting married this fall, remember? I can't leave Vanya to do all the wedding plans alone, can I? I need to be here…"

Angry at his brother's passive reply, Derek said, "Wait a minute, if you're not going to Europe, this is the first I'm hearing of it. Have you made arrangements for Manny to go?" He waited a beat, couldn't resist adding, "Or am I going to cover that, too?"

Oswald hesitated, which wasn't like him. Derek knew his brother loved the business; it was an obsession with him, as was every facet of the art world. He had a passion for collecting, researching and cataloguing the pieces acquired by the gallery; he even wrote the catalog copy, and his private client mailing list was the envy of every art dealer in the city. His reputation and influence had been growing on both a national and international scale. For him to not have his fall plans made, or arrangements already in the works for someone to cover for him, was alarming to Derek. It was simply out of character for Oswald, but, Derek reasoned, so was the whole idea of his brother marrying Vanya. He and his brother never stepped on either of the other's territory in the gallery, but in this instance, Derek knew that his brother had seriously dropped the ball.

"Oz? You there?"

After several seconds of silence, Oswald finally mumbled, "Vanya…and I have decided we want a small wedding…."

Warning bells were now going off in Derek's mind. He felt an apprehensive knot growing in his stomach. "How small?"

"Just you and Edith. And Vanya's father, of course."

Derek forced himself to remain calm. "Where will you be married?"

"Here, in Hydesville, at the Colony."

Trying not to sound as if he was begging, Derek carefully asked, "Will I see you before the wedding? Are your friends throwing you a bachelor party? Or—"

"I really haven't been in touch with many people. There's so much to *do* here...so much for me to *learn*."

Derek had an image of Vanya whispering these words into Oswald's ears. He wanted the sentences to stop, his gut telling him this would not end well.

"—of fact, the reason I really called... I'm quitting the gallery..."

Stunned, Derek said, "What?! You love the gallery! It's your life—"

"No, Vanya's my life now. Manny can take over, he's built a solid relationship with our European contacts. And Jared is good with the international agents, and Sally and Beatrice can split up the U.S. regions."

Derek was unable to process the notion of his brother quitting the family business. He felt numb, was devastated. It was like a death, an end. While it was true that they had an excellent staff that could pick up where Oswald would leave off, the loss of his brother as the personality and figurehead of the David Gallery was going to be explosive news in the art world. He was angry, but also hurt. Why was everything happening so fast? Surprised at his reaction, he wiped tears away.

Finally able to respond, he said, "Oz, I don't know what to say. Maybe it just all seems too much for you, right now, but after the wedding, once you've settled in together… Why not just take a leave of absence for a few months, start in again at the first of the year? Or next spring?" He was pleading now, begging. Was there even a difference?

"No, Derek. I want out. The people are in place, don't worry. Everything's taken care of."

###

After he finished the phone call, Derek told Edith.

"I just don't understand what's going on with him," she said, shaking her head. "Why has he shut us out? Why doesn't he visit us anymore?"

"Vanya," was Derek's one-word answer.

"I don't like her," Edith said flatly, decisively. "I realize that now. She's taken Oswald away from us. Changed him. I mean, *really* changed him, Derek. Forget about him getting married; that in itself is unbelievable, although I can almost accept it now. *Almost.* But he and I used to be pals; he'd call, we'd goof on one another and gossip, but he doesn't call anymore, and he's holed up in that weird Colony place. All because of her."

"Before he hung up, I did get him to agree to meet me for lunch when we get back to the city. Why don't you join us? I could use the company."

Edith pulled Derek close. "'Use the company?' What do you mean?"

"I feel a little awkward talking to him. Like you said, something about him is different."

###

Edith and Derek returned to the city after their time in East Hampton. Lunch reservations were made at Gail's, the East Side townhouse restaurant that featured a garden area in the back. It was one of Oswald's favorite haunts. He was going to meet them there at one. It wasn't until Derek and Edith were seated and had ordered and finished their first drinks that Derek found he was able to relax a little.

"Strange he's not here on time. That's not like him," Edith said, sipping her chardonnay. "It's almost one-thirty."

Derek glanced around at the well-heeled crowd, nodded at some familiar faces. A gaunt man who had just entered the area with the maître d' smiled at Derek, made his way purposely to the table.

Derek realized with a shock that the thin man was his brother.

Oswald must have lost close to fifty pounds. He had always been robust and heavy, always twenty pounds overweight, but now he was barely recognizable. His eyes had the wary, hollow look about them of a sad-eyed animal that had been severely punished. His shoulders were lost in the now-misshapen cut of his Armani blazer, the collar of his custom-made shirt appeared to be three or four sizes too big.

It was as if Oswald David was diminishing in size, wasting away.

He looks haunted, was the first thought that came to Derek.

Edith was startled when Oswald gripped her shoulders from behind, planted a kiss on her. When she faced him, she flinched, drew back, couldn't control what she said. "Oh, Oswald! What's wrong?"

Oswald drew up a chair, the waiter took his drink order. Edith glanced at Derek, their eyes sharing the same distraught concern. A few of the people at the other tables that knew the David's also bent their heads together, began whispering. The beautiful garden suddenly seemed to be filled with poison and unpleasantness. Overhead, a cloud moved over the sun, a shadow crept over the restaurant.

Derek, his voice despondent, said, "Oswald..." But he couldn't finish the sentence, couldn't ask the question, didn't want to know the answer. *Cancer?*

Oswald smiled brilliantly at them, but Derek saw that Edith had to advert her gaze; Derek couldn't blame her. When Oswald grinned like that, the skin tightened and shifted, formed contours that caused his face to resemble a skull. Oz took Edith's hand. When she looked up, Derek saw tears in her eyes. She didn't pull away from Oswald's touch, but he could see she had gone stiff with fear and uncertainty.

"You don't look well," Derek finally stated, trying to pull the attention away from Edith, who seemed trapped in Oswald's gaze.

He accepted his drink from the waiter. "I assure you, I am not sick." He raised his glass, smiled his death-grin. "To my new life!"

They drank, sat in silence, waiting for Oswald to continue. "Obviously, I've lost weight, close to sixty pounds," he finally said. "The food at the Colony is, for the most part, all organic. It's grown and prepared there. I eat a lot of vegetables and fruit, they have a tremendous amount of experimental supplemental ingredients that they use. Herbs, special teas and sauces that they prepare for the meals. And I am trying to please Vanya, and that burns a lot of calories, as you can imagine." He wanted them to join him in chuckling at his mildly bawdy joke, but they only watched him. "But, most of all, walking! That's made all the difference! The healthiest form of exercise! I did a lot of walking in the woods. Oh, the Fox Woods are so beautiful to explore!" He paused, a distant look in his eyes.

What is he seeing? Derek wondered.

"That's how you've come to look like...*this*?" Edith asked, confused. "Oz, you don't think you look healthy, do you?"

He didn't answer, signaled the waiter, they all ordered.

When they were alone, Derek said, "You must see how you look, don't you? I mean, you can understand why people would think you're sick?"

He shrugged. "People think they know so much. They know nothing. They have no idea...." The skull-grin again.

Derek felt a chill even as the sun shone down on their table. Salads and rolls arrived, the conversation drifted about, never anchoring on any topic of significance. Derek sensed Edith had dozens of questions; he knew she was showing tremendous self-restraint in holding back. Oswald seemed intent on getting Edith to talk about what she had been doing the past month; clearly, he was refusing to share any more details about his own life in Hydesville.

After twenty minutes of this, Derek jumped in. "So, tell us about the wedding. All we know is the date and time."

"That's really all there is to tell. October fifth. One o'clock. At the Colony. Just the two of you as witnesses, Vanya's father, the justice of the peace from Hydesville."

"None of your friends?" Edith asked softly. "Surely they—"

"My friends don't understand *anything,* Edith," Oswald said, his hollow eyes intense, haughty with a wisdom they could never comprehend.

Edith said, "Well, Oz, this whole affair *is* hard to understand. Surely if you gave them time? And is there really the need to rush into this marriage? You hardly know the woman—"

"You don't like her, do you?"

"I didn't say that. It's just—"

Don't push it, a hard thought flared through her mind. She cringed, touch her forehead, closed her mouth.

"You both forget, Vanya *knows things,*" Oswald said calmly, a subtle boast in his statement. "She can sense things, Edith. She can see as well as hear. She knew the first time you met that you didn't like her."

"Oz, that's really not fair—" Derek said, upset by how his brother was speaking to Edith. *But it's true, isn't it?* a voice deep in his mind challenged him, pressed him.

Oswald turned to Derek. "And you, you only want to *touch* her. She told me so." He said it so easily, not as an accusation but as a fact, that it took a moment for the words to register.

Edith went pale with humiliation. "Why would she say such a thing?" she murmured.

"Because she loves me. She tells me the truth...about so many things." He leaned toward Derek. "And I *am* trying to satisfy her, I *will* satisfy her, so *stop* sniffing around!" He straightened up, said calmly to both of them, "You know what I've come to realize? In the end, all that matters is that you have someone who loves you."

"But Oswald, we love you!" Edith said, not sure what was happening between them, wanting to rescue him, a drowning man who seemed to fight her every effort.

He set his napkin on the table, stood, his lanky, scarecrow frame towering over them. "If you loved me, then you'd love Vanya. After all, we are *one* now."

Derek stood with his brother, acutely aware of the patrons observing the drama. The whispering, the phone texting; he had the feeling they were on TV being watched.

"Oswald!" he said, knowing it was pointless yet sensing it was probably the last chance he would ever have to reach his brother. How had everything gotten out of control so quickly? Oz vanished from the brightness of the outdoor dining area into the gloom of the restaurant, swallowed up in the darkness as certain as if a door was closing.

Out in the garden, the silence that had fallen over the restaurant broke upon itself, the buzz and murmur of gossip sputtered about for a moment, looked for a foothold, then lurched into high gear like a badly tuned engine.

Edith sat with her hands in her lap, staring at her plate, her face composed in its emptiness. Derek saw a tear fall on her blouse, followed a moment later by another.

In the end, all that matters is that you have someone who loves you.

Terrified at the implication, Derek realized that, in the end, the only person Oswald had now was Vanya Avery.

121

CHAPTER 11.

Over the next few days, Derek and Edith tried desperately to speak to Oswald. He blocked their calls to his cell phone so they took turns phoning the Colony, leaving messages, asking him to contact them so they could discuss the angry confrontation at the restaurant. Only the answering machine picked up at the Colony; by the end of September, their calls had still not been returned.

"I feel so helpless," Edith said one evening. "I wake up in the middle of the night thinking everything about Oswald and Vanya is a nightmare, but it's *real*, and we can't do anything about it."

Derek had finally picked up the binder, was now reading it daily, adding insights and writing down theories as they came to him. It was the only way he could keep his memories intact; it was a discipline and if he didn't do it every single day, things slipped away. He thought the contents might help them unravel whatever had entangled Oswald. He was desperate to see if they had missed anything. He had a horrible, nagging feeling in his gut that time was running out, but he had no idea where that anxiety came from. If it wasn't for the copious notes, Derek doubted if he or Edith would remember every single horrible detail that had occurred to them, or that there even was a village named Hydesville. He had learned so much over the past several weeks, had developed explanations, scratched them out, written new ones. It was an education in madness; if anyone ever read the contents, they would think he was insane.

At first, Edith was convinced it was ghosts or some form of supernatural event that they were encountering, insisted Derek write that down. "You didn't experience what I did in the Fox house," she reminded him. "It *was* ghosts or spirits or something, I'm certain of it. Those Fox sisters were right about what was in their home, it was a poltergeist or something with intelligence that was banging on the walls, making those footsteps, moving things around."

Derek indulged her. They made a list of every strange experience, were surprised that each one could be cross referenced to paranormal activity: Flames turn blue in the presence of spirits, bad phone connections or regularly failing electronics are signs of a supernatural presence as are spaces turning cold in a matter of seconds, apparitions, feelings of being watched, drawers, cupboards and doors opening and closing on their own, footsteps, voices and other unexplained noises.

"We've had all of that," Edith had said excitedly, nodding as Derek read off the list which he had taped into the binder. "I told you it was ghosts!"

After thinking it over, he said what had concerned him for some time. "Yeah, and that's exactly the problem. We have encountered every single one of the things on the list. Just like in those scary movies and books. These are the cliché things you hear about in ghost stories."

"Well, yes. That's because spirits show themselves in these ways. Right?"

"Yes, but don't you see? It's *everything* on these lists we've compiled, it's each item, like a shopping list or checklist."

Edith waited for him to continue.

"It's like the greatest hits of supernatural events. We have zeroed in on all this stuff because it's familiar and expected, but what have we forgotten?"

She thought for a moment. "You'll have to check the notes. I really can't remember every single thing."

"Exactly! That's my point. We get so hung up on the spooky stuff that they divert our attention from other things we've experienced. It's like we have a one-track mind, and everything must fit on the ghost train or we ignore it. Remember the tasteless food, the fire that didn't warm us, *the amnesia*? *Those* are the things that we should be focusing on, but we're not, are we? We're stuck verifying a bunch of cliché things like we're on one of those ridiculous ghost hunter shows—"

"It's a distraction!" Edith said excitedly. "It's trying to distract us so we don't find out what's really going on."

"That's what I'm thinking. If we decide it's a haunting, then we simply are confined by whatever rules that involves. We stop exploring, seeking out the truth. We settle. And all the while, it can do whatever it wants because we're over here, stuck in ghost land. That's what's been bugging me about all the paranormal stuff; I can't seem to get beyond it, it's so big, so huge, and there's so much written about it, but I think we're dealing with something that is using all that supernatural *noise* to hide behind."

"It's like backstage at a performance," Edith said. "That's really what makes the show run, the stage hands, technical crew, and the audience only sees what the performers are doing. We've been looking at the performance, but we need to find out what's going on behind the curtains."

After a few seconds, Derek nodded. "You know, that example is perfect. Whatever this thing is, it *is* putting on a show for us. Think about it: It provides food for us, but it's fake, flavorless, tasteless. And a fire that provides no warmth, it's all stage dressing, all pretend, all make believe. That reminds me. Remember we went to that magic show at the Carlyle a few years ago? The fellow said afterwards at the cocktail reception that all magic is really just distraction—"

"No, *misdirection*!" Edith said. "He said misdirection. Look it up, the meaning."

Derek was at the computer, found the definition, read it to her. "'Misdirection is a form of deception in which the attention of an audience is focused on one thing in order to distract its attention from another.' So, this is really about deception, sending us one direction when the truth is really somewhere else."

They went silent, each pondering whatever it was that was behind what was occurring.

Edith said, "But if it's not supernatural or paranormal or whatever the term is, what is it? What do we call it?"

"It's from some other…realm, I guess, some dimension we've never considered, I suppose."

"And it's terribly smart, or maybe cunning is a better word," Edith said.

"Yes, smart enough to hide itself in the trappings of the paranormal, something it knew we'd be familiar with and probably grab on to immediately."

"It's like it set us up, deceived us, presented us with the trappings of ghosts so we'd follow that path."

Derek wrote all of this down quickly in the notebook in case they suffered another memory loss: *Something from another realm, deceptive, smart, not ghosts or things that go bump in the night.* He finished by writing and underlining the words *It deceives.*

"Don't laugh, but maybe it's an alien, or aliens?" Edith suggested after he had finished.

He shook his head. "No, again, too…easy. It would have done all that abduction stuff, spaceships if it wanted us to head in that direction, plus it doesn't explain everything, the—"

"Maybe it's Vanya?"

Derek looked at Edith, waited for her to continue.

"I mean, maybe *she's* the thing that's causing all this to happen? There is something mysterious, strange about her, but we've been so distracted with the ghost stuff that we haven't really focused on *her*."

He wrote it down, said, "The same goes for the village of Hydesville, the Fox house, the woods and the Keilgarden Colony. It's all part of this."

"True, but I still think it's Vanya," Edith said again. "She's the one thing common to all of this. She sent the invitation, works with the Colony, met us at the restaurant where we spoke so weirdly, was in Hydesville and at the Fox house—"

"—met and plans to marry Oswald next month," Derek said.

"So, who is she and what is her power, why is she doing this?"

"And why Hydesville?"

"And what role do the Fox sisters play, right?" Edith asked. "Their cottage and Spiritualism, the Colony buying their property, the Fox Woods. It seems to be a...a targeted place for all of this to begin; we had to go *there* for it to begin, it didn't happen to us *here*."

Derek said, "That's a good point. So that means the village is a special place. I wonder if there are other locations like Hydesville, or is it unique?" He quickly began typing information into Google, called Edith over to read along with what he found on the screen.

He jotted down the numerous places in the United States that were known to have magical or occult energy or urban legends. They went deep into Native American culture since it was amongst the oldest in the United States, discovered there were other places like Hydesville: The Bighorn Medicine Wheel in Wyoming, Mount Denali in Alaska, Serpent Mound in Ohio, Mount Shasta in Northern California, Dudleytown in Connecticut. But there was no evidence he could find where people claimed they were mentally affected by the locations. No mentions of amnesia, dream visitation or any of the other things they had experienced.

Edith said, "Check Sedona. Remember that trip we took there? It was said to be a place of special energy or something."

That led to a companion site about the ancient Middle-Mississippian village in Wisconsin's Aztalan State Park, along with a dozen other so-called haunted places, but nothing came close to Hydesville.

"None of these places are reported to cause traveler's confusion like Hydesville," Derek said, "and they are always easy to find on maps or GPS."

When he finished transcribing the information, Edith said, "Okay, so it's the *place* that's unique. This thing or whatever it is—whatever *Vanya* is—there's something about Hydesville that attracted it in the first place."

"I guess that would be the Fox sisters, right? I mean, that's what the village is known for," Derek said. "Here's an idea. Maybe it's a place and a time. We know the place, so maybe the time period is important?"

"The mid-1800s," Edith said, "the 19th century. What was different about that era?"

Derek clacked away at the keyboards as Edith wrote down what he said. "Let's see, prior to the seventeenth century, there was only a little interest in the occult and supernatural. When the Age of Reason came along, it pretty much squashed that diminishing worldview, made it outdated and primitive. And the 19th century was an era of technology and science. There was the invention of the telephone, light bulb, telegraph, discoveries like vaccines and germ theory. But interestingly, there was also a profound, renewed interest in religion along with a huge resurgence and a fascination with…the supernatural!"

He turned to look at her; they grinned at one another. "A time and place! It says that even in the midst of great advances in technology and science, people had a new-found willingness to suspend their belief about what was seen or heard or felt."

"Hypnotism!" Edith said abruptly. "Isn't that what we've felt at times, like we were under a spell? When did it become popular?"

A few seconds later, Derek said, "The term 'hypnotism'—which means a sleep of the nerves—was coined by James Braid, a surgeon, in 1842, so the same time period as the Fox sisters. He studied extensively about what he called mesmeric trance."

"And isn't that what the Vanya thing does to us, to Oz? She mesmerizes us?"

Derek thought about it, said, "Maybe because the 19th century had that new-found open-mindedness, it allowed things like Vanya to invade people's thoughts easier? Gave it access to cause them to see and feel things, made them do things against their will?"

"Like compelling Oz to marry Vanya," Edith said.

She wrote as fast as she could, summarizing their conversation and conclusions: The 19th century was ideal for the thing called Vanya to introduce itself to this world since people wanted to believe in paranormal events, they were primed for what happened in Hydesville in 1848 and Katie and Maggie communicating with the dead.

Derek said, "It's fascinating, I think we're right about this! It says here that there was little to no evidence of any rappings or communicating with the dead before the Fox sisters. After the events in Hydesville, one of the most significant religious movements of the 19th century, Spiritualism, had begun, which introduced the belief in ghosts to a worldwide community. It was the only time in our history that it could work since everyone *wanted* to believe."

Edith asked, "But why couldn't the Vanya thing have done it in the 1960s or 70s? There was a big uptick in the occult then, right? All those weird movies and books and music?"

After tapping on the keyboard, Derek acknowledged what she had suggested. "Look at this. It says that in the early 1970s, *TIME* magazine devoted a cover story to the topic since interest in the occult in American culture was so high at the time. But let's think about this. Fascination in the supernatural was so widespread at that time, I wonder if it was too big for Vanya? Maybe it was too much, too many people?"

Edith said, "That makes sense. An isolated community like Hydesville would make it easier for the Vanya thing to distract, misdirect and control people. You think her power is limited?"

Derek nodded. "I do. Think about it. Just you, me and Oz seem to have had interactions with her. Maybe she needs to start small, keep things contained. That explains why so few have heard of her or commented about her. Even if she wipes out their memory, it seems to eventually come back, so if she had revealed herself, others would have eventually known, talked about it, maybe investigated, told others. But it's only been us."

After he wrote that down, he said, "I also sense that the longer she's around us, the stronger she gets. And I think the more she knows about us, the more she can *do*."

"We shouldn't call it a she, Vanya isn't a woman, isn't even human," Edith said. "She's a *thing*, dressed up like a human, wears a disguise to deceive us."

Derek nodded as he turned to a fresh page in the binder. "When the Fox sisters heard the rappings, it was the Vanya thing, deceiving them into thinking it was simply a ghost, a poltergeist or spirit trying to chat with them."

Edith said, "That way, no one would ever look too closely into what it *really* was." She exhaled loudly, smiled. "You know, this all sort of makes sense now, doesn't it?"

Tired, Derek stretched, rubbed his eyes. "Only sort of. We know the Vanya thing uses deception and misdirection, but what does it *want*? Why is it *here*?"

II:
The Impossible

134

CHAPTER 12.

Two days later, after they had once again updated the notes in the binder, Edith closed it, said sadly, "It's like Oz has been recruited to a cult, is getting brainwashed or something. And I know he must be sick with something he's not telling us about; he looked dreadful at lunch."

Her cell phone chimed. Derek leaned back on the couch, watched her as she paced around the room, asking questions, listening to the responses. When she ended the call, her eyes were glassy, bright and dry, as if she had been staring too long at some astonishing image.

"What happened? Who was on the phone?"

"It was my doctor. I went for a check-up a couple days ago. I sensed...I thought that...Oh, Derek...He told me. I'm. Pregnant."

She had said those words to him once before, ten years earlier. It had been an accident, evidence that no form of birth control was totally effective. She had been the one from the beginning who had never wanted children, Derek had felt the same way. She had gone on to have a tubal sterilization to prevent any further chance that a child would be conceived.

Stunned, Derek said, "You're…but isn't that impossible?"

"Well, clearly it isn't!" She almost laughed. "He said that it is rare to conceive and warned that I have about a thirty percent risk of an…ectopic pregnancy."

"What's that?"

"When the egg implants outside the womb. He has some more tests to perform." She smiled weakly at Derek. "I'm in shock. It's all kind of amazing. Just last week, I told her I thought it was impossible…"

"Told *her*? Who?"

"Hmm? Oh, nothing…"

They sat there in the early evening silence, holding hands. Derek kissed her tenderly. "I love you. And you *are* amazing."

Edith started to laugh. "Believe me, I never thought I was *this* amazing! I'm going to have a baby."

"And you *are* okay, aren't you?"

"Yes, the doctor said everything was fine…" She hesitated. "The strange thing is, I'm not really surprised. It's odd, but ever since I had that dream about having a son…it's like I've just been waiting for this to happen, expecting his phone call…"

Although they continued to hold hands, emotionally he sensed she had moved away from him, was standing on her own at the opposite end of the room. Again, he noticed that when she mentioned the dream and the child, it was always her baby, never theirs. *I'm* going to have a baby, not we're going to.

Choosing his words carefully, Derek said, "That really *was* some dream, wasn't it? I mean, you rarely recall what you dream about, do you? But this one really stuck with you, didn't it?" She was nodding, a crooked smile on her face. He finished his thought, said, "But honey, it was just a *dream,* it doesn't mean…"

"Not anymore," she said. "It's not a dream anymore. I'm *really* going to have a baby!"

"But honey…you've never wanted children, you told me that from the very beginning, done everything you could to prevent it." He could hear his voice, the panicky edge to it. He stopped speaking to calm himself down.

Edith was watching him closely. "You're right. But I've changed my mind…"

Derek, desperate to regain ground, shifted gears. "What does the doctor suggest you do?"

"He wants to perform some more tests on the embryonic fluid to make certain the fetus is all right. Then, if everything checks out, he said I should make a decision. And I *know* everything will be fine. Just like in the dream, it's all going to be wonderful. I'm going to have a baby!"

Derek slept fitfully that night, awakening every hour or so to find Edith slumbering next to him. It was after three in the morning. He wished her pregnancy was a dream that he was waking from, like so many of the nightmares they had experienced in the past few weeks.

He was planning to accompany Edith to the doctor for her tests. If the results were positive, if it seemed that she was healthy enough to carry the baby to term, then in June he would be a father. A father! His heart raced at the thought, charged him up to such an extent that he climbed out of bed, knowing that for the moment, sleep eluded him. He glanced back at Edith, who continued to dream.

I'm going to be a dad, Derek marveled.

He made his way through the moonlit apartment to the kitchen. Odd. Two of the cupboards were wide open. He closed them, poured himself a glass of milk. Sipping it, he glanced out the window, noticed lights were on across the avenue in the facing building. *Who else was awake at this hour,* he wondered. What issues or problems had dragged them from their sleep, left them to ponder their fate in the pre-dawn light? He finished the milk, set the glass in the sink, yawned. He left the kitchen, started back to the bedroom.

He saw them in the moonlight.

Three figures, pale, ghostly silver due to the glow of the moon, white starched collars luminous in the night shadows that surrounded them. Their green eyes were incandescent in the dim, shaded space. They stared at him; as in previous encounters, there was an overwhelming sense of *need* emanating from them, a desire for something. Derek recognized two of the specters as the Fox children, Maggie and Katie. Who was the one on the right? Her image wasn't as fully formed as the others, seemed to flicker like a lightbulb about to die out. *This is just a distraction,* he reminded himself. *Simple misdirection.* Still, it was frightening to see the apparitions. He swallowed to loosen his vocal chords, managed to whisper, "Why are you here? What do you want?"

The shapes seemed startled that he spoke; he saw their images falter for a moment, grow brighter in the shadows. Their arms extended, reaching out, imploring him, but for what? Then they merged with the shadows, fading into the gloom. Derek blinked several times, felt dizzy, leaned against the wall to steady himself.

What was that all about? he wondered. *Was Vanya using them to test our theory, confirm to her that we've moved beyond the stage of being spooked by the distraction of ghostly manifestations? Maybe once they know we don't believe they are the source of what's going on, they vanish? I'll have to add that to the binder.*

Then, a tug at his loins. He was aroused. Was Vanya nearby? He recalled the times Vanya had been in his presence, the effect her voice had had on him over the phone the first time they spoke. A dream-image of making love to her surfaced for an instant then sank into the darkness. Was she close, was that why his body was responding this way?

He padded back to the bedroom, intent on putting thoughts of Vanya out of his mind. Edith was still softly snoring. He slipped into bed, his cock still raging hard. He wanted to put his erection to good use. He wrapped himself around Edith from behind, pulling her close, kissing the back of her neck.

"Derek?" Edith suddenly said, her voice sharp, clear, no sense of drowsiness about it. She turned over, slipping easily around in his grasp, began kissing him passionately, taking him completely by surprise. Thrilled, he reached down, found that she was already moist, all ready for him. He pushed her nightgown up, was preparing to enter her…

Vanya smiled up at him, her green eyes gleaming unnaturally in the moonlight that glowed from the window. She pulled his neck down until he was forced to kiss her. Derek tried to turn his head, but it was as if she was sucking the very life force out of him, melding herself to him, joining them in a union he desperately wanted to be free of. She reached over his buttocks until she had maneuvered him inside of her. Vanya curved her legs around his, locking herself into his body, chest to chest, mouth to mouth, groin to groin. She began thrusting herself at him. Her grip on him tightened. He struggled even though his body had fully responded to the encounter.

"Oz is trying, but I don't have much hope," she whispered in his ear, her breath hot. "I want to keep you primed and ready if I need you."

They shook together in unison, he yielded, all thoughts of resisting her vanquished. He felt the first stirrings of a climax approaching. He came closer and closer, moaning and thrashing about in ecstasy, felt himself being consumed by the event, succumbing to the sensual gratification. Even as he rocked in their shared passion, he knew he was also making a choice to experience it to its fullness this time, and also to face the unknown repercussions that may follow, whatever they may be.

Derek thought he heard a voice urgently calling his name. At the same time, the intensity of Vanya's embrace tightened until it was painful. It burned his skin, he writhed about to be free from her. Her nails dug deep into his back. He pushed away from her for an instant to relieve himself from her embrace and—

— Edith was shaking him, calling his name. Derek opened his eyes.

"Wake up! You're having a bad dream," she said.

He sat up in the bed, trembling. Edith fluffed up the pillows behind him. He glanced at the bedside clock. 7:40 a.m. Sunlight filled the window. He had fallen asleep, finally, for a few hours. It had been a dream.

Except for the nail marks that remained on his back.

CHAPTER 13.

The Indian summer that had clung to September was finally shaken off when October arrived. During a beautiful, clear, brisk Sunday afternoon late in the month, Derek and Edith wandered along Madison Avenue, window-shopping, then stopped for lunch at Bistro 60. Some friends from another gallery greeted them, joined their table.

Derek and Edith had decided to wait until Edith began to show before announcing their news. Although the doctor had been extremely optimistic, he had cautioned that the first trimester was the one of highest risk of losing the baby. He told them that all the tests had come back in their favor, that it was not an ectopic pregnancy. If she chose to keep the baby, they should expect delivery around the beginning of June. He assured them that Edith was fine, but he encouraged them to weigh their options, as any expecting couple would. "At this point, you're both doing well. However, due to the robust hormonal therapy you'll be on, very likely total bed rest will be required from about November on."

Following lunch, Edith chatted on the phone with some friends while Derek sorted through the mail. A square envelope was addressed to him, the handwriting unfamiliar. He opened it, pulled out a card. On the front, in gold leaf, were the words *Thank You*. Inside, four words:

He's mine now.
Vanya.

There was no return address. Derek could make out that the envelope was posted from Hydesville. He knew immediately what Vanya was referring to: Weeks had passed and with no word or returned calls from Oswald, Derek had forgotten about the October fifth wedding. Oswald was now married to Vanya.

Derek crumpled up the card and envelope, threw them in the wastebasket. A moment later, he pulled them out, tore them up. Then, realizing he didn't even want them in the apartment, he took the scraps of paper out to the hallway disposal area, dropped them down the chute.

He didn't want any trace of Vanya in their apartment, not even her name signed on a piece of paper. Despair settled over Derek, cloaked him it its gray futility. It was over now, she had won. She had what she wanted; Oswald was hers now. What was the point of any further inquiry into who or what she was?

###

It rained all day on Halloween, thunder and lightning shot across the sky, setting the perfect mood for the ghostly occasion. From early evening, their apartment bell rang or childish knocks were heard on the door. Edith happily doled out candy to the witches, spooks, cats, and super heroes who never tired of shrieking "Trick or treat!" when she appeared.

As the evening wore on, the tricksters outnumbered those who sought candy. The doorbell frequently chimed or frantic knocking was heard, but no one was waiting with an outstretched candy bag. Derek and Edith even lurked at the entry and yanked the door open at the first sound, but never caught the culprits. This went on well past ten, which irritated them both.

Edith noticed Derek didn't immediately write down the strange event. "Where's your binder? Aren't you going to add these weird shenanigans to it?"

"What's the point?" he said. "It's Halloween, isn't that when witchy things are supposed to happen?"

She looked at him, shrugged. "You just seemed so adamant to capture every single thing, that's all."

He sighed. "Okay, I'll write it down." He added the odd event to the ever-growing notations in the binder. He knew it was another distraction, even wrote the word GHOSTS in large letters, then put a thick line through it. *Not supernatural*, he wrote. *It's much bigger than that, uses paranormal events to disguise itself, misdirect us. Don't fall for it!*

After reading over a few of the previous pages, he realized how silly it all sounded; some conspiracy theory written by someone with a tin foil helmet. All the enthusiasm and curiosity had dulled for him; he doubted if there was a need to continue with the project. What was the point? He was going to be a dad, plus he now had to handle everything with the gallery, and who knew if he'd ever see his brother again? He needed to focus on those life changing events, not every little thing that went bump in the night or every bad dream he had. He closed the binder, set it on the shelf, doubt he'd write much more in it. He had better, more important things to do.

By ten thirty, the door knocking interruptions ceased. They climbed wearily into bed to read; Derek glanced through the *Wall Street Journal* on his iPad while Edith studied *What to Expect When You're Expecting*. He glanced at her, smiled as he watched her eagerly devour the contents of the book. After days of soul searching, he had finally succumbed to the idea that he was to become a father, the lifetime guardian to a child. He still was troubled by Edith's about-face when it came to being a mother, especially since she insisted on crediting much of her changed heart to her odd dream about she and Oswald both having babies. But she had been so elated and joyous over the prospect, he had put his concerns aside.

He was going to be a dad.

They turned the light out after eleven, Derek fell asleep almost immediately. His phone seemed to ring seconds later. He fumbled around for it; it took him a few moments to answer. He noticed one of them had left the bathroom light on. He glanced at the time on the iPhone, was surprised to see it was already after two in the morning. He didn't recognize the 315 area code.

He cleared his throat and, trying not to awaken Edith, whispered into the phone, "Hello?"

"Derek David?"

"Yes, who is this?"

"Mr. David, this is Lieutenant Johnson of the Hydesville Police Department. I apologize for calling so late. You have a brother, Oswald David?"

"Yes."

"I'm afraid I have some bad news. Your brother's body has been found in the Fox Woods here in Hydesville."

Derek sat up in the bed, his sudden movements waking Edith.

"Is he all right?" Derek asked.

"No, Mr. David. I am so sorry to inform you that your brother is deceased."

"What? Oh, my God! What was he—"

"Mr. David, I'd rather not discuss the details over the phone. Would it be possible for you to meet with me tomorrow? I know it's a bit of a drive but there are several things I need to address with you immediately, face to face, about the nature of your brother's death..."

Derek hadn't seen or spoken to his brother since their disastrous lunch at the garden restaurant. He and Oswald had drifted so far apart that his death somehow seemed almost inevitable. It was as if Oswald had been clinging to a life raft that had become unmoored and was drifting further into the deep recessives of the sea. Derek could only watch his brother gradually fade from view as he disappeared into the darkness.

And it was all on account of Vanya Avery.

He's mine now.

Why had she sent that card? Derek wondered. Addressed to him, there was a triumphant connotation about it, as if she had been trying to win Oswald over, and she finally had. "We are one now," Oz had said that horrible day at lunch. And it was true: Vanya had taken him away from them and now, Oswald was gone forever.

Derek finished the call, turned to Edith, told her the terrible news. They held one another in shocked grief as they tried to comprehend what had happened. Edith wept and Derek, feeling hollow and sick inside, could only hold her, unable to speak or comfort her, feeling only a deepening sense of loss and despair.

Encircled by mourning, unable to sleep, Derek and Edith, embraced each other as the hours passed and the dark bedroom gradually lightened with the approach of dawn.

###

The next morning, Edith checked on flights to Rochester, the city closest to Hydesville, but the small commuter airline was already booked solid. She wanted to accompany Derek on the five-hour drive, but car travel didn't agree with her pregnancy and Warren was away visiting a cousin in Hartford.

"You know you shouldn't be driving alone," Edith said. "Why don't you just call a car service?"

"Don't worry, if I have even an inkling a spell is coming on, I'll pull over," Derek said. He strongly felt he needed to do this alone, needed the freedom and independence to drive around Hydesville and the Colony, find out whatever he could without the constraints or questions from a driver. He owed his brother to find out everything he could. It was now seven in the morning, he was eager to be on his way. He made certain the notebook was with him; he hoped he'd have a lot of updates to add to it. Edith hugged him tightly, her belly pressing against him, a reminder that so much was soon to change in their lives.

The green sign for Wayne County, New York, flashed by the car as Derek sped north up I-90. Portions of the drive seemed familiar to Derek, as were some of the back roads he had traveled on for the past few hours. Most, but not all, of his and Edith's memories were recovered from the missing days back in early August. Perhaps when his and Edith's recollections were completely restored, the events of the past few months would begin to make some sort of sense. Now it was merely the back side of a tapestry, a chaotic mess of ideas and events, questions and theories.

The first day of November was clear, the surrounding area washed clean after the previous nights' rainfall. Leaves that had stayed past their prime had been struck from the trees by the storm, the black, bare branches looked like cracks against the sky. A sign welcoming Derek to Hydesville sped by the car. He made the turns, followed the streets signs as provided by Officer Johnson in the printed email Derek had in the seat next to him.

The police station, like the vaguely familiar town itself, was a small, unassuming building, appropriate for the little hamlet of Hydesville. Overhead, several black birds called to one another, then took off in flight, darting across the sky in fancy arcs and turns that appeared as if they were showing off. They disappeared over the cluster of rooftops that comprised the main street of Hydesville. Derek looked around, saw a hardware store, Del's Coffee Shop, a deli, the Elite Tailor, a small grocery store, a pharmacy, the red, white and blue spinning cylinder that indicated a barber. Overall, Hydesville appeared to be a slightly down-on-its-luck small town that probably hadn't changed much in fifty years. *Was any of this here when Edith and I visited in August or is it just some set created by the Vanya thing, then put away when it's not needed?* he wondered. Very little of it was familiar to him. He recalled something about the trees, the way the old, cracked sidewalk pitched and rolled, but most of it was foreign.

Tears stung his eyes as he thought of his brother—who thrived on Manhattan's nightclubs, wild social scenes, gallery openings, international travel—spending the last few weeks of his life tucked away in a quiet, out-of-the way village that concealed the Keilgarden Colony and who knew what else. It just didn't make any sense.

He called Edith. The phone answered with a static burst that was so loud, he almost dropped it. He left a voice mail letting her know he had arrived safely. With one last glance at the strangely deserted streets of Hydesville, Derek walked up the steps, entered the police station, hoped for answers.

CHAPTER 14.

Broad shouldered with a chest that strained at his police uniform, Lieutenant Johnson looked to be in his late forties and appeared to spend a good deal of time at the gym. His grip as he shook Derek's hand confirmed that he was familiar with barbells and strength training. He offered Derek coffee, then ushered him into a cramped, messy office.

The linoleum floor was scratched and stained, several wire baskets were overflowing with paper, the walls were covered with memos and wanted posters. Derek sat in a chair that was losing its stuffing, Johnson squeezed behind a battered metal desk that looked as if the ceiling had caved in on it. To the left of the desk was a grimy computer monitor, the kind popular ten years earlier.

"Let me again offer my condolences, Mr. David," Johnson said once they were settled in. "A homicide of this nature requires—"

"Homicide? Oswald was murdered?"

Johnson shifted in his seat, put his hands up to hold back Derek's comments.

"Let me start from the beginning. That's why I thought it was important we speak face to face. Much of this information is sensitive and I didn't want to relay it to you over the phone." He opened a file on his desk, glanced down at it from time to time as he spoke. "Two days ago, October 30th, we received a call—"

"Who called?"

"It was an anonymous tip."

"The caller—"

"Man or woman?"

Johnson looked at him, then back down at the report. "It, um, doesn't say. The caller said that a man was suspended from a tree in the Fox Woods, about a half mile out of town. We investigated, discovered the naked body..."

"Naked?"

Johnson nodded.

"My brother was hanging naked from a tree?" Derek shook his head in disbelief. "Where's his body now?"

"Wayne County general morgue, for holding. You can go there as soon as we're finished here." Johnson glanced down at the file. "We retrieved the body of your brother. We checked the rope for fingerprints, but the fiber strands didn't retain any usable traces." He hesitated, then, reading from the file, said, "Upon examination of your brother, we found semen discharged on his legs."

Derek didn't respond, had no idea where the police officer was headed with the information.

"At first we believed that your brother's death was a suicide. But after we found the semen we thought it might be a case of asphyxiaphilia. Are you familiar with the term?"

Derek shook his head.

"It's more commonly known as erotic strangulation, a method used to achieve a more powerful ejaculation. It's based on the idea that during masturbation, the climax can be dramatically intensified if oxygen is limited at a certain point during the experience. Sort of an orgasm-heightening high."

Derek only stared at the officer, thinking, *Dear God, where is this going?*

Johnson said, "Tragically, it doesn't always have the desired effect. Sometimes the person is found dead, hanging in their closet or from some support beam."

Derek sat up in his seat, rubbed the back of his neck. His thoughts were blurry with horrific, confused images of his brother, his body handing from a tree in the woods. Johnson was still, waited for Derek to speak.

"I'm…trying to make sense of this, but I can't. You're telling me my brother was in the forest, with a rope around his neck, masturbating, and at a certain point, he… jumped off a tree branch to hang himself, just to experience a more intense climax?" He leaned forward. "You're fucking nuts! Why would my brother do that, knowing he'd kill himself?! He had everything to live for! He had just gotten married, was excited about the future, not preparing to commit suicide!"

I'm trying so hard to please her. The phrase came to Derek. Oswald had said that to him. Was that what he had meant? With a sickening realization, Derek wondered, *Was he doing anything he could to—*

"Have you contacted his wife, Vanya Avery? She lives up here, they were both staying at the Colony."

Johnson said, "As I mentioned on the phone to you last night, we tried to contact the Colony, but have not received any word back from your brother's wife. In fact, the exact location of the Colony is in some dispute."

"What do you mean, 'dispute'?"

Flustered, Johnson explained, "We haven't actually located the facility. Yet. To be completely honest, we can't seem to find it."

Derek waited. Johnson shrugged. "The Fox Woods are expansive, the roads and pathways are old, unmarked. The Colony and those who live there are very private people. They live on a hidden compound; they don't want to be found. But we *will* find them, and Ms. Avery; my team is on it right now, but putting that aside, I need some more information from you. There are some things we're not sure about without an autopsy, and that's scheduled for tomorrow."

"What exactly are you looking for?"

"Possible drug use. If your brother was high when he died, if his brain receptors were sending abnormal messages, then maybe it was a drug-induced suicide. But we doubt that, nor do we think it's even possible he took his own life."

Derek waited.

Johnson shifted in his chair, cleared his throat. "We don't know how he got up in that tree, Mr. David. You see, it was close to fifty feet off the ground, and there's no way he could have gotten up there alone. It was a sheer, flat climb to that first branch he was found hanging from. There was no ladder around, no tracks in the earth or evidence that anyone had even been there. And there were no other trees or branches nearby that he could have used to climb up and across."

"I still don't understand."

"I'm saying that your brother needed some help to get up there, and that whomever got him on that branch was probably the one who pushed him off." He paused. "Also, and I don't know how to put it any easier, but your brother's neck wasn't broken; the rope strangled him."

"What difference does that make?"

"If someone had jumped off the branch, the rope would have pulled taunt, would have snapped and broken the person's neck. Decapitation would probably have occurred. But it didn't. The rope was tight around your brother's neck, very snug. The condition has led us to believe that he had been slowly lowered from the branch, not like he had jumped or been pushed."

Shaken by the information, Derek felt anger, rage and a mounting sense of dread and grief begin to overwhelm him. "Who would do such a horrible thing to my brother? And why?"

###

It was late afternoon when Derek left the Hydesville Police Station. Numb from the conversation with Officer Johnson, he was burdened with even more questions and uncertainty.

Outside, it had clouded up. The village looked even more isolated and forlorn than it had earlier, matching his mood. It was unnerving to be so alone in the town. He expected people to be out and about, but the streets were empty. Overhead, the white-gray clouds hovered motionless, as if waiting for a signal to disperse. Despondent over all that Johnson had told him, Derek took a moment to compose himself before calling Edith to update her on the bizarre circumstances that surrounded Oswald's death. His throat tightened, he started to weep as he told her the details.

When he finished, he said, "I need to spend the night here. There must be a library in town and I want to do some research, bolster some of the stuff we wrote in the binder. Maybe I can locate the Colony; I can't believe the police were unable to."

"What if you run across Vanya?" Edith asked uncertainly.

"She should be more concerned if she encounters me! She—or it—killed Oswald. I'll deal with her if I find her," he said grimly. "I'll leave first thing in the morning, stop by the morgue on the way home."

"You be careful," she said. "I don't like you being up there or driving alone. You're sure you're all right?"

"No, of course I'm not all right," he said. "Not at all, especially after all Johnson told me. But I want to find out all I can. I want to put an end to this, whatever it is."

Hungry, he had a sandwich at Del's Coffee Shop, which, like most of Hydesville, was deserted with the exception of a lone waitress and cook. The food had flavor, Derek assumed it was real, but he no longer trusted anything he saw or felt. It could all be a dream or illusion, manifested by the Vanya thing. *Maybe I am going mad,* he thought idly. *If anyone was aware of the ideas in my head, they'd put me away.* He looked at the open binder in front of him next to the plate of French fries, glanced at some of the ludicrous things he and Edith had written over the past few months, wondered how much of it was true, how much was lunacy.

Back out on the street, the air was still, the sky was now a dark gray with the promise of a storm. The temperature had dropped while he'd been inside; Derek shivered, his sports jacket not providing much warmth. There were so many unanswered questions about Hydesville, the Colony, why the Fox sisters kept appearing to him. He had been disappointed with all that Johnson didn't know about Oswald's death, his inability to locate Vanya or the Colony. Could it really be so difficult to find either one in this little town?

He started walking, looking for a library or bookstore, anyplace that would have information about the village. Other than that sole *Life* article, the internet had been pretty useless; he'd have to go old school. He mentally ticked off his goals: *I need to learn about the history of this town, the Fox sisters, the Colony, maybe even find out something about the Vanya thing if that was possible. Then, armed with the facts, I can talk it over with Officer Johnson, work toward a more thorough investigation of what happened to Oswald, and what is happening to Edith and me. And maybe the facts will help assure me we're not crazy, not all losing our minds.*

Then, like an answered prayer, as soon as he finished his list of objectives, he came to the end of the street. Nestled under a cluster of trees was the Hydesville Library.

CHAPTER 15.

The place looked to be either deserted or void of any recent library-visiting enthusiasts. There may or may not have been illumination inside the building; the windows were so grubby it was impossible to see if the lights were on but nobody was home. Weeds had grown up between the cracked pavement, the thin, vertical windows that lined the entry way were filthy with grime. Knapsack over his shoulder, Derek passed between the old, crumbling columns that stood like ancient sentries, guarding the entrance to the building. He tried the front door handle, expecting it to be locked tight. It turned easily.

Once inside, the library spread out before him, was much larger than he had expected. He glanced around the cluttered, dusty space. The dirty windows that lined the building remained in shadow, shying away from the antiquated overhead lights and their chalky, dull glow. Like perfectly landscaped privet hedges, rows of shelves divided the library up into sections. Derek could see two or three small round tables scattered about but didn't get the sense that anyone else was in the building.

The checkout desk was immediately in front of him. He was surprised to see it was occupied by an Elder, a reed-thin woman whom he guessed was in her mid-to late eighties. She had badly cut, thin silver hair that squarely framed her coarse, roadmap face. Her dull green eyes watched him as he approached. A hollow silence hovered over them, amplifying the slightest movement: his footsteps, the rustle of the ancient librarian's dress as she stood, the squeak of her chair as she vacated it, the slow shuffle, shuffle, shuffle of her shoes as she approached Derek.

"Hello," she said immediately, as if she had been waiting all day for Derek to appear. Her one word greeting banged around the large empty library for an instant. Her fingers fluttered nervously at her sides, playing piano scales in the air. The left side of her neck had a boil or growth that was bruised a gray-purple; he tried not to stare.

"I'm doing some research, want some information about Hydesville. Old newspapers, books, anything that will give me a sense about the town, its history."

"That would all be kept in the archives." Her voice was flat, gravely. She spoke the words rapidly, almost like a computer. She gestured Derek to follow her to the back of the library. "It's nice to have someone express an interest in our little village," she said over her shoulder as she led him toward a room with the words *Hydesville Historical Archives* stenciled on it. He noticed that her left leg seemed shorter than the right, causing her to lurch to the side as she walked. Her fingers continued their random movements; he wondered if it was a nervous disorder.

"There's a photocopy machine just outside the room if you want to make copies of anything. I'll be at the front if you need me. We close at eight."

He pushed the door open, stepped into a space that resembled a small, cluttered attic. *The people who call this the Hydesville Historical Archives suffer from delusions of grandeur,* he thought ruefully. Old magazines were stacked in bulging boxes, ancient photo albums lined one corner of the room, yellow and torn newspapers were strewn about, rolls of blueprints were jammed in between bookshelves that were lined with dusty volumes.

He scanned the titles, hoping one would catch his attention. The spines read like titles from historical movies or never-seen documentaries: *The Story of Swedenborg, Edward Irving: The Shakers, The History of Spiritualism, The Career of D.D. Home, Collective Investigations of Spiritualism, Great Mediums from 1870 to 1900, The Society for Psychical Research, Spirit Photography, The Afterlife as Seen by Spiritualists, Hydesville In History, The Career of the Fox Sisters.*

Derek removed the last two books, cleared off the cluttered table, sat down, started to read, began to take notes.

It was close to eight when Derek stuffed the stack of copies he had made into his notebook. The camera on his phone hadn't worked so he was grateful for the photocopy machine. He stretched, his shoulders were tight, heavy. His eyes burned from the time spent reading through the papers, but he also had a certain thrill flushing through him because he had learned a great deal about the town of Hydesville, the Fox Woods, and, most importantly he thought, his brother's death. He slipped *Hydesville In History* and *The Career of the Fox Sisters* into his knapsack, covered them with his binder and photocopies. He closed the door behind him, said goodnight to the Elder at the counter, left the library, relieved that no alarm went off indicating he had stolen two books.

Outside, massive dark clouds covered the sky from end to end, obscuring most of the moon. The trees that lined the area were bent and hunched over even more than Derek remembered, as if they were cringing from what they sensed was approaching. He hadn't planned to spend so much time in the library. Now he needed a place to stay, and a meal. For some reason, the concentrated research had given him a ravenous appetite. In the morning, he'd have another talk with Officer Johnson; this time he'd have specific questions to ask about the Fox Woods. Then, the morgue, followed by the long drive home, but at least he'd return to Edith with some answers.

The first drop of rain splashed on his forehead. A moment later, another one landed squarely on his head, then one pelted him on the cheek. He turned left, toward the part of town he had not yet explored. He jogged down the street, looking for shelter, trying to hide his knapsack against his chest to protect it from the weather.

Within a few blocks, he was in the sparse residential section of the village. The few homes he passed were dark, appeared deserted or gave off a firm, *Not Welcome Here* vibe. No lights peeked out from the windows even if anyone was home. The disturbing image of people sitting around in darkness, watching him scurry past, flickered through his mind. Suddenly angry, the wind kicked up its fury. The driving rain felt like needles and pebbles against his face and hands. Derek pulled his damp collar up, shivering now as he made his way through the onslaught. The sky was black with the rage of the storm. With no streetlights, he stumbled blindly on the cracked and uneven sidewalks. Trees that had been there for centuries had refused to stop growing, so their roots had broken through the old cement walkways, fracturing and twisting them, leaving mounds on the sidewalks like tumors or frozen waves.

Just as he was thinking he should give up, run back to his car parked in the police station, the sky exploded with lightning. Startled, he gasped as he looked up, just in time to see a tree branch crack and hurtle down at him. He dove forward, stumbled to the ground as the limb crashed with a great clamor behind him. Thunder roared like a predatory beast in search of the lightning that had preceded it. Another electrical firework blazed across the sky.

Derek stood, was immediately hit by the force of the wind, which had quickened its intensity. It plowed into him like a linebacker, managed to knock him down again. He fell hard, banging his knees, ripping the elbow of his sports coat. Now soaked, bruised, his clothes torn, he felt helpless and feeble. He summoned all of his reserve, reset his thinking, willed himself to stand, hugged the knapsack tightly. In front of him he was able to make out a mailbox, the lid like a lower jaw hanging open in astonishment, swinging up and down with the wind. He grabbed hold of it to steady himself, then glanced down the neatly kept pathway at the house behind it.

It wasn't any different from the others he had seen as he had dashed through the storm. Modest, with two windows on either side of the front door, a small yard with a few trees, a second or third story attic window. This property appeared to be kept up more than the others. A flower box was near the step-porch, the blossoms now torn lose, scattered about the yard like broken Christmas ornaments. But what drew his attention was that he saw lights inside. He squinted. Incredibly, the front right window displayed a small, neatly lettered sign: ***Room to let.***

Relived at his unexpected good fortune, Derek hurried under the shelter of the meager porch, knocked on the front door.

CHAPTER 16.

No one responded. He didn't see any shadows moving about inside, so he assumed the occupants hadn't heard due to the racket of the storm. He knocked again, longer and harder, fighting to be heard. It sounded like the sky was shattering, ready to collapse.

Then, locks were turned, the door opened. "Come in, come in! Sorry about the delay but the missus and I were in the back parlor."

Derek hurried inside but stayed by the closed door shivering as his wet clothes quickly formed a small puddle. "Thank you! I hope that room is available for the night. I'm Derek David."

"Atticus Doyle," the man said, stretching out his hand to shake. He was in his late fifties. By the look and size of him, he had spent a career in the army or marines. He had the characteristic buzz cut, square-jawed face, sturdy football build and a firm, dry grip that Derek associated with men from the armed forces; a take-charge, no-nonsense type of man.

Whatever his past, he had a solid, welcoming appearance that Derek appreciated after the raging madness outside. Most of all, he was relieved the man was not an Elder. "Yes, the room is available. Any luggage?"

Derek shook his head, started to explain, but Atticus said, "I'm sure we've got some extra clothes you can change into while we dry these for you. Wait here. I'll get my wife and some towels."

A woman appeared a moment later, looking exactly like everyone's favorite small-town aunt: kind, round face, gray hair worn in a bun, healthy bosom topping off ample hips, sturdy legs. She looked Derek over sympathetically. "Hello, I'm Noreen. What a night, right?"

Atticus returned to the entryway with a robe, several thick towels, an assortment of clothing. "Get yourself a nice hot shower, change into these, then come down and join us for a late supper. We'll have your clothes washed and dried before you know it."

###

After the shower had cleansed away the storm scum, Derek changed into the provided clothes, which were a size or two too big, yet the thick fabric was comforting. He almost felt restored to his old self.

He examined the Xerox copies in his notebook and the two books he had taken from the library, trying to determine how much wear and tear the water had done to them. Fortunately, his soaked knapsack had protected them from any significant damage. The outside covers were barely damp, the pages themselves didn't seem too moist. He laid all the items out flat on the wooden desk in his room to help them dry quicker.

While in the library, Derek had been surprised to find an old, tattered *A Line a Day* diary tucked inside the *Hydesville In History* book. The inside pages were devoted to a calendar for 1811. After carefully turning the pages of the parchment, he came across the name of Ann Ryan along with a faded address. He had almost left the journal behind, thinking she had no bearing on the Fox sisters when, upon further examination, he saw mention of the name John Fox in the pages. He soon discovered why he was included in her diary.

He finger-combed his hair in the Doyle's bathroom mirror, thought that, all things considered, he didn't look too much worse for wear. He called Edith, but the connection failed, tried again, got a nasty static discharge, waited, then left her several messages about what he had learned at the library, told her he had found a place to stay the night.

Downstairs, Noreen and Atticus were busy in the kitchen, getting in one another's way as they went about preparing dinner. Soon they all were settled in at the table and began rapidly passing the plates back and forth.

"This is delicious," Derek said, savoring the full flavor of the roast, potatoes, fresh baked rolls. *This must be real,* he thought, relieved. *The food has flavor.* Then it crossed his mind: *Unless the Vanya thing is upping its game, improving its skills of deception.*

"Noreen is a brilliant cook," Atticus boasted. "I rarely get the opportunity to show off her skills,"

"I wouldn't suppose you'd get many guests here in town," Derek said.

"We used to," Noreen said between bites. "Years ago, when the college was still open in Wayne County, we'd have parents and students passing through to visit the campus or for orientation."

"Back then, Hydesville was a busy little village…to pass through." Atticus grinned. "Not many stayed, but many passed through."

"I'm glad you stayed, otherwise, I'd still be out wandering in that storm."

"What were you doing out in that mess?" Noreen asked.

"It's a long, involved story," Derek said, all at once realizing how complicated the path was that had brought him to the Doyle's table.

"We do have time for an involved story," Noreen said brightly, passing the roast toward Derek for a second helping.

"If you want to tell it," Atticus quickly added, giving Derek a way out.

Derek thought about it as he piled more roast on his plate. He, Edith and Oswald had only shared amongst themselves their encounters with Vanya Avery, the Fox sisters and the other odd things that had occurred; it might be a good idea to rehash the circumstances of the past few months with an objective third party such as Atticus and Noreen, see if they could make any sense of it. After all, they lived in Hydesville, maybe they'd have some insights.

"Okay, then," he said, "here goes." He told them about the invitation he and Edith had received in August to visit the Keilgarden Colony, how their trip had at first left them without the ability to recall anything that had happened. "When we returned to

New York, my brother Oswald announced that he was in love and planned to marry."

"How nice," Noreen said, but her expression changed to muted surprise when Derek explained just how unexpected it was that Oswald was planning to marry a woman.

"And of course, we didn't recognize the name Vanya Avery due to the amnesia or whatever it was we had. Are you familiar with her or her name?"

Atticus and Noreen shook their heads. Derek was almost relieved since if they knew her name, he might have actually had to tell them his and Edith's belief that Vanya wasn't even human. *They would send you packing, crazy man,* he thought. *You don't have to tell them everything.*

"She lives in the Colony," he said. When Atticus and Noreen didn't respond, he continued. "Anyway, Edith and I started having these strange dreams and nightmares; we couldn't always tell what was real and what wasn't. A few times, we actually had the same dream, and they all had something to do with Hydesville, and the Fox sisters."

"Why would you dream about our little village?" Atticus asked as he refilled everyone's wine glasses. "And did you ever *actually* visit here, see the Colony or the Fox house, or was it all a dream? I'm a little confused…"

"Stay away from the Colony," Noreen said. "That place—"

Atticus shushed her, motioned Derek to continue.

"It is confusing," Derek admitted. "But yes, we drove up at Vanya's invitation, spent the night in the Fox house."

Noreen shivered. "Ugh, why'd you stay there? Weren't you scared?"

Derek told them about the night in the cottage, what had occurred. "It actually took us many days and weeks of writing down the snatches of memory that returned just so I could tell you all of this. If we hadn't written it down, it all would have been lost..."

He stopped to gather his thoughts, had lost the thread of the story. Noreen was watching him closely.

"You all right?" Atticus asked after a moment.

"Yes, sorry about that. This is the first time I've told anyone everything that has occurred. It's a bit...much, isn't it? Where was I?"

"You said your brother was going marry this woman," Noreen prompted.

Derek's mouth went dry when he recalled the last time he saw Oswald, that beautiful day at the garden restaurant when his brother had appeared, looking drawn and sickly. They had had that awful fight, Oswald had claimed that only Vanya loved him. Derek found himself profoundly despondent, his chest tight with grief and loss; he envisioned his brother hanging alone in the forest, couldn't shake it.

"What is it?" Noreen asked gently. "What happened?"

Derek told them about getting the phone call about Oswald's body being found in the Fox Woods. He didn't go into detail about the specifics but talking to the couple about his brother's death freshened the tragedy, awoke the pain. "Tomorrow I'm going to the morgue to identify the body," he told them.

The three of them sat there in silence for a few moments. Outside the rain pattered down, the storm that drove him to the house settled in as a dull, persistent roar.

"It all keeps coming back here, seems to have something to do with this town, the Colony, the Fox sisters, their house, the woods," Derek said.

"What about the woods?" Atticus asked, leaning forward.

"I spent the afternoon at your library reading up on the area."

"What did you find out?" Noreen asked.

Derek went upstairs to his room, gathered up his binder and the books he had taken. When he returned, Noreen and Atticus were in the parlor sipping brandy, each of them subdued, staring off into space, intently captured by their own thoughts.

"Probably most of what I've learned you already know," Derek said, settling himself and the papers at the table, "but if you'll indulge me, I'll review it again for my own sake to make sure I've got my facts straight." Derek shuffled though his photocopied papers, then began.

CHAPTER 17.

When people talk of Maggie and Katie Fox, little mention is made of their father, John Fox," Derek said, "but he, too, had an interesting and rather tragic life. He was born in 1787 in New York City, moved to Rochester, married Ann Catherine Ryan in 1805. She died in 1811 of a broken neck, the result of a fall from an attic window. They had a son, but for some unknown reason, that father-son relationship was so strained that the child ran away after his mother died, so there's no information on who he is or whatever happened to him."

Derek turned the pages, said, "After the death of his first wife, John Fox moved to Hydesville where he married Margaret Rutan Smith in 1812. They had seven children, six of which survived. In December of 1847, the family took up residence in a house located at 1510 Hydesville Road here in Hydesville. It was Maggie, born in 1833, and Katie, born four years later, who made certain that house and the Fox family name had a place in history."

He looked up at Atticus and Noreen. "This is where the story really begins.

"During the first couple of months, the family slept soundly, although a few peculiar noises were heard at night. Then, in March of 1848, the sounds became distinct and at times alarming. The family reported hearing raps, thumps, footsteps in the cellar, voices calling out to various family members. When Edith and I spent the night in the cottage, we came across Margaret's diary and it confirmed all of this.

"At first, the family thought their neighbors were playing jokes on them, but soon there seemed a malicious nature to the disturbances. It was also obvious that it was impossible for someone to sneak into the house; John Fox had made certain all the doors and windows were locked up tight each night. The police were called on several occasions, they kept an ongoing record, which the paper reported in its police blotter section."

Noreen asked, "How'd the community react when they read about what was going on?"

Derek said, "According to reports, the police and neighbors were sympathetic at first. But on the whole, the town didn't take kindly to the Fox family's stories about the rappings and the voices, or the claims that Maggie and Katie were communicating with the entity. This was an extremely religious area. Anything out of the ordinary or not easily explained was often deemed supernatural or occult in origin, probably in league with the devil."

"Sounds like the same atmosphere that surrounded the Salem Witch Trials," Atticus said.

Derek nodded in agreement. "Anyway, the knockings continued. John Fox and his family were now frightened. They sought help from the community to deal with what were called their 'house hauntings.' The newspapers kept reporting on it, but they were a little sketchy here about exactly what happened next. From what I gather, it seems that some priests visited the Fox home, interviewed the children and parents, and when no occurrences happened in the presence of the religious leaders, they blessed the house and left. I get the sense that they felt the whole thing was a hoax or the result of loose planks or just the girls trying to get attention from their parents."

Derek set aside the newspaper photocopies, thumbed through one of the books. "Let's see...okay, it says here that John Fox began to fight with his daughters over the events. He was ashamed by all the attention it was drawing, he wanted the family to stop talking about it. He even began to suspect Maggie and Katie were being used by the spirits, that they were possibly communicating with a demon."

"Creepy," Noreen said, hugging herself.

"John had another reason to keep the events out of the public eye. He was known to drink. A lot. Whiskey was his poison. The papers said he was a mean drunk, would reek of it, but he wanted to be known as a pious leader of the community. So, I'm sure he hated being the center of attention since his drinking bouts became public knowledge, and his position as a church leader began to slip. But the more the chaos in his family increased, the more he drank. His oldest daughter, Leah, openly defied him. She continued to tell their stories around town about the rappings. Soon, curious neighbors from other villages stopped by. It became a bit of a circus, which infuriated John Fox even more. Hydesville soon became the laughingstock of Wayne County, was called 'Haunted Hydesville' and a 'Ghost Village.'"

Derek turned some more pages. "It seems that while her father was at work during the day—he was a blacksmith—Leah started charging people to tour the family home or to meet her sisters. This went on for months, and the movement grew quickly. Soon, residents in nearby towns claimed to have the same gifts as the Foxes, and Spiritualism quickly spread across America, to England, and, from there, to the European continent."

He looked up, hesitated before continuing. "But that was all to come later. The next part of the story is a bit disturbing."

Atticus glanced at his wife, then nodded. "Go on."

Derek said cleared his throat. "From what I read, although the village had become somewhat embarrassed by the goings on at the Fox home and the crowds it was attracting, it was still a tight-knit community, they worked together, depended on one another, looked out for each other. The neighbors all saw one another in town on a regular basis.

"This book says that in late September of 1848, the entire Fox family apparently dropped out of sight. They weren't seen at church, the children had not attended school, none of them had been in town to get supplies for over two weeks. Due to the suspicious events that had occurred in their home, the family was no longer on speaking terms with many of their neighbors; some thought what was occurring really was Satanic, no longer wanted anything to do with the Foxes. But some of their acquaintances became concerned by the family's absence.

"According to the papers, some neighbors went to call on the Foxes to see how they were getting on or if they were ill or some catastrophe had happened. When they arrived at the property, they found the house overrun with flies and bugs. For some reason, the table had been set—for dinner apparently—a few days earlier. All the food had spoiled terribly. The napkins had been unfolded, the drinks had been poured. It was as if the family had sat down to begin supper, then had simply decided to up and leave the premises. The kitchen was still in disarray from the meal preparation. The front door was wide open when the investigating party arrived."

Derek paused, still uncertain if he should continue. Atticus and Noreen both had their eyes closed, were listening intently, as if it was the first time they had heard this story, were envisioning the events unfolding. Derek picked through his papers, organized them for the next and final section of his story.

"The house was searched. Three of the youngest children were found hiding in the attic, unable to speak, severely traumatized by whatever had happened. The town was alerted, the police came. A search party was organized because it was thought that the rest of the family had been abducted, although no one had any idea of who would have taken them. There was some suspicion it was the Iroquois Indians, but they had been friendly and peaceful for decades. Due to the state of the spoiled food, it was guessed that the family had been absent from the house anywhere from two to five days.

"The search party started on the Fox property, circled outward until they came to the wooded area. Back then it wasn't called the Fox Woods, but where they found John's body is in that area as it's known today."

Atticus and Noreen opened their eyes, waited.

Derek shifted in his chair. "The newspaper reported that the body of John Fox was found hanging from a tree in the woods. The birds had gotten to it, but he was positively identified. His wife and three oldest daughters, Leah, Maggie, and Katie, had simply vanished. Speculation in the town on the murder of John Fox went from one extreme to the other. The favored thought was that John Fox was so enraged by his daughters' refusal to stop talking about the rappings that he had gone mad during one of his drunken binges and killed them, along with his wife. He hid the bodies somewhere, then hung himself out of guilt or insanity."

"Oh, my Lord, that's so gruesome," Noreen muttered. "But that hanging, it's the same way your poor brother died. I am so sorry, Derek."

He felt his throat tighten, his eyes filled. He blinked away the tears. "I need to read through these books more carefully, but just skimming through, I saw that historians suspect that John Fox was suspected of also killing his first wife, Ann Ryan, too, but that wasn't the accusation at the time of her death, it was ruled an accident."

"What?" Noreen said, eyes wide. "He killed two wives and three of his daughters? In this little village?" She glanced at Atticus. "I didn't know any of this! Do you believe what we're hearing?"

Derek jumped in. "That's what I was wondering. You've lived here for so long, is *any* of this familiar to you?"

Atticus shrugged. "No. Other than the Fox sisters and the rapping sounds, that's really all I know. It's a *lot* of scandal to never hear about."

"It wasn't that hard to find this out, either, so I'm surprised the police knew nothing about John Fox and his death, how it was the same as Oswald's. It's so obvious, the similarity…"

A somber mood settled over them. They had become caught up in the strange stories. Derek tucked the pages back into the notebook, closed the binder.

"I blame the Colony," Noreen said suddenly, her voice tight with conviction. She straightened up, looked at Derek, her eyes alert. "I've always thought that place was *bad*."

"Noreen," a warning from Atticus, which she ignored.

"I remember hearing somewhere that Dr. Keilgarden received a *lot* of money—we're talking almost a million—to get it started, to acquire the Fox cottage and the area around it, including the forest where your brother died. It was always kept a bit hush hush as to where he got the funds to buy the Fox property and all that land since those Spiritualist people certainly didn't want to sell the spot where their movement started. But I guess if you offer enough money to someone…"

She glanced at Atticus, then finished her rant. "And after what you told us, I'm thinking Dr. Keilgarden *knew* about the terrible things that had happened there, the family that vanished, the hanging of John Fox. Right? He *knew* about those terrible things and he intentionally bought the cottage and the land and the forest where that all happened, where people died or vanished or experienced such frightening events. Who would do such a thing? That sad, tragic Fox family. It's like he exploited those people. And the Colony builds itself right on top of their misery! And now your brother, once he marries that woman and moves to the Colony, what happened to him is just like what happened to John Fox. It's a *horrible* place, horrible people, no one should go there…"

Before Derek had the chance to process all she had said—and acknowledge to himself that his great-grandfather had been the one to fund the purchase of the cottage, the woods, and help finance the place—Atticus asked if he had visited the Colony yet.

"No, and from what I understand, the police can't locate it, or my brother's wife."

"That's no surprise," Atticus said. "Years ago, all the signs in the area were removed, the roads were no longer maintained so it became very difficult to find your way around. We never saw people from the Colony in the village, so we eventually forgot about them. It was very much out of sight, out of mind."

"Sort of like this whole area," Noreen said sadly, settled now after her outburst. "People moved away, shops closed, the town seemed to empty itself of life…"

"So why have you stayed?" Derek asked, curious.

"We really don't have anywhere else to go," Noreen said. The statement left Derek feeling uneasy for some reason. He waited for her to continue but that was all she said. Atticus yawned. Noreen stared at the floor. It seemed both of them had suddenly shut down.

"I didn't mean to keep you up so late," he apologized. "I have a long day tomorrow, first to the morgue, then the drive back home, so I should get to bed." He stood, stretched. "Thank you again for listening to me, talking this over. I know it all sounds so crazy, but…"

"Not at all," Noreen said, her eyes clear as she faced him. "This is a strange area to live in, we've known that for a long, long time. Obviously, it's somehow…impacted you and your wife. And you've just lost your brother. You needed someone to talk to. Maybe that's why you were brought to our home tonight."

CHAPTER 18.

The next morning, Derek was able to leave the Doyle's by eight. He had been grateful for their hospitality—literally a port in a storm—and their listening ears, but instead of experiencing a good night's sleep, he had tossed and turned; something about Atticus and Noreen had troubled him. The more he had told them of his experiences, the more he had expected to be interrupted with questions or requests for clarification. But for the most part, they had sat there in silence, their eyes closed as they visualized all he was telling them. He had no idea if they believed him or thought he was nuts. Their calm, non-questioning response wasn't at all what he had expected. He thought, *If anyone had told me such a wild tale, I doubt if I'd let them remain under my roof for the night.* The only outburst came from Noreen when she blasted the Colony; that only made him more determined than ever to find the place, see what was going on.

As he started down the sidewalk toward the main part of the village, he sensed he was being watched. He stopped, turned. Atticus and Noreen were at the front window, their faces slightly obscured by the reflection of the sun on the glass. Derek saw a movement from them, returned what he assumed was a wave. He continued down the street, hurrying a bit, wondering why they had been watching him, what had they *really* thought of the story he'd told?

The storm had run roughshod over the village. Branches were scattered about like broken wire hangers, huge puddles of water reflected the clear blue sky like wide-open eyes, staring, unable to blink. The police station was deserted. His Mercedes was where he had left it the previous morning, yet the other parking spots were vacant, the building was void of lights and activity. *Odd,* he thought, *It's after eight; why isn't anyone here?* Derek pulled at the doors. They were locked. He peered into the window. After his eyes adjusted to the dim interior, his heart immediately began to beat anxiously. In the gloom, he could see that the facility had been stripped of furniture. The desks and filing cabinets he had walked between on his way to Johnson's office were gone. From a thin shaft of light, he could discern that the counter was coated with dust and debris.

Impossible, Derek thought. *It's abandoned.*

"I was here yesterday," he whispered into the dirty glass, wanting to hear his voice, a form of confirmation, that he was real, *this* was real. He stepped back. The front of the building was in as bad of shape as the inside. Two of the windows had tiny cracks in them, the few steps leading to the entry were split and chipped, something he hadn't noticed the previous morning. Wires from the outside light had been pulled lose, extended from the fixture like a pile of black worms.

"What the hell is going on?" Derek asked, again needing the sound of his voice. He hurried around to the back. Those doors were also locked. The windows in the rear of the building were all cracked, splintered yet it didn't appear as if the office had been vandalized. But it was obvious that the Hydesville Police Station was no longer in use; it was simply collapsing in on itself, falling apart from old age.

Derek wandered back to the front, trying to figure out what was going on. Overhead, the sky was blue, scraped clean after the previous evening's storm. The streets were deserted. After a few seconds, the silence crept up on Derek, made him jumpy. He felt he was being toyed with, that someone was amused by his predicament. Was the Vanya thing nearby, somehow witnessing his confusion?

"I was just here yesterday!" he said again wildly, this time with a hysterical edge. *Get a grip,* he thought. *Don't go to pieces.* He walked around the police station again, still shaken by how decayed and deserted it was. Derek had had so much to tell Johnson, so many questions to ask, the most important one being why hadn't the officer made the connection of Oswald's mysterious death by hanging in the Fox Woods with the death of John Fox back in 1848? Did he even know about it? There had to be some connection between the two events, no matter how farfetched. He assumed the officer knew the history of the village, would have known how similar the two occurrences were. Why hadn't he mentioned it?

Wondering what to do next, he climbed into the car, started it. He needed to identify Oswald's body at the Wayne County Morgue, but he recalled Noreen's rant about the Colony, knew he had one more destination in mind, one side trip to make. *I'm so close now,* he thought as he backed the Mercedes out of the parking spot.

He called Edith. The scratchy connection broke twice, but he was able to speak to her through the staticky white noise, relayed his evening with the Doyle's. Then: "Before I go to the morgue and start home, I want to check out the Colony. If I can find it," he said.

Edith said, "Don't do that! You heard what Noreen said. I want you home. Let Officer Johnson do that."

"Oh yeah, about that..." Derek told her about the abandoned police station. "I want to visit the Colony, see if I can find out anything about the Vanya thing. I'll be home in time for a cocktail," he promised.

The *Hydesville In History* book had included a rough map of the area, showing the location of the house at 1510 Hydesville Road, its distance to what became known as the Fox Woods, which is where the Colony was. Derek figured he'd give himself a couple hours to see if he could accomplish what the now-disbanded Hydesville police force couldn't: locate the Colony. The David Foundation had handed over a million dollars to establish the compound and had continue to generously fund it over the decades. He was intent on seeing the results of his great-grandfather's investment for himself.

###

Later, with several wrong turns behind him, Derek was surprised to find himself on Hydesville Road. Then he passed the Fox cottage, which looked familiar, indicating that most all of his memory had been restored. Other than the Fox house, there were no other homes on Hydesville Road. *This is almost too easy,* he thought nervously. If he followed the road into the woods as far as he could, it should eventually lead him near to the Keilgarden Colony.

Hydesville Road was an uneven, gravel road that had potholes as bad as those that Derek encountered in the city. Bushes and trees pressed in on both sides of the car. Derek cringed, imagining the branches scraping against the Mercedes, leaving their fingernail-like marks.

The fierce storm from the previous evening had downed trees, created mountains of dried mud. Several times Derek had to get out of the car to pull discarded branches off the road so he could continue. Overhead, the sky remained blue, but a bundle of clouds had formed. Derek didn't see any repair trucks out removing upended trees or town employees cleaning out the drainage ditches. *If this village even exists,* he reminded himself. There were no other cars or people about as he maneuvered the Mercedes along the unmarked streets. Although it was true that most of the signs were missing, the few that remained were enough for him to use as guideposts and thereby estimate where the next turn should be.

A half-mile further on, the trees and shrubbery began to thin out. At the end of the road a sign was posted, the letters faded, blurred after years of exposure to the elements. Derek switched off the car, stepped out of the Mercedes. It was surprisingly warm out for November. A dry breeze kicked up around him. Derek brushed the dirt and grime away from the sign:

KEILGARDEN COLONY

PRIVATE PROPERTY

**NO ADMITTANCE SECURED AREA
TURN BACK**

After the realization of where he was had settled over him, Derek thought of Oswald. This was the place where his brother had spent the last few weeks of his life. Had he been here by choice, or had he been a prisoner? Derek stepped back to better survey the area. The road beyond the sign was paved after a few yards; it led up an incline for a half-mile or so, then curved to the right, was lost from view.

Why would Oswald choose to stay in such a desolate, God forsaken place? Derek was certain the Vanya thing had somehow trapped Oswald here, mesmerized him or something, refused to let him go.

I'm trying so hard to please her. Oswald's voice in Derek's head.

Abruptly, a shadow fell over the car. Startled, Derek looked up, relieved to see it was just a cloud that had stalled in its attempt at passing over the sun. The sense of isolation crept over him again, along with a nagging question: Why had he managed to find the Colony so easily, using a map from a book published in 1917, thirty years before the facility was even founded? That was something neither Officer Johnson nor the news media had been able to do. Yet, here he was.

He climbed back into the car. His mouth was dry, hands and brow were now sweating. He turned the ignition key. The car roared to life.

He drove slowly down the road to the Keilgarden Colony.

CHAPTER 19.

The path eased to the right, the lane began to rise. The incline twisted into a series of turns so sharp that Derek was forced to slow down. The unkempt wooded area pressed in closer as the road narrowed. Fallen branches lined the path; twice Derek had to stop the car, drag the debris off the road. It was clear that it wasn't meant to be traveled by automobile. It was too narrow, the path was gouged with holes and sharp, bulky rocks spiked upward like teeth prepared to shred tires. He'd have to walk the rest of the way.

He secured the car out of habit; there was no one there to steal it, he knew that, but he also took comfort locking it up. The risk of theft was a symbol of civilization, a fact that people were nearby. He wanted to believe that if anyone came across the expensive vehicle, they'd be curious to see where the missing owner had wandered off to, that he wasn't just out there on his own.

Although his footsteps crunched noisily along the pathway, the sounds were swallowed up, suppressed immediately. The unnatural silence tracked him, bore down, hovering and peering like a voyeur. As he walked along, the shrubbery and trees would rustle about, making whispering sounds that were quickly stilled. Overhead, no birds fluttered by. It was all maddeningly familiar to him, yet also vague at the same time, like rereading a book but forgetting the basics of the plot.

This happened at the ClearView Restaurant! he abruptly remembered. *The distorted sounds, the weird hush over the area, lack of birds, animals. When we got out of the car, right before we met that Vanya thing, all this weird stuff happened.*

"Distractions, misdirection, deception," he muttered, a chant as he moved along. "Distractions, misdirection, deception."

He pushed on through the foliage, out of breath a bit due to the exertion. He reached a clearing. At the far end was a gatehouse, some sort of security checkpoint. It was deserted, the door half off its hinges, the inside of the booth was vacant. It had not been occupied in months, probably years. *I remember you,* he thought smugly as he passed by. *I remember some old man, some Elder, pointed us to the Fox house.*

Ten minutes further down the road, he came to the crest of a hill, looked down at a group of buildings. There were four structures, all appearing to be in various states of ruin like the guardhouse. Nondescript, they reminded him of a series of small army barracks. Functional, nothing more. The sloping roofs, the uniform line of windows along each side, the peeling tan paint, the cracked sidewalks that led from building to building all had the look of a military base. The primitive landscaping had grown wild, but he could still detect the intent of the original low maintenance design. The grass that encircled the area was dead brown; even the few trees seemed dejected. Like everything else in the area, it was obvious it hadn't been occupied in some time.

Was this the Colony?

From somewhere, a door slammed. Derek flinched in surprise, looked around nervously. He thought it had originated from one of the barracks off to the right. In the unnatural stillness, the sound was amplified, then quickly snatched away. *Maybe the wind had blown it closed?* he thought. *Surely, no one else is here.* Suddenly anxious, he had the desire to hide somewhere, but there was nowhere to seek shelter unless he ran back to the entangled pathway behind him.

"Justice, Derek. Justice."

The chorus of voices, speaking as one, hissed in his ear. Derek spun around. No one was behind him.

"Derek?"

This time, the sound had come from in front of him. His eyes were open, he had heard his name, but the area remained deserted.

"In the cellar. Justice for us."

Standing in the shadows in front of the second building from the right he squinted, was able to make out three figures. Two were Maggie and Katie Fox. Their dark hair and murky, ankle-length dresses blended in with the shaded area and the faded paint on the side of the structure. Even the brown, dead grass helped to camouflage the children. If they had been attempting to hide from him, the environment surrounding them certainly helped. Only the strange echo of their garbled, pleading voices revealed their presence as it traveled across the space between them. But who was the third woman? Her form hadn't completely materialized, was more of a silhouette of dust and shade. Was it Leah, the oldest sister?

The three remained where they were as if waiting for him, their expressions fixed, their green eyes bright, almost glistening in the early afternoon light. Maggie and Katie leaned toward him, their hands clasped as always, begging for something. What did they need? The Leah apparition—if it was her—continued to flicker and waver. It seemed to be straining to fully manifest itself. Only its eyes seemed suitably formed; they'd gleam, sparkle for seconds, then vanished, only to reappear again like the revolving lantern from a lighthouse.

It seemed like a standoff. Seconds ticked by as the figures watched Derek. He swallowed nervously. A harsh, grainy taste filled his mouth. He spat it out at the same time that a steely courage and determination rose up. With clarity, all at once he knew he was tired of the mystery, the uncertainty. He was here to find out what had happened to his brother, among many other things. Embolden by thoughts of Oswald, Derek started determinedly down the slope toward the specters.

Derek half expected them to vanish as he drew near, yet they remained stationary in the shadows. As he approached, the area seemed charged with some type of vibration, a subtle yet continuous electric current. He felt the hair on his arms and the back of his neck flick, twist about. Once he stood a few feet in front of them, he steadied himself, addressed two of them by name. "Maggie and Katie Fox, what do you want from me?"

At the sound of his voice, the two children moved forward eagerly, hope on their faces. They opened their hands to him, imploring him to assist them. "*Justice*," they finally said, and again interlocked their fingers as if praying. "*In the soil. Justice*," they beseeched him. Leah dematerialized, her piercing eyes the last vestige of her presence. The shadows that surrounded the two girls deepened for a moment, then went black as if a light had been extinguished. The sisters vanished at the same moment, the word "*Justice*" repeated a third time, only a faint whisper. The specters were then replaced by the scent of a light, spicy perfume that whiffed past.

"It's nice to see you again," Vanya said, smiling, her voice low and seductive as she stepped out of the darkness where the three women had stood seconds earlier.

Derek was unable to move or look away from her. It was as if he was discovering her all over again. She was beautiful. He could almost feel her touching him, tasting his lips, stroking his body. *But she's not a woman*, he reminded himself frantically, trying to control his desire for her. With great effort, he managed to form a thought, ask a question. "Was that third woman Leah Fox?"

"You'll find out, but at another time. She is the One who is yet to come." Vanya didn't move closer to him. He sensed she was pulling at him, wanted him to come to her. He felt his legs beginning to make the effort.

He looked away from her, concentrated on the area around him. Her ability to reach into his mind lessened a bit, a relaxed fist. He focused his attention on the buildings, how decrepit they were. Most of the windows were broken or shattered, cobwebs had fanned out where space permitted, curtains hung in shredded fragments, the exterior of each building seemed to be ready to collapse at any moment. He noticed that the paint had not only peeled or faded, but there were actually holes in the structure, areas where rust and the elements had devoured the walls. Looking past the Vanya thing, he saw that the roof of the building directly behind her had partially caved in. Through a broken window, the ceiling debris had been left where they had fallen; there was obviously no reason to repair what was no longer inhabited.

Still avoiding her gaze, he said, "I thought there was a community of children living here."

"There *is* a community." She stepped closer, touched his arm. A surge of craving swept through him. He managed to shut out the thought, *Not human.*

"Where…do they live?" he asked, staring at the ground.

"They—*we*—live here, of course. You just can't see us."

Unable to resist now that she was so close, her hand on him, he looked at her. "Oswald would *never* have lived here."

Vanya said calmly, "Oswald *tried*, that's all that really matters. He did everything he possibly could to consummate the relationship with me, to provide what I needed, what I wanted. You can take comfort in that, Derek. He did all he could."

"And then you killed him."

"No one killed your brother. It was his idea. He chose to go into the Fox Woods."

Derek needed to anchor his thoughts. He focused on his brother, the horrible torment and death he had experienced. "Why? Why did you kill him? What did you want from him?"

"I wanted from him what I'll *take* from you," Vanya said, then licked her lips.

Derek wanted to choke her, feel her throat squeezed between his hands, but first he had to know what had happened. "What did you do to him?"

"I didn't *do* anything. He didn't succeed in what I needed, so he was useless to me, not appropriate for what I needed. I didn't know that when I chose him. But I gave him one last chance because I know he *wanted* to please me. We were running out of time. It was his idea to use a scarf in the Fox bedroom, to help excite himself as it tightened around his neck. Autoerotic asphyxiation would create a powerful ejaculation, would give me what I needed, he swore to me it would achieve what I desired, what he had failed at. I was the one with the better I idea. I suggested he take a rope to the Fox Woods. The power in that location is...*enormous*. I really thought it might work for him."

She took a moment, her thoughts elsewhere, her voice soft with longing. "It was so...*extreme* what he was willing to do for me. There was such history in that place, the very spot where I took out my vengeance on John Fox. I thought that the rage of energy that dwelt there would assist your brother. I told him to go there, prepare himself. If he succeeded, we'd try it on the Fox property. He was so eager to please me, too eager, I guess. By the time I arrived, he had already finished. I had no choice..."

Weeping at her heartless description, Derek asked, "How did he get up in the tree? He was alone—"

"He was lifted," Vanya said simply, her voice thick, deep, watery. "Same as John Fox was. Once the noose was around John's neck, the rope was gathered up into the tree, hand over hand, until he was fifty feet off the ground."

"Who?" Derek choked out the word. "Who…pulled Oswald up?"

"The children of Hydesville," she said. "Maggie and Katie, of course. But there will be others. I told them to lift your brother once I saw that it was too late. …"

Overcome with grief at the way his brother had been deceived and then discarded by the monster in front of him, enraged by her indifferent responses, Derek grabbed her by her shoulders, shook her. "What are *you*? What do you want?"

Derek started to ask another question when she cut him off.

"Stop acting like you have no idea what is going on. You *have* the answers you need, Derek. You know about the Fox Woods. You know there's a power that dwells there. You read about it in the library, jotted notes down in your silly binder, you know what happened to John Fox. You told the Doyle's all about it."

Surprised, he released her, stepped away. "How did you know about all of that?"

"We know what we need to know, Derek. Haven't you figured that out by now?" She had a bemused, patient expression on her face, as if he was some harmless specimen she was studying under a microscope. By a flicker of intuition, he sensed she was wearing a mask. As he watched her, he saw it ripple, slip momentarily from her face. For an instant, he saw her for who and what she truly was. It was far beyond anything he could have imagined. There was an impression of profound intelligence, but it was inscrutable, he could not fathom its origin or its limits, if any existed. It possessed an ancient wisdom of unfathomable intentions and desires. These insights she allowed him to experience for less than a second; they were gone faster than they had arrived.

Shaken, he took another step away from her, then another, continued. Once there was ten feet between them, he said, "Tell me what you are."

She didn't respond, only stood there. With mounting dread, Derek realized that he didn't really want to know anything else about her or it. Whatever the thing in front of him said would be beyond his ability to comprehend. In the brief instant of revelation that he had just had, he'd thought he'd also glimpsed another presence within her that was also attempting to materialize, an entity or something else that was yearning to come forth. He couldn't identify them with a known name, but Derek perceived other apparitions were straining to manifest themselves.

Russian nesting dolls, he thought, picturing them. He recalled reading once that there could be dozens of them, the record being more than fifty dolls within the main figure. All incased in the largest one. How many things were contained inside of Vanya?

All around him, the air was now fluttering in an odd way, shimmering like it does off a hot surface in the summer. A massive form seemed to be pressing against the area, many starving faces crowding against the window of a bakery, hungry to get in. *Break the glass, force their way in,* he thought uneasily. Was the Vanya thing calling to the others to join her or was it a part of herself she yearned to unite with?

Abruptly, he turned from Vanya, severing the connection with her, no longer seeing or sensing what she was revealing to him. He scrambled back toward the more densely wooded area, away from the Colony. Once he was at the top of the hill, he turned, looked down, prepared to see her hurrying after him. She wasn't there. In her place, the three women had returned, standing still as statues, their presence yearning for his attention, his assistance. They stared at him. It was clear they were making a point; they didn't need to pursue him. They could wait. They were willing to wait.

Derek turned, dashed blindly through the brush, off into the surrounding forest, wondering if he would get through the Fox Woods alive.

CHAPTER 20.

Derek barely remembered the five-hour drive home. He had tried to call Edith, but the connection kept breaking so he had left a message that he was on his way. He stopped by the morgue to identify Oswald's body; the autopsy was pushed to later that afternoon so they had no information yet. He was given a card of who to call. The next thing he knew, he was passing the keys of the Mercedes over to Jose, the Park Avenue parking attendant.

"You all right, Mr. David?"

Derek knew he looked like five miles of well-traveled road. His face and hands were scratched from running through the tangled and overgrown Fox Woods, his sports jacket was torn and soiled, as were his pants, his shoes were a wreck. But he had gotten out of there alive; he had even rejoiced at the sight of a sludge of traffic as he had entered Manhattan.

"I'm fine, Jose, just fine," Derek said, handing the man a five-dollar tip.

"Thank you, Mr. David!" Jose said, his face lighting up.

Derek's generous and grateful mood stayed with him as he rode the elevator to the apartment. Edith opened the door, he held her close, inhaled her scent, the very essence of her. God, but she felt good. He squeezed her tightly, released her, pulled her close again, kissed her firmly on the lips. She helped him out of his jacket, then he headed off to shower off the grime, shave, tend to his scratches.

They enjoyed Matilda's famous beef stew, her homemade bread. Derek read to Edith from his notebook, wrote in the new details, told her how he had gone looking for the Colony using the map from the Hydesville book. He described the broken-down state of the facility, the sudden appearance of the three apparitions and Vanya, and his overwhelming fear that something monstrous was approaching the area, most likely summoned by the Vanya thing, a part of itself that it wanted to be rejoined with. Edith nodded throughout but didn't ask any questions.

"I have never been so frightened. It was as if a huge...*swarm* was approaching, some gigantic *thing* on its way to the Colony." He held his quivering hand out. "God, I'm shaking now just thinking about it! That really happened! Vanya—whatever she is— just stood there; she knew that I sensed this presence was coming. She's getting more powerful, Edith, I'm sure of it. And she knows we're on to her, she knew about me talking to the Doyle's, even this binder! Not the contents, I don't think, but that we're keeping track of stuff."

He looked up. Edith wasn't reacting as he expected. Instead, she was watching him with concern. "What? What is it, honey?"

Obviously upset, she stammered out a question. "What…time of day did you see Vanya?"

"It was this morning. Before noon. Why?"

"You're *certain* it was today?"

Derek looked closely at his wife. "What is it?"

Matilda came in to clear away the plates. "Would you like some apple pie, Derek?"

"Yes, that would be fine."

"Edith?"

"The same for her, Matilda," Derek said quickly. "Let's have it in the living room." Once they were settled next to one another on the sofa, Derek asked her what was wrong. Edith looked confused, nervous.

She said, "Listen to me. Early this morning, I got a call. From Vanya. She said she couldn't stop crying, couldn't sleep, she was so upset over Oswald's death, didn't have anyone to talk to, would I mind if she came over. Of course, I told her to come right over."

"What? You invited her here?"

"Derek, I had breakfast this morning with Vanya. Here, in the apartment. *This morning!* She arrived at nine, stayed until just before noon."

"That's impossible…"

Edith didn't respond.

"I saw her, spoke with her at the same time," Derek insisted, "more than five hours away! But why did you let her in? Why invite her—?"

"Matilda and Warren were here, too, Derek," Edith said calmly, ignoring his question. "They saw her." The short silence that followed quickly shifted into a hushed accusation that Derek immediately responded to.

"You're saying you have...*witnesses*, is that it? What you experienced was *true*, while I'm away...hallucinating, having one of my *spells*? Is that it?"

"Dear, calm down, stop shouting. Listen to me. I know you're exhausted," Edith said, trying to sooth him. "I just wanted to explain—"

Matilda arrived with dessert and coffee.

"Matilda, did you prepare breakfast today for Edith and Vanya?" Derek demanded.

"Yes..." She returned quickly to the kitchen to escape the tension in the living room.

Edith remained silent. The coffee, which she always drank steaming hot, cooled gradually in front of her. Derek's fork clicked on his plate as he angrily devoured the pie in a few swift bites. "I don't get it!" he finally said, slamming the silverware down. "Why the hell would you invite this *thing* into our home? If it can appear two places at the same time, what *can't* it do?" Then he thought of something. "Oh, God, the same thing happened when Oswald first met her, remember? We were in Hydesville, he said she was here in Manhattan." He quickly jotted down the information in the notebook.

After a few seconds, Edith said quietly, "Do you constantly have to write in that thing? Look at me. Derek? Maybe...like you suggested, you had, or have been having, spells, and didn't know it? Little ones. Think about it. The stress of driving up there, alone, which you shouldn't have done, maybe it got the best of you? Perhaps you only thought—"

He held the binder up to silence her, the notebook crammed with pages they had written together about their experiences. "We wrote it all down, you and me! Even Oz! We all agreed something was happening! You *know* this isn't about my spells! How can you say that what happened to me the past couple of days is all due to me blacking out but everything else *isn't*?"

"Shhh. Please, stop yelling. I think this because…I guess because *more things* have happened to you. In fact, most things do. And you are under tremendous pressure, what with Ozzie's death, having to take a lot more responsibility with the business…"

"I can't believe you're saying this!" Derek was furious. "I *know* what I saw today, whom I spoke to." He caught his breath, worked to calm himself down. "And you *know* what this Vanya thing is. She's not human. She's gotten into your head … somehow…" His voice trailed off, the anxious pit in his chest swirled into overdrive. *What was happening?* he wondered, aghast at the thought of losing Edith to this deception.

Edith sat quietly, finally said, "Vanya really loved him, you know. It was awful to see her so upset. I wanted to make her happy, so told her I was pregnant. I know we were supposed to wait, but she's family now—"

"No, she isn't!"

"—and she was so happy for me! She told me she would help me since she has so much experience working with children—"

Derek was shaking his head. "That's a lie! There are no children at the Colony. It's a bunch of empty buildings, ruins, with the ceilings caved in, the windows broken, the grounds overgrown with weeds. *Nobody lives there, Edith*! The whole Colony is a sham, it doesn't exist, and hasn't for who knows how long. It's just one of those illusions she created to distract us from what is *really* going on..."

After a moment, Edith calmly asked, "And what is really going on, honey?"

With his face buried in his hands, he shook his head, didn't answer.

Edith was looking at him sadly. "Listen to yourself. What are you saying? It makes no sense."

He didn't answer, wanted the sparks between them to settle down. It wasn't like them to disagree or challenge each other to this extent. It was all so maddening, what had happened to her?

"—really enjoyed her company," Edith was saying. "She made me feel...good. Safe. Secure. I don't know what you thought you saw today, but it wasn't the Colony, and it certainly was not Vanya."

Derek hadn't missed her dig about what he *thought* he saw that day; she didn't believe him, thought he was having spells, not telling her the truth. Fresh waves of panic rose and sloshed about his chest. For some reason, Edith was siding with Vanya, but over what? What invisible lines were being drawn?

"...offered to stay with me, keep me company while I have to stay in bed."

Derek, his thoughts scattered, missed part of what she had said. "What?"

"...and I told her she could stay in the guest bedroom, that we had plenty of space. Besides, you know you have to be traveling soon for that trip to Europe. The office can't do everything, a lot of the events that Ozzie organized will have to be covered by you." Edith smiled warmly at him, the first time she had all evening. "Vanya will move in here when

I'm taking bedrest, help care for me while you're away."

He couldn't believe what Edith was saying.

"Vanya was very generous to offer. Besides, honey, she *is* family now."

"Family? Stop saying that! Don't you remember how you felt about her, the way she changed the way Ozzie was, the way you felt that she stole him from you?" He started to read aloud to her from the notebook of their recollections.

Edith waved her hand dismissively. "Oh, honey, stop with that. Stop it. You're obsessed with those old stories, that silly binder. Listen to me. Vanya was Ozzie's *wife*, she's now his widow, she *needs us...*"

Silly binder, he thought incredulously. *That's exactly what Vanya called it.*

"No! No, no, no!" he cried. "She's *not* moving in!" He was shouting now, trying to wake her up. "God, do you even hear yourself, Edith?!" She was looking at him, her eyes wide with...fear? Was she afraid of him?

Then her look shifted, reformed itself into determination. She sat up straight. "How dare you! Don't you ever speak to me that way, Derek! Of course I know what I'm saying and I'll spend time with whomever I want!"

He didn't think they had ever fought this intensely about anything before. It unnerved him. It was as if the rules of some terrible and mighty game had just been switched up on him. The more Edith spoke, the dizzier and more bewildered he felt; a buzzing white noise filled his head. Edith was his first concern, but he also had to be certain his brother's death was being investigated, learn more about the Vanya thing, the Colony, the Fox sisters, the woods, untangle all the strange events that they had been experiencing for the past few months, and of course, keep the gallery functioning and profitable, which loomed large. So much was going on, all at the same time.

Edith's voice dropped down a notch. "We haven't told our friends like the doctor said, just to make certain I'm all right, and I have another two months to go before we can tell anyone. I'm fine with that, but until then, I would like to have *someone* I can talk to!"

"But you have *me*, Edith…"

She shook her head several times, angry and weary over what she felt she was not able to communicate. Either that, or Derek was not understanding. She puffed out a sigh of exasperation as if he was a child she was addressing, then tried a different tact. "You're not well, Derek. Admit it. You haven't been for some time. We need to get you back to the doctor, get some tests done. I worry for you, about you, and the things you're saying and doing. When Vanya was here with me, I felt closer to Ozzie somehow. It's hard to explain, but just being with her, talking about him, I…," Edith started to cry. "I miss him *so much*…"

Derek didn't hesitate, he held her as she collapsed into him. He felt the significant amount of extra weight she had already put on since discovering she was pregnant. He wished they could tell one of her closest friends, someone they knew and trusted, about her pregnancy, but as the doctor said, there was still a high risk that she could lose the baby and they agreed they didn't want to go through that exposed grieving if something happened. It would be tough enough if they told their friends and the baby wasn't viable, but after the media had briefly and harshly hounded them about Oswald's surprise marriage announcement, he didn't want to ever go through that kind of public scrutiny again.

Edith stirred in his arms. "I'm sorry I got so upset." She reached for his hand, kissed it. "I've got all these extra hormones, you know, so I'm bound to be a little rough and ragged around the edges. A little feisty!"

Derek nuzzled the top of her head, but didn't relax, didn't trust her any longer.

For a moment, they simply held one another, eyes closed, the argument stilled. One of the lightbulbs in a table lamp flickered, dimmed then brightened. Once it returned to normal, the matching lamp repeated the incident. *Evidence of the paranormal or simple misdirection?* he wondered, his eyes narrowed, knowing the answer.

He looked down at Edith. Her gaze was like that of a statue watching him. "Honey?" She was no longer seeing him. "Edith?" Alarmed now, he called to her again, but she remained in some catatonic state, her eyes staring through Derek into the middle spaces. "*Do...as I do,*" she murmured.

"Edith? Honey?"

Again, the lights flickered, dimmed as if straining against an insurmountable force, then blinked on and off before returning to their normal illumination. At the same time, Edith closed her eyes, then opened them.

"Derek?" She looked around the room, bewildered. "What happened?"

"You sort of zoned out on me for a second there," he said looking at her closely. "Are you okay?"

"I felt something...cover me," she whispered nervously, glancing around as if it was still in the room. She sat up. "It was like I was being *embraced* or almost smothered. It was *horrible*! I couldn't move or speak, it was all dark..."

Derek could almost finish her description: The symptoms she described were the same ones he felt whenever he had one of his spells. He rocked her in his arms as she continued speaking, realizing that whatever force had invaded their lives was making it clear that it intended to have both of them, that they were equal targets now.

We're at war, he realized as he held Edith tightly. *It is going to be an all-out war.*

The first casualty was Oswald, but he will be the only one, Derek vowed silently to Vanya as he embraced his trembling, terrified wife.

CHAPTER 21.

The next morning Derek was out of the apartment by eight. It was going to be a full day at the gallery catching up with Manny, working out all the details for his two-week trip to Europe. He wished desperately that Edith could go away with him, but the doctor forbade the idea.

"She's at the point now where I really don't want her to leave the apartment," the doctor had said. "She's doing just fine, but let's not take any chances. And certainly no air travel, just bed rest."

Warren drove Derek downtown. He had always trusted the houseman's judgment, so after mulling the situation over in his mind, Derek asked, "Warren, what do you think of Vanya Avery?"

"Very attractive, bright woman," he said after a beat, glancing at Derek in the rearview mirror. "Edith certainly enjoyed her company yesterday at breakfast," Warren continued, trying to be helpful. "They really seemed to have a good time together. It was nice to see Edith with someone since we haven't seen many of your friends lately."

"Maybe we'll have some people over after the first of the year, once we're sure Edith is okay with the baby," Derek said.

Warren nodded, then added, "But until then, I think it's good for Edith to have Vanya around."

Derek stiffened in the back seat. "Why do you say that?"

"You'll be gone for a couple of weeks, wouldn't it be nice if Edith had the companionship? At least until she can tell her friends about the baby. She seems lonely with no one to talk to."

Derek started to tremble with anxiety, tried to keep his words calm, measured. "Warren, I want to make this clear to you: Under no circumstances is Vanya Avery to ever enter the apartment or see Edith while I'm away."

"I don't understand..."

"Vanya is dangerous."

Warren looked at Derek in the mirror. Waited.

"I don't have it all figured out yet, but she's not who she seems to be." *God, I sound crazy,* Derek admitted to himself. He finished weakly. "I need to know that you and Matilda will back me up."

Derek saw Warren glance at him in the rearview mirror again, his eyes wary.

"What is it?"

"Edith said you didn't like Vanya..."

"Yes?"

"Vanya is your sister-in-law, Derek. She was Oswald's wife. Yesterday when she was here for breakfast, I could tell she was terribly upset over Oswald's death, we all are, and she *is* part of your family now. Surely in her grief you're not going to send her away, shut her out, are you? If you could have seen how well she and Edith got along..."

Derek said. "There's more going on here than you're aware of, or that *I'm* aware of."

Warren didn't respond.

"Don't ask me to explain, because I can't! I don't have it figured out. Yet. But I'm sure of this: Oswald would be alive today if he had never met and married Vanya Avery."

Warren remained silent, pulled the car over. They had arrived at the gallery, Derek grabbed his briefcase.

"I don't have the proof, yet," Derek said as he opened the door. He leaned in before closing it. "But what I said stands: I don't want Vanya Avery at the apartment with Edith. *Ever!*" He locked eyes with Warren, but never got a sense the man would honor his request.

The David Gallery was located downtown in SoHo on Wooster Street. Derek glanced at the window display placards announcing paintings by the Russian-born modernist Myron Lechay were currently on display. He walked through the main floor and upstairs to the private offices. He nodded to the staff who were already busy answering phones, showing work in private spaces, unloading recently received pieces, selling, trading and gossiping over last night's opening or tomorrow's rising star. It was a fast-paced, glitzy world that Oswald had loved and flourished in, one that Derek merely tolerated. He preferred to be in the background, working on the deals, but as he had heard repeatedly, the David name needed a David up front, and that was why he was there.

He settled in at his desk. Manny appeared immediately at the door. "Morning. Start your day with some good news: The Lechay is doing tremendous business. I'm getting lots of calls requesting American modernists he was stylistically related to. Ozzie was right on the money when he said this shit was going to sell through."

"What about the Poons?" A new collection of abstracts that focused on surface textures had been created by Larry Poons and Oswald had insisted on buying the entire series.

Manny shrugged. "Half sold, some spec bids on the others. The Kondo's did better, surprise, surprise."

Derek sighed. Things moved through much quicker when Oswald was there, and even with the success of the Lechay show, they were behind this quarter. Abstracts were Oswald's specialty, he always managed a sell through, so Manny's news was disheartening.

"Okay, let's talk Europe then," Derek said. They spent the next few hours discussing Derek's itinerary, the contacts at the various galleries, their current inventory, the prices they were going for. When they finished, they both stretched, Manny said, "So, how are you?"

"Tired. Not sleeping very well."

"Any update about what happened to Oswald?"

Derek shook his head, not certain how to answer. Since the Hydesville police station had aged fifty years and was abandoned the last time he saw it, he knew there was no investigation occurring. He had tried to get Manhattan police involved since that was where Oswald was a resident, but had been told, "The homicide occurred in Wayne County, we have no jurisdiction there." The administrator at the morgue said their autopsy results were inconclusive; that was all Derek had been told. Even the press had dropped the story after Oswald's death had been reported; it was as if the horrible event, like everything connected with Hydesville, had been erased and forgotten. He suspected Vanya Avery was at work behind the scenes, pulling strings, shutting the story down, making it all disappear using her otherworldly influence. He knew that the only way to find out what had happened to Oswald was to visit the village again, but he wouldn't have a chance until he returned from Europe.

What he had still not been able to determine was why the Vanya thing was after him and his family; and why Edith, now? It was clear Vanya was currently focused on his wife.

Derek rubbed his eyes, tried to clear his head of all these thoughts to focus on the matter at hand, the David Gallery. He stood, told Manny, "I'm going to walk around the office a bit, show my face. Why don't you work up those numbers we talked about, make sure I have my facts straight?" Derek reviewed some papers on his desk that required his signature, then left his glass-enclosed office, strolled the hallways. The phones purred, computer screens were bright with activity, there was the sense of a quiet yet powerful engine running.

Derek wandered, smiling at the staff, all eager, hard-working men and women in their twenties, paid on a generous commission that ensured their loyalty to the David's. He didn't know them all by name as Oswald had, but he knew he would now since he would be spending a lot more time with them. Twenty minutes later, his assistant handed him some messages, one of which was from Officer Johnson in Hydesville. Derek stared at the note. He walked slowly into his office, the piece of paper in front of him like a small flashlight illuminating his way. He closed the door, sat at his desk, called the number, his heart racing. After a moment, a machine clicked on.

"The number you have reached is not in service at this time. Please check the number and dial again or contact the operator for assistance. This is a recording." A sharp dagger of high-pitch static emitted from the phone, startling him. Then all was quiet. *Bad phone connections are a sign of paranormal activity,* he recited to himself, picturing the list, *but I know it's really Vanya trying to misdirect me. I know it's her.*

He redialed, got the recording again. *Was this a sick joke, Vanya teasing him in some sadistic fashion?* he wondered. Simply another trick to confuse him? He reached in his wallet to retrieve Officer Johnson's card to check the number again, but couldn't locate it. Derek Googled the phone number but there was only information for a Hydesville police station in California. He didn't even know if phone operators still existed, but he went ahead and tried.

"Operator. What city please?"

"I'd like the number for the Hydesville Police Department. That's in Wayne County, New York, not the one in California."

After a moment, the operator said, "I have no listing for a Hydesville Police Department. Would you spell it for me?" Seconds later, the operator said, "I'm sorry, sir. No listing under that name."

"How about anything in Hydesville?"

"That's the problem, sir. There is no phone service or phone lines registered in my system with that information. I don't have any listings for a place called Hydesville in Wayne County, New York."

Derek ended the call, his mind fumbling about for solid explanations. He tried to reason himself back to a place where he was certain of what he knew. *I know I was in Hydesville, I know I spoke with Vanya. Even though Edith and Warren and Matilda say she was at the apartment at the same time, I* know *I spoke with her.*

A sharp knock at the closed door startled him; he almost cried out. He did his best to calm his trembling hands as Manny entered the room, sat down across from him. "I've got the schedule all set for Europe and a list of confirmed appointments. Is now a good time to review all of this?"

Edith was withdrawn, quiet that evening. Derek assumed she was still brooding over their argument about Vanya staying with her while he was in Europe. He had hoped that during the day she would rethink the situation, recall all she knew about what had been occurring, come to her senses. He had urged her to read the binder while he was at the gallery, but the chilly reception he received confirmed that she hadn't looked through the notebook, was still blind to the Vanya thing's sly, deceptive methods. The entity was taking over Edith, nibbling away at her until she'd be as lost and robotic as Oswald had been at the end. Derek wanted to cancel the trip, but it was too late, there was really no one to take his place, and after the death of Oswald, it was important for the stability of the company that he be in attendance.

Yes, I am stressed out, have too much going on, he thought as he changed out of his suit and tie, *but I'm not losing my mind, not having spells or hallucinating things.*

Throughout dinner, Edith was coldly civil, asked him about the gallery, his plans for the trip. He kept his answers equally short, annoyed at her attitude, matching her subdued and distracted behavior, all the while trying to figure a way to rescue her from the devouring presence of Vanya Avery. He didn't mention the mysterious phone message from Officer Johnson or his futile attempt to return the call. The realization that the police station in Hydesville—in fact, the whole village—wasn't listed online or with the operator made him wonder if Vanya's power and influence were increasing; were there any limits to her ability? How long until she totally controlled Edith?

"Let's take our coffee into the living room," he suggested. "I like the view of the park, it's so clear out tonight." One of the drapes was closed, which was unusual since it had been sunny all day. He opened it, they settled on the couch. After a few moments of silence, he asked, "Everything all right?"

"Just tired, I guess. The baby...."

He cautiously put his arm around her, hoping she wouldn't resist his attempt at affection. Maybe the human bond they shared would loosen Vanya's grip on her. "How about we have a dinner party soon after I return? By then you should be far enough along that it will be safe to tell the world about the baby. We can have the Donaldson's, the Carlson's, Sherrie and Tim, Betsy and whomever she's dating at the time. How's that sound?"

"Really? Oh, that's a great idea! I can start planning it now, and when you come back, if the doctor says it's all right, then we'll do it soon after." She hugged and kissed Derek; he was reminded again of how childlike Edith was at times in her enthusiasm. Parties, vacation trips, holidays always brought out such bright-eyed eagerness in her that it never ceased to surprise and delight him. It wasn't like her to be cold and aloof to him, or anyone. That wasn't Edith; *this* was Edith. There was still hope.

"I wish you could come with me," he said. "I'll have to travel more and spend more time at the office. Manny keeps reminding me that the gallery needs to have a David 'face,' and I'm the last one."

Edith patted her stomach. "Well, I'm working on changing that."

A sound woke him from a deep, heavy sleep. He laid there, his eyes closed, waiting to hear it again. There. The murmuring of a voice, a low, continuous hum. Derek opened his eyes, glanced at the digital clock. 1:22 a.m.

He yawned, thinking perhaps he had been dreaming. Who would be up talking at this time? He rolled over to embrace Edith. She wasn't there. The area where she would normally lay was cool; she hadn't been in the bed for some time.

In the dim moonlight, he saw a crack of light below the bedroom door. A muffled chortle from the hallway. Edith's voice. He listened at the closed bedroom door. By the rhythm of the conversation, it sounded as if she was talking on the phone. He carefully opened the door a crack.

"...dizzy, nauseous at times in the morning."

He crept down the hallway to hear better. Edith was in the study, speaking into her cell phone. "The saltine crackers help. I have to be careful what I eat because I want to eat *everything* but it doesn't all agree with me anymore." After listening a moment, she asked, "But how can you be certain it's a boy? Really? Hmmm. The doctor kids me, says it's an amazing, growing baby, never seen anything like it..." Then, "Oh, I know, Vanya! Can't wait. But each day just creeps by, like he'll never leave. Two whole weeks together! And then..."

Derek returned to the bedroom, closed the door, leaving Edith alone in the study. He felt sick to his stomach. How often had Edith been calling Vanya, plotting together for her to move in as soon as he left for Europe? The betrayal he felt was so painful that Edith might as well be having an affair with someone. His eyes teared up, a furious anger burned in his heart. How could she do this to him? He sat on the edge of the bed, staring into the darkness, not knowing what to do. Should he confront her with what he had heard, or would his betrayal of her privacy drive an even bigger wedge between them? Had the Vanya thing really taken over to such an extent that he could never trust his wife again? He hadn't thought things had progressed this much, that Edith was so far gone...

He glanced at the door. He couldn't locate the strip of light on the floor. Had she already turned off the study lamp while he was lost in thought? He listened, his ears straining to catch any sounds.

"Derek?"

He gasped. Her voice, behind him. His heart immediately started to gallop. He twisted around. Edith was in bed next to him.

Her voice was thick with sleep. "What's wrong? Why are you awake?"

He looked at the clock. 4:47 a.m.

Where had the last three hours vanished? Was Edith right, had he had a spell, wasn't even aware of it? Or a dream?

"Honey, what is it?"

He turned to her in the darkness, reached under her, felt the sheets.

"Derek, what are you doing?"

The sheets were warm. She hadn't been out of bed.

CHAPTER 22.

He didn't want to leave Edith for the two-week trip to Europe, knowing what she had planned, knowing that the Vanya thing was gradually moving its way into their lives, mentally and physically. He had spoken again to Warren and Matilda, and they had reluctantly assured him they would not allow Vanya into the apartment. He had to trust them, *did* trust them, so was able to leave knowing she was protected from whatever advances the entity planned to make in his absence.

He took the binder with him; he was in desperate need of undisturbed time to continue his research. He was no longer sharing with Edith what he was learning or mulling over. One theory he had was that Vanya's reach didn't extend past the East Coast; there had been no other areas in the United States that came close to the events that had put Hydesville on the map. *Until the Vanya thing removed the village from the map,* he thought, realizing that maybe he was getting close to discovering her secret. Maybe that was why she hid things or made them vanish.

Even with his crammed European scheduled, the late dinners and early morning meetings, he was able to set aside a few hours every day to review the notebook, read the books he had brought with him, update his ideas. He spent one evening reading Ann Ryan's diary, was astounded at the contents and what he was able to glean from her entries.

Whatever the Vanya thing was, Derek realized he had been wrong to assume it had first made itself known in Hydesville with the Fox children. He was able to trace it back to the city of Rochester and John Fox's first wife, Ann Ryan. John Fox was a very devout man, very religious, as was Ann. But soon after they married, for some unknown reason she abruptly denounced her Methodist upbringing. Almost overnight, an interest and fascination in the occult consumed her; the diary was filled with elated discoveries of her newfound beliefs and a devotion to an entity she referred to only as She.

During the first year of marriage, Ann was desperate to have a child, had several early miscarriages, was distraught, thought she was barren. She believed her devotion to the occult and a special ritual she performed had finally ensured she would become pregnant. Her son, Roland, was born late in 1806, her and John's only child.

She raised Roland with a love and devotion of alchemy, hiding their shared passion from her husband, whom she knew would forbid the practices they were involved with. While John worked long hours as a blacksmith, Ann and Roland would play what she called "special games," activities which assisted them in developing their occult abilities.

According to her diary, her husband eventually caught them, forbid them from engaging in what he called the dark arts, beat them both during one of his drunken rages. John considered their actions ungodly, blasphemous. They ignored his demands, took his punishments with defiance, used their gifts to heal one another after his lashings. Their refusal to obey infuriated him. Proud of their developing psychic abilities, Ann and Roland often laughed at John, privately and publicly. Repeatedly, he demanded his wife and son stop their evil practices, but they refused.

Or they couldn't stop, Derek reasoned. *Clearly, Vanya had already captured and controlled them.*

Things escalated one day in 1811. Ann found a locked wooden box in the attic. The outside was very ornate, intricately carved, the work of a skilled craftsman. It looked valuable, almost like a sacred relic; she wondered what it contained. There was no keyhole, no hinge; the container was sealed. Then, whatever was inside, began to move on its own. Scratching, thumps and muffled knocks were heard. Ann was startled by the sounds but also curious. She tapped on the box, was startled when it returned the sound.

Excitedly, Derek thought, *Those same rappings were later used to deceive Maggie and Katie Fox in their cottage in 1848, made them think they were communicating with the spirit realm, but Ann experienced the sounds first in 1811!*

She wrote that she tried to bang and pry the box open, but it remained shut tight. One morning she went to awaken Roland, was surprised to find the box in his room. He told her that he woke in the middle of the night, saw a nice lady with green eyes and golden hair. "She was an angel, right Mommy?" he had asked.

Ann wrote that Roland said the woman was holding the square item out to him like a gift or an offering.

The Vanya Avery thing, Derek thought, jotting the information into the binder.

First appearance was in 1811; it was the thing that made the original rapping noises from the box.

According to her diary, Roland took the box from Vanya. Either he opened it or it was opened for him, Ann wasn't clear in her entry. Inside was a ball. Ann's second to last entry didn't make a lot of sense to Derek. Her handwriting, always legible and controlled, had become sloppy, frantic. From what Derek was able to decipher, Roland had learned from the orb how to levitate. Ann herself made attempts, an effort which eventually cost her her life.

One evening, John Fox came home unexpectedly. When he went looking for his wife, he found her in their bedroom, in a trance, on her back, three feet off the floor. Ann wrote that he screamed at her, said she was bewitched. Then he dragged her up to the attic, locked her in, said she'd remain there until she repented. Ann wrote her final diary entry from that place. She indicated that she could hear her husband in an alcoholic rage on the floor below her, said it sounded like he was speaking to someone, arguing with them, but she assumed it was just the whisky talking.

Ann wrote:

Thank God, I am not alone at this time! She is here, She has arrived in her glory. I will leave my diary for Roland, so he can continue to follow his path to his destination, creating a union child.

Now I will go to the window, follow Her through to the next life. She says Do as I Do, and I shall.

Derek turned the pages. That had been the last entry. He shivered nervously, realized that the familiar phrase "Do as I do" was what Maggie Fox had said when speaking to the entity in March of 1848. When Ann quoted the child, it was in 1811, twenty-six years before Maggie Fox was even born.

According to *Hydesville In History*, Ann Fox was found dead of a broken neck after falling from the attic window. Roland believed his father had killed Ann in a drunken rage, but of course the little boy, only five-years-old at the time, never had access to his mother's diary or he would have known the truth, but John did. He entered the attic after his wife had smashed through the window, found and read her diary, learned all that Ann and Roland had been doing while he was away working. Already drunk at the time, he took his fiery, sloppy rage out on Roland, beat him almost to death, then collapsed, blacked out.

The next day, John awakened to find Roland gone. He contacted the police, saying he had returned home to find his wife had apparently fallen and broken her neck. He said that his son was nowhere to be found, had probably run off over grief of his mother since they had been so close. Ann's death was ruled an accident.

Of course, Derek thought, writing in his binder, *John hadn't killed her—it was the Vanya thing, the "She" who had led Ann to the window—and John had hidden her diary so no one could read her final entry. If they had, they would have thought her mad, would have known the occult practices she and Roland had been involved with, would have wondered if John Fox was also bewitched.*

Derek mulled over who John Fox had been speaking to downstairs while Ann was in the attic. Since Vanya excels at misdirection, she could have appeared to John Fox in some form to keep him occupied while she also manifested herself in the attic to lead Ann to her death. If John had seen the Vanya thing, surely he would have interfered since he was so opposed to the occult and its manifestations.

But why kill Ann Ryan? Derek wondered. *Was she simply* used *by this Vanya thing just to gain entry into our world and then discarded when she was no longer needed? She provided a son, but he soon disappears from the story. What was Ann's part in this? What role does Roland play? Whatever happened to him?*

Derek paced his hotel room, speaking aloud, working through the puzzle. If everything came back to a place and time—Hydesville and the 19th century—and the Fox sisters were literally what put the village on the map, then somehow Vanya needed to get John Fox to leave Rochester and move to the little town. The Fox children *had* to be born in Hydesville.

Then it dawned on him: John Fox left the city—or was driven from it—because of his sullied reputation and the suspicion that clung to him over the death of Ann. According to the *History of Hydesville* book, although Ann's death was ruled an accident, suspicion had simmered in town that John Fox, in one of his frequent drunken rages, had actually killed his wife, and perhaps his son since he was never found. No charges were ever filed, but his blacksmith business began to shrink along with John Fox's once sterling reputation. He wanted a fresh start, so he moved east to the tiny hamlet of Hydesville.

Derek let the thoughts settle over him, tried to fit the pieces of the puzzle together. He summarized what he knew, wrote it in the binder, realized how outlandish it sounded: The Vanya thing has the ability to read minds, plant destructive thoughts in our brains, it can create illusions we think are real, it can comb through our past, see into the future. It has a plan, it has a reason for being here. It wanted to be impregnated by Oswald for some reason, killed him when he failed.

Now, it's after Edith. But why? Derek looked through the binder for another hour, crossed out some passages, updated others. He swallowed, it burned going down, tasted of…alcohol? Was it whiskey? He sniffed the air. Pungent scent of smoke, wood. He grimaced until the flavor and smell receded. He never drank whiskey. This had happened before, this harsh flavor appearing when he'd seen the apparitions at the Colony. *It was John Fox's drink of choice,* Derek reminded himself. *Maybe it's evidence he's near or wants to impress something on me?* He jotted the idea down just as the thought came to him, *Burn down the Fox house.*

In the notebook, he wrote down, *Return to Hydesville, burn down Fox cottage.* He underlined the words so he would not forget.

CHAPTER 23.

When Derek returned from Europe two weeks later, the plane landed at JFK in the middle of a light snowfall, early in the morning. The flight had been delayed two hours due to the weather, which had only added to Derek's anxiousness: he desperately wanted to see Edith. He had tried to call her every day from Europe yet usually it went to voice mail. When he reached Matilda or Warren, they said she was napping. Of course, he didn't want to disturb her, so he tried to make his calls when she'd be awake, but that was difficult due to his own busy schedule and the time difference.

The few times he had gotten through, he had been bothered by their brief conversations; she hadn't sounded very animated or excited to hear from him, she seemed disinterested in the news he shared with her about the trip. She didn't ask him how the auctions were going or what he was purchasing or who he had had dinner with or meetings with, things she would have always chatted with Oswald about.

When he'd ask about her, she was vague, said she was fine, yet she sounded half asleep on the phone or slightly confused, as if she had just awakened. She didn't sound like herself. Something was going on. He had asked Warren and Matilda but even they seemed evasive, saying only that she was following the doctor's orders, was resting well or napping. Everything was fine, they assured him. He knew something was wrong, knew the Vanya thing was gaining its control of her, but he thought there was still a chance to free her once he got home.

Warren met him at the airport gate; Derek's heart sank. He immediately knew something was up. "What happened? What's wrong?" Crowds jostled around them, Derek grabbed Warren's arm, pulled him off to the side.

"Edith is *fine*," Warren said. "It's…something about the baby, it's growing at an incredible rate. It's exhausting Edith, sapping her strength. That's why she hasn't been able to speak with you much, didn't have much to say. The doctors are monitoring her, she's on some medication that leaves her a bit loopy. But they say she is okay."

Once they were in the car on the way home, Warren glanced in the rearview mirror. "Edith took to feeling badly soon after you left. She had a dramatic loss in her weight even as her stomach began to expand. Matilda knew something was wrong, called the doctor. When he saw her, he was astonished by her condition."

"Why wasn't I told about this? Why isn't she in the hospital?" Derek demanded, his heart racing, his mouth dry with anxiety. Couldn't the car move any faster?

"It isn't safe to move her. She's surrounded by equipment. The doctors have said—and they told me to tell you this—that Edith really is fine. It's just the rate that the fetus is growing; they've never seen anything like it. It appears to be the size of a six-month-old—"

"Six months!"

"—and yet it's a normal, healthy, fully formed six-month-old baby," Warren finished quickly. "Edith insisted we not tell you. She didn't want to worry you, said she was concerned about you, knew you've been under so much stress lately…"

She has that right, he thought darkly. They sped along in silence. Warren cleared his throat, looked at the road ahead, not glancing at the rearview mirror, didn't want to see Derek's reaction when he told him. Finally, he blurted out, "Edith started calling Vanya as soon as you left. Then—"

"What?!" Derek felt as if he had been punched in the gut. He gritted his teeth, was going to respond but Warren broke in.

"Edith said it didn't matter what you had said. She told us that you weren't yourself these days, were making wild accusations. That you had been seeing things…"

Warren told him that Vanya Avery had moved in while he was gone. Derek stared out at the traffic, his mind filled with a roar, his thoughts in chaos. Despair settled in. He found it hard to accept that the three people he loved and trusted so completely had so totally betrayed him. And that's what it was to him, a betrayal. But Edith's comments that he had been seeing things, that hurt the most, actually stung.

She chose to side against him, to undermine him, when he was only looking out for her.

Warren had continued speaking, his voice broke in on Derek's thoughts. "The first day, Vanya came over in the early afternoon. They talked, had lunch in Edith's room. We left them alone. By the sound of their voices, they seemed to just be enjoying one another's company. It seemed very... normal, we didn't think it was causing any harm, was nothing to be concerned about. Matilda and I, we talked about what you had said, but it seemed okay, Edith was so happy and relaxed. But soon after, Edith started to become withdrawn and moody. Then she had terrible nightmares, was in great pain and discomfort. Matilda tried to comfort her, but Vanya was always there at the bedside first. Vanya explained to us that since the baby was kicking and growing so rapidly, it affected the nature of Edith's dreams, it was nothing to worry about."

"How the hell would Vanya know? She never had children." Derek was seething now.

"Matilda has a lot more to tell you; some of it I can't quite believe since I didn't see it or experience it myself. But one thing both of us have noticed is how the lights keep blowing out. I must have replaced every lightbulb at least twice. I've called the repair people, but they can't find anything wrong. I don't know what it means or why it happens..."

I do, Derek thought miserably. *It means nothing, it is simply a distraction from the main event that is happening right under our noses.*

Warren caught Derek's eye in the rearview mirror, saw his misery, his anger. "Vanya didn't want the doctors near Edith, said she would care for her until the time of birth. And she seemed to be helping, she really did. The doctors are still on-call for when she goes into labor, but even when they last checked, they were astounded at how well Edith was doing, considering the size and rapid growth of the fetus." He hesitated, then said, "We're so sorry, Derek. You were right. We never should have let Vanya into the apartment. I've seen some things, Matilda has, too. She—"

"Is Vanya here, now?" Derek asked, sickened that he'd have to see her.

"No, she left earlier today, knew you were coming home. Said she'd give you and Edith some privacy."

###

Derek was desperate to see Edith. The elevator seemed slower than usual. He barely acknowledged the operator, really didn't have the energy for small talk. The doors finally opened. Derek hurried through the small, marble foyer that led to his apartment.

"Edith? I'm home." Silence swallowed his greeting. He sat his knapsack down by the door, took off his jacket.

Matilda called out, "Derek, come here, quickly! Your bedroom!"

Derek rushed through the living room, down the hall, his heart pounding hard. Matilda had sounded terrified. He rounded the corner. Matilda was crouched next to the bed as if in prayer. In fact, she appeared to be appealing to a higher power by the look of her grasped hands. Derek moved closer, then stopped when he saw a stranger on his bed.

Where was Edith?

The woman's face had a damp, waxy appearance to it, a pale sheen as if she were under tremendous pressure. Her black hair resembled a bristly shadow that framed her face; portions of it had been tightly swept up in a half-hearted attempt at a bun. Her eyes were closed yet he saw rapid movement beneath her lids, as if she were dreaming violently.

"Where's Edith?!" he shouted at Matilda, who continued to mutter prayers. "Who is this?"

The woman on the bed opened her eyes. "Derek! Thank God…you're here!" She started to struggle and squirm, made panicky, jerky movements, yet was unable to rise from the mattress. Derek peered closer; he knew the voice. Impossibly, it had sounded like Edith but the figure before him didn't resemble his wife. Her face seemed longer, thinner, paler, her complexion oily, it almost glowed in the dim light. He stepped nearer, curious why she was thrashing about.

"Derek, for God's sake, get me *loose*!" Edith screamed.

It *was* her, but there was something wrong about her wide, blazing eyes. Brown eyes…were they now hazel? Derek guessed his wife was having a fever dream or some reaction to whatever medication she was on; how else to explain her erratic behavior?

She continued to grunt as she struggled in the bed. Then he saw a thick white clothesline was wrapped several times around her waist. The sheets that covered her hid most of the rope, but when she strained against it, Derek could see the coils pressing around her greatly enlarged stomach. Although he had only been gone two weeks, Edith's pregnancy had progressed at an astonishing rate.

His foot connected with something. He looked down, saw a child's rubber ball roll toward the end of a frayed piece of the rope that touched the floor. He immediately made room between the medical equipment that surrounded the bed, began loosening the restraints. A hand gripped his arm.

"Don't!" Matilda said. Her strength and insistence surprised him, her grasp tightened. He stopped fiddling with the bindings.

"UNTIE ME!" Edith screamed, her voice a thick, low roar. The picture next to the bedside table came loose from the wall, crashed to the floor, showering Matilda with fragments of glass. The woman cried out, tried to stand, but instead she stumbled violently to the side as if pushed by invisible hands. Derek carefully led her to the door. Matilda leaned on him, clung to him, crying steadily, murmuring prayers. Edith continued to thrash around on the bed, demanded to be untied.

"What is it, Matilda?" Derek pleaded with her. "What is going on?"

"Don't untie her!" Matilda said frantically. "I have seen her—"

He gently led her out of the room into the kitchen where he confirmed the glass hadn't cut her. He told her he'd be back, to stay where she was. He didn't know if she heard him or even knew where she was.

Once in the bedroom, he watched the rubber ball suddenly lumber across the room to the corner where it stopped. He wondered where it had come from, was distracted by Edith. Her chest was heaving, her breathing raspy. Her eyes almost glowed a radiant, polished green. *Like Vanya's eyes,* he realized dully. *Dear God, am I too late?*

He worked quickly at the knots. Edith lay still, gazed at him with the gratitude a child would bestow upon a father fixing a broken toy. When the bindings were undone, he pushed them aside. Edith squirmed about on the bed until, with Derek's assistance, she was sitting up, her belly huge, grotesque in its appearance. She took a few moments to rub her arms and stomach where the clothesline had left deep marks. Holding her ice-cold hands in his own, he was shocked by her appearance.

Up close, she looked even worse than when he first saw her. Dark circles were under her eyes, her skin was blotchy, had a glazed, rubbery feel to it. For all the increased size to her stomach, her weight elsewhere seemed to have fallen off. Under her nightgown, her shoulders appeared bony; even the skin on her hands seemed papery and rough. There was a stench that hovered over her of shit and body odor and… something else. *Stress?* Derek thought crazily, *and terror. What's happened to my wife? Where's Edith?*

She finally managed to speak, her voice a weak whisper. "If you hadn't been her… Matilda…something is wrong with her. She has become so strange lately. Ask Warren. He's seen it…And now this. I was taking a nap, the next thing I knew…she's tying me down on the bed. What if there had been a fire? I could have died. Oh, God, Derek, I could have lost my baby…"

Feeling helpless, Derek cast about for a response, finally said, "But what put the idea in her head to do this to you?"

Edith started to answer, then stopped, calmed herself. "Ask her. No idea what she's thinking…But so glad you're home. Promise…you'll never leave me again." She closed her eyes, exhausted, whispered, "Go ahead, ask Matilda why she tied me up."

CHAPTER 24.

Matilda was in the kitchen, still visibly shaken, trying to calm herself with a cup of tea. She looked up, startled, when Derek entered the room.

"Oh, thank God, it's you! I thought she got loose. You didn't untie her, did you?"

He sat down across from her. "Matilda, what's going on?"

She sipped her tea, placed her hand on her breast as if trying to slow her rapidly beating heart. "There's something terribly *wrong* with Edith, and this apartment. Did Warren tell you?"

"It doesn't matter what Warren said. I want to know why you had Edith restrained on the bed." Matilda reached again for her tea. Derek saw her hands trembling. Her shoulders sagged, her hands shielded her face as she wept. "Matilda? Listen, you have to tell me."

It took her several seconds to regain control. She wiped her eyes on a napkin, cleared her throat, then began to speak very quietly, as if she was telling Derek a secret.

"I just wanted to save her, Derek. That was why I tied her to the bed. *To save her*."

"Save her from what?"

"From going to the window, from climbing out…" She reached for him to quiet his questions. "Let me finish, let me tell you what happened. After Vanya moved in, I started to…see things, see *people*, here, in the apartment. I saw two children wearing long dresses with high collars, from a long time ago. And there was a man from the same time period. He had a beard, dressed like an Amish man.

"I'd see their reflections in the mirror, or at the end of the hallway I'd hear the rustle of something and there would be the girls, adjusting their long dresses, just watching me. I know this sounds crazy, but *I saw them…*"

Derek listened, wondered why she was seeing Maggie and Katie Fox, curious who the Amish-looking man was.

"One afternoon, I felt a chill in the apartment, traced its source to the area around your bedroom. I went to see if a window was open. When I went in, there they all were: the two children and the Amish-looking man! He was pointing out the window, which *was* open, and the two girls had their arms around Edith. I knew Edith could see them, too, so I wasn't imagining them! I called out to Edith. She turned to me, said, 'My name isn't Edith, it's Ann. And John wants me to join him. Outside.' And then she started to stagger toward the window."

Frantic thoughts flashed through Derek's mind. *Why was Edith trying to re-enact Ann's leap from the attic window? Was the Amish man an apparition of John Fox?*

Matilda said, "It was all so strange, like a dream I was in but one that I was also watching. I wasn't able to react, couldn't speak or move. The man urged Edith toward the window. The two children held her back. Then, the Amish man and the girls simply …weren't there. At the same time, I heard Warren return home. Of course, I told him what I had seen but by the time he came back to the room with me, Edith was asleep in bed, holding some old child's rubber ball. I didn't know where she got it or why she was holding it. I took it from her, I'm certain I did, but it keeps reappearing."

Derek thought of the rubber ball Roland Fox had discovered in the sealed box, the one Vanya had opened for him. Could it be the same one or was there more than one? Why was it here?

Matilda took a sip of tea, seemed calmer. "And from then on, I was aware that the ghosts—they are *ghosts*, Derek, this apartment *is* haunted—were around, each of them looking for their opportunity to be alone with Edith. The children wanted to protect her, the man wanted to do her harm. And then they started to move things around in the apartment, hiding my cleanser or mixing up my cooking ingredients. Warren says I'm getting old and forgetful, that I leave the cupboards and drawers open, too, but it's not me, Derek. It's them! I'm certain of it. In your study, the drawers are always open and I know you don't leave them like that, do you? And did he tell you about the lightbulbs? That's them, too! I know these are signs of the supernatural, of spirits, I've looked it up! We need help…"

Derek wanted to tell Matilda how wrong she was, how *small* her thinking was, how much bigger the Vanya Avery thing was than simple supernatural occurrences, how she deceives, misdirects people. He wanted to show her everything that was in the binder, but there was no time. Plus, she had given him a new piece of vital information he had to mull over: John Fox—the Amish-looking man—didn't want the baby Edith was carrying to come to term, he wanted to destroy it, have her leap out the window, repeating how Vanya had led Ann Ryan to fall to her death. Was it some form of sick poetic justice John Fox was attempting? The death of Ann Ryan had caused him to move to Hydesville and remarry, resulting in the birth of the Fox sisters and ultimately the Spiritualist movement, which provided camouflage for whatever the Vanya thing has planned. Would the death of Edith and the child she carried end what Vanya first introduced back in 1811? Derek rubbed his forehead, wanted to stop thinking that way, frightened that he wasn't able to.

Matilda was saying, "…twice last week I saw Edith standing by the window, stroking her stomach. I could see she was in great conflict over something. She was holding that old ball again, murmuring to herself, fingering the window latch." Matilda's face and hair were in disarray due to her crying and distress. "And *that's* why I've restrained her, for her own good. I knew she was thinking of harming herself. I know it looks wrong and it's terrible, but if she is tied down, then she can't jump. *I am trying to save her.* You didn't untie her, did you?"

"Of course he did," Edith said from the doorway, filling the space. Derek and Matilda both jumped.

Derek stood, put his arm around Edith. "Are you all right? You know you shouldn't be out of bed." The housekeeper, who had remained seated, cowered under Edith's glare.

"I'm fine." Edith's voice was weary. She gestured at Matilda. "Did she tell you her stories, about seeing ghosts, me threatening to jump out the window? How could you do this to me, Matilda? I love you so much…" Edith began to weep, turned her face to Derek's shoulder.

Derek quietly suggested that Matilda gather some belongings, stay with some friends or at a hotel for a few days, until they got things sorted out. She nodded immediately, hurried from the kitchen. Derek wondered how any of them would ever get over this event. He had grown up with Matilda and Warren, they had been with he and Edith all of their married life. They loved one another, were family…

"Thank you, darling," Edith said, raising her head, sniffing back tears. "I feel so sorry for her, no idea what's wrong with her." She embraced him, was surprisingly strong, her stomach huge, solid and firm against him.

The front door closed. Derek heard some fumbling about, knew Warren had entered with the cart, piled high with his luggage. He'd forgotten all about the houseman in his haste to get into the apartment, couldn't believe all that had occurred in the short time since he had arrived home.

Once Derek had Edith settled back in bed, he found Matilda at the front door, wiping tears away with a tissue. A small suitcase rested at her side. Warren was awkwardly holding her, murmuring to her. The three of them walked to the elevator, pushed the button.

Derek said, "Let me know where you're staying, we'll talk, get this all cleared up. You know this is a terribly stressful time for Edith."

Matilda said something.

"What?"

She looked at him, her face red, the tears flowing freely. "Oh, Derek, can't you see? That's *not* Edith anymore."

The elevator doors opened. Matilda quickly stepped away from Derek. He wasn't fast enough to save her, but he knew instantly that something was wrong.

No light illuminated.

There was no operator there to greet them.

The doors opened to black space.

There was no elevator car waiting.

But Matilda, in a hurry to leave the place that had caused her so much distress, stepped immediately into the empty elevator shaft. Her feet touched only air as she fell away. The horrific image remained permanently etched in Derek's mind.

For the rest of his life, whenever he had a nightmare—and he would have them most every time he fell asleep—Matilda being swallowed by the darkness would always appear somewhere in the dream.

Derek and Warren staggered back from the elevator shaft, horrified at what had happened. Derek called the front desk. Moments later, several employees of the building appeared. Within ten minutes, the police and an ambulance had arrived.

Two hours later, Derek closed the door, rested his forehead against it. He and Warren had told the police and the building staff the same story over and over. Pending a full investigation, the officers ruled the death was an accident based on their preliminary findings. The elevator was placed out of commission.

Derek checked on Edith, who remained asleep, the machines that surrounded her all quietly keeping watch. Warren was in the kitchen, slumped over the table, a half-finished scotch in his hand. It was only noon, but Derek pulled a glass down from the cupboard, joined the houseman at the table to share a drink. Both men were traumatized by what had occurred.

"Nobody can explain how it happened, can they?" Warren finally said softly.

"No, they can't, not yet, anyway. They think maybe it was a short on the signal riders, so a false 'car available' impulse was given when there really wasn't a carrier there."

"Makes no sense. You know that. The elevator operator controls it. How could it have arrived with no one inside?" He hesitated. "No. It was *her*."

Derek knew without asking whom Warren was referring to.

"So, you know? Suspect?"

"I know that whatever you suspect about her, you're right. We should have listened to you."

"It's all so crazy, not sure anyone would believe me if I told them all that was going on."

Warren asked, "Did you know that Edith fired Matilda, and the only reason she was still here was because of Vanya?"

Derek shook his head.

"Matilda has done this before, restrained Edith while you were away. I came back from doing errands one day, they were yelling at one another. Edith had managed to get loose, told Matilda she was to pack her things, leave immediately. I guess Vanya had been away when it happened so when she returned, she and Edith spoke to Matilda. The door was open, I listened in. Couldn't really believe it, but Edith actually apologized to Matilda, said she wasn't fired, that she understood we were all under a lot of pressure with the baby coming and the extra work it all required."

"Vanya intervened to *save* Matilda's job?" Derek asked. "That doesn't make any sense."

"Maybe it does." Warren stared into the amber liquid for a moment. "Maybe if Matilda had left, had been dismissed, she'd still be alive today, would still be suspicious, still able to do something about Vanya. By keeping her here, you know that saying, 'Keep your friends close, your enemies closer...'" His eyes were red with tears and exhaustion. "Whatever is going on, we have to get out of here. Now."

"But Edith can't travel in her condition..."

"I have a cousin in Hartford that I'm going to stay with," Warren said, ignoring what Derek said. "I packed, made arrangements while you were talking to the police. Get Edith, come with me." He stood, Derek hurried after him as he headed for the front door.

"But the doctor said Edith can't be moved in her condition now, or she could lose the baby."

"She shouldn't have that baby, Derek." Warren stared at Derek intently for several seconds, as if searching for something. "If you're lucky, Edith will lose that baby or whatever it is that is growing inside of her." He gave Derek a piece of paper with his cousin's address and phone number on it. "If you need anything, call or come here, all right? I think we'll be safe here."

Derek checked on Edith. She appeared to be sleeping normally, the large mound of her stomach now her defining characteristic. He examined her face closely; she did look different, her bone structure seemed longer, narrower, her eyebrows were thicker, matched her dark hair. Even her nose seemed pinched, turned up a bit. And her lips, even in sleep, appeared to be thicker, almost as if she was pouting. How had the transformation occurred, and why?

He had just closed the bedroom door quietly when his phone rang.

"Hello, Derek," Vanya greeted him. "Glad you're home. I wanted to give you some alone time with Edith. I'd love to see you…"

He told her he wanted to see her, too, somewhere in public. His sorrow over Matilda's death and anger at what Vanya had done to his wife bolstered him.

"The steps in front of the library at four," he said. He hoped that meeting between the lions that guarded the doors of knowledge would symbolically work in his favor. Desperate for answers, still hungover a bit with jet leg and the horrific events that had occurred since he'd been home, Derek took a quick shower. He wanted to be alert and prepared for his meeting with Vanya.

CHAPTER 25.

Before leaving the building, Derek slipped one of the porters he was especially friendly with a twenty, asked him to check on Edith every thirty minutes, just to ensure she was resting. "Call me if anything changes. I should be back in an hour or so," he said.

Derek arrived at the library first. He quickly mounted the steps, removed himself from the crowded, active section, wanted a little privacy. It was the week before Thanksgiving, the brisk, 40-degree weather was just the thing to send people out in packs. The clear sky added to the buoyant mood; everyone seemed to be in high spirits as they hurried about. In contrast to the festive mood that surrounded him, Derek's own life had taken on a bleak and frightening tone.

He couldn't help reflecting on what had happened in the few hours he'd been home that morning; the strange transformation of Edith, the bizarre things Matilda had told him including the information about the Amish-looking man he had assumed was John Fox, her sudden, tragic death, his revealing conversation with Warren, who had then departed for Connecticut. Without the maid and houseman, he was truly left by himself to battle Vanya Avery. Before he left the apartment, he had added every new revelation to the notebook, still hoped the information would lead to an insight that would reveal what the Vanya thing was planning.

He was jumpy as he waited for her, highly apprehensive, feeling as if a trap door would spring open unexpectedly at any moment. From out of the swarming crowd, she arrived, striding up the steps. She gestured at the stone lion off to the right and the one in front of them. "Did you know the lions have names, Derek? Patience and Fortitude. Those are two traits I've had to develop over the years." Vanya settled down beside him on the steps. She was dressed in a red and black wool skirt, with a stylish coat closed up tight over her chest. Her perfume was coy and aggressive at the same time, beckoning him to inhale all that it promised. She was beautiful.

People continued to move up and down the steps, but no one seemed to notice them. Derek wanted his words to be direct, on point. "I've asked before, but you've never answered. Who are you? What do you want? Why me, and Edith and Oswald?"

"I told you back when we were chatting at the Colony. You already have all the answers," Vanya said, smiling, her bright green eyes flashing with delight. "Don't you remember? I sent a letter to you back in August, inviting you and Edith to visit the Colony, attend a dinner in appreciation for the money your great-grandfather had given us to start the organization back in 1948, followed by generous grants every year since."

He nodded impatiently as she spoke.

"I told you to meet me at the ClearView Restaurant for lunch—"

"Yes, I remember all that," Derek said dismissively. "It was so quiet there when we spoke, it was as if our words were in a vacuum or we were trying to speak under water. And Edith felt someone was watching us. It was you, right? Somehow, you were there, watching us before you appeared, making the sounds go haywire. You and the Fox sisters were present. I'd even seen shapes of the three of you, a silhouette, in the forest a few times."

Vanya didn't respond, wanting him to figure it out himself. She watched him, her eyes ablaze with interest.

"In the restaurant," Derek continued, "I saw a painting of three women, didn't know who they were at the time. Now I know that two of them were the Fox sisters, Maggie and Katie, but who was the third figure? I'm guessing it was their older sister, Leah, right?"

"Yes, She is the One who is yet to come," Vanya said with solemn reverence. She drifted off for a moment, her thoughts captured by what she had just announced. She blinked, mentally returned to the hard, cold steps on the library. "She is part of the Fox family. As are you."

"Me? I'm not part of that family, never even heard of them until—"

"—until I invited you to the Colony," Vanya finished. "Do you think all of this has been some random accident, without planning? Without patience and fortitude? We sought you, Edith and

Oswald for a *reason*, Derek. Aren't you beginning to see that there is a very strong purpose behind all you're experiencing?"

"'Purpose'? No, not at all. Just a lot of confusion. Like when we got into our cars to drive to the Colony after lunch at the ClearView, you took off speeding, lost us almost immediately."

"You were never lost, Derek. You were actually on your way home, back to your family; you just didn't realize it at the time."

Frustrated with the evasive conversation, he said. "Why do you keep saying that? My last name is *David*, always has been. No relation to the Fox family. None."

"Really? How far back can you trace your name?"

Derek thought for a moment. His father, Bernard, was the only son of Simon David, the son of Maxwell David, but further beyond that, he had no idea, had never checked, no reason to.

"Just to my great-grandfather. Why?"

She smiled. "Why indeed." Vanya looked away, gazed at the street. A group of tourists rushed up the steps behind Derek, brushed against him, laughed at one another, in a hurry to get inside the library. She turned back to him. "You really should be more curious about things, Derek. For example, who is the father of your child?" Before he could form a response, she said calmly, "The answer is: You're *not* the father, which means he's *not* your child."

Derek recalled Edith's dream about having a baby, the uncomfortable feeling he had because she never did say it was his baby or their baby, it was always only *her* child.

Vanya leaned closer. He inhaled her perfume. She whispered, "Don't you remember?"

And then, with great might and power, the images, the voices, the memory, sprang open in his mind: The Fox house—

"Edith? Come downstairs..."

—Edith in the arms of an old, disfigured man—

"Edith? Am I going to have to come up there to get you?"

Edith in the cellar with her back against the wall, both her arms extended over her head, held in place by Vanya's father, as he thrust into her, crying out, "Do as I do!"

"Remember?" the Vanya thing teased, its voice bringing him back from the obscene event in the basement to the busy activity of Fifth Avenue, the hard, cold steps of the New York Public Library. "Now do you remember whose baby it is?"

Appalled at the suggestion, he said, "No! That was all some kind of dream, hallucination, a nightmare you created..."

"A dream?" Vanya said. "No, it really happened, Derek. All of it."

He tried to make sense of what she was saying. She leaned in closer, her green eyes wide with excitement.

"You're doing this," he insisted, face to face to whatever she was. "There is no Hydesville, no Colony. It's in ruins, I saw it! You're making all this up."

"Am I?" Vanya said, her eyes bright, animated. "Back in 1848, where do you think Maggie, Katie and Leah Fox and their mother vanished to? Who do you think was calling from the cellar? They want justice, Derek. Only you can provide it for them."

"They're *dead*," he managed to say. "There are no ghosts or hauntings, it's all *you*, making this stuff up in my mind!"

"If it's all in your head, then maybe Edith is right and you're going crazy," Vanya said. "Is that what you want? To lose your mind and any sense of reality? Or do you want the truth, want to know who you are, what you did, and why I must have you?"

She watched him for a moment, then whispered, "You keep asking who *I* am, but you should be asking who *you* are. The past has *all* of the answers you're looking for."

Then she leaned closer, softly kissed him. Her tongue flicked over his. His crotched tightened, his erection thickened, hardened. He pressed his lips over hers, his tongue filled her mouth. In his mind, he envisioned making love to her, pushing deeper and deeper into her, becoming one with her, giving her everything she wanted, everything Oswald was unable to provide, abandoning himself to her, allowing her to consume him, yielding to whatever she wanted—

A spicy taste filled his mouth, he sniffed a whiff of oak. The fleeting presence of John Fox empowered him. He shoved Vanya roughly away as he coughed. He shouted at her, "Get away from me! You'll not have me, you'll not take from me!"

"You!" she cried, enraged, but Derek sensed she was responding to someone other than him, someone only she could see. He moved sideways on the steps a couple feet from her, allowed his head to clear of the images, her scent, the coarse taste. No one seemed to have noticed his outburst.

He looked around. She was gone. Left alone on the steps, the holiday crowds stepping around him, he pondered what she had said: *You should be asking who you are. The past has all of the answers you're looking for.*

248

III:
The Consummation

CHAPTER 26.

Derek walked home in a daze, unaware of the cheerful crowds that jostled about him. He was in his own world, a soundless bubble of mystery, confusion, fear. It was now dark, store lights spilled out on the streets in squares of white and gold and green and red. Pre-Christmas Santa Claus's of the Salvation Army variety rang their bells while excited children pulled at the hands of exhausted parents. But Derek saw and heard only a muted version; his mind was racing about as if he was trying to complete a scavenger hunt, but the list of collectables was lost.

The porter said Edith had been fine, sleeping peacefully. Derek nodded at the elevator operator. He entered his apartment, was immediately struck by the heavy, muffled silence, like an immovable force he was compelled to wade through. Warren and Matilda had always been a welcoming presence; with them gone, it was like some of the warmth and life of his home was absent. He glanced down the hall; for some reason, the lights in the study were on. He hurried to the bedroom, flicked on the bedside lamps; each bulb exploded. The glow of the moon provided weak illumination. The sheets and cover quilt were twisted about. Edith wasn't in the bed.

"Edith?"

"Here I am..."

In the darkness, he was uncertain which direction her voice had come from.

"John?"

A slow chill inched up Derek's back. He looked to the corner of the room by the window. There, in the black shadows, stood Edith, her hand on the glass, caressing it. He could see by the glow of the moonlight that she was wearing a dark, full length gown, her hair was piled tightly to the top of her head.

"John, why did you do it?"

"Honey, it's me. Derek..."

"The children, John. Your flesh and blood. The cellar. Why did—"

"Edith." He grabbed her gently by the shoulders, turned her around so she would face him. He recoiled. The woman in front of him no longer bore any resemblance whatsoever to his wife. The hatred and rage that were etched in her face were like a physical blow to him. He released the woman, repelled by her.

"Why do you call me by that name, John?"

Derek was hesitant to touch the woman. "Will you get back into bed?" he asked. "The doctor said you should be resting, remember?"

"You're worried about your son," she said warmly, with affection, the anger gone as she placed her hands on her stomach. She accepted Derek's arm as he led her to the bed. "Roland will be pleased that you care about him..." She settled back, he covered her with the comforter.

Derek shuddered, tried to gather his thoughts which were beginning to dissipate. *It's all madness,* he mused wildly. *I thought I had lost my mind, but what has Vanya done to Edith, what has become of her? Possessed? Inhabited? Does she think she's pregnant with Ann Ryan's son, Roland?*

He looked down at the woman. Edith thought she was Ann Ryan, believed Derek was John Fox. Derek decided it was best to enter his wife's world, take hold of what she believed was true, join her reality. He addressed her as Ann, asked her who was the father of the baby she was carrying, wanted to know if Vanya had told him the truth.

"Father is the father," she said simply, like a child reciting a poem. She leaned up in the bed toward Derek. By the silvery-white sheen of moonlight, he could see her eyes were huge, a vibrant emerald color, fully dilated, insect-like in their intensity. Not Edith's eyes. "I shall be its mother. A new family will be established, a family of union children. We will begin and will forever continue what you sought to end."

Union children? Derek thought, puzzled. *What was she talking about? The phrase was familiar.*

The woman in front of him continued to stare eagerly into his eyes. Derek gently settled her back on the bed where she promptly fell asleep. Other than the quiet click of the medical equipment, the apartment was silent.

Think! he told himself as he paced the living room. He didn't know what to do next, felt immobilized by too many choices, too much information. He knew he needed to make one more trip to Hydesville. He remembered writing in the binder the need to burn down the Fox cottage; that he could do. He would also visit the library again, see what else he could find out about John Fox's background, how it connected to his own, if it did.

You should be asking who you *are. The past has all of the answers you're looking for.*

"Yeah, yeah, or more misdirection," he said, but admitted that Vanya had been oddly insistent that there was something for him to discover. Most of all, he was aware of an undercurrent of urgency; this couldn't wait, he needed to decide what to do and do it—

He coughed, gagged as a whiskey flavor burned its way down his throat. Doubled over, he sank to his knees in front of the sofa. His thoughts blurred, were suddenly a frantic cauldron of voices calling out, insisting, demanding action be taken. He gasped for air, felt he was being pulled down, drowned beneath a surface of consciousness. Forced to listen, to see, he tried to turn away from the sickening visions, but they kept reappearing like the spinning images on an evilly unbalanced slot machine.

Seconds, maybe minutes passed. He squirmed in despair, wept. Then, the unsettling mental pictures subsided as quickly as they arrived. Shaken and reeling from the dark commands that seemed to have come from within him, Derek clutched his head, clenched his jaw in discomfort.

"What the fuck was that?" he cried, shaking. Although his mind still churned with the distorted ideas, a thought, then a plan, quickly formed. Derek squeezed his eyes shut. *God, no!* He could never do that to Edith—

—It's not Edith—
—or his own son—
—It's not your son—

For most of the night, Derek updated in his notebook all that he knew and suspected about the Vanya Avery thing, John Fox, his first wife, Ann, their son, Roland, and John's second wife, Margaret, and their children Katie, Maggie and Leah, as well as Hydesville. He also reviewed everything that had happened to him, Edith, Oswald, Warren and Matilda, made sure it was current.

He read over many of the passages, knew it sounded like the writings of a crazy person, but was grateful he had had the foresight to collect all the information into one binder. If anything happened to him, there would be detailed information as to what had occurred. He found a box, put the notebook in it, wrapped and addressed it to Warren in care of his cousin in Connecticut.

Early the next morning, Derek checked his reflection in the bathroom mirror.

"You're sure about all of this?" He was looking at a madman. His eyes were red, bloodshot, dilated, rimmed in crimson, soulless, on fire with a mission. His face was sickly pale, and he hadn't shaved so there was a grainy quality to his image. The realization of what he was doing made him sick, he began heaving and gagging, finally vomiting several times into the toilet.

He cleaned himself up, began pacing back and forth, from the bedroom to the front door. He rubbed his hands together to help offset the icy chill that seemed to have suddenly taken up permanent residence in the apartment. *Misdirection,* he thought. He stood in the middle of the living room, shivering. He reached into his pocket, fingered the car keys. The craving ache to drive upstate returned. Dreading what he was about to do, all that he was prepared to set in motion, Derek hurried out of the apartment.

He left the parcel for Warren with the porter who assured him it would be messengered to Connecticut and received that day. Derek had tried texting and calling Warren's phone to alert him that the binder was coming, but when the call connected, it only emitted some brittle and ear-piercing bits of white noise. *Distraction,* he thought, not at all bothered. It was to be expected, common place now.

His hands were trembling behind the wheel of the Mercedes. The garage attendant had looked at him strangely when he had handed the car over. *I'm a mess,* Derek admitted to himself, *outside and inside. I'm a mess, a wreck, a danger to society, to myself.*

At a stoplight, he squeezed his eyes closed. Tears leaked out as he thought of what he had done, what he had left behind.

There was little early morning traffic out of the city. Within minutes, the car was able to race up the bleak landscape of I-80 West. He turned on the radio, tried to lose himself in the weather report, traffic updates, stock news, the headlines. But it was all just words, a foreign language. He focused on the road ahead of him, wondered if he would be able to find the village. Hydesville seemed to appear and disappear at will, but he sensed that it would be there this time. Waiting for him. Challenging him to find its secrets.

CHAPTER 27.

The exit for Hydesville was easy to miss.

The sign for the village was weathered, the elements had had their way with it over the years; the paint was faded, blistered, the backing support beams showed through in the upper left-hand corner. Wild shrubbery had grown up around the signpost, partially obscuring it from view. For whatever reason, Hydesville was not a place that wanted to be easily found.

Derek drove right past it, had to double back to make the turn. The GPS didn't recognize the information he had punched in, only got him as far as New York State Route 14 North, which was about ten miles from the village. The five-hour drive had left him stiff, his emotions were frazzled. Several times he wanted to turn around, drive home, stop what he had started.

The nearer he got, the more solid his recollections were; most all of his memory had returned. Derek wasn't surprised that the main street of Hydesville was deserted. On his right was the abandoned police station. It was hard to believe that he had actually spoken to someone there just a few weeks ago. Officer Johnson had seemed so real...The police station was now just an abandoned place.

The thought came to Derek to call 911. All he had to do was contact them, they would be at his apartment in five minutes...

He started weeping, briskly pushed away the tears. No, he'd finished what he needed to do as quickly as possible, then return home to Manhattan.

Five minutes later, he parked the car across the street from the library. The sky was steel gray, the air was cold, with a thirty-degree bite to it. There was no wind to speak of; it was as if the environment had stagnated, turned in on itself. He shivered, tightened his coat, walked hurriedly toward the building. Once inside the quiet old property, Derek didn't hear any sounds other than his footsteps on the warped wooden floor.

"Hello?" No response, not even a brief echo. His voice was swallowed up whole. "Anyone here?"

Then he saw the note on the desk: *Derek, you know where to look.*

The message unnerved him. He was certain it was from Vanya; she seemed to be one step ahead of him. Did she know all he had planned, could she read his mind? *Probably*, he thought. *If so, I'd better lock up my secrets.*

He stood at the checkout desk, pondered how to do it, how to create something in his mind that was like an impenetrable safe. After he discarded several ideas, he went about envisioning a simple wooden crate. He added the word **SECRETS** to it, bold, stenciled letters on each side. He'd think of that crate, not its contents, hoped that would work to hide from the Vanya thing what was happening in Manhattan.

He exhaled with relief, started on his way. His footsteps seemed especially loud, jarring and clumsy in the empty building. The door to the *Hydesville Historical Archives* was ajar. Inside, he saw the same boxes and stacks of photo albums, small wooden chests, crates, heaps of newspapers, file folders, odds and ends of clutter that had been there last time he had searched for some answers. But everything was coated in dust and grime as if he had never been there. In the corners of the room, shadows hovered.

A genealogy was what he was looking for. He started in on the pile closest to him. On top was a weathered, mildewed photo album. Underneath, several file folders of newspaper clippings. Immediately, his hands were grimy from the filth and dust. It took him almost fifteen minutes to sort through the items. He was beginning to taste the grit in his mouth when he came across a file marked *Fox*.

Excitedly, he pushed aside a pile of journals to make room for himself at the desk, sneezed as the dust scattered. The first document was a marriage record from Rochester, stating that John David Fox was joined in the holiest of matrimony to Ann Catherine Ryan, in the Year of Our Lord, 1805.

It took Derek a moment for the information to register.

John David *Fox?* A stone of dread plummeted from his throat to his chest. Anxiously, he thought, *I never saw that middle name before. His middle name, my last name? Is this the connection Vanya had hinted to me about? Am I related to the Fox family?*

Hands trembling, rattling the fragile pages, the next document was a second wedding record from Hydesville, this time joining John David Fox to Margaret Rutan Smith in 1812. A rustling sound from behind startled him. A stack of newspapers spilled over onto the floor. He fetched the top page. The *Rochester Times* of April 15, 1811 stated that Mrs. Ann Fox suffered a broken neck after falling from the attic of the home she shared with her husband, local blacksmith, John Fox. According to the paper, *"The couple's son, five-year-old Roland, is missing."*

Derek sorted quickly through the stack of papers, found a follow-up story that reported that a search party had been assembled to find the boy, but it was unsuccessful, he was never located. A month later, one short notice read, *"overcome with grief and remorse following his wife's tragic end and the mysterious loss of his son, blacksmith John Fox plans to move from the area."*

He continued to examine the contents of the file, came to the 1806 birth record for Roland David Fox. With a shaking hand, he held it close. In the small, cramped and dusty room, Derek read the name several times, not wanting it to register, not wanting it to be true or accurate. It became a mindless chant in his brain. *Roland David Fox, Roland David Fox, Roland David Fox.*

Nervously, Derek thought, *like his father, his middle name, my last name. What's going on...?*

Derek contemplated Roland and John Fox's lives as he walked about the small room, trying to figure out the connection to his own family. He paced the room, speaking aloud as he tried to piece together the information. "Roland David Fox. You run away, your father never pursued you because he feared your practice of alchemy, was probably glad you were gone. And you were glad to be free of him. Let's say that you're taken in by another family, raised by them, you never reveal who your father is. Since you despise him, want no connection between the two of you, maybe you go so far as to change your last name? Maybe it was as simple as removing his surname? At some point, you become just Roland David. Is that what happened?"

The words hung in the air for an instant, then escaped the room. Derek looked around, needed more. A hefty, thick white book caught his attention. *Holy Bible* engraved in raised gold letters on its cover. Had it even been there a minute ago? Derek began casually flipping through the scripture. In the section that separated the Old Testament from the New, he came across pages that listed the births, baptisms, confirmations, marriages and deaths of the Roland David family. He scanned the information, saw that very late in his life, Roland David married twenty-two-year-old Sarah Elizabeth Connor in 1827. After five miscarriages, they finally had a son, Thomas, in 1830.

Derek forced himself to say aloud what he was seeing. "Roland David was my fourth great-grandfather. Thomas was my third great-grandfather."

He continued to skim down the listings, seeing his second great-grandfather, Graham was born in 1860, then his great-grandfather Maxwell, was born in 1910, and then his grandfather, Simon, whose wife, Hope Washington, gave him a son, Bernard—his and Oswald's father—in 1960. All sons according to the record, no daughters, or none that survived.

Bernard David married Sissy Dunton in 1980. Derek found it upsetting to see his parent's names in the book, along with the dates of their death due to the car accident just after he had graduated from college. Then a slow chill fingered its way up Derek's back. Someone had updated the family tree with the births of Oswald in 1981 and Derek in 1983. Who had found this old book in Hydesville and done that?

"Finally getting your facts straight?"

Derek spun around, dropped the Bible. Vanya was standing in the doorway.

"I told you that all of the answers were in the past."

It took him a moment to compose himself, praying she couldn't pick the truth out of his brain, but he sensed she was beginning to. He envisioned her trying to pry the lid off of his **SECRETS**, seeking a way to see what was inside. He willed himself to turn his thoughts away from that subject, said, "I guess these records validate what you said. I *am* part of the Fox family. John David Fox was my fifth great-grandfather, and with Oswald gone, I am the last of the Fox bloodline."

She nodded, looked pleased.

"But I still don't know what *your* connection is to me. Or Edith, or the Fox family. What is your role in all of this?"

"It's simple, really. Like you said, there's a bloodline," Vanya replied, still speaking from the doorway. "It didn't matter if Roland changed his name, it's only through the blood that a generation survives. And there's *memory* in blood, Derek. In that Bible you were looking at, scripture says that the 'blood cries out.' Blood has a voice, it can testify to justice. And injustice. Blood never forgets, it always demands justice…"

She stepped aside, vanished from his sight. He rushed after her, banged his elbow against the doorframe. The pain seared his arm, he cried out. Where had she gone? He hurried out to the main floor of the library, glanced around, listened, but all was silent. A scent of oak drifted past. A harsh, grainy taste suddenly filled his mouth, he gagged, coughed, spat it out. The thoughts all came in a rush: He needed to get in his car, see if he could locate the Colony; maybe that's where the Vanya thing went, or the Fox cottage.

Burn down the Fox house, he reminded himself as he jogged out of the building.

Once inside the Mercedes, he looked in the mirror. His eyes were bloodshot, filled with anxiety, his face had grime and dust and dirt on it from his library investigations. He started the car. It purred out its steady, low grade hum. He had transportation, he could go wherever he wanted. He could give up; it was a five-hour drive home. The clock was always ticking against him if he wanted to arrive at the apartment in time—

SECRETS

He shut down the thought, turned away from the crate in his mind, forced himself to resist the Vanya thing's efforts to unlock what was hidden.

Again, the coarse taste filled his mouth. *Thank you, John Fox!* he thought. He slammed his hands down on the steering wheel, shattering whatever stupor was creeping over him. He had much to do. He needed to destroy the Fox house, but first he had to get to the Keilgarden Colony, deal with Vanya. Before his thoughts could scramble again, he put the car in motion. He didn't know where he was headed or exactly how or where he'd find Vanya, but it felt like the right thing to do. A form of clarity was beginning to settle in place.

Within minutes, a huge forest spread out around him, the Fox Woods. The trees seemed to thicken and populate the landscape as rapidly as he drove past them as if he was creating them, seeding them. *Or was the Vanya thing creating all of this, knowing it's where I wanted to go?* he wondered, uncertain whether or not to proceed. But he realized that at the same time the place was being revealed, the area also seemed familiar to him, two images being laid over one another, compared and matched. The thick, spicy flavor of whiskey returned. Soon Derek surmised that he may be seeing the woods as John Fox saw them when he entered them for the last time in 1848. He would certainly know the area that was named after him; if anyone could locate the elusive Keilgarden Colony, it would be John Fox.

Derek proceeded, didn't have to think twice about which way to turn when he came to the numerous forks in the road. The abrasive taste would fill his mouth, he'd have a sense of which way to steer the car, and he'd continue deeper into the foliage.

With a lurch, the automobile suddenly accelerated up an incline. He hadn't touched the pedal. The Mercedes seemed eager to make it over the grade. Derek loosely held the wheel as it seemed to drive itself, crashing its way over the wild road, tree branches scratching against the sides.

The car jerked to a hard stop, tossing Derek forward. If it hadn't been for his seat belt, he might have collided with the windshield. The Mercedes turned itself off. Derek sat there, waiting for a sign of what to do next, listening to the tick, tick, tick of the engine as it cooled down. He smacked his lips several times, waiting to see if the taste of his saliva would change. After several seconds with nothing happening, he climbed out. The automobile was slanted sideways, the front left wheel wedged into a hole. Derek leaned against the door for balance. The road was hard and dry, a mess of potholes. Football-size rocks were littered across it like giant crumbs.

The quiet forest ominously stretched out in all directions, shadows of green, shadows of black. Disoriented, he wondered how had he driven in so deep, so quickly? Had he followed John Fox's directions correctly? In the eerie stillness, he felt the area pulling at him, attempting to draw him into its darkness. Overhead, the dull sunshine was flat, as if it was being filtered through a dirty glass bottle. It was warm out, too; strange for November.

The car was firmly entrenched in the road, would take him no further. He couldn't imagine walking back through the dark woods. The narrow path in front of him edged up at a sharp angle. He couldn't see over the precipice, but he knew his only option was to head toward that blind horizon. He leaned into the steep incline, started up, slipping and stumbling over the loose rocks in the road. Soon, he was actually gasping for air as if he was at an elevated altitude. He hadn't thought the knoll was that high, would require such effort. When he reached the crest, he paused, looked back. It must have taken him several minutes to make the climb, yet when he looked down, the Mercedes was less than twenty feet below. *Vanya again?* he mused, *playing with time and space?*

From where he stood, he could see the section of the Fox Woods he had passed through. He shivered. It looked even more menacing, the trees standing like unearthly warriors, their shadows impossibly black and thick, almost three dimensional. There was no way he would ever go back that way.

It was coming. The woods were eagerly, impatiently waiting to greet and embrace whatever the Vanya thing was calling. Looking at the trees made him anxious; something that shouldn't be seen was about to appear. Derek scrambled over the top of the ridge, trudged forward, wanted to get away before the thing Vanya was summoning arrived. Would it be a separate entity or another part of herself? He recalled the image he had had of her as a Russian nesting doll. He shuddered.

At the crest, he had to catch his breath, take in the view. He rubbed his eyes. But what he was seeing remained, hadn't dissolved, wasn't a mirage or hallucination.

Below was the Keilgarden Colony, but not the decrepit ruins he had visited before when he had encountered Vanya and the Fox sisters. Then it had looked like the deserted and ramshackle library and Hydesville Police Station, an abandoned place of decay.

What he saw now was a vibrant, active, thriving community with dozens of people, mostly children and young adults, milling about neatly manicured lawns, walking between recently constructed buildings that were freshly painted. The Colony appeared as it was in 1948.

Derek cautiously started down the hill.

CHAPTER 28.

The closer he got, the greater detail he saw in the clothing, the haircuts, the way people spoke to one another. One of the dormitories had a radio on; Derek thought he heard some old crooner singing. Perry Como, maybe. A swooning company of girls joined in on the song's chorus. A group of boys were seated in a circle on one of the cement walkways concentrating on marbles while another played jacks. Girls pumped their legs on a swing set that was built for eight, others jumped rope alone or double-dutch. Children ran about shrieking, enjoying tag, hide and seek, or red light, green light. No one appeared to pay Derek any attention; for a moment, he wondered if he was invisible.

He stopped in front of two girls knitting, his shadow falling squarely between them. They wore peter pan collar junior blouses, poodle skirts with their socks rolled down to their ankles, dirty black-and-white saddle shoes. They were whispering, giggling together as they worked on their argyle sweaters. Behind them was a well-landscaped dirt road. Several boys were bent over the hood of an old Model T automobile. The guys were all elbows and arms as they operated on the vintage car.

The girls stopped their activity, looked at Derek.

"Hi-de-ho!" the attractive brunette said. She was wearing red lipstick, her hair was pulled back neatly. "My name is Joan, this is Molly."

No black nail polish, nose ring, tattoos or green hair, something he associated with so many modern teenagers. It was like watching an old film or stepping into a Ray Bradbury time-travel story. Derek smiled uncertainly, nodded at her pleasant greeting. "I'm Derek. I'm looking for someone. A woman."

"What's her name?" Molly asked. "We know all the girls here. And the boys, of course!" She and Joan giggled. "Sorry, we're kinda khaki wacky!"

"Her name is Vanya Avery."

"Oh, sure! Vanya's staff. She's probably over at RB."

"RB?"

"Rec building," Joan said. "It's the last one on the right there."

Derek started along the neatly landscaped lane. To his right were large dormitories, which resembled army barracks. Brilliant patches of flowers— yellow daffodils, red and white tulips, giant purple crocus, a fantastic mix of blue, pink and white anemones— were scattered throughout the compound; all appeared to be thriving, even if they were out of season.

And who knew what season it was, Derek wondered, *or what year. I know I'm somewhere in the 1940s by the look of things. It was November when I left Manhattan this morning. What month is it now?*

To his left was an open activity field, where young men were tossing a football around, girls were chatting in groups, children were calling to one another as they played red rover. All the residents of the Colony wore clothes from the time when Truman or Roosevelt were President, listened to music from that era, spoke in the lingo of that period. It was unsettling, yet he didn't feel threatened. They all seemed pleasant enough and when he'd catch anyone's eye, they'd smile and nod, not at all surprised or curious to see him. He supposed he had expected to see the children doing odd things with their psychic abilities; these kids just seemed like regular youth from the '40s. If it wasn't for the decades-old appearance of everything, it would almost seem that he had stumbled upon the private campus of an exclusive school.

The recreation building was painted a bright yellow. He quickened his pace, was drawn to it. His mood lifted. He relaxed. *I could spend the rest of my life here*, it suddenly occurred to him. *I could settle down here and never leave.*

"Hello, Derek."

Vanya Avery was dressed in the modest fashion of the 40's, a simple flower print dress that extended down below her knees. Her blonde hair was neatly pinned back, there was an essence about her that was much like the inviting nature of the building she had just emerged from: secure, nurturing, comforting, wise. She was lovely.

"Welcome," she said simply. "Welcome home."

"Home?"

"Come inside."

She reached for him. He felt the instant erotic pull when she touched him; it shimmered throughout his body, coiled at his groin, stiffened him. It was sexy the way she held his hand; he liked how she took charge. She led him inside to a large, casual living space. A black and white television set was on. The voice over on the nine-inch screen announced it was broadcasting *The Growing Paynes* starring Ed Holmes and Elaine Stritch. "Sponsored by Wanamaker's Department Store!" exclaimed the announcer.

The front page of *The New York Times* was on a coffee table in front of the TV set:

TRUMAN DEDICATES IDLEWILD INTERNATIONAL AIRPORT

Idlewild, Derek remembered as Vanya pulled him on. *That's what JFK International Airport used to be called...*

Three boys were slouched on the floor with their backs against the sofa, all peering at the latest issue of *Hot Rod*, pointing at the article one of them was reading aloud from. "It says right there that it's Dick Vineyard's Little Beauty!" Opposite the boys, a teenage girl was deeply engrossed in the *Calling All Girls* magazine. None of them glanced at Vanya or Derek as she led him past them.

From the dorm rec room, then down a hallway, they passed a series of closed doors on either side. The further they traveled from the living room, the gloomier and narrower the passageway grew; it was hard to see where they were headed. He stumbled several times. She gripped his hand tighter, quickened their pace in the near darkness. She seemed able to see clearly in the dim light. It was an awfully long hallway, Derek realized with mounting unease.

"Where are we going?" he finally asked.

Her pale white hand dragged him forward relentlessly. He was unable to release himself from her. Gradually, the blackness that surrounded him dissipated. Faint light materialized. The end of the impossibly long corridor appeared. They stopped in another living space, but much smaller.

Vanya released Derek's hand. He looked around. By the flickering glow of a peculiar, blue-tinged fire, he was able to make out a bookshelf, some paintings on the wall, a rocking chair, a tattered sofa. A very humble dwelling, not at all welcoming, no effort made to spruce it up. The dull fire—with its eerie blue flames—danced in the stone fireplace, yet there was a chill in the air that seemed to be expanding as it drove the temperature down, down, down.

"What is this place?"

"It's home, John."

With a start, Derek recognized where he was, the Fox house.

From upstairs, a door closed. Derek heard two sets of heavy shoes slowly clump down the staircase. The ominous sound immediately terrified him. He looked wildly about for a place to escape. Vanya watched him, her face composed. Her pupils were hugely dilated, blotting out the familiar green, now only two cold black marbles.

The leaden pair of footsteps grew nearer. *"John? We have something to show you."* The deep, guttural voices echoed about the room.

Maggie and Katie Fox appeared at the bottom of the staircase. Derek staggered back as if struck; a powerful desperation emanated from them. He glanced anxiously from Vanya to the children. She moved toward the two girls, joined them. The one in the middle, Katie, placed her hands protectively around each women's shoulder. The three of them watched Derek with tremendous anguish. The force of their despair continued to pour forth, all of it directed at Derek.

Frustrated, tired of guessing, he asked, "What do you want?"

"*Justice. In the soil.*" They spoke as one, their voices tight, close to tears, their dark images at times fluttering, rippling in the dimly lit room.

"I don't know what you mean…"

The heavy rustle of the sisters' long dresses scraped the floor. They moved forward as one. He stepped away until his back touched the far wall. He could go no further. Pressing his hands against the battered and scarred wood, he felt an iron latch.

Vanya and the children were now just a few feet in front of him. Tremendous waves of pain and sorrow encircled them; he felt their grief, wanted to comfort them, free them from whatever had bound them to the cottage. They didn't speak, but he sensed they would continue to move nearer to him until he'd have to seek refuge on the other side of the door.

Their intent was obvious: to drive him into the cellar.

CHAPTER 29.

Derek slammed the cellar door behind him, was immediately assaulted by a variety of sharp odors. It was a mix of smells which led to stark images of their sources: the stuffy and stifling scent of ancient grime and mildew; putrid water trickling down jagged, unfinished stone walls; the decayed shit of rats, mice and other animals; the aroma of exposed rot from splintered wooden support beams; the scurry of glistening insects and the moist, sluggish movement of worms.

Underneath all of it was the sour-sweet putrefaction of long-buried human remains that had settled into the very foundation of the cellar. *This must be where John Fox buried Margaret and his daughters,* Derek thought, something he had suspected for some time. He had written as much in his notes, but it had only been a theory that he had been trying to piece together. He wondered if digging up the remains of Margaret, Katie, Maggie and Leah Fox—and exposing John Fox, their father, as their murderer—was the justice Vanya and the apparitions were so intent on? It sounded like the hackneyed plot to every ghost story he'd ever read, every scary movie he'd ever seen, but he had added the idea to his binder of information. And now he found himself ready to find out if any of it was true.

He tried not to gag on the odors, instead concentrating on making his way carefully down the antiquated wooden stairs. Each plank he stepped on yielded dangerously on the old staircase. Every time his foot stepped down, he'd hear a creak and groan, threats of breakage, collapse. He took it slowly, mindful of every sound.

Behind him, he didn't hear the door latch being lifted or any indication that he was being pursued. He expected to stumble about in pitch-blackness, but his eyes quickly adjusted due to a faint light source that had manifested itself in the center of the cellar floor.

With great relief, he finally stepped onto the safety of the solid dirt floor, exhaled. The shimmer of illumination that had faintly guided him down the stairs was just a few yards ahead of him. It was a muted green glow that flickered under a pile of debris. Derek moved forward, immediately tripped over some stones. Cursing, he rose, brushed himself off, felt something quickly scurry over him. He shivered with disgust.

It took several seconds before he was able to control his jittery breathing. He continued toward the light source, stepped gingerly in the dimness, was soon standing over an area of the cellar that was littered with old packing crates, battered luggage, what appeared to be a moldy box of rags. The greenish light emitted faintly from under these items.

Derek spent a few moments clearing them away, flinching with revulsion at the various things that scrambled over and about his hands and arms. An occasional squeal or squeak of surprise confirmed that the creatures of the dark were not accustomed to having their home disturbed.

When the area was sorted, Derek stared down with uneasy wonder at the glow below the dirt. It was as if someone had buried a lantern a few feet under the ground, its pale rays still beaming after...how long? If he was correct, and this was the burial spot that he had been led to, the earth had not been disturbed since September of 1848.

He got down on his knees. He began scooping out handfuls of dirt, ignoring the texture of the heavy, clammy soil and the insects that were burrowing deeper into the dirt or frantically up his arms. His breathing became ragged as the hole grew deeper, the illumination brighter. Soon, his back was aching from leaning into the hole, which was now almost two feet deep. The unpleasant warmth of the cellar had him sweating profusely yet he continued, knowing there would be no relief until he uncovered the bodies of Margaret Fox and her daughters.

The stench intensified the further he dug. Soon he was almost four feet into the hole. The light was exposed enough so Derek could look above him, get a better sense of his surroundings. What he saw overhead made him cringe. Packed and sealed tightly together like small black and brown purses, dozens of bats clung to the ceiling. They were motionless yet even in the dim light he could see that their bodies were pulsating with life. *How'd they get in here?* he wondered. There must be a broken window or some other opening for them to enter and exit. *And I'll find that spot,* he thought, somewhat relieved. He wouldn't have to return upstairs to Vanya and the Fox children; he'd escape the same way the bats did.

He resumed his digging, tried not to think about the dozens of repulsive winged creatures that slept just a few feet over his head. With renewed vigor, he removed great handfuls of dirt and rock and debris from the cavity. He concentrated on his panting, making it into a mindless rhythm, tried to ignore the horrible foulness that confronted his senses. *It's almost over,* he thought. *Almost...over.*

His hands came in contact with a smooth shape about the size of a grapefruit. Grunting with effort, he pulled it lose from the tightly packed earth. The neck, shoulders and rib cage of a skeleton came, too. He cried out, dropped the skull and its attachments back into the hole. They clattered hollowly. The light burst forth in a damning radiance. The sudden illumination shocked the winged residents of the cellar into wakefulness.

Derek could see by the emerald glow that next to the skeleton he had uncovered—Margaret, on top, protecting her children?—were two more, turned on their sides, facing one another. *Probably Maggie and Katie,* he guessed. He was certain a fourth skeleton, Leah, could be found but he was out of time. The light that beamed from the uncovered graves irritated and excited the bats. A nervous chattering and rustling was heard overhead. Once one bat had fluttered its wings, the rest followed.

He cringed as the entire ceiling begin to move, flutter, eventually squeal and squeak in unison. Like a cape blowing in a hurricane, the bats rushed about the confined area as one, their wings whipped into frenzy. Derek watched to see which way they were headed since he planned to follow. They flew past the staircase to the far end of the cellar, then were gone.

When the last bat had vanished and the area was still, Derek climbed cautiously out of the hole. The unknown source of the light under the dirt appeared to be fading; Derek noticed he couldn't see the ceiling as clearly any longer. Perhaps the glow was only to show him the way to the skeletons. Now that he had uncovered them, there was no more need for the guiding illumination. The crimes of John Fox had been exposed.

"Justice," he said, exhausted, wiping his forehead with the back of his hand. "So, all of this—everything that has happened—was to lead me here, to find the skeletons?" He spoke into the space around him, bewildered, still uncertain. He had lost so much, his brother, Matilda, Edith at home now—

SECRETS

—and he had thought it was all going to be part of a much bigger intent on behalf of the Vanya thing. Was this her plan, her purpose, to drive him to locate the remains of Margaret Fox and her children? If that was her goal, then it really had been all about ghosts seeking justice. Nothing more than that. He had been *so wrong…*

"John…"

He spun around. Behind him, the voices spoke as one. In front of the hole where the skeletons rested stood Maggie and Katie Fox.

"Listen to me," he pleaded, "I'm *not* John Fox!"

Then, for the first time, the sisters smiled. It was a ghastly sight in the near dark of the cellar. The strange green glow that emitted from them wavered, rippled; it made it appear as if they were under water. He saw their shoulders shaking with mirth. They placed their hands over their mouths to quiet the laughter. They stepped toward him. Where was Leah? He understood Margaret wouldn't appear, she was not part of John Fox's pure bloodline, only joined to him by marriage. But Leah, where was she?

And why were the Fox children giggling?

Vanya stepped out of the darkness behind them. Derek shouted to her, "What's going on? I've done all you wanted! I dug up their bodies, freed them, given them the justice they demanded, exposed John Fox for what he did to them. What more do you want? Just go back to the Colony, leave me and Edith *alone*—"

"The Colony?" Vanya said, "What Colony?"

"What?"

"Does it even exist?"

Bewildered, Derek said, "I was just there! You led me here after I saw it as it was when it was brand new."

"Or was that all an illusion, Derek? Maybe it—perhaps all of this—was something we introduced to you in one of your spells." She smiled warmly. "Have you ever considered that?"

He shook his head, wanted to clarify his thoughts, make sense of what he knew to be true. "But...I saw the article about the Colony in *Life* magazine! I have records, documents from my great-grandfather that confirm he helped establish and fund it! *I saw it*, both in ruins and how it appeared when it was new, back in the 40s!"

Vanya said, "Those things you read in the newspapers and books, what you and others thought they saw, what if none of them exist? Even the history of my dear Fox sisters was made up. They weren't buried alive with their mother in this cellar in 1848. They spent *decades* telling their lies, deceiving newspaper editors, a judge on the New York Supreme Court, governors, scientists, Christian ministers. They took the deception far and wide until the whole world was fooled, then I laid them to rest in the 1890s.

"Think about it, Derek. What if it was all in your head? What is real and what is just a dream world I created? Can you discern between the two? How will you handle it if you admit that I just made it all up? You believed each illusion. Would you think you were mad?"

"But Edith was with me, we wrote it all down. And Oswald...Oswald knew all of this! And Matilda and Warren knew things!" Derek insisted, wildly grabbing at whatever he knew to be true, whatever he thought he and others had experienced.

"Oswald and Matilda are dead. And Warren...well, patience and fortitude. As for Edith, she's...different now; you know that. No living person can confirm what you believe to be true, Derek. Only you. And whatever you wrote in that binder, if it's ever found and read, it will simply be considered the ravings of a madman..."

Derek was relieved that she didn't know he had already sent the notebook to Warren.

Vanya continued, "But none of that matters any more. My only desire was to get you back to this village, this house. And you came, just as I wanted."

"What do you mean?"

"You were losing interest in me, Derek. You were feeling overwhelmed with the gallery, becoming a father. I needed you *here*. I wanted you close to me."

He thought about it for a moment. "That's why you killed Oswald? Knew I'd drop everything to come here to find out what had happened to him?"

"He failed in what I needed, but he could have lived, I suppose. But like I said, your curiosity was fading. Seeing your brother lifted, pulled up into the trees by the children of Hydesville, ensured that you would come running back to me, to this place. And you did. Then, I had you spend some time in the library, learning what I wanted you to know." She smiled. "You had taken the bait, you were hooked; we just needed to pull you in deeper, to keep you *hungry* for more."

Derek heard her but wanted to finish what she was saying to confirm it for himself. "What about that night I spent with Noreen and Atticus?"

"I wanted you to summarize all you had learned, to discover all that you did *not* know, so you would realize that there was more to find out, more mystery to solve in this little village that doesn't exist on any map," Vanya said. "Unless we want it to."

"*Everything* that occurred was to keep me coming back?" Derek mumbled as his sense of the real world rapidly fell away from him. His voice sounded so small, so helpless. How could he ever fight this thing? What was he really up against? It was huge. How could he stop it?

The image of the **SECRET** crate rose up; he mentally pushed it back into the darkness.

Vanya watched him.

"It was *all* a lie?" he asked. "All of it, just to lead me here??"

"Or a trap, or you could call it bait. And it worked. You're here, aren't you?"

Devastated by the revelations, he felt himself collapsing inside. He swallowed. It burned all the way down. He gasped at the rough, grainy taste, started to cough, his eyes stung with tears. His words were a roar. "*NO!* Not in my house! Your power, not in my house!" The sounds coming out of him were not from his own mouth, someone was behind him, shouting *through* him. The voice was much deeper than his own, there was a thick, heavy edge to it, a stiff, hard warning that weighed every word.

Startled, Vanya backed away, stumbling on the dirt in her haste. Derek could feel the presence of John Fox inside of him; it was like the boldness of a nightmare, one that was only going to increase in substance until the dreamer woke with a scream. Bolstered by the forceful entity, Derek took an aggressive step toward the Vanya thing. His foot smashed through an old wooden box. Something scooted out. It rolled toward Vanya. Her expression changed from fear to delight. She quickly snatched it up.

She held the old rubber ball reverently in front of her as if it was a sacred relic. "Within this sphere is the One who is yet to come. We have been desperate to find this, to restore Her!" Vanya looked intently at Derek. "It's happening. It will happen *today*. I will have your child, Derek. I will have a *girl*, she will join with the son Edith carries now. Then they will consummate, shall cover this world with our powers. It will all belong to *us*..."

There was a dull radiance about her. Slowly and seductively, she removed her dress. She unsnapped the buttons that ran down the front, allowed the garment to slip to the floor. He stared at the fullness of her breasts. She looked at him, her body perfect, supple, ready to be devoured by him. She was magnificent.

"Come to me, Derek. Taste me. Consume me."

His desire for her was immediate, complete. He felt his body respond. This was what he wanted, what he had always longed for. He wondered, *Why did I ever resist?* She was beautiful. His mind dark, single focused, lusted for her. She reached for him. She unbuckled his pants, quickly released what was straining with such craving for her. He gasped with pleasure as she held it.

"Finally," she murmured. She pulled him toward her. "The consummation must occur here, on this hallowed ground." He moaned, felt himself yielding, sliding into the abyss.

He coughed. The abrasive taste filled his mouth. He sensed the steel presence of John Fox. Feeling as if he was surfacing from the depths of the ocean, Derek managed to extract himself from Vanya's spell. It was like pushing against a glass window until the effort of the pressure finally made it shatter. He shoved her back into the darkness of the cellar. She stumbled against a support beam, fell hard to the ground. Behind her, Derek saw Maggie and Katie move to her side.

Abruptly, his mind fully cleared. Derek looked at the cowering, naked body of the Vanya thing, had no desire for it. He swallowed. No taste of whiskey. He was on his own now, knew he had to get away while he could. He pulled his pants back on, dashed to the far end of the cellar where the bats had fled. As he had suspected, there was another way out. A window had broken through, a two-foot wide crack in the stone foundation provided ample room to escape. He squirmed out, scratching his arm on the rough, jagged stone.

Once outside, he deeply inhaled the fresh air, his heart pounding. He rested against the tree in front of the Fox cottage, giving himself a moment. The house glared down at him. From the cellar, he felt the dark black presence of the Vanya thing vibrating its wrath, small explosions of fury that pounded and shook the earth. At any moment, she will be out, nothing would stop her from achieving the consummation she demanded.

He had to act quickly.

CHAPTER 30.

Derek stood in front of the cottage as the enraged sounds continued from the cellar, louder now. She was nearer to the surface.

He quickly focused on what the Vanya thing had told him. She had talked of a consummation that must occur between the two of them, something Oswald had never been able to achieve. It had not yet happened between he and Vanya either; never in his dreams or illusions. She had said that it *would* happen, so she was not yet pregnant. *And never will be by me,* he swore. Derek knew the Fox bloodline would end with his death one day. There was no male heir. Although he was still sickened by how he had left Edith—

SECRETS

—he forced his thoughts to swerve in a different direction, away from the image of the crate, away from what it contained.

Derek whispered, "John Fox, you were right to fear and denounce your first wife, Ann. Your son, Roland, did. But like me, you never knew that you were already in a trap, had no choice but to move to Hydesville, never knowing that it was planned all along that *this* was to be the place you and Margaret would birth the Fox sisters.

"It *had* to be in Hydesville, *had* to be during that time of history. But even back then, somehow, you discovered what the Vanya thing was, tried to put an end to it in 1848 by destroying your wife and children. Her revenge was to hang you in the Fox Woods as she did my brother. But I'll finish what you started, I'll burn down this house, this sacred place. This will be your vengeance, and mine, for what this thing has done to those I love."

Derek felt in his pocket to make certain the matches were still there. He sensed the spicy aftertaste of whiskey, grinned. John Fox was with him, confirming his thoughts. Derek knew that what he was about to do was the right thing.

Destroy the cottage. Burn it down.

He hurried down the walkway back into the Fox house.

The cottage caught fire faster than he expected.

He had assumed it would defy him, but he had no trouble lighting the matches—no sudden drafts appeared to extinguish the flames—and the old clothes he had set alight in the second-floor bedrooms had offered no resistance.

"Come down here. We have more to show you."

He glanced at the cellar door. It was a trick; nothing to see down there anymore.

"Do we have to come up there and get you?"

After a moment, a heavy footstep. Then another. Even over the gathering roar of the fire, he could hear the sounds of the girls slowly clumping up the steps. But it was just a distraction; he needed to stay focused.

Smoke from upstairs was now beginning to push its way into the first floor. He could hear the hungry crackle as the teeth of the fire consumed all in its path; he envisioned a lawn mower aflame, the blades greedily chewing up the second floor. He was certain the fire could be seen from outside by now, but there would be no fire trucks to the rescue, no ambulance, no gawking neighbors. No one lived in Hydesville anymore, and even though he stood firmly and solidly on the landing of the Fox house, he wasn't fully persuaded the floorboards—or the town—even existed. Like waking from a dream, too often they had simply evaporated from his mind, from history, from maps, GPS systems…

The noises from the cellar were now a thick and menacing chorus. The children's call to him reverberated through the walls, cut through the flickering snarl of the flames.

"Open up. We have something to show you…"

The basement door handle rattled.

It was like they were on some film loop or were hosting a residual haunting, simply repeating themselves. *I've already heard the joke,* he thought to himself. *I know the punchline.*

"Go away!" he finally shouted, couldn't help himself.

Overhead, a crash followed by a muffled *whoosh*! as the flames found something new to devour. Thick gray clouds were now rapidly billowing down the stairwell like huge tumbleweeds. He was sweating from the stifling heat. The house seemed to be closing in around him. He started coughing. His chest was tight, he began gasping for air. The old property was now an inferno. The kitchen ceiling to his right blasted open as the second story storeroom crashed into it. The tremendous pressure of the fire shattered windows. The place was collapsing around him.

The walls trembled, split…

The blaze, having found the first of the gasoline on the stairway, licked it up. The fire exploded, devoured the fuel in one gigantic gulp, creating a raging fireball. Derek staggered toward the front door, stumbled out onto the porch, gulped the fresh air while his heart pounded frantically. The trees were heavy with leaves, the grass on the front lawn was green and healthy, the sky was a light, friendly blue. When he had left Manhattan earlier that morning, it had been a cold, gray November day with the promise of snow predicted for later that evening. Now, it appeared to be early May.

The Vanya thing, always tricking us, confusing us, deceiving us, he thought.

"Hello, Derek."

He turned. Vanya was standing there, composed, calm, as the house burned. She was ravishing. He could see the flames reflected brightly in her green eyes which sparkled like fireworks. Immediately aroused, all he could do was gaze at her. She stood so tantalizingly close that if he took only a few staggered steps, he could be touching her. That was his greatest desire, to hold her, embrace her…

Behind him, the furious heat began to blister his back. Black smoke suddenly poured out of the house, river rapids of molten lava. Overcome, he fell to his knees, gasping for air, coughing, choking. He collapsed onto his back, cried out as his scalded skin touched the earth. His eyes stung, he closed them just as he heard Vanya murmur something seductively to him. Then she was upon him, clawing at his pants, struggling to remove them again. Even in the midst of almost inconceivable pain and blistering, Derek remained aroused as the fire began to consume his body. He opened his eyes. Above him, Vanya thrust against him as he deeply penetrated her. She was lost in some dark euphoria, her murmurs of pleasure were animal-like, triumphant as the consummation was enacted.

"This is finally our day!" she cried out. Derek wondered why the phrase was so maddeningly familiar, yet he couldn't grasp its meaning or where he'd heard it before.

From behind Vanya, two images manifested out of the cloudy murk. Maggie and Katie Fox stared down at him, smiling, their hands resting on Vanya who continued to push passionately against Derek. He felt himself began to surge toward climax, was unable to stop it. He gasped when he finally released all that Vanya had required from him. Dazed, spent and depleted, his resolve faltered, his thoughts drifted to the **SECRET** crate, its contents. Even as the images inside the wood box briefly flickered across his mind, the Vanya thing immediately pounced, quickly accessed and explored them for an instant before he was able to slam the **SECRET** shut, push it back into the shadows.

Vanya's expression changed. She had seen something of what he had left behind in Manhattan.

"What have you done?" she demanded. "What did you do to Edith?" she screamed. "What have you done to my child?" Enraged, she unleashed her fury, began to tear his body apart. He struggled weakly, knowing it was useless yet found a grim satisfaction and confirmation in her reaction. Yes, it was unforgiveable what he had done to his wife, but he had ended what the Vanya thing had begun back in 1811 with Ann Ryan.

I'm sorry, Edith, he thought, weeping. *Please, please forgive me.*

He gagged at the taste that filled his mouth, but it gave him lucidity in the midst of the excruciating pain. He heard the gruff, elated voice of John Fox whisper to his mind, remind him, *It's not Edith, that's not your wife.*

Derek's final thought before he lost consciousness was how innocently it had all begun, just a few months earlier, with a simple invitation…

PART TWO

"I beg of you, Sir Arthur, do not jump to the conclusion that certain things you see are necessarily 'supernatural,' or the work of 'spirits,' just because you cannot explain them...."
—Harry Houdini, 1922; a plea to his friend Sir Arthur Conan Doyle

294

IV:
The Proposal

CHAPTER 31.

Eight months later, behind schedule and in a rush as always, Sheila Irving stepped out of the shower, slipped, fell, cracked her head on the floor and died alone. Naked.

"And ten pounds overweight," Sheila muttered as she frantically dried her hair. A long time ago, she had formed the habit of narrating her life by creating headlines in her mind. Yes, she had to admit, she was probably a little overweight. Maybe a few pounds, but nowhere close to ten. She smiled at her still-firm breasts, pleased they didn't dance about too much as she brushed back her hair.

At thirty-five, she concluded that she still looked pretty good. Moved well on a dance floor. Could still catch a few glances when she entered a restaurant. And, most importantly, she continued to have the stamina to rush all over the city at a moment's notice.

She pulled on her short terry cloth robe, started to apply her makeup. "*New York Times* reporter can still pass as fashion model. Or star as one of those reality TV housewives. You've probably seen her on one of the women's channels or interviewed on NPR. She's close friends with lots of very famous people. She says she's not jealous of her friends' successes. Is glad that—"

Her phone chimed. Sheila answered. Always did, never screened.

"Ms. Fontaine? Ms. Joan Fontaine? Cary Grant here."

"I'm sorry, Ms. Fontaine is at a fitting right now," Sheila said, grinning. "This is Barbara Stanwyck. May I be of assistance?" Her boyfriend slash fiancé slash old movie buff slash best friend Kevin Jackson always seemed to call whenever she was in a hurry. Which was always.

"Ah! You're out of breath," he said. "You're in a rush, you're off somewhere, so my timing was perfect."

"Of course, you're psychic."

"It's a gift."

"And I love you for it, among many other things, but—"

"What are you wearing?"

"Guess."

"Let's see. You've probably just showered…"

"Amazing!"

"…so…that too-short robe? And your hair's dried by now. And it's been brushed back, right?"

"Incredible! But really, I *am* in a hurry."

"Destination?"

"Derek David."

"Ugh. That gruesome, weird story. You poor thing."

"Yep, poor old me."

"Tell me all about it over dinner tonight?"

"Atlantic Grill at eight?"

"It's a date. I love you."

"Then marry me already!"

She ended the call, grabbed her digital voice recorder, note pad, file folder of background information, rushed to the elevator. When she reached the lobby, she hurried past the doorman.

"Go! Go! Go!" he cheered and pump-fisted her on as she breezed by with a smile flash, then she was out the door. It was late morning, so taxis were available, no need for Uber. She figured she had about five minutes from her Upper West Side apartment to the Park Avenue digs of Derek and Edith David. She told the cab driver the address, settled back, pulled out the copy of the *New York Times* article from last fall:

FIRE DAMAGES HISTORIC HYDESVILLE LANDMARK

Hydesville, NY, Nov. 20 – One of Hydesville's oldest homes, the Fox cottage, said to be the birthplace of Spiritualism, was damaged by fire on Friday.

One badly burned, unidentified man was discovered under the collapsed front porch and has been taken to the burn unit at Rochester General Hospital where he is said to be in "extremely critical condition." Arson is thought to be the cause and it is not known if the hospitalized man is a suspect.

The farmhouse came to prominence in 1848 when two young girls, Maggie and Katie Fox, claimed they could communicate with the dead through a series of "intelligible rappings." They soon took to holding séances throughout the area, which eventually led to the founding of the worldwide religious movement known as Spiritualism. The Fox sisters later admitted that they caused the sounds themselves.

In 1948, the property and surrounding area were sold to the Keilgarden Colony, a privately funded institute known for its research into the psychic ability of children.

Calls to the Colony were not returned.

Sheila tucked the article back into the file. The unidentified man who had been found under the collapsed roof and had just barely survived was later confirmed to be wealthy art dealer, Derek David. Sheila was on her way to interview his wife to find out what really had happened. She glanced over the rest of the backstory she had pieced together. She knew it all by heart, more or less, but she was feeling a bit apprehensive about the interview, as if she was about to take an exam for which wasn't really prepared.

The same afternoon that Derek David had been terribly injured in the fire in Hydesville, his wife, Edith, had prematurely given birth to their son, Roland, in their Manhattan apartment. For some never-explained reason, Derek had tied his wife to the bed, torn out the doorman phone and all the landlines and taken Edith's cellphone with him, leaving her with no way to call for medical assistance. It was her sister-in-law, Vanya Avery, who had called the police from Hydesville, alerted them to Edith's condition. The officers and a medical emergency team had arrived at the David's apartment just in time to help deliver the baby. It had been a complicated pregnancy and a dangerous delivery. One of the officers had stated, "If we had shown up just five minutes later, things wouldn't have turned out well at all."

Derek's horrific behavior had never been explained. All Edith would say was that he had been acting strangely for months, had been devastated over the death of his brother, Oswald. "They had been very, very close. I don't think Derek ever fully recovered from Oswald's passing," Edith had said in a brief statement.

Of course, grief has sent many people into an unhinged, downward spiral, Sheila reasoned. *But still, to drive five hours upstate to burn down an old house, while leaving your pregnant wife tied to a bed? Who does that?*

"Here you are," the driver said, pulling up to the address she'd given him. It was a beautiful, mid-July day, yet as the cab pulled away, a cold shadow of unease passed abruptly over her. She shivered under the bright sunlight. Perplexed at the curious sensation, Sheila hesitated on the pristine Park Avenue sidewalk, the feeling of anxiety taking tighter hold. *What is going on?* she wondered.

This wasn't at all like the Sheila Irving she'd come to know and love all these years. The happiest thoughts came when she thought of Kevin, so she chanted breathlessly to herself, "Kevin loves me, Kevin will marry me, Kevin will go down on me tonight if I'm lucky, lucky, lucky…"

But it didn't work. The sensation of dread remained, even tightened its grip. It was stubborn; she felt like she was hip deep in the ocean and a power wave was about to knock her over, hold her down, smother her. "Deep breath, deep breath, happy thoughts, happy thoughts," she mumbled, confused by what was occurring.

I'm going to faint, she realized. *Right here on Park Avenue, I'm going to collapse.* Her legs felt weak, numb and tingly. *I can't pass out on Park Avenue in front of one of the most expensive buildings on the block,* she thought as she tried to make her way into the lobby, her stomach churning as her world spun like it was the Tilt-a-Whirl ride at the carnival. *Am I pregnant? Did Kevin do this to me? Is feeling creeped out and freaked out one of the early signs of pregnancy?*

"Ma'am? You all right?"

Startled, she looked up, faced the doorman. A curious, concerned yet suspicious man. He didn't want her losing consciousness, either. Her face automatically tightened up into what she hoped was a smile and not a grimace. Trying to get her mind working again, she thought, *Delusional* New York Times *reporter on Park Avenue manages to control the heebie-jeebies or the onset of pregnancy symptoms, quickly recovers her poise, calmly speaks to puzzled doorman.*

"Yes. Hello. Sorry, I was just feeling a bit dizzy. I'm here to see Derek David."

The doorman's face folded up for an instant. "Ma'am? Mr. David? He doesn't …he doesn't have visitors anymore."

She shook her head, trying to steady herself, clarify her request. "I'm sorry, I mean his wife, Edith David. I have an appointment with her. I'm Sheila Irving of the *New York Times,*" she said, knowing the statement acted as key to the city. Any city. Especially this city.

"Let me call up. You feeling better? Why don't you sit down for a moment?" She followed him into the plush lobby while he phoned. Her watery legs firmed up, the weird feelings that had attacked her and demanded she yield to their demands seemed to have attached themselves to some other paranoid New Yorker. *What had all that been about?* she wondered uneasily. *Something in the air, in my head?*

Unnerved by the odd experience and grateful for the chance to sit and compose herself for a few seconds, Sheila refocused on Edith and Derek David, thought over what she had read. Lots of questions remained. No one had ever been able to determine why Derek was in Hydesville or how he had gotten himself trapped on that front porch while the house burned around him. Also, what to make of the mysterious Vanya Avery? She had been briefly married to Derek's brother, and was now pregnant. Oddly, she had stated that the baby she was carrying was *not* Oswald's. "Out of respect for the privacy of the father, I won't reveal his name," Vanya had said.

It's all so reality TV, Sheila thought. Or so *Peyton Place* as Kevin would have suggested. The whole story was more *National Enquirer* or *New York Post*, both of which had written unauthorized stories about what had happened, but Edith had reached out personally to the *Times*, promising an exclusive.

The doorman called to her. "Ms. David asked me to send you right up." The elevator was at the end of a short hallway, was occupied by the operator who smiled and nodded professionally at her. Without being told a word, he seemed to know where she was going. They didn't speak as they swished their way rapidly up the building. But the quiet only lasted about four seconds; silence was not Sheila Irving's style.

"So, do you ever see the David's?"

Startled, the man flinched. Sheila wondered if it was the custom of Park Avenue residents to never speak to their elevator operators. It sure would be her custom if she had an elevator man in her building. Like the doormen, she bet they knew everything that went on; she'd chat them up all the time.

"I see Ms. David and Ms. Avery," the man said quietly. "But never Mr. David anymore. Not since the accident." The man's face twisted slightly, remembering something very distasteful, then it returned to its bland expression. Obviously, at one point, he *had* seen Derek David after the fire; it hadn't been a pleasant experience.

The elevator stopped with a muffled ping on the twenty-seventh floor.

"This is where the David's live," he announced. Again, tingling, nervous dread swept over Sheila. She felt her heart pounding much too hard, too quickly. *Breathe, breathe, breathe.*

What's wrong with this place? she wondered, *or is it me*? Images from one of Kevin's favorite films popped up: A couple making love on the floor of their unfurnished apartment, eccentric, nosey neighbors, a weird dream on a yacht...

Rosemary's Baby.

That's it, she thought as she stood nervously in front of the opened door to the David's apartment. *I feel like I'm in the Dakota, about to meet Guy and Rosemary Woodhouse.*

CHAPTER 32.

The door to the David's apartment was ajar. Although it was the only unit on the floor, Sheila had expected to knock, assumed a butler in a black, double-breasted suit would greet her. *And he would announce me,* she thought, *just like in the movies that Kevin loves so much.* She called out a hello.

The door immediately opened wider, startling Sheila. It was as if someone had been waiting for her, wanted to surprise her.

"Yes?" The woman standing there was beautiful. Astonishingly gorgeous. An astounding cross between the sophisticated beauty of an Audrey Hepburn and the slow-burn sultriness of Marilyn Monroe. She was also hugely, gigantically pregnant, yet carried it so well you were dazzled by her appearance, barely noticing her rotund shape. There was a luscious, Mother Earth fertility that radiated about her. It was like an absurd R. Crumb drawing from the 1960s, a caricature of a female who was all enormous breasts, expansive hips and full, round, pouty lips. There was an overpowering sense of… something that Sheila wasn't able to identify immediately. Then it came to her: Nourishment. *To suckle from this woman's body would bring sustenance and insight unlike anything—*

Embarrassed and mortified by where her musings were headed, Sheila thought, *What the hell is going on with me? And how long have I been staring at this woman? Only seconds I hope, but there is no denying that her presence demands all of your attention.*

The healthy glow that exuded from the woman was mesmerizing. The dark emerald pregnancy gown was simple yet stylish, a muted paisley design that gently accented the woman's most striking feature, her eyes. They were bright, impossibly green and vibrant. They sparkled with light, intelligence and allure. For a few seconds, Sheila was unable to look away.

"You must be Sheila. Hello, I'm Vanya Avery. Won't you come in?"

They shook hands. Sheila couldn't form any words of greeting. She was speechless, no idea why. There was a low-grade humming in her head; had it been there all morning? Vanya's strong yet feminine grip was nothing more than the usual social formality, but it upended Sheila. She couldn't think of a thing to say. Kevin said she was second cousin to Audrey Meadows, the always talkative and brash actress best known as Jackie Gleason's wife on *The Honeymooners*. Sheila talked, that was her thing, but she felt totally shut down and mute, flustered and transfixed by this woman. She was aware of a subtle, moist buzz between her legs, a pleasurable sensation that was growing fiercer. The crazy realization she admitted was that she was sexually attracted to Vanya Avery; she wanted to be touched by this woman, kissed by this woman, to take whatever was offered to her—

What is wrong with me? Sheila screamed in her mind for the umpteenth time that morning. She followed Vanya down the hallway, still mute, eyes locked on Vanya's plump yet still well-formed buttocks as it bustled back and forth in the perfect-fitting pregnancy gown. Was it Sheila's imagination—or wishful thinking?—that Vanya was walking with a bit of a seductive twist, showing off her oversized yet flawless hips and backside to their best advantage? *You're hopeless,* Sheila chastised herself. *Speak up! Stop leering at this woman. Get a grip.*

"Why don't you have a seat in here? I'll get Edith."

Sheila looked around the well-appointed living room, relieved to have a few moments to herself. She needed to get her act together; ever since she had arrived at the building, her body had been acting funny, and bizarre thoughts along with an aggressive, wild libido had emerged. She thought, New York Times *reporter has series of mind-altering strokes yet continues to pursue the story until she is found dead, her fingers stiff and brittle over her keyboard.*

From the twenty-seventh floor, she gazed down on Central Park. The magnificent view, the bright sky, the line of traffic far below, reminded her that no matter what was going on with her, it was still a beautiful July day outside with millions of people crammed together on the island. *That's normal,* she thought ruefully, *I'm not normal at the moment, but everything else is.*

She looked away from the view, glanced around the room, found herself squinting. It took a moment for her to realize that something was wrong. There was a dimness that hovered over the area, a thin dusting of gloom. *That's odd,* she mused. The windows were clean; they sparkled against the blue sky, but the room seemed suddenly very shadowy, as if the natural light from outside had just dimmed. *Maybe the glass is specially tinted?* she thought, looking closer. Something else was offsetting but she wasn't able to recognize it right away.

After a few seconds, it came to her: It was so quiet. The term deafening silence came to mind. It was as if normal, everyday sounds were being sucked away into some void. Even on the twenty-seventh floor, there should still be the faint clamor of the traffic far below. Horns, trucks rumbling, police or ambulance sirens. This was, after all, New York City. Even birds made a racket on such a perfect day.

Then she realized that the only noise she did hear were ones created by her, and they were all wildly amplified. Her own breathing was louder, more noticeable, as if she had cupped her hands over her ears to magnify the breaths. She opened her bag, rustled some papers; it seemed as if the contents were broadcasted through a Marshall amp. She held the pages still; the unnatural, blaring racket ceased. She crinkled them together; the response rustled about the room like someone tearing wallpaper away. Gently, she took out her digital voice recorder, placed it on the coffee table, switched the lever to be sure the power worked. Each movement was as if pots and pans were being beaten. Every exaggerated and overbearing sound made her feel awkward and clumsy. She swallowed; even that creaked and gurgled as if played through a loudspeaker.

Sheila tried to ignore her thundering heartbeat. She wanted to figure out what was going on, how to get it—whatever *it* was—under control, how to make it stop, how to start speaking again. She knew she was still recovering from whatever strange feelings had come over her outside on the street, and then the powerful sexual charge that had been ignited between her and Vanya. That had been weird. Sheila had never been with a woman, never felt an attraction or desire. Until now.

She adjusted the voice recorder, opened her notepad, swished through the pages, flinching at the over-amplified clatter. She shook her head, tugged at her ears, wondering if some internal organ was causing her hearing to be impacted, her emotions to become unhinged.

A movement by the doorway.

"Hello! I'm Edith David. I'm so sorry to have kept you waiting."

Sheila smiled as pleasantly as she could under the conditions she found herself in, nodded politely at Edith's suggestion of iced tea. She sipped her drink, noticed that the clink of the ice cubes was not unnaturally magnified. It seemed that for whatever reason, the weird amplified volume seemed to have abruptly ceased, all had returned to normal when…When what? Perhaps when Vanya and Edith had walked into the room? *Weird,* Sheila thought. *Weird, weird morning.*

Sheila dove into the thankfully mundane chitchat, grateful to have her voice back, to feel more or less like her usual chatty self, glad to be over the mesmerizing oddity of meeting Vanya Avery; nothing like that had ever happened to her before. It was in such a contrast to meeting Edith David, who was just your average, thirty-something year old woman, pleasant-looking but not the alluring, magnetic attraction that Vanya had been. Plain Jane compared to Raquel Welch.

The three women conversed for several minutes, then Vanya excused herself, returned a moment later with Edith's eight-month-old son, Roland. She handed the infant to Edith. He was a darling baby, happy, gurgling contentedly in his mother's arms, looking about the room with delight. Sheila noticed that he was especially fond of Vanya, frequently reaching out to her, squealing with delight.

"I hope my little girl will be such a good-natured baby," Vanya had said.

"Oh? You know the gender of the baby," Sheila had said, jotting down the information.

"Yes, I'm certain it's a girl!"

"And when they grow up, we plan that they marry each other!" Edith had said. Both women had laughed.

"And they'll have *lots* of children!" Vanya had said.

Edith had chimed in. "They'll start a revolution!"

"They'll change the world as we know it!" Vanya had added.

Sheila had cringed inwardly at the effusive statements but said aloud that the women certainly had big plans for their children's future.

Vanya had patted her stomach affectionately. "The past has been so difficult and *uncertain* that we both think the future is the one thing we want to be *certain* of."

Edith said, "Vanya had become a dear friend while dating Oswald, and she has now become a very close family member and companion during this very difficult time." She took Vanya's hand. "Now I feel like she's the sister I never had." They had exchanged a glance, then Vanya had asked if Edith wanted Derek to join them.

"Certainly," Edith had said, telling Sheila, "I hate to leave Derek out of anything that Vanya and I do."

Vanya said, "I'll get him."

When they were alone, Edith confided to Sheila, "You know, a lot of papers wanted to talk to us, the legit ones like yours as well as all the tabloids and the online bloggers, TMZ and so on. They were all sniffing around like dogs, but we wanted the *Times*. And we wanted *you* in particular."

"Why me?"

"Because you're fair," Edith said simply. "And we think you'd be open to new experiences."

"I don't follow."

Edith leaned closer, whispered, "And most importantly, we know your—"

"Here we are!" Vanya exclaimed as she wheeled in Derek David.

In the seconds before she turned to face him, Sheila recalled that she had only read the descriptions of Derek since no photos were ever released. She remembered the elevator operator's strained expression when she had asked him about seeing Edith's husband.

Nothing could have prepared Sheila for what sat before her.

CHAPTER 33.

Sheila didn't know how she did it, but she had somehow managed to suppress and swallow the scream that had threatened to rise out of her throat, the one that was ready to burst from her mouth, the one that could probably shatter every window in the room. Its size and momentum were in proportion to what she was staring at, what was seated right in front of her.

He barely looks human or even living, she thought, *more like a piece of road kill that is being kept alive for some reason.*

In the wheelchair was the armless, legless body of what remained of Derek David. The flames had devoured most of the tissue and bone from his limbs, so they had been amputated. What was left had been savagely burned although extensive skin grafts had helped to keep his torso intact. Much of his lungs and vocal chords had been destroyed when he had inhaled the burning substances from the house, so he was attached to a respirator, was unable to speak. He was blind and hairless, with both eardrums burst. Edith had declined having facial cosmetic surgery done. She had told the doctors and the press that she knew the processes were terribly painful; hadn't Derek been through enough?

After four months in the hospital, the staff had agreed that nothing else could be done for him there. After the horrific way he had treated his wife, they had at first been surprised and then impressed with the daily visits from Edith and Vanya. The women's visits must have made a difference on a subconscious level since the doctors were astonished by how quickly he had stabilized. In mid-April, it was unanimously recommended that he be sent home. Even though he could not speak, see, hear or communicate, it was hoped that perhaps—on some level—he would sense he was in familiar, loving surroundings and that would provide him some form of comfort.

Since there was an ongoing risk of infection, Edith told Sheila that the doctors had shown her and Vanya how to debride the skin twice a week and apply an antibacterial lotion three times a day. The army of equipment that surrounded him while in bed monitored all of his vitals, a portable respirator ensured a flow of oxygen. It beeped twice. Edith quickly knelt down, adjusted a knob. After watching the meters for a few moments, she said, "Okay, I think we're all set."

Edith settled next to Vanya, said, "As we were saying, planning a happy and secure future for our children is the best way we can think of to overcome all this tragedy. Vanya's daughter is due next week. We plan on naming her Margaret Ann Avery."

"You won't be using your married name?" Sheila asked.

"No," Vanya said. She hesitated. "I...don't think it would be right since Oswald and I were never able to successfully consummate the marriage..."

Although she inwardly cringed—*TMI!* she thought—Sheila wasn't surprised. Oswald's sexual orientation was public knowledge, and it had never been explained why he would suddenly marry a woman. "So, if Oswald isn't the father, who is? If you don't mind me asking."

Vanya glanced at Edith, raised her eyebrows, a silent question. Edith took her hand, said, "The father is someone we both love very much, despite all that has happened." Vanya nodded. Both women looked at Derek.

Cautiously, as if she was walking on thin ice that was preparing to break, Sheila asked, "*Derek* is the father?" *Something is really, really wrong here*, Sheila thought, carefully keeping her expression bland. *The rich are different*, she mused, *and creepy and sick and twisted.*

"It wasn't by choice," Vanya was saying softly. "You see, he—"

Edith squeezed Vanya's hand, said, "My husband was having some sort of... breakdown at the time. He wasn't well, hadn't been for several months, was having hallucinations, wasn't sleeping much, was making wild accusations..."

"But in fairness, I've always felt partially...responsible for what happened," Vanya said quickly.

Edith looked at the floor, shook her head.

"Why is that?" Sheila asked, not completely tracking the conversation. *Were they implying Derek had raped Vanya?*

Vanya looked at Edith. "This is so awkward, but from the first time we met, Derek seemed to be…attracted to me, *interested* in me."

Edith said, "It's true. Derek was obsessed with her." Her voice was low, heavy with tragedy. "And yes, Derek *is* the father of Vanya's daughter."

Before Sheila could respond, Edith jumped back in.

"Let me see if I can explain what happened. As I said, Derek had these very vivid dreams, was imaging things, seeing things, but they were very real to him."

"They started to take over his day to day life," Vanya added. "He mixed up what was real and what was a dream."

Edith said, "Then, when I became pregnant, he was convinced that it wasn't his child—"

"Whose child did he think it was?"

"He was always vague about that," Vanya said quickly.

"But he *is* the father, isn't he?" Sheila pressed Edith.

Ignoring the question, still caught up in the story she was telling, Edith said, "I remember he told me several times that the baby I was carrying should not be born. It was all so horrible to hear, so hurtful. And in his confused state, he felt my pregnancy and his obsession with Vanya were all somehow tied to Hydesville and its history, and the Fox house. He felt if he destroyed that house, then everything would return to normal."

"Whatever normal meant to Derek," Vanya said sadly.

"What does the Fox house have to do with any of this?" Sheila asked, shifting her position, sitting up straighter. "That all happened so long ago. Why burn it down? What was he hoping to accomplish?" She thought, *Obviously, he was having a mental breakdown but who wouldn't, hanging around these two?*

Edith hesitated, clearly embarrassed. Sheila knew that it was best to be silent, let the person take their time. It was like fishing; sometimes, you just had to wait. Finally, Edith began speaking, her tone almost apologetic. "Most of Derek's imaginings were focused on Maggie and Katie Fox and Hydesville. For some reason, Derek felt that the Fox sisters were after him. Haunting him. He claimed that he heard their voices, saw apparitions of them, dreamed about them, thought they were after him for some reason, wanted something from him. I know it all sounds so strange, but he was *very* serious about it all. He even wrote down his theories in a notebook."

"May I see that?" Sheila asked.

Edith shrugged. "We can't find it, think he took it with him to Hydesville. It was probably destroyed in the fire." She glanced at Vanya. "Soon, it seemed everyone around him was part of this conspiracy. Even Vanya, and of course, the child I was carrying, our son."

Vanya said, "But I think it got worse after Oswald died. That's when Derek became so obsessed with me. His behavior became so bizarre, he had all of these conspiracy theories. I was concerned over Edith's safety because of his thoughts about the baby. I moved in with her—"

"I invited her," Edith inserted quickly.

"—while Derek was away in Europe on a buying trip," Vanya finished. "I wanted to be certain Edith was well cared for."

"There was hell to pay when he returned," Edith admitted. "It really sent him over the edge. He was convinced that Vanya was evil, a part of this haunting or whatever he thought it was..." Edith seemed to shut down, her words slowing, then ceasing altogether. Sheila didn't really buy the act; she had interviewed hundreds of people, found that when they stopped speaking to "compose themselves," they were usually just pausing long enough to double-check and confirm that the lie they were unspooling was being accepted.

"Derek finally...just lost it," Edith said at last, looking directly at Sheila. "It was so painful to see. He raved that Vanya was dangerous, not to trust her, insisted he had to destroy anything and any*one* connected with the Colony, claimed the Fox children were after him. It was all so awful. He believed that it had all started in Hydesville at the Fox cottage, so he went there to burn it down."

Sheila turned to Vanya. "You were there in Hydesville when Derek set the place on fire, right? Tell me what happened, what you saw."

CHAPTER 34.

I was at the Colony," Vanya said, her voice tight, terse as if she was under cross-examination. "I went for a walk, saw Derek's car parked at the Fox house. I went to see what he was doing there. He had just returned from his trip to Europe. I had left their apartment to give them some privacy. I knew Edith's baby was due any day, so I wondered why he wasn't home with her. When I got inside the cottage, I heard some noises in the basement. He called for me to come down there, kept insisting. I was worried about him, so I went down the stairs. The place was filled with the smell of freshly turned soil; he had been at it for some time."

"At what?"

"Digging, He said he had found something he wanted me to see."

"What was it?"

Vanya shrugged. "Nothing, really. He had been digging, saying he was looking for the bodies of the

Fox children and their mother, Margaret. He had this crazy idea that their father, John Fox, had had killed them, buried them in the cellar. Derek was frantic, sort of babbling, acting crazy, telling me that he would find them, dig them up, set them free, give them justice. Then they would leave him alone, that *I* would leave him alone, not haunt him anymore."

Sounds like the plot to a Lifetime movie ghost story, Sheila thought, resisting the urge to roll her eyes.

"He was holding some rocks in his hands, said they were bones, now the sisters were free, and he was no longer afraid of me. I was concerned about Edith, asked how she was, who was with her. He told me that she wasn't well, there was something wrong with her, she was different, had changed, that the baby she was carrying wasn't his. It was the same crazy things he had said before. Then he said not to worry, that he had taken care of both of those problems.

"That concerned me, so I asked him what he meant. He said he had made certain that Edith couldn't escape the apartment. He had cut off her ability to contact anyone in the building or call for medical help. I was shocked, couldn't believe he'd do this to his wife and son. I knew I had to get help, so I ran back upstairs."

Vanya was speaking rapidly as if she was reliving the experience or reading aloud from a suspense novel. Sheila watched as the two women grasped hands like they were on a carnival ride that had suddenly gotten very scary and dangerous.

"I made it only to the front porch before Derek grabbed me," Vanya said. "He pulled me to the ground. All the while, he had this terrible, twisted look on his face, like he was going to laugh or scream at any second. I was terrified. He continued to hold me down, all the while he had that horrid expression. When he was…finished with me, he just pushed me aside. It was as if I wasn't really there. I was in shock, could barely move. He went back into the house. I managed to stand up. I could hear him splashing something around, then I smelled the gasoline. I knew I had to get help for Edith so I called the police in Manhattan."

"Vanya saved my life, and the life of my baby," Edith said quietly, awe in her voice. "Roland is *alive* because of Vanya."

"A few minutes after I made the call, I smelled smoke, saw the flames," Vanya said.

"Where was Derek? Did you see him?"

Vanya shook her head. "I called the fire department but kept my distance. I didn't know what else he might do to me…"

The two women fell silent, as if a truce had been reached.

Sheila had just finished up her notes when Edith said, "He was so mixed up, was so paranoid—"

"But why are you making *excuses* for him?" Sheila demanded, knowing she shouldn't get emotionally involved in the interview, tried to remain calm. Unable to help herself, she turned to Vanya, blurted out, "And I'm sorry, but why are you bringing the child to term? If he…forced himself on you, surely—"

Bizarrely, the women broke out into wide, benevolent smiles at the question.

"Because it's the last of Derek's bloodline," Vanya said eagerly. "So, of *course* I'm keeping his baby! The opportunity…there is thought to be *tremendous* psychic power in his family."

In her eagerness to speak, Vanya struggled to sit upright, was forced to move her massive bulk which proved to be a challenge. Once settled, she said excitedly, "You see, from the very beginning, Derek's great-grandfather was intrigued with the experiments at the Colony and helped fund it because he knew there was evidence of psychic abilities in his own family."

"Did Derek or his brother have these abilities?" Sheila asked Edith.

"Unfortunately, other than Derek's mysterious blackout spells—the cause of which has never been diagnosed—neither he nor Oswald had any unusual experiences or psychic skills that they ever mentioned."

"But there's hope!" Vanya said. "We don't yet know exactly how the gifts are passed on to each generation; the abilities seem to be inherited on a random basis, and they don't always manifest themselves." She glanced at Edith; the women both smiled fondly at one another. "But it's hoped— fingers crossed!—that either Roland or my little Margaret will have the abilities."

Edith said, "Or *both* of them, if we were to be so blessed!"

Sheila couldn't believe what she was hearing, waited for the women to burst out laughing. She wanted them to tell her that the wild story was just some sick joke they had told to see how far they could go with it before admitting it was all a ruse. Instead, they only sat there, waiting for her to respond or to ask her next question.

Not trusting herself to speak civilly, Sheila counted to five silently, thinking: *That's the strangest, most sick and twisted reason for bringing a child into the world that I have ever heard.* So far, the interview was a complete waste of her time since the story was sheer madness. It was so far off the rails that they should have just gone to the tabloids, made some money, then sold the rights for a movie to the SyFy channel.

Vanya abruptly asked, "What do you know about the Keilgarden Colony?"

"Not much, really. There's one old article from *Life* magazine online, but that's really it, other than the nonsense the *Post* and *National Enquirer* published."

Vanya explained, "I ask because I first met Edith and Derek due to my association with the Colony. I worked there as sort of a public affairs spokesperson. My father was one of the original associates of the founder, Dr. Charles Von Keilgarden. I invited Derek and Edith up for an appreciation dinner to acknowledge the seed funding his great-grandfather had provided."

She straightened up in her seat. "Soon after, I met Oswald. We fell in love, at first sight. He *loved* it up there," Vanya said warmly, her voice softened with wistfulness. "It relaxed him. We had such wonderful times together. It was a classic love affair, just like in the old movies you like so much."

Sheila wondered if she had heard correctly. *How'd she know I liked old movies? Had I mentioned that earlier when we were chatting?*

"I think, for Oswald, it was the first time he had ever been in love, with anyone," Vanya continued, her voice tight with emotion. "He had never fully experienced the emotional passion, the way it can be all consuming. I love how Shelley put it, 'Soul meets soul on lover's lips.' That's what we were, instant soul mates. It was as if we were devouring one another, wanting to spend all of our time together, every moment. For our brief time as a couple, it was as if no one else existed. And he was always trying so hard to please me…" Her voice trailed off.

Sheila looked up. For a moment, she thought Vanya was going to begin weeping.

Edith asked gently, "Have you ever been in love?"

Sheila nodded absently, wondering if she was dreaming this entire interview. Never had she met such eccentric characters.

Vanya leaned forward. "Then you know what it's like. You can't wait to be with him, there's a thrill when you first see him or hear his voice on the phone. The small jokes you share, the private glances. All of that was what Oswald and I shared. But only for a short, short time." She brushed back a tear. It didn't work: Sheila didn't believe a word she was being told, it all seemed scripted, staged for her benefit. And a sick and disturbing scene too, especially the implication that Derek had raped Vanya in the fit of some paranoid delusion.

The fact checkers are going to love this, she thought.

During the entire time the women had told their strange story, Sheila had been acutely mindful of Derek's presence in the room. Mute and immobile, the only noise from the wheelchair was the rasp of the machine that was breathing for him. Although she didn't look directly at him, she was always aware that he was hearing every word they spoke.

No, he couldn't, she realized with a start. *The fire had burst his eardrums.*

Distracted by her thoughts, she had missed part of what Vanya was saying. Thank God for the recorder.

"…know that Oswald and I were in love," Vanya said, "and how can love ever be a bad influence?"

Silence followed the question. Derek's machine hissed. Sheila realized that Vanya wanted an answer. "Well, I suppose any type of obsession can be dangerous because it tends to push away any sense of reality, becomes single focused," she said slowly, wondering where she was headed. "Especially if it comes between an already established and close relationship, like two brothers share."

She suspected that Derek and Oswald had been tight all their lives. They had inherited the hugely successful gallery, worked long and hard to keep it growing and prosperous. Anyone who came between them would be seen as some sort of threat, at least at first, she supposed, especially a woman who claimed that Oswald had fallen in love with her.

Especially a woman like Vanya Avery.

"In theory, what you say is true," Edith said, "but I was there. I saw how… *transformed* Oswald was when he met Vanya. I've never seen him so happy, so settled, so at peace. He was so in love—Vanya was a *wonderful* influence, not a bad one—and he was so delighted to have finally found someone…"

"Well, if he was so happy," Sheila asked gently, ready to dig in, wanting to get to the point, "then why do you suppose he hung himself or who do you think killed him?"

Vanya didn't answer the question, she asked one. "Do you know anything about the Fox Woods? There are powerful forces there—"

"I've heard the stories," Sheila answered dismissively, recalling the absurd *National Enquirer* exposé that had run. "But I don't believe in the supernatural. Oswald David's death was awful, and I *am* sorry for your loss, but I don't believe some evil force compelled him to those woods to hang himself. And I don't believe he was blissfully happy with you, Vanya. Otherwise, like I asked, why would he do such a thing or who do you think was out to get him?"

"At the end, I think Derek may have contributed to Oswald's state of mind," Edith suggested. "You see, Oswald knew of Derek's attraction and obsession with Vanya."

"Derek thought I was not a good match for his brother," Vanya said. "He had this idea that I was changing Oswald or sort of brainwashing him, I guess. Derek was suspicious of me."

Sheila mentally agreed with Derek's assessment. She didn't like Vanya Avery either; the woman gave off a strong whiff of superiority along with the silent implication that she was pulling one over on you, but you were far too stupid to ever suspect you were being played. Edith's obvious infatuation with the woman was also troubling, but that only reminded Sheila of her own odd and disturbing attraction to Vanya when they had first met.

Disgusted by what they were implying, Sheila said, "You think Derek wanted Vanya for himself so he convinced his brother to kill himself or hired someone to do it?"

"Derek was in a dark, terrible place," Edith said. "Look what he did to me, his own wife? There's no reason not to believe that he might have said some things to Oswald…"

"Any proof of this?" Sheila asked. *I'll need a long shower after this,* she thought, *to wash off the filth of these women and this story.*

"No," Edith said. Vanya only shook her head. "And the crime—or suicide or whatever it was that happened to Oswald—remains unsolved."

The hiss of the machine attached to the wheelchair caught Sheila's attention. She couldn't resist stealing another glance at the stone-still, almost lifeless form of Derek David. When they had wheeled him into the room, there was something Sheila had been aware of right away that she knew was absolutely impossible. It was a sense that he was still somehow very much aware of all that was going on around him. There was a presence about the poor man, keen intelligence even though it was inconceivable for him to communicate in any way. He couldn't speak, hear or see, yet somehow, he remained alive. The doctors said his brain was still functioning, although they were not able to say for certain to what extent. They knew he could probably still reason, process information, recall memories; he could still *think.* But he was forever unable to communicate. Of that, they were certain.

But still, the feeling lingered with her that he was *aware.* His personality had filled the room like the knowledge that something incredibly valuable was kept locked in a closet. You wanted to see it, have access to it, but were unable to get close even though you knew it was there, just tantalizingly out of reach.

Sheila glanced at her notes. She wondered if she could make any sense of the strange story that had been told, salvage anything from her notes and the recording? She felt the need to assert herself, finish the interview in the world of facts, timelines, eyewitnesses. The phrase *the upper hand* came to mind. *Yes, that's what I want,* she realized. *I'll be like Bonita Granville from those Nancy Drew movies of the 1930s.*

She closed her note pad, grabbed her recorder, gathered her belongings. Intent on leaving the interview and the apartment in a professional manner, she said, "Thank you, both, so much for your time. I'm sure this has all been painful to recount. I really appreciate your speaking with me. I'm not saying I understand or even believe everything you've told me. Just being honest with you. I'll have to get collaboration from Derek's employees and friends. And the police, of course, up in Hydesville and the Wayne County Coroner. Much of this just seems…*too much.*"

Even as she sat upright facing the two women, her voice sounded as if she was fading away, a flutter of dizziness nudged past her. *I gotta get a physical immediately,* she told herself. *Something is wrong with me.*

The women seemed surprised at her abrupt announcement that the interview was over. "But…you *can't* leave!" Edith cried out like a disappointed child refusing to go to bed. "We haven't discussed the proposal with you."

"Proposal?"

Vanya patted Edith's hand. "Let her go. For now. It *has* been a long morning. I'm tired. We'll speak to her again."

No, you won't, Sheila thought.

Edith nodded obediently. "Yes. Yes, of course. Vanya's right. We'll be in touch with you, Sheila."

Fifteen minutes later, the cab pulled up to Sheila's apartment. She paid the fare, walked into the air-conditioned relief of her building, grateful for the respite from the mid-July heat, glad to be home and away from the craziness of the morning.

She thought of Derek David again, as she had during the ride home. *What a nightmare existence. To have the ability to remember and reason, but never be able to communicate your thoughts to anyone.*

She checked the mailbox. Nothing. Too early.

She pushed the elevator button. Waited.

My God, Sheila thought seconds later as she stepped into the elevator, shuddering at the question that had just crossed her mind.

My God, I wonder what Derek David thinks about all day?

CHAPTER 35.

O nce Sheila was in her apartment, she was suddenly overcome with exhaustion and a yawning fit. It was after two; she should transcribe her notes and the contents of the digital voice recorder while they were still fresh in her head. After all, her boss would want the contents even though he'd never run the story. Even if it was posted for the *Times'* secondary online site, it was too weird for the Gray Lady.

She had turned her phone off during the interview, had been too disturbed and preoccupied on the ride home to check messages. She scrolled through email, read her boss's text about a new assignment he wanted to discuss with her, clicked on the voice message Kevin had left.

"Hi, Boris Karloff here. I have made 8 p.m. dinner reservations in my name at the Atlantic Grill. I thought I was so clever using Karloff's name, but the kid on the phone didn't know who Karloff was! I feel old, babe, and I hate millennials more every day.

I look forward to the always fascinating Elsa Lanchester joining me this evening as we talk about your creepy interview."

Sheila grinned. Happiness and calm replaced the weight and tension that had settled over her shoulders. Kevin could do that. Did that, all the time. He was her fixer upper. He helped her to think straight.

She brought a soda to her computer, hoping the caffeine jolt would keep her focused. She typed her reporter slug at the top right of the page—Irving/Sheila—then added David Notes so they'd know where to file the mess after it was spiked. *They'll* never *want me to pursue this craziness,* she told herself. *Nor do I.*

If she concentrated really hard, she could have it all done by five. Then a short nap—*why am I so tired?*—a shower, Atlantic Grill by eight. She smiled. Dinner with Boris. Boris and Elsa.

"One day, I shall *be* the Bride of Frankenstein."

Sheila woke at 6:30 p.m.

Strange dreams had left her disoriented. A sheen of anxious perspiration enveloped her. She stretched, her sore muscles uncoiled. *Why am I still so sleepy?* She felt like she was crawling out from under a pile of invisible weights, as if hundreds of blankets had been piled on her. She yawned, reached for her phone, saw she had missed a phone message, pushed the speaker button, tensed when she heard the voice.

"Hello, Sheila! Hope you had a good nap."

It was Vanya Avery.

"We so enjoyed meeting with you today! And we still need to speak with you about our proposal. It'll only take three months of your efforts. We'll pay you, of course. Very handsomely, too. I promise, it will be well worth your time. You left so quickly before we had a chance to tell you about it. We'll be in touch again, soon. Goodbye, for now."

As the sentences poured out of the machine, Sheila had found herself backing away, step by step, putting distance between her and the voice speaking. By the time Vanya had finished, Sheila was in the kitchen, her shoulders pressed into a corner, trembling. She noticed one of the drawers was open, as was a cabinet. She closed them with sharp bangs, distractedly thinking, *How had those crazy women known I'd taken a nap?* followed by, *Did I mention I was going to before I left their apartment?* She wondered why the phone hadn't woken her up when they called. She never put it on mute except when she was with Kevin. To hear Vanya's voice in her apartment really bothered her, made her feel as if someone had trespassed into her life, rifled through her purse, read her diary.

"Okay," she said weakly, "stop overreacting. First things first, Miss Sheila. Shower. Collect your thoughts so you don't sound too insane when you relay the story to Boris. You want this guy to marry you one day, so your psycho-side needs to be kept well-hidden a bit longer." She continued to talk to herself as she clicked on the cable news to keep her company while she showered.

As the TV pundits shouted at one another, she pushed the print button, then stepped into the shower while the pages were spat out of the Epson. She decided she'd take her notes along to review with

Kevin over dinner. After all, he asked to hear about it.

She dried herself, curious why she didn't hear the TV, checked, saw the mute image was on the screen. She disengaged it, the political panel continued yelling in mid-argument. Puzzled how the sound had been silenced, she shrugged, applied her makeup, dressed, gave herself a once over.

"You do yourself proud, Elsa," she announced, snarled and hissed at herself as the bride of Frankenstein had done in the movie. She snatched the papers from the printer tray, turned off the machine, glanced at the top page, then quickly sorted through the others. They were all blank except for the header. She looked closer.

"Can't be," she whispered, realized she sounded like a frightened little schoolgirl. An old, childhood memory, buried and safely tucked in, put to bed for so many decades, suddenly stirred. The past reached out, joined hands with the present. Her nerves jangled, the printouts in her grasp started shaking uncontrollably.

At the top right of each page, the same words appeared. It read almost like a sentence. Mesmerized, wanting to look away but unable to, her eyes locked into the nine words that had replaced her slug line, and the strange statement they made:

Sheila Irving / We know your face touched the ceiling

She immediately sensed the message came from Vanya and Edith. "But why them? How could they know?" Shelia whispered to herself, scanning the words on the pages. "No one knows…"

We know your face touched the ceiling.

"But they knew I took a nap," she reasoned, "or am I just making links where there are none?" The strange feelings she had before she entered Edith's apartment that morning brushed past her, the apprehension, the anxious uncertainty. She looked again at the papers she held: The statement that had replaced her header was like a long-held secret told. The words riveted her. She sat in a chair sorting through the identical, repetitive sentences as if searching for a pattern or hidden meaning that might explain it all.

We know your face touched the ceiling.

###

Uber left her off a few blocks north of Atlantic Grill on Third Avenue. It was one of their favorite restaurants. She thought a short walk might help to clear her head. She wanted to be able to tell Kevin a coherent recounting of her day and the odd events. It wasn't easy to come up with logical explanations—she had tried—but she didn't want to present the story as a blithering idiot, either.

She arrived early. Mr. Karloff wasn't there yet. Would she care to wait at the bar? Sure. She settled on a barstool, nodded to Nancy, the bartender, ordered her usual, scrolled absently through her phone. Nancy raised her eyebrows, turned away to pour. Without looking at the drink set before her, Sheila sipped, gagged, almost spit it out.

"Ugh! Nancy, what *is* this?"

"Whiskey neat."

"What? Why? I never order whiskey."

Nancy yanked the drink back. "You said whiskey. I figured you were trying something new."

"Certainly not whiskey! Blah! Can I have some water to rinse out the foul taste?"

"Oh, come on. It's not that bad. You just had a sip."

"Yuck! Let me have my usual, Hendrick's and tonic."

"Who are you tonight, anyway?"

"Elsa Lanchester."

"Never heard of her."

"*Bride of Frankenstein*?"

Nancy shrugged, set the G and T and a glass of water in front of Sheila, went off to serve another customer.

Weird, Sheila thought, sipping the drink. *I would never order whiskey.*

A man put his hands on her shoulder, kissed her neck. "Hello, my bride," Kevin said.

"I wish."

They kissed. The phrase *Irish eyes are smiling* flashed across Sheila's mind as it always did, automatically, when Kevin appeared. His eyes were always happy, it seemed, gleaming with good cheer. His reddish-brown hair was always in place. Even the traditionally Irish "sprinkle of freckles" was conservative and orderly, just enough to keep him boyish looking with a slightly mischievous edge. He was solid, secure.

My boy, she thought fondly, feeling better as soon as he touched her. He settled her, relaxed her, always calmed her down. If she was known to rock the boat, he was always on an even keel. He caught Nancy's eye, ordered a Grey Goose on the rocks.

"Sure you don't want a whiskey neat?" Nancy teased.

"Funny lady," Sheila smirked. "Careful, everyone, the barkeep is a little hard of hearing tonight."

"Explain," Kevin said. Sheila told him about the drink mix up, then spent the next few minutes trying to make sense of her day: the strange feeling of dread that had settled over her before she entered the David's building, the unnatural silence in the apartment, followed by the amplified sounds that emanated from her.

"You aren't a little church mouse, you know," he kidded her. "I mean, I wouldn't say you're exactly quiet as a mouse or—"

"I'm serious about all of this," she said, then remembered how dim the room had been even though the sun shone brightly outside, waited for his response.

"Um, okay. I must be missing something. You're researching a story about people from the 1840s who hear spirit rappings and talk to spooks and start the whole rage for séances and Ouija boards and ghost hunting shows, so of *course* you're going to spook yourself, hear weird things, see weird things. You're predisposed to it. It's a mindset. What you need to do…."

She sighed, feeling like she wasn't getting through. Kevin worked in real estate where walls were always upright, bricks met neatly, floors were firm, everything was built on a solid foundation. What she was about to tell him was more like a crazy time amusement park funhouse, full of distortions, the unexpected and the unexplained. She started by informing him about the strange tales relayed by Vanya and Edith.

Kevin took a moment to process what she had said. "Vanya said Derek *raped* her? Do you believe her?"

Sheila shrugged. "I don't know. I don't really *want* to know. The whole thing—the whole morning—was too crazy to figure out. I know the paper won't want it. It belongs in *Ripley's Believe It or Not!*" She looked through her bag, pulled out the papers she had printed out, but didn't hand them over. "I typed out my notes, took a nap. When I woke up, there was a message on my phone." She turned away, finished her drink.

Kevin touched her arm. "And?" She looked at him, her eyes glistening.

"Hey, what is it? What's wrong?" Concerned, he rubbed her shoulder gently.

She felt safe as his calming influence took hold of her. She needed this, needed him. "Okay, this next part really frightened me. It's something that no one knows about me. Something I've never even told you."

Kevin frowned.

"Is it a bad thing? Like you have other boyfriends, or a good thing, like you have a lot of money?"

"Neither. It's just something that happened to me once. An experience I had. As a child. I've never told anyone about it."

The hostess appeared; their table was ready. Once they were seated and had ordered a bottle of wine, Sheila said, "Let me backtrack a sec. Like I said, I took a nap after I transcribed the notes from my interview. When I woke up, there was a voice message. From Vanya." She stopped speaking. He could see she was terribly troubled by something.

"The message she left…asked if I had had a good nap," Sheila managed to say. She waited for Kevin to respond. He leaned toward her, expectantly, a blank look on his face. He didn't get it. "Kevin, how did she know I had taken a nap?"

"Oh." He settled back. "Maybe you simply told them you were heading home to take a rest?"

"Nope, didn't happen." The wine arrived. Sheila was exasperated with herself; the story was coming out all wrong, she sounded like a fool. She stared at him, irate. "And to think I'm considering marrying you one day!"

"Only if you're really, really lucky. Now, let me see the papers you are so tightly holding. Are they about your childhood experience?"

"These are the notes I had typed up. Seven pages." Looking at the crumpled printouts in her hand, seeing the same sentence on each page, gave her a fresh tremor of alarm. She handed them over.

Kevin quickly sorted through the papers, glanced at her. "'*We know your face touched the ceiling.*' What does that mean? Why'd you type it in the header?"

"That's just it, I didn't. I just put in my name, left the title as 'David Notes' to identify them when they got filed away. But this is what printed out, just the slug, none of the content from my interview."

"What about your notepad and the recording? Have you checked them?"

Sheila nodded. "They're fine, they both contain notations from my interview and the audio." They each finished off their glass of wine in one gulp. The waiter refilled them.

"Okay, now I get it. Yes, it's very weird," Kevin agreed, lining up his silverware until each piece was set at the same exact height. "Any idea what, '*We know your face touched the ceiling'* means?"

"That's what I'm going to tell you."

"This is your childhood thing?"

She nodded. "When I was eight or nine, I used to have these really vivid dreams of flying or floating. I'd rise off my bed, sort of drift about the house, usually visit my parent's room, see them sleeping or I'd fly over the cat dozing in the living room or the dog on the kitchen floor."

"Flying dreams are common, aren't they?"

"Yes, they are, and I remember it was kind of fun. I would wake up having the sensation that it was all real. I could feel it, right here." She placed her hand over her chest. "It was always a pleasant feeling, a *release*, like when you cry at the end of a movie."

"No idea what you're talking about. Men don't cry at movies."

"Well, I think you know what I mean. It was never scary or frightening. It felt okay. At least at first."

"Uh oh."

CHAPTER 36.

After a few weeks, the flying dreams turned…darker somehow," Sheila said. "I didn't have that good feeling anymore. I no longer felt like I was flying alone; I sensed there was something with me. I started to wake up in the middle of the night and…I'd be...hovering over my bed."

Kevin waited for her to continue. "You mean, you thought you woke up, but you were still dreaming you were floating?"

"No, I wish that was it, but I'm certain I was awake."

Their salads arrived. Kevin focused his attention on spearing several bites before he spoke. "You know it's impossible for people to fly, right? We can't even hover."

"Kevin," she said, a warning. "My parents saw me."

"Okay…"

"One night when I woke up, I was already outside their bedroom door. I must have been…three feet off the ground. I remember they slept with the door always partway opened so I sort of swam into it, nudged it all the way open. I didn't really understand what I was seeing them doing…"

"Oh, Lord, I'm afraid to ask."

"Shut up and listen. Yes, they were having sex. My father was on top of my mother, they were naked, the sheet pushed to the bottom of the bed. I remember there was something violent about it, my mother was moaning. I thought he was holding her down for some reason. Against her will. It was frightening, weird. Kind of disturbing…"

"Ya think? And you were…right there above them, looking down from the ceiling or something?"

"I was. And then my Mom opened her eyes. She saw me. I remember it seemed to take so long for her to react. The moon was bright and full that night, so the room wasn't at all dark. She *did* see me, yet neither of us spoke or reacted. I remember I was about a foot above them, I had moved in closer—it was like I was swimming—since I was concerned she was being hurt. And then, all at once, it was like she *really* saw me, knew I was actually there. She screamed, kept screaming."

Sheila could see Kevin was transfixed by what she was saying but she had no idea if he believed her. Her parents had died years ago in a car accident, she had no siblings or any other eyewitnesses to verify the incident, or what occurred afterward.

"What happened?"

"Dad reared up off of her when she started screaming. Of course, his back smacked into me, which caused him to cry out. They both ended up cowering on the floor by the bed. I remember he was holding her as they stared at me. He finally managed to call my name. He was so…composed, like I had simply climbed onto a counter and needed to get back down. My mom was crying hysterically, trembling in his arms, but he kept telling me, real gentle, to, 'Come down now, honey. Come down.'"

"'*Come down*?'"

Sheila nodded. "Yeah, as simple as that. And I did. I mean, I don't think I consciously knew how to control it, but something about his voice allowed me to just settle back onto their bed. It really was like swimming."

"What did he do?"

"He asked if I was all right. When I said I was, he told me to go back to my room. I remember how big their bed was; it took a moment to get my footing, climb to the edge. I heard my Mom weeping into his shoulder. He was trying to calm her. I walked away, feeling a bit dazed, trying to make sense of what I had seen, my mom's reaction. I got back under the covers, waited for him. When he came in, he sat on the edge of my bed in his t-shirt and boxers, asked me again if I was okay. I said I was. He kissed my forehead goodnight."

"Ground pepper?" the waiter asked after placing their entrées before them. They both nodded absently. After he left, Kevin asked, "So did you talk about it with them the next day?"

"No. The next morning, my mom slept in, which was something she never did. I think she wanted to avoid me, not address what had occurred. Dad fixed me breakfast, never mentioned what had happened."

After a couple bites, Kevin said, "Do you think maybe it was a dream, maybe that's why he didn't mention it?"

Sheila looked at him, suppressed the irritation, felt it smolder "It was *real*, Kevin!

"What happened next proved it, to my parents and to me. It was no dream. It really happened." She waited a moment, made sure he was with her. "A few days after that experience, I was literally jerked out of my bed one night, ended up next to my dresser, easily fifteen feet away."

Kevin stared at her; she had lost him. After a beat he said, "Honey, really? Jerked across the room? Like in a horror film?"

Ignoring him, she said, "The noise and my crying woke my parents. They rushed to my room but just before they came in—"

"—the door slammed in their faces, right?"

She turned her attention to her meal, furious. Her chest tightened in rage; she wished she had never mentioned anything to him. She felt foolish and very, very alone.

After a moment, he reached for her. She stiffened. He withdrew. "Honey, you know I've seen a *lot* of films and everything you're describing is classic ghost cinema cliché stuff, okay? The levitation, the doors slamming, being jerked from your bed. All of it. You have to give me a *chance* to believe you, right? I mean, I *do* believe you, but cut me a little slack, okay? I need time to catch up. You've lived with this, I'm only just hearing about it."

He waited. She wouldn't look at him. They ate in silence, the conversations around them suddenly louder since they were not speaking. Silverware clinked on their dishes, they sipped their wine too frequently, felt awkward with one another, like ill-fitting clothing. Finally, speaking to her empty plate, Sheila said, "The bedroom door closed with such force, it splintered the frame. And it stayed closed, like it was locked or barricaded. My parents were pounding on it, shouting my name but they couldn't get to me. I was trapped with this …thing."

Kevin listened.

"Remember when I said that I thought something was with me when I experienced this? Well, now it made itself known. I couldn't see it, but I knew it was there, keeping the door closed." She shuddered, rubbed her arms. "It was so awful... I was so scared. I just curled up in a ball next to my dresser where it had thrown me. I was crying, telling it to go away, just go away. Soon I was shaking so much I couldn't say anything."

The waiter came, cleared their plates. She continued when he left. "My parents never gave up, they kept crying out for me, saying they loved me, that they would get into the room, kept asking if I was okay." She closed her eyes at the memory. The waiter offered a desert menu, Kevin declined for both of them. When they were alone, Sheila opened her eyes.

"Then…then it touched me. I felt it tug at my left arm, like it wanted to lead me somewhere." She looked directly at Kevin, wanted to force him to believe her. "Its touch was so cold, it burned. It felt sticky, clammy like that slime toy we played with as kids."

"Like *The Blob*?" Kevin suggested, trying to be helpful. Her look shut him down.

"The first contact was almost gentle or hesitant. But when I resisted, it had no patience for that. I was immediately jerked away, yanked up from the floor. I screamed, my parents grew even more frantic as they tried to get into the room.

"It somehow got behind me and…started to lift me. It was like I was in some crane that was just pushing me rapidly upward. We lived in an older home, the rooms had plenty of height, so I must have been at least fifteen feet off the ground. It held me like I was some tiny creature in its gigantic, formless hand. My folks kept pounding at the door, trying to get in. At some point, my dad had gotten an ax, was smashing his way into the room. By the time they broke in, my body was jammed up against the ceiling. I remember it was my nose that hurt the most, it was smashed flat. God, I can recall this all so clearly! My tears were tickling my ears as they ran down the sides of my face.

"I couldn't turn my head to look at my folks or even speak, but I knew they were far below me. I heard a scrapping sound; my dad had dragged a ladder in. He kept unfolding it; it would collapse over and over. He cursed, told my mom to hold it steady—God, I remember so much of this!—but it never stabilized. Whatever was holding me up didn't want me to be rescued. It wanted me to stay where I was."

Kevin was fully engaged in what she was telling him. When she took a moment to collect her thoughts, he asked, "How long do you think this was going on?"

"About an hour, maybe? Long enough to make it impossible for any of us to think it was a dream or hallucination. When you're suspended for that long with your face smashed into the ceiling of your bedroom, you can accept the fact that the situation you're in is really happening."

"Did they try to get help, the neighbors or—"

"Call the fire department?" Sheila smiled. "Instead of a cat stuck in a tree, they requested assistance getting their levitating daughter down? No, I don't think they really knew what to do. They dragged furniture under me when the ladder wouldn't unfold but whatever they brought over to step on to try to reach me was shoved aside or broken in two.

"And then I had this feeling that it was…unclenching itself from me. It was like when the sun rises, all the darkness and shadows gradually start to withdraw and fade away. I felt like a spell had been broken. I was slowly lowered back onto the floor. My folks hugged me so hard, we just embraced, didn't let go. We were all sobbing. It felt so good to be held by them, to be touched by…humans. That sounds weird, but that thing had me in its grasp for so long that it had left me feeling contaminated or like I needed a shower or something."

Kevin sat back in his chair. He hadn't realized he had been so tense while Sheila had told her story. She asked him, "You know that photo of my parents on my dresser? When you first came over and saw it, you were surprised when I told you they had died so young. Their hair was already gray. Remember?"

He nodded. "Yes, they looked much older than their age."

"I always thought it was a myth that traumatic experiences can rapidly change your appearance. But they do, and this event aged them. I noticed it while we were all hugging one another that day. Both of their hair had gone from brown to white-gray. In just an hour."

Kevin reached for her hand. This time she held his.

"Talking about it for the first time with someone, I realize how much I miss them. I wish they were here with me now, wish they could have met you." She leaned forward. "You do believe me, right? I know it all sounds like a movie to you, but it really happened. It's important you know I'm not lying, not making it up. I'm telling you the truth."

Kevin smiled, so in love with her. "Yes. Yes, I believe this all happened to you. I think you had an extraordinary paranormal encounter. I don't understand it, but yes, yes, I believe it really happened."

They reconsidered dessert and coffee, lapsed into a comfortable silence as they shared the strawberry chocolate molten cake. After they had cleaned the plate, Kevin said, "So why do you think '*We know your face touched the ceiling*' appeared in your notes?"

Sheila shook her head. "Unless I wrote it subconsciously—which I didn't—I have no idea why or how the sentence appeared."

"But you're convinced it somehow is connected to Vanya and Edith?"

"Probably. No, absolutely. Between the creepy experiences outside their apartment and all that went on while I was with them, they certainly have some role to play in this. It still bothers me that they knew I was taking a nap."

When the check appeared, Sheila snatched it. "My treat." After the waiter had taken the bill and her credit card, she said, "Well?"

"Well, what?"

"Any hints, clues or suggestions as to what is going on?"

"One question: Are there any more strange tales from your childhood you want to tell me?"

She shook her head. "Nope. That was it."

"And nothing else odd ever happened to you after that?"

"Let's see, I met you…No, nothing. Mom and Dad had me sleep with them for a few weeks, of course. We were all still terrified by what had happened, they didn't want to leave me alone. But I had no more experiences. Plenty of nightmares, though, but that's fine; I'll take bad dreams over the real thing any day."

"So why did it happen?" Kevin asked as she signed the check. "Why you? What do you think it all meant? You've had all these years to think about it…"

"No idea. Never found out. And I haven't *wanted* to think about it, wanted to forget it ever happened. Never told anyone about it until now, until you."

Kevin said, "So how do you think Vanya and Edith found out? And how'd they do it, get the words to change on your notes?"

"I have no clue, that's why this all bothers me so much. There's something spooky about the two of them and their whole freaky story. I'm glad that I never have to see them again."

"But I thought the paper wants you to write about them, that's why you went there. Didn't they request you specifically?"

Sheila waved her hand dismissively. "Their allegations can't be substantiated, the whole sordid tale is a little too lowbrow, too grotesque. But if they insist I do it, then I will come down with the flu, be generally unavailable. They'll have to assign it to someone else. I'm done with Vanya and Edith."

At the bar on their way out, Nancy waved them over.

"There was a strange guy asking after you," she said to Sheila.

"Strange how?"

"Like he suddenly showed up out of nowhere at the serving hinge, glared at me until I went over to see what he wanted."

"What did he say?"

"Just your name."

"What did he look like?" Kevin asked.

"Older guy. In his fifties. Very dark eyes, bushy eyebrows. Long, narrow face, big nose and chin. Hair was shoulder length, thick, combed straight back from his forehead. Sideburns a little excessive. Overall, old fashioned in appearance. Shabby suit. Reminded me a little of what the Amish look like."

Sheila was surprised at Nancy's detailed response. "That's so vague; can you be any more specific?"

The bartender grinned. "Please, do you know how many times a night I get asked about other people or if a blonde with a green purse was here? I have exceptional powers of observation."

"Does he sound like someone you know?" Kevin asked Sheila.

"No, not at all. I'd remember someone like that. What did he want?"

"No idea. He said your name, I said, 'Yeah, what about her?' He just kept looking at me, didn't say anything. Gave me the creeps. Someone called for a drink, I turned away, told them just a second. When I looked back, he was gone."

Sheila asked, "He just left?"

"No, he was just…*gone*. Like he vanished." She shrugged. "Poof. He disappeared."

CHAPTER 37.

Outside the Atlantic Grill, Sheila glanced nervously up and down Third Avenue. She was unsettled about Nancy's story of the Amish man asking for her. It had been a weird day, she wanted it to be over, wanted all the strange events and people to leave her alone.

Ten minutes later they entered Kevin's apartment. There was a high-pitched beeping in the kitchen. The light in the microwave was on, the door was unlatched, the timer flashing. Kevin closed it, cutting the chirp in mid-sound. "That's weird."

"Why was it on?"

"No idea. I last used it this morning when I needed to zap my coffee." He opened and closed it several times, checked the timer to be sure it was working.

Sheila had spent many nights there, so she had kept some clothes and toiletries in the closet. While she changed into an oversized t-shirt and comfortable sweatpants, Kevin poured them each some Sambuca.

"Your bathroom lights just blew out," she said as she joined him on the couch, nestled herself in his arms.

"All *three* bathroom lights? Did you replace them?"

"I don't know where you keep the bulbs. It's not my house. I'm simply informing you of the damage. Now, if we were married…"

He left to replace the bulbs. When he returned, he said, "By the way, I don't like the idea of that strange man looking for you. Or the fact that you used to float around as a child, spy on your parents having sex. Just so we're clear…"

She elbowed him. "Don't make fun of me!"

He kissed her forehead. "Sorry, I couldn't resist."

His phone rang. He fumbled for it, glanced at the number.

"Who is it?" Sheila asked.

"No idea." He set the phone down. It went silent, then pinged a moment later, indicating a message had been left. He activated voice mail with the speaker on.

"Hello Sheila. Sorry to bother you again—"

"It's Vanya!" Sheila cried, sitting up, sloshing her drink onto her fingers.

"—but this really can't wait. We've decided to make our proposal to you right away, before I have the baby. Edith thinks we should meet tomorrow morning. Let's say ten o'clock, here at her apartment. See you then."

"How'd she get my number?" Kevin asked, staring at his phone. "Sheila? How'd she do that?"

"No idea. I didn't give it to her! I never even mentioned your name. How did they know I was with you, to call now—"

"—unless we were followed? Maybe that Amish guy was hired by them to follow us?"

"But why? Why didn't he just wait for us at the bar like a normal person would?"

He could feel how upset she was. He asked, "What's the proposal she mentioned? Any idea?"

Irritated, she said, "Oh, who cares! Ugh, I can't believe they are doing this, stalking me like this! There's *no way* I'm seeing them tomorrow, or ever."

"They sound like they're expecting you."

"They can wait until hell freezes over, I'm *not* doing the story! They can leave me messages all over town but it's not going to happen!"

Kevin put his hands up in surrender. "Okay, okay. And as for getting my number, maybe they have some gizmo that takes the data off your phone without you knowing it, like those credit card hackers do all the time. It was probably activated at their apartment. No big deal, I'll just block the number. Watch."

###

"How about breakfast at Sarabeth's?" Kevin suggested the next morning. "My treat."

"You're on."

While Kevin watched CNN, Sheila showered, her thoughts inexplicably drifting toward her parents. It had been twenty years since their deaths; she had been fifteen at the time. She ached for them now, a physical sorrow. They had been driving upstate, a weekend to themselves to celebrate an anniversary. Her mom's sister, Letty, was caring for Sheila while they were away and…

In the shower, she squeezed her eyes closed, tried to block out the old memory. She had successfully locked away so much of her childhood and adolescence that only her parent's death remained vivid and intimate. And painful. Full color agony in a faded world of gray or black and white memories. She turned off the water, dried her hair, found that the sadness in her heart was lingering. She hadn't thought of her folks with such emotion in a long time.

"I miss you," she whispered to them as she rubbed the steam off the bathroom mirror. She began to narrate her life story as she applied makeup.

"Following the loss of her parents, Sheila Irving was lovingly raised by Letty, her mother's sister. Then, when she was eighteen, Ms. Irving went to college. When she was twenty-five, her aunt died of a stroke. Five years later, Sheila met Kevin and everything has been good since then. *Great* since then. Fantastic since meeting Kevin. Ms. Irving works at the *New York Times*, has a fabulous boyfriend slash fiancé who is a successful real estate broker. One day soon she shall be happily married, will live happily ever after." Pleased with her reflection, she reached to turn off the bathroom lights just before all three bulbs exploded.

"Shit!" she cried, startled.

From the other room, Kevin called out, "You okay? What happened?"

"Your lights. Again."

She joined Kevin in the living room. "Sorry. I mean, I didn't do anything, but…"

"That's weird," Kevin said. "Those are expensive, too, and I don't remember them ever blowing out before. I'll have to get some after work today." Then, giving her the once over, he said, "Hey, nice,"

She checked her phone. Groaned. "I have a voice mail…"

"It might not be them." He put his arm around her.

She engaged the speaker function.

"Good morning, Sheila," Vanya Avery said. *"Don't forget, ten o'clock at Edith's apartment. I'm certain you'll be intrigued by the proposal she and I have prepared for you. Oh! And I keep forgetting to mention something. It's about your parents. They weren't alone in that car."*

Sheila didn't want to hold the phone, almost dropped it when it went silent. Kevin grabbed it as she backed away from him, settled slowly on the sofa.

"What did she mean?" he asked helplessly.

"I don't know," Sheila whispered, her thoughts puckered with images of her parents.

They weren't alone in that car.

Sheila knew Kevin was speaking to her, but he seemed so far away. She wondered what Vanya could possibly know about her parents and the accident, it had happened so long ago. If they weren't alone in the car, who had been with them?

"Then I'm going with you," Kevin said, buttering a freshly baked biscuit.

"Oh. I don't know," Sheila said, pleased with his response.

"Well, I *do* know. I don't want to be left out of this strange little adventure you seem to be on. If you're going to find out what Vanya knows about your parent's death, I want to be there. Plus, I'm curious to meet them, learn about this proposal they keep talking about."

Sheila nodded. "I also want to find out how they know my every move."

"And how they got my phone number," Kevin added.

"Do you think we're being followed?"

He shrugged. Nodded. "Probably the Amish guy. And I was thinking, he most likely is the one who remotely bugged our phones and computer lines."

She giggled. "He's read those nasty emails and texts you've sent?"

"Oh, sure. Forwarded them on to Edith and Vanya, too. I'm certain of it. In fact, our apartments are probably *packed* with hidden surveillance equipment."

They grinned at one another.

She said, "I wish it was true. It would explain so much."

"A logical explanation, you mean."

"Yeah, but I know there's something else going on."

"I agree. That's why I'm going with you."

They hailed a cab, sat in silence holding hands as the taxi careened up Madison Avenue, then over to Park.

"Who are we?" Sheila asked.

"Huh?"

"Characters. Just between us, we need to be people other than ourselves for this caper."

"Why? What's wrong with just being us?"

Sheila squeezed his hand "I'd feel better, more like we were pulling one over on them if we could assume different, secret identities."

"Okay, give me a second." He stared out the window. A grin formed on his face. It grew wider. "Got it! Witty! Sophisticated! Intelligent! They are always in danger yet always come out alive and well!"

"Who?!"

The driver said, "Here's your stop."

Kevin paid the fare. They stepped out in front of the building.

"Hurry up! Tell me!"

"I'm William Powell. You'll be Myrna Loy."

"The detective couple from *The Thin Man* series!"

"Yep. They never got hurt, got in and out of all sorts of jams, solved every mystery, and always ended the day with several cocktails."

Arm in arm, they marched passed the doorman, into the lobby.

"We're here to see Ms. David," Kevin said boldly.

"Yes, Mr. Jackson, they're expecting you."

All of Sheila's jaunty confidence fled. *How'd they know Kevin's name and that he would be with me?* she thought uneasily.

CHAPTER 38.

Kevin had the same questions, shared them with Sheila once they were in the elevator.

"Obviously, our apartments *are* bugged," he murmured. "We'll have to get a security firm to check them out."

"But why would they do that?"

Kevin motioned with his eyes toward the operator. Sheila nodded, remained silent until they had reached the David's floor. Once they left the elevator, he said, "I don't know why they're keeping tabs on us, but it seems that Vanya knows a lot about you. Your childhood experience with levitation, the events surrounding your parent's death. This really is a job for William and Myrna." He rang the buzzer for the David's apartment.

Sheila smiled. "I don't remember *ever* having a case this intriguing, do you?"

"Right on time!" Edith exclaimed cheerfully as she opened the door. She introduced herself to

Kevin, not at all surprised to see that he was with Sheila. "Promptness is a form of respect, and I appreciate that," she said as she ushered them into the living room. "Please, make yourselves comfortable."

"We can't stay long," Kevin said firmly. He and Sheila remained standing. "We came for two reasons. First, to find out what Vanya knows about the death of Sheila's parents. Secondly, we wanted to let you know that Sheila won't be pursing the story and to no longer contact her."

"She can't speak for herself?" Edith asked, an edge to her tone even as the smile remained. "And what 'story' are you talking about?"

"The one you and Vanya told me yesterday," Sheila said, grateful that Kevin had spoken first, cleared the way. "Your allegations that Derek raped Vanya, his nervous breakdown…"

Edith frowned. "Oh, there must be some misunderstanding. That's not what we want you to write about. No, not at all. That was all merely background. It was provided as an explanation as to what happened to my husband. Please, won't you be seated? We should really clarify all of this. You see, we have *another* project, an exclusive for you, actually. A longer, historical and investigative piece I suppose you'd call it."

Sheila shook her head. "I'm not interested. Really, I came here only to find out what she knows about my parents."

"We'll pay you $100,000 for three month's work," Edith said with the same easy manner used to announce the weather. "I'm sure that makes it at least worth discussing before you turn it down. Doesn't it?"

Kevin and Sheila glanced at one another.

"Um, that's very generous," Sheila said, "but I'm still not interested."

"We won't offer you more," Edith said, a warning. "If you think delaying an answer will increase the amount, you're mistaken. Let me have Vanya join us. We can discuss it in more detail. Excuse me."

Kevin said, "I guess they won't take no for an answer."

"I almost wavered," Sheila admitted. "That's a *lot* of money."

"Would it bother you to hear her proposal? Now, I'm curious."

"Why not, right? We're here and I'm declining it anyway. All I really care about is finding out what she knows about my parents and getting their gadgets off our computers and printers. And getting those martinis at the end of the day."

Kevin took her hand, pulled her close, kissed her.

"That detective couple, they were married, right?"

Kevin said, "In the movies, *everybody* was married—"

"I'm sorry…I wasn't able to greet you," Vanya panted from the doorway. "But… I need to rest. The baby. Is due. Any. Day."

Sheila was stunned at the rapid deterioration of Vanya. She looked exhausted. Her complexion was oily and pale. She was leaning on Edith's arm as she slowly made her way into the room. She eased her huge, pregnant bulk gradually into one of the overstuffed chairs. It was hard to believe that only 24 hours earlier Sheila had thought Vanya resembled a potent, cosmic Earth Mother. She had radiated robust health and sexual vitality. Now she appeared to be nothing more than a dangerously bloated, perspiring woman with hollow eyes and a sickly, almost yellowish glow about her skin. *And I'm not at all attracted to her,* Sheila thought with relief, glad she had never mentioned that incident to Kevin.

"Are you sure you're all right?" Sheila managed to ask after Kevin had been introduced.

"I'll be. Fine. Once baby Margaret arrives."

Sheila took a moment to settle her thoughts, then said, "There are a few things we want to talk to you about. First, I want you to tell me what you know about my parents. Your message said they were not alone in the car. What did you mean by that?"

"No, first we will discuss…the proposal," Vanya insisted, trying to compose herself.

"No." Kevin pushed back with equal intensity. "Answer Sheila's question."

Vanya turned to Kevin, looked him over.

At the same instant, a thought appeared in Sheila's mind, a rapidly approaching warning sign: *She'll devour him one day. One day, Vanya will simply eat him alive.* Unnerved at the terrifying image that had formed, she glanced at Edith. She too, was carefully looking over Kevin, sizing him up, almost examining him, then her gaze settled on Vanya, waiting for her response.

"I *will* tell you…about your parents," Vanya finally said. "I promise. But first we want to discuss the proposal Edith and I have. Really, I insist."

Sheila looked at Kevin. He shrugged slightly. It was checkmate, they both knew it. "All right," Sheila said. "Tell us."

Vanya said, "What Edith and I are proposing is that you come to Hydesville with us for the next three months. Write about the Keilgarden Colony, the history of the organization, the importance of what occurred with the children at the Fox cottage in 1848, why the village is so highly regarded by Spiritualists, and, most importantly, write about our children, Roland and soon-to-be-Margaret."

"We'll pay you $100,000," Edith reminded her.

Confused, Sheila said, "But what story could there possibly be about Roland and your newborn?"

"That will actually be the focus of the story," Vanya said excitedly. "You see, Roland and Margaret will be part of a new generation known as union children."

Kevin asked, "What are 'union children'?"

Vanya said, "They are the result of the union of one individual, usually from the Colony, who exhibits significant, extraordinary psychic abilities, and someone from outside the community. These offspring are extremely rare, something the Keilgarden Colony has been desperate to produce for decades."

After thinking this over for several seconds, Sheila said, "You're claiming that Roland is a union child because either Derek or Edith have these psychic gifts? Is that right? Are you psychic?" she asked Edith, who shook her head. Sheila looked at Vanya. "And either you or Derek must have these abilities in order for Margaret to be a union child, correct?"

Edith glanced at Vanya, who nodded. Edith leaned forward, said quietly, "I guess we should tell you the truth, full disclosure for the story. Derek *isn't* the father of my son, Roland."

Confused, Kevin and Sheila asked at the same time, "Then who is Roland's father?"

Vanya shifted about, trying to make her bulk more comfortable. Edith adjusted the pillow behind her, murmured, "You really should lie down."

"Yes, I can feel little Margaret trying to push her way out. The little dear wants some *room* to move!" Vanya said fondly. She looked at Kevin and Sheila, her green eyes dull with exhaustion. "I'm sure this is confusing for you. Let me explain."

She took on the tone of a schoolteacher or tour guide. She reminded them that the Colony was established to study and nurture children with proven psychic abilities, including telekinesis, telepathy, clairvoyance, precognition, ESP, all realms of the preternatural physical and paranormal sciences.

"How many children are in residence now?" Kevin asked. "And you're saying that over the years, *none* of them produced one of these union children?"

"Tragically, for some unknown reason, we have a very high rate of miscarriage and infant mortality," Vanya said sadly "Once the children have grown and left the Colony, we've tracked them, of course, but unfortunately, only two union children have been born, both female, which doesn't work for us, as you can imagine."

Before Kevin could ask more about the union children, Vanya shifted again to make herself more comfortable, put her hand up, indicating to wait before he spoke. "To answer your question about the number of children who now reside at the Colony, the counterculture of the 1960s really impacted our work; very few remain. People everywhere suddenly became open to alternative forms of belief, psychic abilities, occult practices; it was no longer mocked or ridiculed. Soon, our community was no longer unique or exclusive. The work we did, the effort we put into it, simply wasn't recognized for its value since so many were doing it—or trying to—throughout the world. Summerhill School in the UK, the L'Abri community in Switzerland, the Waldorf schools in Eastern Europe, the Naropa University in Colorado, the Delphian School in Oregon. The list goes on and on, yet none of these institutions has produced the potential we see in Roland or Margaret. That's why the birth of these union children is so historic, so important to what we've desired to achieve all these years."

Sheila said, "You make it sound like you were actively involved all these years..."

"I was."

Kevin said, "What? You're not old enough. You're what, only in your early or mid-thirties?"

Edith giggled suddenly, a sharp, startling sound.

Vanya smiled broadly as she stroked her stomach. "I was born at the Colony," she explained. "If you haven't guessed, I am a union child myself, the descendant of a powerfully gifted individual from the community. His psychic scores in a variety of areas tested off the charts."

"Your father?" Sheila suggested. Vanya nodded. Sheila wondered about Vanya's mother, if she had special abilities, but before she could ask, Kevin jumped in.

"Sounds like these gifted adults were used to...*breed* union children, because of their psychic abilities," he said, appalled by the idea. "Like a super race. No offense."

"None taken, and they weren't exactly…*adults* as you might define them," Vanya demurred. Unclear of what she meant, Sheila was going to ask but Vanya continued. "But I think now you understand why little Margaret will be so special and important since she is the union of myself and Derek." She closed her eyes, grimaced. A shimmer of perspiration materialized over her face. She went pale, her breathing turned raspy, labored.

Concerned, Edith asked, "You all right?"

"Give me. A moment."

The room was silent. They all watched Vanya attempt to rally. She massaged her stomach, murmured to herself, to the unborn child. A smile would crease her face at times, then etch itself into a grimace. She attempted to correct her erratic panting by puffing out gasps of air as if she was in early labor. She began to rotate her head about as if her neck was stiff with pain. Gradually the color returned to her face, the glossy sheen departed, her breathing steadied again. She opened her eyes. "Ah, better now. But my daughter is making it clear her time is *soon*."

"Mommy?"

A young boy stood in the doorway. Dressed impeccably in a blue and white polo shirt, white shorts, tennis shoes without socks, and holding a half-eaten bagel, he looked like a Ralph Lauren model. "This is dry," he said, holding up the bread. "Can I put some jam on it?"

Edith extended her arms out. He rushed to her embrace. She pulled him close, pulled him onto her lap.

"Of course you can, sweetie! But first I want you to meet our guests. This is Ms. Irving and Mr.

Jackson. They're going to be staying with us for a few months in Hydesville."

Her eyes bright with love and affection, Edith said, "This is my son, Roland."

Sheila was confused by Edith's introduction. *No, that can't be Roland,* she thought. *I saw him yesterday. He was born back in November, so he's less than a year old. This child is at least two.*

CHAPTER 39.

Roland had a huge smile on his face. He pointed to Kevin. "You'll play with me in the woods, won't you?"

A buzzy low hum filled Kevin's head. His eyelids became heavy, closed. In the blackness, he had a vision of he and the boy surrounded by tall, thick trees that hovered over them, seemed to bend down, peer at them. Forest shadows materialized, impossible in the pitch dark. Kevin saw an oddly shaped thing with three peaks shuffle toward them. It resembled—

"Kevin?" Sheila asked.

He jerked in response to her voice, was barely able to open his eyes, they were so heavy. He closed them, could still see…the Fox Woods? Where Oswald David had died, hung from a tree? Was that where he was? He recalled the gruesome story Sheila had relayed to him over dinner. His mind kept shambling about in a daze. He leaned forward, partly opened his eyes, peered closer, deeper at Roland.

The boy shimmered, flickered in and out of focus. Kevin saw that the child wasn't even—

"Honey? Are you okay?" Sheila's touch brought Kevin out of the trance. The connection with Roland snapped.

Kevin turned, nodded at Sheila, rubbed his forehead, smiled weakly to let her know he was okay.

She said to Edith, "Who is this? I met Roland yesterday, remember? This boy is too old to be your son."

Edith was massaging the child's shoulders. "This *is* my son," she assured them. He continued grinning shyly at Kevin, as if they were sharing a secret.

Vanya explained, "Union children, such as myself, sometimes *age* differently, sometimes very rapidly, especially when they are young, sometimes slower when they are older. It doesn't always happen, of course. But for Roland, he matured very, very quickly when he was inside of Edith. Margaret seems to be taking her time. Once they reach adolescence, the process slows down a bit..."

"I don't believe you," Sheila said sharply. "You're saying he aged from an eight-month-old to a two-year-old *over night*?"

Edith and Vanya nodded.

"Do you have any other explanation?" Edith asked.

"Yes, that you're making it all up for some reason. The kid's an actor, a different child, playing a role."

"Mommy," Roland whined, bored with the conversation. "You said I could have some jam!" Edith agreed, took him by the hand. He passed by

Kevin, beamed a smile at him. "We'll have a good time in the woods! Just you and me."

Kevin backed away from the child.

After Edith and Roland had left the room, Sheila turned to Vanya, exasperated. "You don't need me to write any of this. The history of Hydesville, the Fox sisters, the Colony, the story of your children. If what you are saying is true, take them to a hospital or clinic. They can study them, document their growth, have it peer reviewed, prove it to the world. I can't do that. I'm not interested."

When Vanya didn't reply, Kevin said, "No more phone messages, either. I've got a buddy who can debug our apartment; he'll find and remove any spyware you've installed on our computers. Leave us alone. Oh, and call off the man you hired to tail us."

"What man?"

"The Amish-looking man. The one with the old-fashioned clothes. Don't play innocent with us, Vanya!" Sheila was angry now. "We know—"

Vanya's face had gone dangerously white. With a strangled cry of anguish, she collapsed into the sofa. Kevin and Sheila rushed over to the couch where she was beginning to slide to the floor. Her tongue was protruding thickly from her mouth. Behind her flickering eyelids, they could see rapid, frantic movement.

One of the oil paintings on the wall behind them came loose, crashed to floor. Sheila let out a startled cry. A portion of the wall had torn away. It crossed her mind that the damage made it appear that the picture may have been wrenched free in a fit of rage.

Sheila glanced back at Vanya. Kevin had managed to settle her back onto the sofa. "Is she okay?"

"No, I think something is really wrong with her."

"I'll find Edith," Sheila said.

Kevin was uneasy being left alone with Vanya. It was unpleasant having to sit so close to her. Her sheer mass, the odd sounds of her terrible wheezing, the strange sheen to her skin, her semiconscious state made him uncomfortable, but he knew he had to remain near in case she became worse. Behind her closed eyes, panicky activity raged on as if she was having terrible nightmares. Her plump bosom heaved as she labored to breathe. She groaned, murmured, twisted about on the sofa. He watched with disgust as the fleshy folds around her neck distorted the lines of her face, making her appearance more angular at times. He blinked, rubbed his eyes, not sure if he was seeing correctly. For seconds at a time, he barely recognized her, as if her features were shifting right before him. The color of her skin would darken then the texture seemed to develop ridges and deep crevices. Her arms and legs seemed to—

He looked away, closed his eyes, tried to stabilize himself. It was the same dreamlike unsteadiness he had experienced with Roland. *What was taking Sheila so long?* He swallowed nervously, tasted bile that blazed harsh. His tongue burned with it. He sniffed, could almost smell it. Was it whiskey? He looked around for the source of the scent; it was strong, like the open bottle was right under his nose. Lightheaded again, he settled next to Vanya on the sofa, closed his eyes, waited for the spinning to stop.

After a moment, he felt better, opened his eyes. He looked over. She was worse. Her face had a vacantness about it, a green tinge that blurred as her body shook and trembled. Her mouth was set in a grim line of pain. She whimpered.

It would be best to put her out of her misery. The thought came to Kevin like a simple text from his phone. No emotion to it, just something to consider, a suggestion. After all, she was in horrible discomfort, she and that baby she was carrying. *Two birds, one stone.* She groaned. He could put both of them out of their misery right now. Kevin reached down to comfort her. "There, there," he whispered, his voice thick with concern. "Soon it can all be over."

It would be so easy. The thick throw pillows she had leaned on for support were right there, but he'd have to act quickly. Soon Sheila would return with Edith.

Do it!

"Do it!" The voice, heavy, masculine, urgent, startled Kevin; it had been said *through him.* His voice, but he hadn't formed the words. The grainy alcohol smell accompanied the command.

Kevin placed the pillow over Vanya's face.

Push!

"Push," he muttered. The stink of the dark brown liquor rose up as if from the sofa. Kevin gagged at the stench as Vanya weakly tried to resist him. Her muffled cries turned to rage. She freed an arm, scratched blindly, deeply into his right forearm. He reared back in pain, the pillow flung off of Vanya as her arms extended upward.

Edith and Sheila rushed into the room, just missing the struggle. They hurried to Vanya's side, helped her up from the couch as she regained consciousness. Kevin massaged his arm, wondered what had happened to him. He had never felt such an urgent frenzy before, all of it directed at Vanya. He could still detect the bitter taste and scent swirling about him like agitated gnats.

While the two women ministered to the now-recovered Vanya, Kevin glanced over to the damaged wall. There was a five-inch hole in the plaster where the painting had been torn loose. It was as if the same rage he had experienced had yanked the frame away.

My God, what happened to me? he wondered, the dizziness returning for the third time, closing in around him for a moment. He was horrified by his actions. Neither Sheila nor Edith had seen his attempt at smothering Vanya; she had appeared to be unconscious during the act, only awakening at the last instant.

A clichéd expression came to him, one with a literal meaning he had never really thought about before: *What's gotten into me?*

"You're sure she doesn't need a doctor?" Sheila asked nervously a few minutes later. They had managed to settle Vanya in her bed, were all watching her closely.

"No, it's just important now that she rests," Edith said easily. "Nothing should be upsetting her. I wonder…what *were* you talking about before she collapsed?"

"I was telling her that I wouldn't be doing the story."

"That…wasn't what upset me," Vanya murmured weakly from the bed. Edith leaned in close. "What *did* upset you, dear?"

"They said a man…was following them…old-fashioned clothes …"

When Vanya finished describing the Amish man, Edith straightened up, grabbed Sheila roughly by both arms. "You've *seen* such a man? Have you actually *seen* him?"

"No, we haven't seen him. We were at a restaurant, he mentioned me to the bartender. Who is he, Edith? What's going on?"

Sheila thought she glimpsed a shimmer of fear in Edith's eyes. The phrase *Slave, not servant*, crossed her mind, but she wasn't clear what that meant. Vanya fell into a restless asleep. Edith led Sheila quickly out of the bedroom. They rejoined Kevin who was dully examining the damaged wall, tracing the hole with his finger, weaving on his feet, barely able to keep his eyes opened. Sheila noticed immediately how tired he seemed, almost dazed; all the fight seemed to have gone out of him.

"Honey? Are you okay?" Sheila put her hand on his shoulder. They both turned to face Edith when she asked them to tell her more about the man.

"That's really all we know, just what the bartender said," Sheila said.

"Tell him to stop following us," Kevin said, his energy somewhat restored. "Call him off, tell him to leave us alone."

Edith shook her head dismissively, began pacing the room. "We didn't hire him. I *can't* call him off."

"If you didn't hire this fellow to follow us and mess with our apartments and computers, then how come Vanya knows our every move and what we've been doing?" Sheila demanded.

Impatiently, Edith said, "Do you really think Vanya would have to resort to such arcane devises? She's already told you. She's a union child, she has…abilities, can do things, cause things to happen." She glanced back and forth between them as she rapidly spoke, could see the scorn on their faces.

Sheila rolled her eyes, said, "Oh, please Edith! I don't know how she found out my parents died in a car accident; I guess through Google somehow. And I don't know why she would say they were not alone in the car. Maybe just a tease to get us over here to see you both so you could trot out this bizarre story, show us some neighbor's kid, claim he's your son. But special powers?"

Edith was about to respond, Sheila talked over her. "And look, it's horrible about what happened last fall and Derek's injuries, but I gotta tell you, there is something seriously…wrong, or off, about Vanya. I'd stay away from her if I were you. And I'm telling you now to keep away from Kevin and me. No more phone calls and tell the Amish guy to leave us alone or I'm contacting the police."

Having said all she could think of, she turned to leave.

And screamed.

Standing directly behind Kevin was the Amish man.

Her shriek shook Kevin fully out of his stupor. He rushed to Sheila. She was trembling, so terrified she was unable to speak. He turned around to see where she was looking. "What is it? What did you see?"

But the Amish man had vanished.

Edith stepped closer to them, whispered, "Was it him?" Her voice was tight with dread. She glanced nervously about the room.

Sheila, her voice muffled, her face pressed into Kevin's shoulder, said, "He was standing there, right behind you. I thought he was going to harm you…"

"No," Edith murmured bitterly. "He's not here to harm you. He's wants Roland. And Margaret and Vanya. And me, I suppose."

"Who *is* he?" Kevin asked, angry at the riddles and peculiar explanations. He kept his arm tightly around Sheila's shoulder.

Edith said weakly. "If he can manifest himself *here*, in her presence…"

"This is nuts," Kevin whispered to Sheila. "Let's get out of here." He maneuvered her to the door.

From behind them, Edith's voice suddenly frail, fading, said, "He's found us, he won't leave us alone until…"

Kevin and Sheila hurried down the hallway, past the kitchen and study, were just turning into the entry way when they heard the sound:

Hiss. Clink. Hiss. Clink.

Sheila recognized the sound of Derek's respirator.

He was in the study, his back to them in his wheelchair, positioned in front of the window. Motionless. The only sound was the machine that breathed for him.

"Kevin, wait." All at once, Sheila had the overwhelming desire to rescue Derek, to take him away with them, to protect him. She entered the room slowly, not wanting to startle him, but realized he wouldn't even be aware she was there. Then, impossibly, his head moved slightly side to side. She heard someone giggle. She crept deeper into the study, saw that Roland was kneeling before Derek. He had his hands up under what was left of Derek's raw, blistered chin. The boy was moving the lifeless head about as if it were a marionette puppet with the strings severed.

"Won't ever hurt my Mommy or Aunt Vanya," Roland was saying. "Won't ever stop us…"

"Roland!" Sheila shouted, rushing to the wheelchair, Kevin right behind her. "Leave him alone! Roland! Take your hands away from him!"

The boy didn't flinch or seemed surprised to see them. He kept his hands poised under Derek's jaw. He stared at Sheila. "I play with him *all* the time," he said matter-of-factly, his tone and speaking ability more like that of a ten-year-old. "Just to remind him of what happened, of who won, of who *will* win. I do all *sorts* of things to him." He stood, released Derek's head, which lolled to the side.

"Get away from him!" Sheila said, barely controlling her rage. She wanted to strangle the child, then take his lifeless body and toss it out the window. How could he torment such a helpless man?

Kevin said, "Get out of here, now!"

Roland ignored Sheila, looked directly at Kevin. "We're going to play together in the woods, just like Oswald did." He gazed down at Derek's face one last time, then dashed out of the room, calling over his shoulder, "See you in Hydesville!"

CHAPTER 40.

Come on," Kevin said urgently, grabbing Sheila's elbow. "Let's get the hell out of here."

"But we can't leave Derek! You heard what Roland said. He…plays with him, does things to him…"

They were standing a few feet behind the wheelchair, both reluctant to approach the occupant.

Hiss. Clink. Hiss. Clink.

"Tell me the truth," Sheila said. "Be honest. Don't you feel there is *something* in this room, right now, a sense that he's *here*, alert, somehow aware of his surroundings? No matter how impossible it sounds, that's what I felt yesterday, that this man is still, somehow, *aware*."

"I don't know. Maybe. But we need to *go*," Kevin said urgently. "Those women are crazy!"

Sheila had an idea. "I want to try to communicate with him."

"What? How? We need to get out of here." She waved off Kevin, glanced nervously at the doorway. No sign of Edith or Roland, and Vanya was still hopefully sleeping. Sheila stepped around until she was standing in front of Derek. She steadied herself, then hunched down until she was face to face with him.

His neck was raw, chicken bone-skinny, seemed too fragile to support the weight of his head. His face resembled a dried-up apple that had rotted; terribly scarred, misshapen, it was a dead thing that had somehow removed itself from the grave. His nose had been sheared off from the fire; the bone had been cut flat since there were no plans for reconstructive procedures. His nostrils were covered over with raw-looking tissue that protected the membranes. An image of Lon Chaney's unmasked Erik from *Phantom of the Opera* was the closest image Sheila's mind could conjuror.

Hiss. Clink. Hiss. Clink.

Derek's mouth had been recreated into a slit that had been permanently formed into a stiff, dried grimace. Inside were blackened gums, gray teeth. The fire had destroyed his eyes; with no plastic surgery performed, the doctors had decided to simply sew protective tissue over the sockets. The impression was of a madman grinning wildly in his sleep. He had a brown blanket draped over what little was left of his torso. Tubes from the respirator and a nutrition supply were tucked under the covering. If she could look beyond the horrific disfigurements to his face and body, she could almost believe that it was just a crippled man asleep in a wheelchair.

Hiss. Clink. Hiss. Clink.

Instinctively, she thought, *He probably has* all *the answers to the questions that keep piling up.* Was he really the father of Vanya's child? Why would she make up such a malicious lie? Why had Derek tied his pregnant wife to her bed, removed all forms of communication in the apartment, hoping to deprive her of medical assistance? Why would he put his unborn son and wife in such life-threatening danger? They both might have died. Why was he so intent on driving five hours north to burn down the Fox cottage? Was he just a sick, delusional man who had experienced a mental breakdown like Edith and Vanya had said? Or did he go to such horrific extremes because he knew something strange was going on, was convince its origin was in Hydesville, maybe centered on the Fox property?

What do you know, Derek David? Sheila pondered.

Hiss. Clink. Hiss. Clink.

She knelt down on both knees, supporting herself by grabbing hold of the wheelchair's frame. "Derek?" she said, knowing he couldn't hear her, but still hoping nonetheless. "Derek, is there any way you can communicate with me?" She didn't know what kind of response, if any, she expected from the disfigured individual before her. Did he have any capacity for reasoning or processing all that was going on around him? She continued to stare into his mangled countenance, knowing he couldn't see or hear, was unable to speak. Yet she refused to ignore her own flickering intuition: somehow, Derek *was* aware of their presence in the room with him.

"Derek?"

Clink. Clink.

Seconds passed. The only response was a mechanical one.

Frustrated, her shoulders slumped, Sheila chided herself. *What were you expecting? For the vocal chords to somehow repair themselves so he could speak? Or perhaps he would grow arms and hands and fingers, begin signing his thoughts?* She didn't believe in miracles, but that was what she needed. Disappointed, she stood up, shrugged at Kevin. They had been there too long already. Still, she was glad she had tried. They turned to leave the room.

Clink. Clink. Clink.

Something…

"The respirator sounds different," she said. The hissing sounds continued as oxygen flowed into Derek's lungs, yet the metallic clinking was louder, more defiant.

"Come *on*," Kevin hissed. "Let's go!"

Clink! Clink!

They turned as one.

"Is something wrong with it?" Sheila hurried back to the wheelchair, glanced at the dials on the machine, no idea what she was looking for. Then a pinpoint of an idea began to expand, then grew, fully dawning on her. "Maybe he can somehow communicate through the machine!"

Clink! Clink! Clink! Clink!

She faced Derek again. Excitedly, she said, "If you can understand me, clink twice."

Clink! Clink!

"Oh, my God," Kevin said, joining her. He recoiled in repulsion at his first full-frontal glimpse of Derek David.

Sheila continued, "Derek, once for yes, twice for no. Are you in danger here?"

Clink!

"Then we'll get you out of here."

Clink! Clink!

"No?" Kevin said, careful to keep his gaze on Sheila, avoiding Derek's face.

Clink! Clink!

"You're in danger here but we're to leave you, is that correct?" Sheila quickly said.

Clink.

"Is there anything we can do for you?"

Clink.

"Great," Kevin muttered, "he can only answer yes or no, so how do we figure out what we can do to help him?"

Sheila plunged ahead. "Is the Amish man good or bad? I mean, is he good?"

Clink.

"So, we don't have to be afraid of him. Is he here to…help us somehow?"

Clink.

Kevin asked, "Is Roland your son?"

Clink. Clink.

"Are you the father of Vanya's baby?" Sheila asked.

Silence for a moment, then:

Clink.

"Did you…rape her?"

Clink. Clink.

"He didn't," Kevin said, "yet he is the father? I don't—"

Sheila tried: "Were you…forced to be the father?"

A loud *Clink.*

"That was a solid yes," Kevin said. "He is not Roland's father, he *is* Margaret's father, but he didn't want to be. Who is Roland's father, we never found out."

"Can't ask that and get a yes or no answer," Sheila reminded him. "Derek, are *we* in danger here?"

Clink.

"I knew it," Kevin said. "Should we stay or go? I mean, should we leave now?"

Clink.

"Okay, you heard the man," he said, tugging at Sheila's arm.

"Wait! One more. Derek, will you be all right if we leave you here?"

Clink.

"I still don't understand," Kevin whispered. "He's in danger here, yet he'll be all right if we leave him. But come on, let's do as he says and get out of here."

From the study, they hurried down the corridor to the entry way. Once they were out of the apartment, Sheila pushed the elevator button while Kevin kept watched. The apartment door remained closed. The elevator operator kept his eyes forward, back stiff. They arrived in the lobby seconds later. The doorman greeted them warmly. "Nice visit with Ms. David and Ms. Avery?"

They both nodded, flat smiles stretched on their faces.

"And that boy, Roland. Isn't he a tiger?!"

"Oh, yes," Sheila agreed, suppressing a maniacal laugh. "They grow up so fast these days, don't they?"

CHAPTER 41.

Once they were outside in the July sun, Sheila and Kevin looked up at the bright, cloudless, white-blue sky. On both sides of Park Avenue, traffic and pedestrians hurried up and down the streets. After the dim environment of the apartment and the odd events that had transpired, it was disorienting to be on the sidewalk with all the noise and humanity. For some reason, they each felt slightly perplexed; half-awake, half asleep.

It took Shelia a few seconds to steady herself. She had no idea why she was on Park Avenue with him. "Kevin?"

"What the—" he started to say but stopped when he saw Sheila's bewildered expression.

"What are we doing here?" she asked him. "How—"

He pulled her close, out of the path of the people scurrying past. "Breakfast?" he said doubtfully. "Weren't we going to breakfast? Have we…"

Their recollections were both on hold, just blinking nonsense images. They recalled the previous evening together, the night at Kevin's. And then…

And then standing on Park Avenue.

Kevin glanced at his watch. 11:45 a.m. Something nudged his thoughts. "I have to call my noon appointment, tell them I'll be a little late…"

"SoHo!"

"What?"

"I have an interview this afternoon, in SoHo," Sheila said. "I just remembered…"

They both went silent, watching the busy crowds around them, all intent on heading up or down or across the avenue. They all had a place to go, knew where they had to be and why.

"Why are we here?" Kevin asked. Sheila gazed up at the apartment building they stood in front of. The address meant nothing to her. She turned to Kevin, saw his puzzled expression, assumed his thoughts were as useless and blank as hers.

Sheila spent the rest of the morning reviewing notes, preparing for her afternoon appointment. She tried to stay focused, keep her mind occupied on the interview, but her thoughts kept sliding back to hers and Kevin's morning memory lapse. They had called and texted one another several times to see if either had unlocked any recollections, but no breakthroughs had occurred. They decided against seeing their doctors since whatever it was had happened to both of them.

"Must be airborne," Kevin reasoned. "Neither of us had a bump on the head."

"Can amnesia result from inhaling something?" Sheila wondered. She did some topical searches to see if there had been any recent accounts of memory loss in Manhattan, but nothing showed up.

When she arrived home from SoHo, it was after five. The bed was unmade which was odd since she always made it first thing in the morning. Always. Besides, she had spent the previous night at Kevin's; they both remembered that. She lived in a secure doorman building, knew no one had been in her apartment. Still. She checked the other bedroom and the closets. Finally straightened up the bed. Maybe she had forgotten to make it.

Kevin called, invited her to dinner at his place, insisting it be followed by a sleep over. Sheila showered, dressed, still had time to kill. She poured a glass of wine, was flipping through *Vanity Fair* when her phone rang. It was Suzy, one of her best friends. They chatted a bit; when Sheila ended the conversation a few minutes later, she finished her wine in one gulp, sat there, thinking, pondering.

It was maddening. She knew how she had spent her afternoon but for the life of her, Sheila Irving could still not recall what had happened that morning.

They spent all of dinner—Kevin's famous artichoke pasta—talking about their troubling lapses of memory but could find no explanations between them. Like an itch in the brain, it was out of reach.

After they cleared the table, they settled on the couch. Kevin clicked on the TV. The cable was out.

He got up, fumbled with the wires, rebooted it, scrolled through the recorded shows. "Let's waste some time."

Two hours later, they were snuggled up in bed. "What's that?" Sheila asked, touching his right forearm. There was a slash mark, three-inches long that seemed slightly inflamed, maybe even infected.

"Where did that come from?" Kevin said, confused, sitting up. "I never even noticed it."

"It looks sort of like fingernails. See these two lines going down? Who scratched you?"

"No idea."

Sheila went to the bathroom, returned with a plastic first aid kit. She cleaned and dressed the wound. "Whatever happened this morning, the more I think about it—or try to think about it—the more I get the feeling it's really, really important. Like this scratch on your arm, someone—or something—did this, and yet you can't remember who or why."

Kevin agreed. "It's like my thoughts are being blocked. Whenever I think I'm getting close, bam! The memory gets all jittery. It's like when you get close to an electronic no trespassing fence; the nearer you get, the stronger the charge becomes to push you away."

He turned off the bedroom light. They talked a bit longer, soon grew drowsy, settled in for the night. Seconds later Kevin was snoring softly. Sheila followed him into a dreamless sleep.

The next day, neither mentioned the memory lapse. They didn't even recall it had happened.

###

The traditional, high velocity summer temperatures crept into Manhattan, reaching full force by the third week of July. The humidity pounced by the end of the month. The sweltering days engulfed the city at first light, and it wasn't until after ten at night that temperatures dropped below seventy. The streets shimmered with mirage-like waves of smoldering, stifling oven-heat. People moved about slowly in an exhausted daze; tempers flared, patience simmered to nothing. Throughout the city there was a sense of catastrophe, as if the walls were closing in. Something was bound to give; it was just too damn hot.

Sheila was dreading having to venture outside into the disgustingly heavy and humid air, but she had to meet with her boss, Gerald, at the *Times'* office. He had said he wanted to talk with her about an "intriguing" assignment—his words—and that bothered her. He wasn't the type of editor to use words like that; he'd been around too long, seen too much, done too much, written too much to find anything truly intriguing.

Still, his phone call had…well, intrigued her.

That evening, Kevin was already seated at the restaurant when Sheila arrived, fifteen minutes late.

"Don't touch me, I'm a sweaty, sopping mess," she said immediately. She smiled at the hovering waiter. "Hendrick's, tonic, rocks, lime. *Very* cold. Please." She turned to Kevin. "I'm late, I'm sorry. The traffic and blah, blah, blah."

He pouted, pretended to be miffed. "You didn't even have the courtesy to text me."

"I figured I could tell you in person."

He lifted his menu, gently fanned her. She closed her eyes, enjoyed it. Gulped her ice water, held the glass to her forehead to cool herself down. When her drink arrived, they toasted, sipped. She settled back with a sigh.

"Better?" Kevin asked after a moment.

"Much. Wish I had a walk-in freezer, though. That would be where I'd spend most of my day, most of the summer. I *hate* going out in this weather."

After they ordered, Kevin said, "I know you have huge, big news, but me first. What would you think about a little time off in August? No need to deal with the hassle of the airport or anything, just get out of the city, cool off for a week or so. We haven't had time away in a while."

"Funny you should mention that. It leads right into my huge, big news. I'd love to go away with you and I think I have just the spot, all expenses paid. I had a most interesting discussion with Gerald today. He was sent a proposal that I was supposedly copied on but never received. It's a story assignment."

Their salads arrived. After a few bites, Kevin said, "How does your assignment fit into my idea of a getaway. Or should I ask, where am I going?"

"What would you think of going upstate with me for our little vacation?"

Kevin smiled. "That's exactly what I was going to suggest! I thought we'd head north, too. I looked into Castile, Lake George, Saratoga Springs. Where's your project?"

"A little town called Hydesville."

"Hmmm. That was not on my list." After a moment, Kevin asked, "Why's that name familiar?"

"I know, right? I thought the same thing. Then Gerald gave me some background material and I remembered. It's that town where that art dealer, Derek David, burned the house down last fall, remember? That weird, gruesome story?"

It took a moment, but Kevin started nodding. "Right, right. He was caught in the fire, badly injured."

"And his wife was left here in the city, in labor, tied up alone, in their apartment. But she managed to safely give birth to their son, Roland. Now she and her sister-in-law have moved to Hydesville and are living there with their children."

"Children?"

"Vanya Avery, Edith's sister-in-law, has a daughter."

"And where's Derek?"

"He's with them. Can you believe it? Even after what he did to his wife, she chose to stand by her man, care for him."

"So, what's the story you're supposed to write?"

"Gerald's very excited because it's going to be an exclusive. But what's amazing is that Vanya and Edith specifically requested that *I* write it. Here's the kicker: They'll pay me $100,000 for three months' work, the *Times* will run excerpts, but it will eventually be published! I'm going to write a book!"

Kevin was trying to keep up with Sheila's enthusiasm. "That's a lot of money! What's the book about?"

"About the Spiritualist movement, how it started in this little village upstate, was known as the Hydesville episodes—"

"The what?"

"The Fox sisters heard these ghostly rappings in their cottage in the 1840s, started to communicate with the spirit, it was called the Hydesville episodes."

"Okay…"

"And I'll write about the formation of the Keilgarden Colony a hundred years later and—"

Not sure how he knew, Kevin blurted out, "The Colony is that place for kids with psychic powers, right?"

Sheila looked at Kevin. "How'd you—but, yeah, that's the place. Anyway, I'll take a leave of absence from the paper, Gerald already okayed all of this. Can you believe it? The *Times* will serialize what I write, both online and in the Friday edition and in the Sunday magazine!"

"And Gerald thinks there's enough interest in this for you to take three months off for research and live up there? It doesn't…"

Sheila was nodding vigorously. "Doesn't sound like Gerald, right? Exactly! But he told me he always found spooks and hauntings sort of fascinating, he did some research on the internet, said that other than an old *Life* magazine article, there is virtually nothing about the Colony, no in-depth, legitimate stories about it, just some junk the *Post* and *National Enquirer* made up after Derek was found."

Kevin listened as Sheila kept talking, wondered why it all seemed so vaguely familiar, couldn't recall where he had read it or heard the story, but he knew all about the circumstances. The local papers and media must have covered it more than Gerald had said. Sheila was obviously excited about the assignment but something about what she was telling him didn't sit right.

"And you're going to move up there for three months?"

She nodded happily. "But I want you to come up with me, help me settle in. It can be that getaway you were talking about."

"How far is Hydesville?"

"About a five-hour drive," Sheila said.

He couldn't think of how to respond, finally said, "Sounds like a great opportunity. But three months. That's a long time apart—"

"Before you know it, I'll be home."

"That's not the point…"

"Gerald has already put everything in motion. I'm excited. I *so* want to do this. Can you believe it? I'm going to write a book!"

The waiter brought their main courses. Kevin wondered why Sheila was so immediately sold on the project. Sure, the money was incredible, but he had been bothered that she was so indifferent about being away from him, didn't even want to discuss it with him before accepting the assignment. How could she so easily leave him for three months? They'd never been apart that long in their five years together. Of course, he could go up and see her a few times but she didn't seem that eager for him to visit.

She shouldn't do it; that's what his gut said. Sheila continued to express her excitement about the book, didn't seem to notice that he wasn't sharing in her passion.

It was like he wasn't even there.

CHAPTER 42.

They left the restaurant, strolled into the evening blast furnace.

"Oh, yuck," Sheila said. "How many times a day can a person sweat before they completely dissolve?"

They sauntered slowly up Columbus Avenue. Kevin was disappointed to learn she was scheduled to leave next Monday. It was Thursday night. It was all happening so fast but at least he would be driving up with her, getting her settled, staying with her for a week.

The homeless man appeared out of the shadows. Heat seemed to radiate from him, along with body odor, the musk of shit, and an under scent neither of them could recognize, a grainy, smoky odor. A filthy face surrounded dark eyes, the dirt was oily, appeared to be smeared on. Long greasy hair gave him the appearance of some type of Rasputin mad monk.

Sheila grabbed Kevin's hand, took him with her as she hurried past. The side street was deserted, oddly quiet, secluded. The deli was open, but she didn't see any customers inside. No cars were whizzing past. It seemed like the street had been closed off to everyone except the three of them.

"Your parents weren't alone in the car," he called out, his voice following closely after them.

Sheila felt a tug on the back of her memories; something tried to dislodge and swim to the surface. She turned, stepped cautiously toward him. "What about my parents? What do you know?"

"It can see as well as hear," he said, his voice somewhat garbled, his very presence in front of them tenuous, the darkness behind him bleeding through.

"Tell me about my parents!"

"Keep the children away from the ball," he whispered.

A car's horn startled them, shook them out of the encounter.

Around them, it was as if the city had suddenly sprung back into action after a brief lull. The deli was now filled with customers, WPLJ was blasting out a steady bass beat. Lights from apartments beamed down on the area, couples and kids strolled the streets. Sheila and Kevin looked at one another, felt as if they had been under a spell. A man jostled Sheila, broke them completely out of their stupor. She glanced over her shoulder at the shadowy area where the man had been. All she saw was darkness.

Your parents weren't alone in the car.

Kevin had heard that odd phrase before, but couldn't remember where or when, had no idea what it meant.

###

Monday morning dawned gray with a blanket of humidity shrouding the city. Thunderstorms were in the forecast. It was hoped the impending downpour would help break the lingering heat wave.

They had loaded Kevin's Volvo the night before with mounds of luggage, most of it Sheila's. She was told she wouldn't need a car in the village, but transportation would be provided at her request. At five minutes to seven, they left his building for the garage, both dressed in shorts and polo shirts. "Okay, you're the navigator," he said as he steered the car into the street. "Where are we going, how do we get there?" They had been told that the GPS was unreliable and to follow the directions that had been emailed to Sheila from Gerald.

Four-and-a-half hours later, Sheila said, "Okay, merge here, then we take Route 14."

Kevin rolled his shoulders, trying to ease the tightness. It had been a long, tiring drive. The directions were easy to follow but there were so many twists, turns, on-ramps, off-ramps and back roads that he imagined they would have been hopelessly lost if they hadn't had specific information on how to get to Hydesville. The further north they drove, the more isolated and alone they felt. The flat, unchanging scenery that unfolded monotonously around them had begun to be disquieting; they were piling up miles but were they getting anywhere?

"How much further?"

Sheila rattled the sheet of directions, peered closely. "Actually, I think we're almost there. Fifteen minutes, maybe? Stay on New York 88."

Kevin glanced about the bleak countryside as it sped past. They were now in Wayne County, just south of Lake Ontario's shoreline, a place known as the Burned Over District. As Sheila had informed him from what little research she had had time to do, in the mid-1800s, the townships were known for housing their share of cults and waves of religious revivals. The fiery preacher Charles Finney declared the region had been so heavily evangelized that it was a "burnt district" with no unconverted population or "fuel" left to "burn" or people to convert.

"Weird area, isn't it?" Kevin said to break the silence that had crowded up the car.

Sheila nodded. "I was thinking the same thing. Not a lot of cars."

"Nope. We haven't passed any in quite a while."

The dusky cloud cover that had greeted them at dawn in Manhattan had followed them north. The air was cooler yet there remained a heaviness about it, a sense that anything done too quickly or suddenly would result in an onslaught of rain. *Tread lightly, don't make any waves or sudden movements* were phrases that kept creeping through Kevin's mind. The area seemed ready to bite back if disturbed.

Sheila pointed out a weather-beaten wooden sign. Kevin made the turn, the Volvo crunched up a small hill. At the top of the uneven path, another notice stated *Hydesville.* Below them were a half-dozen small, one-story buildings that made up the town proper. Sheila was reminded of photos she'd seen of the 1920s and the Dust Bowl days, images of forgotten towns that people were forced to give up on, literal ghost towns. Around them was the brooding atmosphere of neglect, isolation.

"This is it?" Kevin said after a moment, stunned. "*This* is where you are going to spend the next three months of your life?"

"I…guess so," Shelia answered, her voice small, uncertain.

"But this is nowhere. This is in the *middle* of nowhere…Why would anyone want to live here? Especially with a new born and a nine-month-old…"

While Kevin spoke, and the car idled, thoughts rattled around Sheila's mind. *Should I be here? Is this what I should be doing? Did I make the right choice? Did I even* have *a choice?* It had always bothered her that the proposal was never received by her directly. Gerald had read, reviewed it, said he had spoken with Vanya and Edith at length on the phone, handled all the contract negotiations, the financial matters, approached the board on her behalf. In fact, when all was said and done…well, all *was* said and done before Gerald had ever approached her with the assignment.

"Hey, are you with me?" Kevin's voice, from a distance, brought her back. He waved his hand in front of her. "Are we ready to make our grand entrance?"

Sheila nodded. Kevin gave the car a shot of gas.

The Volvo descended into the village of Hydesville.

V:
The Village

CHAPTER 43.

The Volvo rocked side to side as it bumped its way down the incline. Kevin frowned. He did not have a good feeling about this.

"I guess I was expecting a nice old-fashion village with gift shops, a diner, an Indian cigar statue in front of the general store," he said, gritting his teeth as he squeezed the steering wheel. "More of a resort where we'd spend lazy afternoons on a lake—is there a lake?—walks in the woods…"

"There *are* woods all around us," Sheila said, trying the lighten the mood.

At the bottom of the hill, he continued down Hydesville Road toward a cottage with the address of 1510. "That's the Fox house, right?"

"Yep. That's the address."

Lumber was neatly stacked at the side of the property next to a blackened pile of debris. Sawhorses and tools were scattered about, some tentative attempts at landscaping had begun. The two-story cottage was separated from the road by a wood rail fence. Two twelve-paned windows bordered either side of the front door. Horizontal wood slats framed the dirty brown, tired-looking home. A circular attic window and the upstairs windows were pitch black. The place had a lonely feel about it, gave off the impression that it wanted to be left alone.

Kevin parked the car. The silence was immediate, a noise unto itself. He could hear his heart beating a little too fast. They climbed out of the Volvo. When the doors closed, the sound cracked sharply though the hushed, isolated countryside. They both flinched.

He reached for her hand. "Sort of quiet wouldn't you say?"

"Like a library."

"Or a morgue."

"Oh, that's perfect. Maybe I should be writing this down?"

They stood in front of the Fox cottage. He squeezed her hand, she returned the sentiment. They stepped onto the cramped porch, their footfalls on the wooden planks sharp like hammer blows that were quickly swallowed up in the silence that swelled about them.

He leaned into the wood door frame, sniffed. "Funny there's no lingering smell from the fire."

"That was last fall," she said. "Long time ago."

"Smoke from a fire never really goes away."

Before she could knock, Kevin said again, "It's so quiet. No birds, no wind in the trees. It's like there's nothing here to *make* a sound."

"Except us," Sheila said as she rapped on the door three times. After several seconds of silence, she said, "Is anyone here? Should we just go in?"

Kevin stepped off the porch, backed away until he could see to the second floor, then checked the side of house. Two windows upstairs, two on the first floor. They mirrored the gray sky, squares of blank slate. "I don't see any movement from upstairs. Knock again..."

"Never mind. It just opened."

He quickly joined her back on the porch. "Hello?" he called to the three inches of open space between the door and the frame. "Anybody home?"

Sheila whispered, "When I turned back after looking at you, it was opened."

Off in the distance, thunder rumbled like a beast searching for prey. It grew louder, closer, landing in the front yard with a low growl.

"That was...weird," Sheila said nervously. She pulled Kevin closer.

"Just rolling thunder," Kevin said, pretending he knew what it was. "Come on, let's go in." He wanted the privacy of shelter, suddenly felt they were being observed. Once inside, Sheila pushed the door closed while Kevin felt around for a light switch. It was gloomy, all shadows and blackness. His hand rasped against something sharp, brittle: torn wallpaper. By the faint illumination of outside light through the windows, he could see that the paper had come off in the palm of his hand. As their eyes adjusted to the dimness, they peered closely at the crumbling strip he held between his fingers. Portions were curled and burned, sections were mere ash that drifted away into the murky darkness of the house. He sniffed again. "Still no smell of smoke. This doesn't make any sense."

Sheila said, "Maybe it wasn't burned as badly as was reported."

"Certainly doesn't look like it," Kevin said.

Sheila moved further into the tiny entryway. To her right was a second room. Behind her, she could hear Kevin still muttering to himself as he shuffled about. The windows in the area she wandered into were partially covered by tattered drapes. The inside of the house looked like it probably did back in 1848 when the Fox's called it home. She couldn't believe *this* was to be her home for three months. She pulled the curtains aside to allow in the dismal early afternoon light. Dust erupted. She backed away, coughing and choking.

Kevin called out, "You okay?"

"Yeah, but not only did they not restore the house, they didn't even bother to clean in here. I don't get it…" She crooked her elbow over her face to protect herself from the filth. With the other hand, she pulled the drapes wider to get more sunlight into the room. Portions of the fabric tore free where she grasped them. "How old are these curtains?" she murmured as she looked out the window at the front yard.

"Kevin! The car's gone!"

They ran outside, looked up and down the street.

"Who could have taken it? We didn't even hear it start up!" Sheila said frantically.

"We don't hear anything around here, remember?" Kevin said angrily. "The sounds are all muted or something."

"Look," she said, watching the sky. The clouds continued to tighten together, grew denser in their formation, darker. "I don't feel any wind or breeze, but the clouds are moving about."

Kevin followed her upward gaze, nodded. "Yeah. Add that to the mystery of the stolen or vanished car."

The first raindrops, seconds later, were thick and cooling.

She pulled at Kevin. "Come on, let's get back inside."

"It's like hail!" he said as their footsteps thudded hollowly across the porch.

"Why's it so dark in here?" he asked, rubbing his hand against the windows to scrap off the dirt as the downpour clattered against the house. Even removing the dust and grime didn't lighten the room. The interior of the house seemed to be encased in permanent dusk or was intent on repelling light.

Sheila led him into the room she had been in earlier. The tattered drapes now met in the middle, the area was again shrouded in darkness. "I had just pulled those curtains open."

"I can fix that," Kevin said. He pulled them apart, but the space remained dim as if the windows had a murky gel over them. They watched the rain, listened as it thundered upon the rooftop.

"Hope the house doesn't leak," Sheila finally said.

"Shouldn't with the new roof they put on," Kevin said, "unless it just *looks* like a new roof but it's only the old one, patched over."

The storm blossomed in intensity, bellowed louder. Trees bent, twisted in agony, branches were given a good shaking, leaves were ripped free, swirled about like playing cards. Streaks of lightening cut through the darkness. Kevin put his arm around Sheila. She was tense, nervous.

"It's just a storm," he said gently. "Don't be scared."

"I'm not scared," she replied, kicking his shoe.

"Of course you're not. Let's try again to see if we can get some lights on. There must be a light switch around here somewhere." There wasn't.

Back in the entryway, they could make out a narrow staircase in front of them that led up into blackness. They looked out the narrow windows on either side of the front door, hoping to find the Volvo once again parked in front of the cottage. But the shadowy, storm-swept street was an empty battle zone of driving wind and rain. Tree branches were down, smaller ones were twisting and rolling about like the thin, spiky and dangerous limbs of gigantic insects. There was an alien, foreign appearance to what was going on outside. Sheila and Kevin both backed away from the window at the same time.

To their right was the tiny kitchen. They searched about in the shadows, opening drawers, cupboards until they found some candles and matches. Soon they were huddled around a small circle of illumination, flickering colors that tended more toward cerulean than yellow or orange.

"That's better," Kevin said. "I guess." He studied the flame. "Must be very old wicks, that's why they are burning bluish."

"You know that how?"

Kevin grinned sheepishly, shrugged.

Sheila sighed. "Anyway, now we have all the comforts of home."

"I guess it's too much to expect a working telephone in here…"

"Oh no. Where's your cell phone?"

"In the car," Kevin said. "Yours?"

"In the dashboard of your car."

"Oops," Kevin said. "You know, I don't understand why Edith and Vanya wanted us to arrive by one, and then they are not even here to meet us."

"Maybe they wanted us here in time for the storm?" Sheila kidded. "You have to admit, it kicked in pretty quickly after we arrived." The candlelight flickered dangerously. They each cupped their hands around the flames.

"Did you notice if there was anything to eat?" Kevin asked. "They did offer us lunch but haven't come through."

The small ice box was empty. In the far corner, shrouded by shadows, was a pantry door. Sheila opened it, peered inside. "Empty."

Tree branches suddenly and loudly raked insistently against a small kitchen window. They both jumped.

"Nowhere to go but up," Kevin said when they had recovered from the jolt. "Let's see what's upstairs."

CHAPTER 44.

They started up the wooden stairs, each of them holding a candle. Their wavering purple lights barely penetrated the heavy gloom. The wall was to Kevin's left, the bannister was on Sheila's right. There was an ancient, threadbare carpet on the steps; it barely cushioned their hesitant footfalls. *Shuffle…Thud… Shuffle…Thud… Shuffle…Thud…*

Kevin's candle lit up an old, oval-framed photograph of three girls from the mid-1800s. He moved his light closer to the wall. "Are those the Fox sisters?" he asked after a moment. Sheila examined the figures who gazed solemnly at her.

After a moment she said, "That's them. The one on the left is Maggie, and that's Katie in the middle. But I don't know who the third woman is."

"I thought you were an expert on this stuff?"

"Not really. Everything they sent me, all the background stuff they supposedly passed along, Gerald read it over. He didn't share it with me, said it would be better for the story if I discovered it as I went along. I barely had time to do any background on Derek and Edith, let alone the Fox sisters. Just what I found on Google."

They continued, their candles bobbing circles of bluish light in the blackness, their footsteps scraping up the old wooden steps. They reached a tiny landing part way up.

But from the ground floor, a slow, regular tread continued.

"Shh! What's that?" Kevin said, turning quickly. His faint candlelight didn't provide much illumination. Sheila clutched his arm. Something creaked. He took a step back down the stairs, lowered his candle, peered into the darkness below them.

"Who's there?" he demanded.

A shoe scratched the wooden step, the footstep hesitated, then was still.

Sheila tightened her hold on Kevin. Someone or something was slowing tracking them up the stairs. Nervous, Kevin's hands were sweaty; the candle could slip from his grasp if he wasn't careful. Sheila's steel-like clamp on his arm wasn't helping him retain his grip. He wanted to whisper to her to ease up a bit, but he didn't want to look away from whatever he couldn't see in the darkness below. He managed to carefully back up until he was once again on the small landing with Sheila. The combined glow of their blue-tinted candlelight barely reached halfway down to the first floor. Kevin wanted to see more, but he didn't want to walk down the steps into the thick shadows.

The storm had eased off a great deal, but the rain continued to patter on the roof. The wind rattled, scraped branches against the house. Kevin and

Sheila blocked out all noise except for whatever was on the stairs below. Seconds passed. Neither of them moved. Their ears were tightly tuned for any approaching sound from the blackness down in front of them.

Their breathing gradually returned to normal. Their arms were tired from holding up the candles. Sheila's hand cramped from gripping Kevin so tightly.

"Why don't we continue upstairs?" Sheila finally whispered. "Whatever it was, maybe it's gone."

"Or just…waiting," Kevin answered. He didn't want to admit that he was afraid of turning his back on whatever had been stalking them. Sheila tugged on his arm. Reluctantly, Kevin turned, they maneuvered past the cramped landing, started up the stairs.

In front of them, advancing swiftly: *Thud.. Thud…Thud…*

Sheila screamed. She backed into Kevin, he dropped his candle. The flame went dark. They had only Sheila's meek, flickering blue light surrounding them.

"Something touched my foot!" she said, her voice tight, panicky. Kevin took her candle from her trembling hand, lowered it until he found his on the floor, relit it. By the brighter illumination, he knelt down to see what had touched her. He saw it, reached for it, stood up. "This is what you felt."

She took the object cautiously as if it were a trap that was about to spring open. It was a child's ball. They examined it by the twitching flames. It was about eight inches in diameter, filthy with age, dust, grime. They peered at the toy by the faint glow of light they shared, turning it over, examining it for what, they had no idea. Sheila carefully put it down on the tiny window sill on the landing, making sure it was secure, wouldn't fall off.

"It rolled down to us from upstairs," she whispered. "What made that happen?"

"Maybe it just got caught in a breeze or something," Kevin said quietly, "and bounced down the steps."

"Or maybe there's someone upstairs."

He thought about it. "Let's keep going. We haven't heard anyone on the second floor, but we think we heard something on the stairs following us up."

They held their candles high. Once they were on the second floor, their lights illuminated a short hallway with three closed doors. The floorboards squeaked and creaked as they made their way down the passage. One door opened to a storeroom, the other to a small room with twin beds, the last to a master bedroom. They checked under the beds and in any places to hide, found no one.

Sheila was surprised to find towels laid out in the large bedroom. She lifted them, sniffed them. No dust. "These are freshly laundered."

Kevin pulled back the bedspread, looked over the sheets. "These feel new."

"I think this is our room," Sheila said.

"But do they really expect you to live in this creepy old house for three months? No electricity or plumbing, no Wi-Fi. How are you supposed to write, with a pen and paper by candlelight?" They set their candles down on the large dresser in the corner. She opened the drawers, a hollow, raspy sound. Empty. Empty. Empty.

"If we had our luggage, we could put our clothes away," she said lightly, trying to steady her voice. "Plenty of room."

"The closet is empty, too," said Kevin. "Lots of hangers. Like the finest hotel—"

Clunk.

The heavy bedroom door had closed.

Sheila, illuminated by the two candles on the dresser, looked at Kevin. "Was that the wind? The same breeze that pushed the ball down the stairs? Go find out."

"Why me?"

"Just go!"

Kevin walked as quickly and as quietly as possible through the murky darkness to the door. He hesitated, then briskly opened it wide. It emitted a pained squeak. There was no one standing in the doorway. Relieved, he hurried back to join Sheila. It felt good to be near the light of the candles; something about the black shadows in the room bothered him.

After a moment, they watched the door slowly close. The shabby latch connected with a hard, heavy *clunk.* Louder this time, more insistent.

Kevin squeezed Sheila's hand. "The door isn't balanced, of course, it's so old. Probably warped so it swings closed all the time." He crossed back to open it again.

Sheila nodded. "That's a logical explanation." She checked out the tiny, square window that overlooked the backyard. Nature was still giving itself a pretty severe lashing; the storm was busy, its activity blocking out most of the weakened sunlight so it was like dusk. Her reflection in the opaque window was surprisingly easy to make out. The candle in her hand provided a warm, almost sensual glow. She smiled, made a face, stuck out her tongue. "What have I gotten myself into?" she muttered.

Sheila turned, watched Kevin move about the room, heard his foot connect with something. An ominous rumble as it scurried ahead of him, scooted under the bed.

"My turn to be brave," Sheila said. She got down on her knees, lifted the bedspread, lowered her candle, peered into the gloom. After a moment, she said, "Oh, shit," pulled out the child's ball. She stood, handed it to Kevin. "Logical explanation, please?"

Kevin frowned. "Same ball?"

Sheila nodded. "Explain, please. How did the ball we left on the landing below climb up the stairs, sneak into this room?"

They both looked into the dark frame of the opened door, waiting for it to close again. Sheila said, "Let's get out of here. I don't care how much they are paying me."

"But we have no car…"

"We have legs. We can walk."

"In this storm?"

After a moment, she said, "What storm?"

And then they realized the silence that encompassed them. Womb-like, it pressed in. No patter of rain, no tree branches clawing at the house, no wind seeking its way between the cracks in the foundation. They went to the bedroom window. The clouds were breaking up. The late afternoon sun, as if scrubbed clean by the storm, illuminated the area by its yellow glow, exposing trees that had been shredded and upended. The foliage looked exhausted, beaten by the storm, flung about like discarded toys.

"We can walk to the village," Sheila said excitedly. "There wasn't much there, but there's got to be a phone, and people."

They hurried out of the bedroom, bluish lights from their candles flickering wildly by the sudden movement. Down the short hallway, then down the stairs, candlelight surrounding them with a few feet of light. It lit up the photo of the Fox sisters for an instant, then the three girls were plunged back into darkness.

Before they reached the first floor, they stopped on the last step, wondering if anything still waited for them in the shadowy gloom before them.

"Okay?" Kevin asked.

"Yes. Okay."

They moved quickly across the floor. *Dashing through the snow*, came crazily to Sheila's mind. Kevin opened the front door. The clean, fresh air and strangely weak afternoon sunlight greeted them like an uneasy wall of relief. They hurried off the porch, feeling like children freed after the last day of school. They tossed their candles onto the damp lawn, heard them hiss as the wicks went dark. Once they were on the street, they clasped hands, turned as one, faced the Fox house.

After a moment, Kevin said, "Do you think all that weird stuff was our imagination, or ghosts? Or?"

"What do you mean? Or what?"

"The ball moving around, the door opening and closing, something following us up the stairs. All of it. We didn't imagine it, and I don't believe in ghosts, so maybe someone was there just trying to scare us."

"But why? And we searched, didn't find anyone."

Kevin shrugged, rubbed his eyes, "I don't know. I think it could have been rigged. After all, they want you to write a book about this place, this haunted house. Maybe they want to start things off with a bang, you know? I just hate to…"

"Jump to conclusions because we can't explain something? I agree, but I'm not doing that. They can throw all they want at us, try to scare us, but I am going to write an honest, first-hand account about all of this. I won't take it at face value or just write about what I feel or we feel or what makes my hair stand on end. This is an important assignment, and I'm going to do a great job writing about this village, this house, all that happened here."

"Hey, I'm on your side!" Kevin pulled her closed. "If anyone can figure this out, you can." He kissed her. She hugged him tightly, wouldn't let him go.

After a moment he said, "What?"

She pulled back, looked deep into his eyes as the sun shone weakly behind him.

Solemnly, she said, "What's going to happen to me when you return to the city and I'm here all alone?"

CHAPTER 45.

Kevin carried the child's ball as they started down the street.

"Why'd you bring that?" Sheila asked.

"Didn't it seem to you that it *wanted* to be taken? First it rolled down the steps from upstairs. Then, after we left it on the landing, it somehow managed to roll *up* the stairs until it was outside the bedroom door. Next thing we know, it's under the bed. Persistent little thing, right?"

The rustic avenue was pitted with puddles of water. Other than their footfalls on the cracked and uneven sidewalk, the only sounds were the leftover smatterings of raindrops splattering from the trees, bushes, telephone poles; their irregular *drip-plops* sounded like someone hungrily smacking their lips in anticipation of a meal. The afternoon sky remained ashen and dull. The sun strained with all its might, but it remained bleak outside, as if the area was covered in a dirty dome that was almost impenetrable to light. A stillness hovered about the surrounding area; the countryside might as well have been holding its breath. They passed small homes that were overgrown with shrubs and weeds. Trees pressed down hard. Windows were caked with grime, they stared blankly at Sheila and Kevin.

Then, a voice, young, with a sing-song lilt to it. They looked at the disheveled house from where the sound had come. The front yard was a ruin of twisted grass, the large picture window was shattered.

"…find it!" The words carried easily in the hushed atmosphere. They stepped closer, peered through the overgrowth, saw a boy of about four or five. He was bent at the waist, frantically searching the tall weeds, muttering to himself. He stomped about the yard in a nervous panic. He was wearing a blue and red checkered plaid shirt that was rolled to his elbows, black jeans, black tennis shoes. His brown hair was heavily slicked down, didn't budge an inch.

"Find it! Find it! Find it!" he cried out, his voice shrill, a hysterical edge to it.

Hidden by the tall, unruly shrubs, Kevin and Sheila continued to watch.

"You *know* we need her. Find. It."

The ominous tone sent a chill swiftly down Sheila's back. How could such a young boy possess so dangerous and commanding a presence? And to whom was he speaking?

"Do you think he's looking for this?" Kevin hissed in her ear, holding up the ball.

"But it's so old," she answered. "Hasn't been touched in a long time."

The boy's search took on a wider and wider area of the yard. He continued to chide someone out of their line of vision. Curious, Sheila and Kevin pressed in nearer.

When they finally caught sight of him, he was close to the rear of the house, standing defiantly in front of a shape out of their range of sight.

"If you're working with that awful man…," he said menacingly. He waited for a response. When none came, he turned around, faced Kevin and Sheila. He didn't see them even though he was headed right in their direction. They were surprised by the boy's expression. They expected to see a tear-stained face, red with childish fury, a furrowed brow, pouty lips, snot nosed. Instead, his green eyes were bright with determination, his mouth was set in in a grim expression of concentrated anger.

He kicked his way through some broken branches. Water from a hidden puddle exploded around him. He yanked a plank free from the old house; it cracked loose like a shot fired. He held it high. It was sturdy, about the size of a tire iron, but he had no trouble maneuvering it about. He used it like a sword, slashing it through the air a few times, getting familiar with the weight of it. After several stabbing motions, he seemed satisfied. He turned and hurried back to the corner of the house.

It wasn't until then that Sheila and Kevin crept in past the shrubs, were able to see who he had been speaking to.

Someone slouched in a wheelchair.

"You know where it is. I want it, now!" the boy shouted. He darted forward until he was behind the figure. He raised the tree branch high over his head. Then, before Kevin or Sheila could call out, he smashed it down on the disabled person.

Kevin immediately crashed through the overgrowth. "Stop it! Stop it right now!"

Startled, the boy turned. The thick branch remained upraised. *How can he lift that?* Sheila wondered as she followed Kevin briskly across the yard.

"*You've* got it!" the boy cried, delighted. He dropped the branch, ran to Kevin, who quickly hid the ball behind his back. The child's face immediately transformed into malevolent rage, so hateful that Kevin and Sheila stepped back.

"I want the ball! It's *mine*!" The boy moved toward them. "Give it to me!"

He sprang at Kevin's legs, forcing him to the ground. The ball rolled into the bushes. Sheila went after it while the child and Kevin struggled. Kevin easily pinned the boy, but he didn't give up, continued to thrash about, spitting, biting, cursing. His rapid, twisted movements made it seem at times that he had too many arms or legs. Kevin would later tell Sheila that he didn't feel like he was wresting a child, it was more like some larger, unseen force had joined them.

Sheila grabbed the boy's legs. She was slapped across the face. The force knocked her back. *How'd that happen?* she wondered, rubbing her jaw. She heard a sharp crack of a sound. Out of the corner of her eyes, Kevin grunted, fell hard to the ground. The child was standing over him, the branch in hand. Sheila scrambled toward him. He saw her, kicked out hard, connecting with her shoulder. She cried out in pain.

Enraged, Kevin rose up, slammed his fist into the boy's face. He went limp, lost consciousness immediately. Blood was flowing, the nose had been smashed flat. A dark bruise was already coloring most of his face as the swelling began. Sheila joined Kevin as they looked at the child, both of them panting, hearts pounding hard.

"Are you…okay?" she asked, her voice trembling. Kevin grimaced and shook his head.

"Something…" he said, trying to reach around. He pulled up his shirt, exposing his back.

"Oh, my God, Kevin! There are bite marks all over your back. There must be a dozen of them." She looked down with disgust at the boy. "You little shit!"

"He didn't do it," Kevin said quietly. "I had him pinned. Something else climbed on my back. I could feel the weight. There were hands or talons or something. It was strong. It held on, I couldn't shake it." He spat onto the grass. "Also, it spoke. Or at least I heard someone whisper in my ear."

"Whisper what?"

"I think I heard a voice say, '*Soon, you'll be mine.*'"

She looked at him, didn't know what to say, couldn't think of a response. "Whose voice?" she finally asked.

He shook his head. "I might have just imagined it. There was so much going on, there *is* so much going on."

They leaned against one another in the yard, calming down.

"Where's his damn ball?" Kevin asked.

"Right here. I wish we knew what was so special about it."

"Hello?" a friendly, female voice called from the other side of the hedges. "Is someone there?"

"Yes!" they cried out, pushed their way through the bushes to the front yard.

An attractive blonde woman was standing on the grass with a baby stroller in front of her.

"Sheila and Kevin, I'm so sorry for the delay in welcoming you," she said. "I'm Vanya Avery." She looked at their disheveled appearance, the mud on their hands and faces, their torn clothing. "What happened? Why aren't you at the Fox house? I was looking for you. Where'd you find that ball?"

"There was a boy," Kevin started to explain, then abruptly cried out, "My God, the person in the wheelchair!" He and Sheila rushed over, found the figure slumped to one side. It was a man. They turned away in shock, both loathed to look too closely at the disfigured man. The only sound that issued from the figure was the gasp of the portable respirator that was hooked to the back of the wheelchair. The blow from the tree branch had grazed his forehead, but it was what little that remained of his body that horrified them.

Vanya had followed them over, watched them calmly.

"What…happened to him?" Sheila could barely get the words out.

"We've got to get him to a doctor!"

"Derek doesn't need a doctor. He was being cared for by Roland. Have you seen him?"

"Who's Roland?" Kevin asked. "Was he that—"

"My nephew. He's five and his mother, Edith, had left Derek with Roland. They love to spend time together and—"

Sheila said, "He was beating that poor man!"

Kevin told Vanya about the fight that ensued, led her to where he had knocked Roland out. The boy was gone. The only evidence of the scuffle was the disturbed area of dirt, the damage done to the shrubs as they had fought one another.

"I broke his nose," Kevin admitted, "but his behavior, his cruelty to that man—"

"Roland has great resilience. He'll be fine."

Kevin and Sheila were surprised by Vanya's unconcerned reaction to the news about the beating of her nephew. The sound of Derek's respirator—*hiss, clink, hiss, clink*—broke into their conversation. Sheila and Kevin knelt down to examine him.

"He needs a doctor," Kevin said again over his shoulder.

"We don't use physicians here. We take care of our own."

"No, he really *needs* a doctor," Sheila insisted, standing, facing Vanya. "And we need our car back, too."

"You don't need your car, nor do you need to worry about Derek or anything else while you're with us," Vanya said lightheartedly. "First of all, there's nowhere to go, nowhere to *be*, so having a car is pointless. And secondly, we're paying you a good deal of money for the next three months. The contracts are signed, the funds are deposited."

"And we need a cell phone," Sheila said quickly, ignoring all Vanya had said, pushing past it. "Ours were in the car. We have to call—"

"No cell towers here, no service," Vanya said.

"Then a landline?"

Vanya shook her head, "Sorry, no working phones. We don't—"

"But those are telephone poles!" Sheila pointed.

Vanya didn't take her eyes off Sheila. "The lines don't work. Besides, we don't need phones, Sheila. We have other ways to communicate."

"How? Banging messages on drums?" Kevin asked sourly, then thought, *Something about the woman was familiar; her mannerisms, voice…*

"No, I was going to say we have more intimate ways to interact with one another."

"Then communicate that this guy needs medical attention! And bring me back my car! I'm not part of this deal," Kevin said.

"What do you mean? Of course you are." Vanya reached into her baby carriage, pulled out a large envelope, removed a set of legal papers. She sorted through them until she found what she was looking for. "There," she said.

Kevin and Sheila scanned the paragraph of the contract that dealt with the deadline and payout schedule. A second section indicated an additional $50,000 that was payable to Kevin Jackson, identified as a research assistant.

"I never saw this before!" he said wildly.

Vanya said, "It was notarized. Perfectly legal. And binding."

Kevin's heart was pounding hard as he turned the page. He and Sheila frantically skimmed the contents. There on the bottom, below her scrawl, Kevin saw his signature. A legal, binding contract.

Vanya interrupted their examination of the papers. "Why don't we get you settled in? I need to get Margaret home, Edith will want to look after Derek, patch up Roland whenever he surfaces. I'm sure you're both hungry and tired after your trip. May I see that ball?"

"I think we'll hold on to it for now," Kevin said. "Until we have a better idea of what is going on."

Sheila had been as shocked as Kevin to see his name signed on the contract, but she was immensely and secretly relieved to know he would be with her for the time she was in Hydesville. The idea of staying alone in the strange little village was more than she could bear.

"I never signed that," Kevin managed to say, helplessly, as Vanya started down the street. They had nowhere else to go, so they followed, keeping their distance so they could speak privately.

"I don't understand Roland's age," Sheila said, "Wasn't he only born last November, so why would this five-year-old kid say that he was Roland? It's impossible."

"And why does Vanya go along with it?"

They lapsed into silence as they pushed Derek, both weary of asking questions that never had any answers. Kevin focused on Vanya, how great she looked in the tight jeans she was wearing. They embraced her long legs, rode her ass perfectly. She had wonderful hips, and a waist he would love to put his hands on. He thought he heard Sheila speaking, ignored it. All that mattered now was spending time alone with Vanya; he imagined what she looked like naked, her taunt stomach, how he would lick, suck and explore her body, working his way down as she wrapped her legs around his neck, pulling him in deeper. And he would plunge in hard, so hard for her, exploring the depths of her rich darkness. He felt his pants shrink as his dick thickened. His mind roamed free; it was like he was out on the edge of some broken wheel, flung free, beyond where he had ever imagined before. Circling and swinging back and forth, her thighs tight around his neck, like the coils and knots in a rope, tightening, a climax beginning to surge forth; he saw it all from the dizzying heights of the tall trees. Yes, the forest, the woods, the Fox Woods. That's where they'd be. And. Then. One. Last. Gasp.

Kevin squeezed the handles of the wheelchair as he came, his legs quivering. He stumbled.

"You okay?" Sheila asked.

He blinked several times, looked around, bewildered, disappointed. What was he doing here, on the sidewalk? He has been in the woods. Somewhere in the woods, high above, he had looked down, he had seen…

"Honey, are you okay?"

Sheila touched his arm. The contact brought him completely back. His hands, tight around the padded chrome of the wheelchair handles, ached from gripping so hard. Half a block in front of them, Vanya was pushing her carriage, Sheila was on his right. He had gone away somewhere, a fugue state, some sexual fantasy—or was it real at some point? Real enough that—

His pants were moist, sticky. *What the hell?*

"Hey! Earth to Kevin! Tune in. You're scaring me. What's going on? Where are you?"

"Everything all right back there?" Vanya called out. She stopped, turned to face them.

Kevin said to Sheila, "Just now I…I had some weird dream or vision. I was in the woods, high above. I was looking down…" He realized he couldn't tell her how the dream had ended, couldn't tell her about the erotic fantasy he had had about Vanya.

"Coming?" Vanya called out. All at once it was clear to him what was familiar about her. Vanya's *voice*. When he had been wrestling with Roland, there had been a voice in his ear, hot, seductive, powerful.

Vanya's words, a promise sworn to him: *Soon, you'll be mine.*

CHAPTER 46.

ere we are!" Vanya announced two blocks later. When they caught up with her, they were in front of a modestly decorated two-story home set back from the street. It was by far the best-looking property in the drab village of Hydesville; it was the only dwelling that had a sense of life about it. Yellow with brown trim, the front yard was landscaped with a variety of shrubs and bushes, a healthy green lawn appeared to be recently mown. There was a shiny clean wheelchair ramp that led to the front entrance. It gleamed and sparkled in the sunlight.

"Edith?" Vanya called out. "We're home. And we have company." She lifted the baby from the carriage. "This is Margaret." The newborn had her mother's bright green eyes, golden hair. Sleepy-eyed, she stared back intently at Kevin and Sheila. No curiosity, just observed them. She turned abruptly to face Vanya.

"Mama, where's Roland?"

Sheila didn't believe what she heard; Margaret was no more than a month old, but she spoke.

"Roland was playing rough with Kevin," Vanya answered calmly. "Kevin thinks he might have hurt Roland." Margaret turned her little, fragile head to Kevin. She opened her eyes wide, glared at him. Vanya patted her daughter's head. "There, there, sweetness. Roland is okay. He's gone off to heal." She turned to Sheila. "She's very protective of her older cousin."

"How…can she speak?" Sheila asked, stunned. She peered closer, certain it was a trick.

"It's a prank," Kevin said doubtfully; he had seen the baby speak, but it was impossible.

"Of course she talks. She's a union child. You do *remember*…what a union child is, don't you?" Vanya's eyes glittered at them, a sudden kaleidoscope of bursting emerald colors.

Then, suddenly, it was as if a dam broke. Everything came rushing back to them, a roar of memories. They each knew the other was experiencing the same information overload, facts overflowing, flooding and soaking them with returning recollections, insights, as if gallons of water were being poured into a small tumbler. They recalled that peculiar morning in July when they found themselves on Park Avenue after meeting Vanya, Edith and Roland, standing on the sidewalk with no idea how they had got there, or why.

Eyes wide, Kevin said, "This isn't the first time. We've met you before!"

"At Edith's apartment!" Sheila said, her heartbeat accelerated. "Roland was there, too!"

Vanya and Margaret watched them with interest as they struggled to process what was occurring.

Kevin stammered, "What happened to us? Why…did we lose these memories?

"Because neither of you would have been willing to come here if you knew everything at once," Vanya said. She smiled. "I've done this before, learned that small increments of knowledge work best. Little bites. A trail of breadcrumbs to lead you here."

Sheila touched the side of her head, grabbed Kevin's arm. "The Amish man! Remember him?" She turned to Vanya. "Something about him frightened you."

Kevin's heart was racing. He sensed they needed to act quickly before their thoughts clouded over, turned to mush again. They needed to get away. "Vanya, I want my car back. We are leaving, *now*. I don't care what kind of…*mind control* you are able to perform on us, we want out of here!"

Vanya said coolly, "There is no *out,* Kevin. For you or Sheila. Hydesville is all there is. For right now, anyway."

"You can't keep us here as prisoners! People know where we are."

"And they know they won't be seeing you for three months."

"What do you mean?" Sheila asked fearfully.

"Your lives will simply go on without you. Your bills are all being paid on time, your jobs have approved your absences, your friends know of your plans, know you'll be out of touch for a while…"

Frantically, Kevin looked around, tried to figure a way out of the situation. Sheila was holding his arm with one hand, Roland's ball with the other. Vanya and the child only watched them, not moving or speaking. The only sound was the *hiss, clink* from Derek's respirator.

"This is *home*," Vanya said after several seconds, sensing they had given up. "This is our little corner of the universe. As far as we're concerned, Hydesville is all that matters. For all of us." She gave Margaret an affectionate squeeze.

"Now, enough talking," Vanya said briskly. "Let's go inside, have our first meal together."

The house was sparsely furnished. To the right of the entry way was a small living room that contained a sofa, two upright chairs. No pictures on the walls, no knick-knacks, decorative items, photos or personal artifacts. It reminded Sheila of a motel unit; functional, nothing more.

Vanya said, "Make yourselves at home. I'm going to put Margaret down for her nap. Edith?"

"Right here. Hello!" she said brightly, appearing seemingly out of nowhere, materializing in the passage between the living room and hallway. "Vanya said you were here. How nice to see you both again."

"We were just leaving," Kevin said, reaching for Sheila's hand.

"No! Don't let them go, Mama!" Roland had appeared behind his mother. Sheila and Kevin stared at him. He was fully recovered from his violent wrestling match; his face and nose showed no evidence of his scuffle with Kevin. No bruises, puffiness or redness.

Alarmed, Sheila wondered, *Dear God, has he aged, grown even more?*

He stepped in front of Edith. She rested her hands on his shoulders, smiled proudly at her son. "I want my ball," he demanded.

He's definitely older, Sheila thought, amazed at the realization. *He's taller by a few inches, thicker, a growing boy...*

"Why is the ball so important to you?" she managed to ask.

"It was a gift that needs to be opened," Edith said quickly, before he could respond.

Kevin directed his request at the boy. "Give me my car back."

"But if I do, you'll try to leave us," Roland said simply. He looked up at his mother. "What if they go away? What happens then?"

Edith patted him, comforting him. "Don't worry, dear. They'll stay."

"You know, the Amish man is here," Sheila suddenly said. Kevin glanced at her. "On the way over, we saw him hiding in the bushes of one of the homes."

Edith and Roland stiffened; Sheila thought she heard tiny gasps from them.

Kevin picked up on Sheila's story. "Seems like wherever we go, he follows. So, if we leave here, he'll go with us, back to Manhattan. Wouldn't you rather have him far away from you?"

Roland started to speak. His mother's hands tightened on his shoulders, silencing him. He winced, frowned.

Soon he won't be so easily quieted, Sheila observed. The thought of an uncontrollable, full-grown Roland David was unsettling.

Kevin held the ball in front of him. Roland's eyes lit up. Although still grimy, the toy rapidly changed when it was displayed for them all to see. A dull gleam materialized as if a light had been turned on inside, weakly illuminating the layers of filth.

Kevin's hand trembled but he continued to grasp the ball as they all looked at it with fascination. Roland's mouth opened in awe as his hands reached out. He took a step toward Kevin. He was mesmerized by the object that had taken on a life of its own.

Edith had the converse reaction. Her eyes flickered with awareness, recognition, but also wariness. Sheila sensed that if the woman could, she'd flee the room, the village. *Slave, not servant,* Sheila thought idly. It was puzzling why the dull glow of the ball provoked such dissimilar responses. *Whatever that ball is, Roland should never have access to it,* she thought.

The boy shuffled toward Kevin, a rapt expression on his face, his eyes wide with desire, his hands reaching eagerly. "Lee…Ahh," he said breathlessly. "Lee…Ahh," his voice deep, with a rich baritone quality. Almost a man's voice. The boy had fallen into a trance. Behind him, Edith clutched her hands to her chest; Sheila saw she was trembling. Kevin nervously stepped back from the approaching child.

Sheila looked around for a way of escape. She glanced out the living room window, was startled at what she saw. Kevin's Volvo sat parked in front of the house. She grabbed his hand, they dashed out of the room. Once outside, Kevin groped in his pocket for the keys, his hands shaking in panic. Roland's footfalls pursued them. Edith wasn't with him. Vanya was nowhere in sight.

The car rumbled to life, lurched away from the house. In the rearview mirror, Roland stood in the middle of the street, hands as fists, enraged. The Volvo raced back through the town. The square black windows of the old homes watched dully as the car sped past. The sky remained slate-gray; the heavens over Hydesville were perpetually dreary, unnatural silence permanently blanketed the area.

Kevin pushed the buttons to get the navigation system going. Sheila grabbed their phones.

"Fuck! They are both dead!"

"We can charge them from the car, hook one of them up," Kevin said, waiting for the map to materialize on the screen.

"They aren't connecting," Sheila said. Both phones remained dead. The navigation screen was simply an endless loop of flickering waves.

"What about the email directions we used to get up here?" Sheila dug through the glove compartment, found the pages, looked at them.

"What?" Kevin asked. "What's wrong?"

Sheila had bowed her head, closed her eyes, exhausted. She told him that each page now only showed faded, undecipherable directions. All the twisted back roads, confusing exits, entrance routes and turns they had so carefully navigated earlier that day would now have to be executed without the notes, only from memory.

"Okay," Kevin said, pounding the steering wheel with the palms of his hands. "Okay, okay, okay. We can *do* this!" He glanced at the gas gauge. "Little over half a tank, enough to get us on our way, get us out of the area. Let's remember how we got here. I think before we came over this hill, we arrived from...from that direction. Right?"

Sheila glanced where he was pointing, nodded. They turned, sped along the road, consulted one another, made another turn. At a split in the road, they stopped the car, discussed options, agreed on which direction. It went on like that for an hour. Slow, hesitant progress. They breathed a bit easier with each mile put between them and Hydesville.

After another twenty minutes had passed, Kevin switched on the headlights, wondered why they were still on the narrow, twisty rural roads. "I thought by now we'd be on the main thoroughfares." He tried to keep the uncertainty out of his voice.

"I know, I don't remember being on these backroads for so long. Do you think we made a wrong turn somewhere?"

By seven-thirty, it was nearly dark outside. The late summer sun was fading even faster than usual. The gas tank was almost on Empty. Kevin chose not to look at it, tried to push down and away the anxiousness that fluttered about his stomach; it was like a living thing seeking a place to settle in for the night. They drove in silence. The headlights cut through the blackness in front of them. No cars passed. No lights anywhere along the road. They were alone in their own little universe. Between them in the car, the ball continued its faint, steady illumination.

Sheila glanced down at the toy. "Is it brighter? Or does it just seem that way since it's so dark around us?"

Kevin agreed with her, thought the yellow-green glow had enough power to provide an otherworldly luminosity in the car, strong enough to show the tense anxiety lined in Sheila's face. He reached over, took her hand. They had tried the radio several times but were unable to snag any signals. They continued barreling through the pitch black, Kevin driving as fast as he could.

It was eight-thirty when the car began to sputter, choke. The red Low Fuel light had begun blinking fifteen minutes earlier. The engine groaned a bit. They had just reached the top of an incline on a narrow lane. They were able to coast gently down the hill. The tires crackled and crunched on the uneven dirt road. Kevin turned the wheels to the right so they were on the shoulder. The Volvo rolled to a stop, the engine ticked a few moments, then was silent.

He turned off the headlights. The glowing ball was their only source of light.

He peered into the darkness. "See anything outside your window?"

She strained, looking into the night. *Did* she see something? A faint square of blue-yellow light behind a window? She mentioned it to Kevin, he squinted, agreed, grabbed the flashlight out of the glove compartment. They exited the car. He aimed the beam of light around to get their bearings.

A tree towered in front of them.

Then, the edge of a cracked, blistered old sidewalk came into view.

"A sidewalk in the middle of these backroads?" Kevin muttered.

Sheila suddenly moaned. "Oh, no..." She slumped against him.

"What?!"

"I know where we are..." Even in the deep black night, she knew. It was a familiar place. Her words were garbled, caught in her throat. The darkness bore down on them. Unable to speak because she didn't want to say the words, she took the flashlight from Kevin, pointed it in front of them. She raised the beam.

It flashed off one of the grimy, dimly lit windows of the Fox house.

434

CHAPTER 47.

They turned their backs on the cottage, hurriedly crunched their way across the road they had just crossed, the flashlight in Sheila's hand flailing its light all over the night as they ran.

"Where's the car?" she asked frantically. They hunted up and down where they had left it, but after a few moments, knew it was gone, vanished again, along with their dead cell phones and the glowing ball that Roland was so desperate for.

It started to rain.

"Of course," Kevin said, defeated. "It *wants* us to go in the house. It's the only shelter around here."

They hurried back over the now-muddy road, followed the glow emanating from the rooms of the house until they found their footing on the Fox porch. Once they were inside, they took off their jackets to dry by the fire. Candles were lit in the parlor; it had been their odd, flickering yellow-blue glow that Sheila had seen from the car.

"Who lit these?" she asked. "And the fire? Who knew we were coming?"

In the kitchen, more wicks were burning. A pot of stew was simmering on the wood stove, bread was on the counter along with plates, utensils, an opened bottle of wine. Wearily, they set about eating and drinking, didn't comment on the fact that the food had no flavor. It wasn't bad tasting; it was simply tasteless. But the provisions did stop the gnawing hunger.

When they finished, Kevin put out the fire. They clomped upstairs to bed. They shed their clothes, washed their faces by candlelight in the basin of water that had been provided by their unseen hosts. Cleansing the stress from the day settled them both a little. They climbed into bed, blew out the candles, held one another.

Eventually, they slept, their first night in Hydesville.

###

Kevin opened his eyes to gray morning light. He glanced at his watch: Just before seven. He nudged his thoughts, wanted to see if his memories were still intact. He knew at once where he was, what had happened the previous day, every impossible and nightmarish event. Next to him, Sheila continued to sleep, yet there was a tautness about her face, a grimness that revealed she wasn't at rest.

She stirred, murmured something, opened her eyes. Looked around, turned to him. "I remember everything. Do you?"

He nodded. They got up, poured water from the jug on the counter into the basin, washed up as best they could. Sheila started to pull on her top from yesterday.

"No need to wear that again," Kevin said quietly, pointing at the closet. All their clothes had been transported from their suitcases in the car to their room where they were now neatly hung. Sheila opened the dresser drawers. Each was filled with their undergarments, t-shirts, everything neatly folded, stacked. The thought that someone else's hands had touched her clothes bothered her more than the mystery of how they had appeared in their room.

"No wonder Derek tried to burn down this house," she said. "This is enough to drive anyone crazy."

"Who knows what state of mind we'll be in after three months."

"That's a pleasant thought."

"Here's another one," Kevin said. "Since they've taken the car, Roland now has his ball. Isn't that what the Amish man warned us against, didn't he say 'don't let the children get the ball.'"

"I wonder if that means they will leave us alone now?"

"Doubt it. They are after something more. We have to find out what it is and put an end to it."

"Like Derek tried to put an end to it?" Sheila asked. "We know how successful he was."

Downstairs, breakfast was ready for them: coffee, oatmeal, bread and jam, all as tasteless yet filling as the previous nights' dinner. They had no idea who their unseen host was. When they finished eating, they stepped out on the front porch. The skies were dark, brooding; the heavens angry.

After a moment, Sheila said, "Another beautiful day in Hydesville. What do we do next?"

"As your paid assistant, I think we should get to work, start the research, figure out what's going on."

"Okay, then let's find a library."

They were surprised the front door to the old building was unlocked.

"Hello?" they called out, their voices landing flat in the obviously deserted library. Pale light tried to push its way through the long, tall windows. Everywhere there was filth, long abandoned cobwebs. The air was stale with the smell of ancient paper and dust. Disinterest and neglect hovered over the space, along with a profound silence, the kind a stern librarian would relish. Their footsteps creaked and squealed on the aged, uneven wood floors as they explored.

Rows of shelves lined up on either side of them. In the back, racks of newspapers were mounted on poles like flags to discourage theft, glass cases contained old manuscripts. To the right were a number of tables, chairs, a librarian's check-out counter.

Kevin asked if Sheila had any idea what they were looking for.

"A light switch, to begin with," she said.

"Really? I doubt it." He shuffled about the dim area for a moment. Sheila heard a click. The overhead lights blinked on.

"Wow, electricity. You were right." Kevin said. "I vote we sleep here tonight."

"Maybe they have Wi-Fi, too," Sheila kidded.

"And computers, landlines," Kevin said. "Come on, let's stay focused. We're here to research, so let's search."

They made their way to the rear of the library. A small office space in the back had the words *Hydesville Historical Archives* stenciled on it. Along one wall were several ledges crammed with yellowed manuscripts that were slumped tiredly against one another. Framed and faded city maps were attached to a bulletin board. A large oak desk in the middle of the room was piled with more papers, old books and photographs, and a thick white tome with *Holy Bible* engraved in gold letters on its cover. A portion of the ceiling had collapsed, so much of the room was littered with debris.

"I'll check the shelves if you want to sort through this pile on the desk," Kevin said. He started to search through the documents, almost immediately called out, "Bingo!" He held out a book to Sheila. "Your research assistant has done it again. I present to you the diary of Margaret Fox!"

"Maggie and Katie Fox's mother?" She snatched the book, excitedly started to thumb through it.

"Odd that it was sitting there, right on top," Kevin said as he peered over her shoulder. "Maybe it found me."

The faded ink on the dried-out pages was a challenge to read, but the handwriting itself was composed by someone with excellent penmanship. They spent the next several minutes reading aloud how the Fox sisters first experienced the ghostly rappings, with Margaret communicating with it by saying, "Do as I do," and then Katie declaring, "It can see as well as hear!" When they finished, Sheila closed the diary. "Creepy, huh?" She kissed Kevin on the cheek. "This diary is a real find. Thank you, assistant. Now, back to work!"

They each returned to their areas of exploration. Sheila pulled a stack of ancient photographs close; they were eerie, the old, stoic faces gazed back at her, unblinking. *And be grateful for that*, she mused, *because if they did blink, you'd scream.* "Didn't anyone ever smile in the olden days?" she muttered as she sorted through the images. Behind her, Kevin coughed, sneezed, cleared his throat as he stirred up dust and grime, searching through the shelves.

Soon, Sheila was lost in her efforts. The only sound she was aware of was the paper rustle of the thick cardboard-mounted photographs she was sorting through. She was perspiring lightly in the stuffy room; there was no ventilation, no air ducts or windows.

Kevin had ceased from his coughs and throat clearing. Out of the corner of her eye, Sheila saw him hunched over the table.

"Find anything?" she asked, still intent on the prints in front of her. No response, not even one of his indifferent grunts. She continued to check the photos. Then, all at once, she felt a tingling on the back of her neck, as if a tiny insect was exploring, looking for a place to bite. She shivered, shook her head, brushed at her collar.

Nothing there.

"Kevin? Any luck?"

She turned around. He wasn't there. In the instant she moved, whatever the shape was that she thought was her boyfriend had vanished. Kevin was sitting against the far wall of the room, comfortably seated in a chair, thumbing through a tattered scrapbook. She started to say something to him, then shook her head. *Get a grip. You're tired, you're freaked out, you're seeing things. Just focus on the task at hand.*

Two stacks of photographs remained. Soon she was back in the groove. Several minutes passed. Then, the shape materialized again. This time, to her left. She didn't turn her head, continued to look at the pictures, swallowed hard. There was definitely something there, a figure sitting, wrapped in a black shroud. Sweat trickled down Sheila's face, stung her eyes. She was afraid to wipe it away, didn't want to startle the thing, didn't want it to move, didn't want it to come any closer.

This is ridiculous, she chided herself. She kept her head down, managed to sneak a look to her left, barely tilted her head. Whatever it was, it was still there, maybe even nearer. She was certain that if she turned suddenly, she'd catch it in full view an instant before it would vanish. And she really didn't want to see it, only wanted it to go away.

She pulled the last stack of photographs toward her just as a second dark shape appeared to her right. She was surrounded now, one on either side. She almost tore a brittle photo in half, her fingers where shaking so much. The figure on her left shifted slightly. Did she also hear it? The rustle of…of what? Clothing? Was there someone or something actually there, a physical presence? Which one should she look at first? Should she call out to Kevin? Maybe that would help break the spell or would he only think she was losing it if there was nothing there? *And you know there's nothing there,* she told herself. *You know it's just your imagination freaking out on you.*

The thing to her right moved, seemed to increase in size as if it was standing up. It was approaching her. Desperate to look, but terrified at what she might see, Sheila forced herself to continue sorting through the photographs. *When I'm finished looking at the last picture, I'll turn and check out both sides. There will nothing there.* It was almost like a nerve wracking game to her, pretending to pay no attention to whatever apparitions had gathered on either side of her.

The shape on her left rustled again. What was Kevin doing? Where was he? Did he see the things but was too frightened to warn her? Only a handful of images were left to sort through. All she wanted to do was finish, bolt off the chair, dive into Kevin's arms. Why wasn't he saying anything? Was the scrapbook he had been reading *that* interesting?

Three pictures left.

Sheila willed herself to comprehend the image in front of her, restrain her hand from shaking so she could see clearly. A woman in a rowboat, staring at the camera, not smiling. *Of course, no one smiled back then.* Next, a couple in front of a house. Looked like the 1920s based on the clothing, the woman dressed like a flapper, the man in a single-breasted, slim fitting suit and hat. *Was he smiling?* Sheila peered closer. *Yes! We have a winner; the man was actually grinning. Good for you.*

Trembling, she reached for the last photograph. It had been enlarged, printed on heavier stock. She lifted it to exam closer. At last, something was familiar. Just as she started to inspect it, two heavy, frigid female hands, one on either side of her, suddenly touched her wrists.

CHAPTER 48.

Sheila screamed, dropped the photo.

Even after her shout, the two ghostly hands remained. She could feel their weight as they each cupped the top of her wrists with their palms. Female hands, soft, fleshy, freezing, not clammy, more like marble, like flesh *made* of marble. Living statues that had come to life. There was a pressure to them, a strength, a dimension.

I can feel them, she thought madly during the split seconds of contact. *Why hadn't Kevin come running? Hadn't he heard me shriek?*

All these observations roared through her like the river of blood that was pounding in her mind. The two hands had touched her at exactly the same time, as if letting her know that yes, they were real, they were both with her in that room, and the large photograph she had been holding was the one they wanted her to look at carefully.

"Kevin!" she finally managed to cry, backing away from the table, the hands sliding from her, fading, gone. She looked frantically at both sides of the room. No female apparitions were there.

"Sheila?" Kevin's voice, from the other room, followed by the squeak of a chair, his rushing footsteps, his appearance in front of her, his eyes wide, questioning, concerned. "What is it? Are you okay?" She fell into his arms, almost toppling him over. She kept pushing against him until they were out of the small room.

"Where were you?" she finally demanded.

"It was so warm and stuffy in there, I went out to the main library to get some air. I told you…"

"I never heard you."

He looked closely at her. "What happened?"

Still in shock, she allowed him to lead her over to one of the study tables. Once they sat down, she told him what had happened.

When she finished, he asked, "Where's the picture you dropped?"

"It must still be on the floor; I think it fell off the table. But I'm not going in there."

"Don't worry, allow your assistant to fetch it."

Kevin hurried off. Sheila leaned back in the chair, hugged herself, examined the tops of her hands where the women had touched her, rubbed them furiously. Kevin returned, sat down at the desk. Together, they looked at the photo of the three figures. "This is the same one we saw on the staircase landing in the Fox cottage, isn't it?" Kevin asked.

Faded writing indicated the image was from 1852. It depicted three relaxed, composed subjects and was captioned as Maggie, Katie and Leah Fox. Maggie's expression was sophisticated yet withdrawn, Katie's was straightforward, haunting in its intensity, while Leah's wry hint of a smile almost made it appear that she was mocking her sisters and whomever looked at the photograph.

Now that Sheila had a chance to study it more closely, she said, "Yes, it's the same photo and I think the two apparitions I saw were Maggie and Katie." She pointed to the long black dresses the women were wearing. "When they touched me—if it was them—I saw the sleeves of their dresses, and it matched what they are wearing here in this photo. I'm sure it was them." She rubbed the tops her hands again, then tapped her finger on the third woman in the portrait.

"How do you know it wasn't Leah, why only the other two sisters?"

A heavy thud from the archive room.

"Sounds like a book fell from a shelf."

Immediately, Sheila said, "I'm not going in there. That's what assistants are for."

Kevin said, "I figured as much. Seems like this library is doing all the research for us. We just sit here, it tosses photos and books at us."

He squared his shoulders, started toward the room. He peered in, spotted a book on the floor. He would have tripped over it if it had been there before. He hurried in, fumbled twice before he could grasp it. He glanced at the spine: *Hamlet of Hydesville in 1848.*

Seconds later, he knelt before Sheila. "Your book, madam."

On the title page, Sheila read aloud, "Hamlet of Hydesville in 1848 by Bob Hoeltzel, Town Historian. Copyright 1957." They found a chapter about the Fox family, skimmed through pages, learned that a man named John Fox worked as a blacksmith, married Ann Ryan in 1805, they had a son, Roland, in 1806. In 1811, following the tragic death of his mother, Roland ran away.

Sheila continued to carefully look through the old book, found a section, said, "Let's see, in 1812, John Fox married Margaret Rutan Smith and they had five children. Their first born was named Leah."

"The sister in that picture that you think *didn't* touch you," Kevin reminded her.

Sheila nodded. "Yeah, and I'm not sure why, but I definitely think it was Maggie and Katie, just those two. Leah…didn't seem to be around."

She picked up the story, read, "Four other children followed, Maria, Elizabeth, David, and another who died in infancy." She skimmed some paragraphs, then started again. "Like most people in the village, John and Margaret were religious, attended the Methodist church. But John was no teetotaler; he had a passionate love for whiskey, was known to be an alcoholic, had violent outbursts."

Sheila had a flash of insight; a piece of her memory fell into place. "Whiskey."

"What about it?"

"Remember that night we had dinner at Atlantic Grill? Nancy said I ordered a whiskey…"

It took him a moment to catch on. "You mean you think John Fox *inspired* you to order that drink? Come on, Sheila …"

"Think about it. Maybe he did, to get my attention. Maybe it was his apparition than manifested to Nancy, the Amish fellow, and later, to us, as that homeless guy. Someone from the 1800s would look Amish to most people today, and he appeared just after I interviewed Edith and Vanya. That very evening. Ever since then, sometimes when

I swallow, I have this weird taste in my mouth. It burns, like whiskey. Maybe it indicates he's near or something."

Kevin thought it over, finally admitted, "Okay. Well, yeah, and… now that you mention it, the same thing has happened to me a couple times, that taste in my mouth. So maybe you're right."

"And it supports what Derek indicated to us at Edith's apartment, when he confirmed that the Amish man, John Fox, was on our side."

They went back to the book, flipping pages, reading that two more children were born to John and Margaret Fox, Maggie in 1833 and Katie in 1837. Following the well-documented ghostly rappings of 1848, their oldest sister Leah immediately took charge of her younger siblings, began to manage their budding careers as Spiritualists. She took them far beyond the farmhouse in Hydesville and led them—for a fee of a few dollars—into dim séance rooms and vast lecture halls. Soon the girls were making more than one thousand dollars a year, with Leah taking a percentage of their earnings. Ultimately, she made her sisters' a place in history at the same time she prospered and flourished off their abilities.

Sheila said, "So, Leah was their manager. Sounds like she worked them hard."

Kevin said, "And that's who Roland was calling for when he kept saying 'Lee. Ahh.' when he was transfixed with the ball."

They looked at one another, neither wanting to say what they were thinking. Finally, Sheila said, "You think he was trying to summon—"

"Probably," Kevin said.

"This is so crazy," she said. "All of it. But it also makes sense. The reason we haven't seen Leah yet, why she didn't touch me just now, is because she hasn't been…called forth or something. Right?"

After a moment, Sheila went back to the book, found where she had left off. "Five years after the documented Hydesville Rappings, there were no fewer than thirty-thousand mediums. By the end of the 1850s, 'table rapping' had become a nationwide craze. The *New Haven Journal* reported that there were forty families in upstate New York who claimed to have the same gifts as the Foxes, and there were more than one hundred spirit mediums in New York City alone. Eventually, millions of people worldwide—including Thomas Edison and Sir Arthur Conan Doyle—had accepted spiritualism's central tenant that the human spirit survives death and can communicate with the living."

"Whatever happened to Leah?" Kevin asked.

"Let's see…here it is. Leah eventually married a wealthy banker. She herself was a much sought-after spiritualist who traveled in well-heeled social circles, held séances for the likes of Horace Greeley, James Fenimore Cooper, Washington Irving, and Henry Wadsworth Longfellow. Wow. While she prospered socially and financially, Katie and Maggie Fox both fell on hard times. Exhausted by the constant traveling to prove their gifts, always on the defensive when accused of being charlatans, they began to drink, were unable to schedule as many meetings, and then decided to bring the entire movement to a halt so no one could make money off of it.

"On October 21, 1888, with Katie in the audience, Maggie appeared on the stage of the New

York Academy of Music. It was a packed house. A despairing, bloated Maggie Fox stated that, 'I am here tonight as one of the founders of Spiritualism to denounce it as an absolute falsehood from beginning to end, as the flimsiest of superstitions, the most wicked blasphemy known to the world!'"

"I guess that settled it," Kevin said.

Sheila nodded. "According to the *New York Herald*, there was a stunned silence. Maggie later followed up with a written statement that spiritualists dismissed as the ravings of a drunk. Since séances were the only way the Fox sisters were able to make a living, a year later Maggie recanted her confession and Katie distanced herself from it as well. But the damage to their own reputations cut deep; the vast majority of mediums turned their backs on them, did not refer clients. Both women succumbed to drink and drugs. Katie died in 1892 and Maggie passed away in March of the following year, both of them buried in pauper's graves. Leah died before the girls, in 1890. She was 76, was buried in the Greenwood Cemetery in Brooklyn."

Sheila closed the book, rubbed her tired eyes. "So, the Hydesville Rappings. Like you, I'm confused now. Were they real or faked by the girls?"

"Fake," Kevin said uncertainly. "Right? I mean, Maggie said they were fake."

"But if it was all fake, then what is going on, what are we experiencing? Why are we here, why are we researching a subject that fell out of fashion at the turn of the last century?"

"Lee. Ahh. " Roland's voice called out.

"What's he doing here?" Kevin hissed as he glanced between the stacks of books. "Where is he?"

Sheila looked around, then pointed. "There! He's in the archives' room."

CHAPTER 49.

The boy was facing them, appeared to be in a trance or half-asleep. They saw a slick wet patch of goo around his feet. The rubber ball was releasing an obscene discharge, resembling vaporous yoke from a broken egg. The material was a shimmering flesh color that bubbled slowly out of what remained of its container. Wisps of its discharge floated upward, gathered at the ceiling. Kevin tried to grab what was left of the ball, disrupt what Roland was attempting, but the heat radiating from it—waves of invisible, scorching flames—made it impossible to touch. He threw a book at it in an attempt to impede its progress, but it only bounced off as if hitting a force field.

"Lee. Ahh."

The expanding mass at Roland's feet responded to his voice. He was conjuring Leah Fox, calling her into existence. With his head down, eyes half-closed, Roland remained unaware of Kevin and Sheila. He slowly, breathlessly chanted the name over and over.

"He's doesn't even care we're here," Sheila said, repelled yet fascinated as she watched. "He's doing it right in front of us just to show that he *can*."

"Come on," Kevin finally said, "this is a waste of time, let's get out of here."

Sheila grabbed the enlarged photo of the Fox sisters and the book about Hydesville. They dashed out of the small room, ran toward the exit of the library. Once outside, they saw that the storm was now gone, the streets reflected the rain that had shed itself from the clouds. For the first time, they saw the setting sun over the village. The rays of light were harsh, creating strong contrasts; thick, blunt black shadows against a gleaming, scrubbed-clean surface. Everything had been washed raw; the broken windows and weathered walls of the abandoned homes beamed, the winds had swept the streets free of refuse.

But Sheila noticed that something wasn't right; something about the area had changed drastically. What was it? She looked around, up and down the street. Things were different. There had been a definite change. *Why is this street freaking me out so much?* Sheila wondered, still distracted by something.

"The trees!" she finally shouted. "It's the trees!" She watched it dawn on Kevin. He nodded quickly. "Yeah, the leaves on the trees. Red, yellow, thick, heavy, about to fall."

"Exactly! Fall! It's fall, and it was *August* when we went into the library."

"Just a couple hours ago."

"Seems like it's September out here."

"Late September," Kevin added, glancing around. The shadows crept closer even as the rapidly setting sun continued to shine. It had already begun to slink behind the mountains that surrounded the village. Around them, the air was beginning to cool as the fall evening settled in for the night.

"*That* wasn't here before, was it?" Sheila pointed across the street where, crouched on the corner, there was a blue metal *New York Times* newspaper rack with a plastic cover. Kevin followed her over. She lifted the lid, pulled out the paper. They bumped heads reading the date.

"October 17?" Kevin said. "From twenty years ago."

Oh, no, Sheila thought. The date was tragically familiar to her. The newspaper was from the year her parents were killed, was slugged the very day after their death.

She turned immediately to the obituaries. Looked for the familiar two-paragraph mention of her parent's accident, the one she had clipped out and stuck away with some family photos. Kevin put his arms around her as he read over her shoulder:

CAR ACCIDENT KILLS WESTCHESTER COUPLE;
UNIDENTIFIED FEMALE MISSING

Valhalla, NY, Oct. 17 Tuesday evening, a car driven by 41-year-old Sam Irving broke through the guardrail at Route 22 near Valhalla and plunged 100 feet into the reservoir. Also in the car was Mr. Irving's wife, Rachel. Witnesses claim that a third person, a woman, was also seen at the wreckage, although her whereabouts are not known. The Irving's teenage daughter was at home.

Visibility was good that evening, the roads were clear of debris and there was little traffic. An investigation into the cause of the accident and efforts to locate the unidentified woman are underway.

Sheila turned to Kevin. "This *isn't* the original article! There wasn't anyone else in the car. This isn't right. It's the same lie Vanya used to get us to come for the second interview. It isn't true!" She hurled the newspaper violently to the sidewalk. The wind scooped the pages up, scattered them down the street.

"It was just a terrible car accident," Sheila insisted. "Aunt Letty told me about it that night. There was no one else in the car or she would have said something."

It was near dusk now. With no street lamps or stores or homes illuminated, the shadows were spreading quickly.

Kevin said, "Come on, let's find a place to spend the night. I don't want to stay at the Fox cottage again."

They started down the street. Sheila looked back. "I hope Leah stays in the library with Roland."

"But you know they won't," he said somberly as she grabbed his arm tighter. "They'll be out and about, sooner or later. And now we know why the Amish man—"

"You mean John Fox?"

"Yeah. John Fox. Now we know why John Fox warned us not to let the children get the ball."

"I wonder why Leah was the last of the three Fox sisters to materialize?" Sheila asked.

"From what we read, she seemed like the marketer of the sisters. Remember, they were really just children at the time. She was the brains behind the deception, kept them on the road, showing off their fake talents."

Sheila nodded. "I guess. Roland sure was desperate to bring her back, wasn't he?"

They passed one deserted property after another, but they were all secured. Kevin rattled the front doors, knocked, tried the windows, but no response, no access. In the time it took them to walk two blocks, the sun fell behind the horizon, leaving a dark red glow across the streets that soon merged with the darkness. A luminous moon shown down, creating shadows that were Kevin and Sheila's constant companions.

"Weird that all these empty homes are locked up tight," he murmured.

"Add it to the list of weird," Sheila said.

"If we don't find one unlocked soon, I'll break a window."

Hungry and exhausted, they trudged along, their footsteps echoing in the night air. Then, from the upstairs window of a house at the end of the street, they heard a sharp tap, knuckles on glass. They glanced up. Again, *Tap, tap.*

The moon's brilliant glow on the window made it impossible to see who or what was making the noise.

Tap, tap.

They saw the glass in the window shimmer, then half of it went black as the window was raised. "Wait for me!" a man's voice called to them urgently. "I'll be right down."

Sheila and Kevin exchanged a worried glance. In the stillness, the sound of the front door being unlatched could be clearly heard. The door opened; candlelight shimmered for a moment. A flashlight beam swept over the front yard. The figure kept the ray of light focused on the ground in front of him as he maneuvered down the porch steps. His slow, careful, stiff-legged walk indicated that he was an older man. When he reached the sidewalk, he hesitated. The shaft of light rose sluggishly, shaking as it made contact with them. His hand was trembling. He was frightened.

"I'm Warren Adler," he said. His flashlight found their faces, traveled the length of their bodies, finally settled on Sheila. She put her hand up to block the glare.

"Sorry," the man said, lowered the beam, stepped closer.

After they had introduced themselves, Sheila said, "Your name. It's familiar."

"I was Derek and Edith David's houseman and driver." He stopped. His voice cracked with emotion when he said, "And Sheila, I'm...oh, Sheila, I'm your uncle."

In the darkness, Kevin heard Sheila's sharp, surprised intake of breath. It took a moment until it dawned on her. "Oh, my God! You're Letty's bother!" She stepped forward into the older man's arms; he returned the embrace. Kevin moved closer, not certain what was going on, cautious about accepting the claim the man had made. It was all too much, too fast.

Kevin hesitated, then said, "You've never met, have you? Do you...have any proof of who you are?"

"Kevin!"

The man nodded. "It's okay. I understand how strange this must seem. Let me tell you why I'm here. Maybe that will help put you at ease. I've been keeping an eye on both of you, from a distance, ever since you got into town. Sheila, I wasn't sure how to approach you. And I'm sure you're wondering…where I've been all your life…"

Kevin watched the man, waited for him to continue. Sheila was dazed by the news. Having been an orphan most of her life, the discovery of a living relative would mean the world to her, if what Warren said was true.

"I remember reading about you in some of the newspaper articles," she said. "You left about the time Derek fled to Hydesville, right?"

"Actually, a little before that. After the housekeeper, Matilda, had…an accident, I was afraid I would be next, so I left. I think Vanya Avery—"

"You know her?" Kevin asked.

"Oh, yes." He waited a beat. "Sheila, that's the other reason why I wanted to talk to you. Vanya knew your aunt, too."

"What? She knew Letty? How?"

Warren said, "Actually, their relationship is why you're here, why you're a part of…all of this. Vanya found you—and now *wants* you—because of your Aunt Letty."

CHAPTER 50.

What does Aunt Letty have to do with *any* of this?" Sheila asked, her voice hushed, small. *I'm like a scared child,* she realized, *listening to a ghost story by the campfire.*

Outside in the quiet evening, the three of them spoke in muted tones, as if afraid they might be overheard. The silver-white moon gleamed overhead. Where they stood, they projected three thick black shadows onto the front yard.

"It all goes back to the experience you had as a child," Warren said guardedly. "Do you know what I mean?"

When Sheila didn't respond, Warren said, "I know about what happened to you, Sheila." He hesitated. "The levitation. Letty and I were in touch back then; she told me." He sighed. "There's so much, I'm not even really sure where to begin…"

A silence settled over them. Sheila shivered. Kevin pulled her closer.

Abruptly, Warren said, "Look, there's no need to do this outside. Come in, spend the night, I have plenty of room." He sensed their hesitancy. "Please, we're going to have to trust one another. *Please.* I need you, and I can help you figure out what's going on. We really don't have much time."

Sheila squeezed Kevin's hand, urged them forward. Clouds drifted over the moon. In the sudden darkness, Warren used the flashlight beam to guide them up the walkway to the house. Once they were inside, he lit three candles, handed them around.

"As you've discovered, some places have electricity, some don't," he said. "This one doesn't."

"What about phones?" Sheila asked. "You have any that work?"

Warren shook his head. "None of the landlines work. I must have tried them all. And with no cell towers, no cell phone service."

"I bet even if there were a dozen cell towers around this village we'd still get no signals," Kevin said.

"Probably right," Warren agreed.

The bluish flames flickered, splattering shadows against the walls.

Kevin said, "Let me ask you something. Any idea why the fire and flames here in Hydesville always have that blue tint to them? I've never seen anything like it."

"I've read that flames turn blue in the presence of spirits," Warren said simply.

"Lovely," Sheila said.

"Really? Where'd you hear that?" Kevin asked.

"From Derek's notes."

Sheila asked, "What notes?"

"He and Edith filled a binder with what they experienced. He did a *lot* of research, wrote it all down. Before he went to Hydesville the last time, he had the notebook messengered to me, said that I needed to read it immediately. It was filled with their experiences with Vanya, Hydesville, the Fox sisters, the cottage, their memory losses, the supernatural events around them, his theories. Everything. It was all in there."

"Vanya and Edith thought those notes were lost or burned up in the fire," Sheila said. She turned to Kevin, "Did you hear that? Derek and Edith had memory loss, too."

Warren said, "It's from his notes that I learned about the blue flames being an indication that an entity is nearby. Derek had a *lot* of ideas about the events he and Edith were experiencing, initially thinking they were ghosts and supernatural manifestations. Some of it seemed a little paranoid to me, some was pretty disturbing. At first, he believed it was all paranormal. He thought that bad phone connections, exploding light fixtures, drawers and cupboards opening and closing on their own, odd things like that, were all evidence of the presence of something unnatural. I know it all sounds crazy, but—"

"Oh, not at all," Kevin said. He and Sheila shared how they had experienced many of the phenomena Warren had just spoken about.

Sheila said, "But you just said 'at first' he believed it was all paranormal stuff. He doesn't anymore?"

Warren shook his head. "No, he came to believe in an entirely different theory, that the supernatural things were just a deception, a misdirection to distract him from what was really going on. He thought there was some ancient, evil power behind all that we're experiencing. By the time this thing, this entity, is finished, it'll leave us unable to tell the truth from the lie or what is real from what is counterfeit."

Sheila and Kevin stared at him.

Warren rubbed his forehead, cleared his throat. "I know that's a lot to take in. Why don't I get some dinner together while we talk? Just don't expect it to taste like much."

"We've noticed that too, that there isn't any flavor to the food here," Kevin said. "Any idea why?"

Warren poured them each a glass of wine, opened some cans of soup, sliced some bread, talking the entire time. "What I'm about to say is going to sound crazy—I use that word a lot, don't I?— but bear with me, all right? Maybe you won't be too hard to convince since you've already experienced your share of bizarre and frightening events."

They nodded, Sheila adding, "Yes, you can safely assume that."

Warren smiled. "Okay, here goes. I'll start with the tasteless food. What I have come to believe and what Derek wrote, is that like everything else here, it's just an illusion of reality. It's like Whatever or Whomever controls this place, wants everything to *look* normal, even though it isn't. It's like it's putting on a play and we're just acting in it, so it gives us food that looks real but it's fake, creates sounds that may be familiar to us, but not quite right. It's all a bit of a trick, a counterfeit."

Warren studied them for a moment, trying to gauge their response. They watched him, waiting for him to continue.

"There's something…strange and powerful about this area," Warren said. "Surely you've felt it? Derek did a lot of research and found that there are several places in the United States that are known to be areas of magical energy or power, but nothing like Hydesville."

"There are *other* places like this village?" Sheila asked, shifting uncomfortably.

"Yes, but if you were to stack up all of the documented supernatural activity in these places, nothing would even come close to Hydesville. And of course, this village seems to disappear or go into hiding at times, unlike those other locations which are always easy to find on maps or GPS. I've even wondered about the Colony, does it even exist?"

Kevin glanced at Sheila, eyebrows raised in curious disbelief.

Sheila looked at Warren. "I still don't understand—"

Warren put his hands up, smiled weakly. "I know you have a lot of questions, and I'm not setting any of this up very well." He looked at Sheila. "Before I get too deep into Hydesville and its history and what Derek believes, let me back up and tell you what role I think *you* play in this, how you ended up here."

The dim sapphire light from the candles revealed Warren to be a balding, average looking man in his late seventies. *Nondescript, someone you'd never look at twice*, Sheila mused. *Except, he's my uncle.* She hated to bring it up, but had to know, wanted to fill in all the blank areas she could.

She asked him, "Before you start, tell me how long have you known about me, that you had a niece?"

Clearly uncomfortable and embarrassed, Warren said, "When your Mom—my sister, Rachel—gave birth, Letty told me. I'm…so sorry, Sheila. After your parents died, I tried to get close, offered to help her raise you…"

"You did? What did she say?"

"She refused, was still angry with me for all the years I was *not* involved; we had a very strained relationship. I can't say I blamed her, but she could be stubborn about things. You were a teenager, had just lost your folks and I guess she didn't want to overwhelm you with something new to adjust to, namely me. Then, after she took you in to raise you, she pretty much shut the rest of us out of your lives, kept you to herself. Not that we were knocking to get in, but she made it clear she wanted to be alone with you. I'd hear from her very rarely. After her stroke, nothing at all. But you were everything to her. She loved you so much…" He reached out. Sheila held his hand, wiped the tear from her eye, smiled at him through the flickering flames.

Kevin asked, "Do you know anything about another person in the car with Sheila's parents? A woman?" He explained what Vanya and the John Fox apparition hand hinted at and what they had read in the obituary.

Warren shook his head. "No, I never heard anything about that." While they ate, he went on to explain that he, Letty, and Sheila's mother, Rachel, came from a large, old-fashioned Catholic family. Seven brothers, three sisters. They were good, loyal churchgoers so when Rachel married Sam, who was Jewish, the whole family entered a war zone.

"Back then, marrying someone outside of your faith was a big, bad deal," he explained. "Especially if they weren't Catholic."

Warren said that lines were drawn, unforgivable things were said. When the battle was over, Letty was the only one who would speak to Rachel. Even then, it was on rare occasions. The rest of the family were at wildly different stages in their lives; some were moving away for college or work or exchanging marriage vows in other states. Everyone pretty much lost touch since they were so scattered about."

"No wonder Mom rarely spoke about her siblings," Sheila said. "I had no idea there was so much drama in my family."

Kevin said, "You never asked about them?"

"No, I was just a kid, so I think any questions I had were shut down pretty quickly."

"Your mother was so much younger than me by the time that she married Sam, we had simply gone our separate ways, lived our own lives," Warren said. "And I know she was terribly hurt by all that had been said about her marrying Sam. But then one day, after several years of silence, Letty called me in a panic about you. Rachel had told her about your levitation; your Mom and Dad had been petrified, didn't know what to do. The experience itself was terrifying for them but they were more concerned about you, imagined the worst, wondered what would happen if it occurred outside; would you just keep floating away? By this time, Rachel no longer went to Mass, had no idea if the Church would help them if she asked them. Sam never went to temple. They had no one with religious knowledge to turn to, no idea *what* to do."

While he spoke, Kevin watched Sheila by the bluish candlelight. She was eagerly listening, nodding intently as Warren seemed to confirm what she had always known or suspected but forgotten or blocked from her memories. Kevin reached over, rubbed her shoulder affectionately. She smiled at him, but her eyes were sad.

Warren said, "Rachel was desperate for help, wanted to talk to someone, so she called Letty, the only sister she was in touch with. Letty said she'd do some research on people experiencing paranormal events and get back to her. Letty told me she was in the library a few days later when a woman asked her what she was doing with such a stack of books on the occult. The lady had large, green eyes, with the sort of gaze that could mesmerize you. It was Vanya, of course. They started talking, soon Letty told Vanya everything..."

Sheila shuddered, now adverse to hearing Vanya's name. Then she blurted out, "'*We know your face touched the ceiling!*' That was the message on my computer, the one that I printed out. *That's* how Vanya knew that I had levitated, from what Letty told her that day at the library all those years ago!"

Warren's hand was suddenly shaking as he refilled their wine glasses, the bottle clinking nervously on the glass.

Sheila watched. Alarmed, she asked him, "Warren? What is it you're not telling us?"

CHAPTER 51.

After he had set down the bottle, Warren said quietly, "I didn't want to alarm you, but I think Vanya believes *you* are a union child. That's why she's after you. You know what they are, don't you?"

"She told us," Sheila said. "But never said she thought *I* was one. How could I be? Neither of my parents were psychic or had any abilities or connection to the Colony. They would have told me or would have known how to handle the weird things that happened to me. It was all a surprise to them."

Warren thought over what she said. "So, when you levitated, it wasn't at all by choice or of your own desire, correct?"

"No, God no! It was terrible, a horrible experience…"

"Then…I guess I was wrong or Vanya is mistaken," he said after several seconds. "Which is odd; I didn't think she made mistakes. Or maybe she has some *other* plan to use you, some other reason she brought you here…"

Alarmed by what Warren said, Kevin asked, "How would Vanya *use* Sheila? For what purpose?"

"I'm still not entirely certain," Warren admitted. "Remember, she uses misdirection to hide her true intentions. It was the same when she infiltrated Derek and Edith's lives. At first, they were distracted by all the supernatural events they were experiencing and the memory loss. It was only gradually that they began to realize she was behind it all, using all the paranormal shenanigans as a way to hide her intentions. They had no idea why she was after them or what their connection was to Hydesville or the Fox sisters."

"What was the connection?" Sheila asked. "Why *was* she after them?"

"It's complicated, but I think I have some of it figured out. I've had plenty of time to do research, discovered something major that I suspect Derek found out before he tried to destroy the Fox cottage: Turns out his fifth great-grandfather was John Fox. When John's only son changed his last name to David, the Fox lineage was lost to history. I found an old Bible in the library that traced the family genealogy, confirmed everything. Derek is the last of the Fox bloodline."

Sheila and Kevin looked at him.

"Seriously?" Kevin said. "Derek is actually *part* of the Fox family?"

Warren nodded.

"But, so what," Sheila said after a few seconds. "I mean, why is that important?"

"There's something in the Fox bloodline that this Vanya thing is after," Warren said. "This area and that Fox house in particular have some strange power coursing through them, as do the Fox Woods. It's like a sacred area or something. Whatever Vanya is up to, it must all begin here. She wants to harness it. Derek called it a consummation, a union between this inhuman thing and a human."

"Slow down," Sheila said. "How would that even happen?"

"She needs a host with the Fox bloodline to begin with," Warren said. "That's why she was after Derek and his brother. When Oswald wasn't able to provide what she needed, she discarded him, went after Derek. This thing takes a human form as Vanya Avery and it was in that form she had Derek's child, Margaret. And Vanya used her father to impregnate Edith."

"Where'd *he* come from?" Sheila asked.

Warren said, "I think she created him herself. Rather, this thing created what it needed in order to exist here and begin to work its plan."

After a few seconds, Kevin said, "If I'm understanding this, Roland and Margaret are both union children, right? They were the offspring of two humans, Edith and Derek, and the inhumans from the Colony, Vanya and her father."

"Correct. And you've seen how quickly they age, which is another concern. It doesn't happen with all of them, but these two are aging rapidly. Soon Margaret will be able to reproduce. She will have an offspring known as a *pure* union child since it's the result of two union children mating. Each new generation is more powerful than the previous one, and each will age faster and faster so they will reproduce at an accelerated rate."

Sheila said, "Once the pure ones arrive, they won't need us any more, right? The human species will no longer have any purpose for them."

Warren hesitated a moment, nodded, then said, "The pure union children will be…monstrosities. Their minds will be linked as one, and their psychic abilities… beyond anything we could ever imagine. Derek believed Hydesville will be used as sort of a safe, incubation area for them, a controlled environment. Once there are enough of them, they will spread out to the surrounding areas, take them over, then assume control of the state, fan out throughout the country and eventually, the world."

"Just like the Spiritualist movement did," Kevin said. "It started here, now its beliefs and practices are worldwide."

Warren agreed. "Exactly. Vanya's following the same plan she used on the Fox sisters."

"And it's all based on deception," Sheila said.

"Started by *children*," Kevin said. "But why the Fox bloodline? Why them?"

"I'm still piecing everything together, but Derek wrote about a consummation that needed to occur here in Hydesville, on the Fox property. It's where Vanya gets her power, it like a charging station for her. Since we know that deceit is at her core, the deception of the Fox sisters is what attracted her to Maggie and Katie in the first place, like a moth to a flame.

"It's incredible when you think about it: In 1848, these two girls are stuck here in Hydesville. They are bored, they innocently begin to make sounds, pretend they were talking with the dead. This Vanya entity has been waiting in this place for who knows how long, decades, centuries. She's patient.

Ultimately, that is her greatest power, along with using supernatural phenomena to distract from her true intentions. I'm guessing she's deep in hibernation when she becomes aware of this grand deception occurring in Hydesville. Attracted to their lies, Vanya tricks the children into thinking it's *really* happening, that they actually *have* this power. She uses her paranormal sleight of hand, mixes the girls' tricks with a dash of her own magic.

"For a few decades, the girls make some money off of it, fooling thousands of people, spreading their lies all over the country and soon the world. This only makes Vanya stronger. She feeds off the deception. Then, forty years after Maggie and Katie first created the rapping sounds, they admit the entire experience was a hoax. By then, there were *millions* of confirmed spiritualists across the planet who had been tricked, which makes what the Fox children did the greatest deception humankind has ever known." Warren turned to Kevin. "And you're right, it was all started by a couple of children!"

Sheila said, "I get it. It's the deception in the Fox bloodline Vanya needs. It's like she wants to bottle it, reproduce it, spread it throughout the world."

Warren leaned closer to them. "If what Derek wrote in the binder is correct, and I think it is, we can't let these pure union children reproduce." His eyes were tired, red-rimmed with exhaustion, yet his voice was now filled with the conviction of a zealot. "We have to destroy them before they mature and reproduce. That's what Derek knew, what he tried to stop by burning down the Fox house, destroy the sacred place where they needed to mate, the inhuman with the last of the Fox bloodline. Like I said, there's something about that property—and this village, this area—that is powerful, more than any other place in the United States, probably on this planet."

His words lingered in the air.

"My head hurts," Sheila said wearily to break the grim silence. "Seriously, I can't even process most of what you're saying."

Warren smiled. "You're right. I've had months to take this in, mull it over. You've had just over an hour to process it. But there's one more thing I have to tell you. This entity is dead set on conjuring up *all* of the Fox children, but its first priority is Leah because she was thought to be the most cunning, the ringleader of the fake Spiritualist movement. She made a lot of money off of her sisters and that religion, worked tirelessly to push the deception out far beyond Hydesville.

"However, we're fortunate to have two things in our favor: First, they haven't been able to locate the sphere that Leah resides in, and second, even when they do, Vanya can't call forth a Fox family apparition, only a union child can do that."

"They found the sphere, Roland's already done it," Kevin announced, then explained what had occurred in the library.

Warren's shoulders slumped. "We have so little time, then. Everything is escalating. Once Roland and Margaret consummate and produce a pure union child, we can't even begin to imagine what horrific things they will accomplish. Vanya's plan—"

"What *is* Vanya?" Kevin asked. "Some creature from, what, outer space, another realm or dimension?" He threw his hands up, bewildered, exasperated. "Remember, I work in real estate, not *The Twilight Zone*."

Warren thought for a moment, then said, "Entity is the best word I could come up with. It means 'a thing with a distinct and independent existence.' That's what she is, a *thing*. She uses the costume of a human woman to sexually attract her prey. I know that she—or this thing—needs to start small, can only interact with a handful of people, maybe two or three. But the longer she's around—"

"Wait, I don't understand something," Sheila said. "Vanya says she's a union child, so why can't she bring forth these apparitions herself?"

"I think it has something to do with her mother," Warren said. "Some defect, perhaps. With everything I've learned on my own and from the binder, there's no information anywhere on who her mother is, where she came from. Maybe the consummation didn't work correctly, some problem with the mother—"

"What if she didn't have a mother, as we think of one?" Kevin said. "I mean, we're thinking in human terms, with our logic. What if she was more like a—"

"She's lying," Sheila said. She looked at the two men. "It's that simple. She's not a union child, or at least as she's defined them. That's why she can't call forth an apparition. She's lying."

Warren grinned. "You're right! It's so simple! It's who she is, a liar, so why wouldn't she lie?"

"Okay," Kevin said, "but what about John Fox, the Amish man apparition? We know he's opposed to everything Vanya and the Fox sisters are up to, so where did he come from? Surely not from them. Who called him forth?"

"Hmm," Sheila said. "Good question. I hadn't thought about that." After several seconds passed, they all shrugged, lapsed into silence. Kevin was about to say something, but Sheila blurted out, "*'It can see as well as hear.'*"

Warren and Kevin looked at her.

"The diary! Remember? The Margaret Fox diary. Whatever the thing was that was communicating with them—the Vanya thing—one of the girls held up fingers without speaking, asked it to count them, and it did, correctly. It could *see* them *and* hear them." She said to Kevin, "That explains how they messed with me in the beginning, how they knew I took a nap, somehow changed the words I wrote, were in the area when I was with you."

Sheila turned to Warren. "Like you said, this entity knows what our world looks like, tries to manufacture something we'd recognize. I'm guessing that if it can create counterfeit things that we are familiar with—like bread and soup and wine—there's really no limit to what it can manifest."

The candle lights in the kitchen flickered as if from a sudden draft.

"That's correct, what you said, but I want to circle back to the most important thing for me, which is to find Derek," Warren said. "He is the entity's prized possession because of his bloodline, so Vanya will keep him close to her, protecting him from us until Margaret is old enough to mate with Roland."

"Which could be any day," Kevin said, "based on the rate they are growing."

Warren sighed, nodded. "There's so much more to do, to learn. I thought I had accomplished a lot since I've been here, but—"

"How long have you been here?" Sheila asked.

"I left Derek's last November, went to my cousin's home in Connecticut. Then Derek sent me his notebook. After I read it, I drove up here that same day. I had to help him if I could."

"You've been here all these months, hiding out in this house?" Kevin asked.

"I stayed put because I didn't know what else to do or who might be after me. I read the binder over and over, did my own research. There are dozens of old books in the library about this village and each one has a piece of the story. It was like assembling a jigsaw puzzle with no idea of the final image. But after I saw Derek attempt to burn down the Fox house, I had no choice but to find out—"

Sheila said, "You *saw* him do that?"

Warren nodded, told them that once he was in Hydesville, he managed to find the Fox house because of a map Derek had drawn. "I couldn't find Derek, so I just waited across the street from the cottage since I knew he'd show up eventually. I saw his Mercedes arrive, but I remained hidden, since I still wasn't sure all that was going on or what he planned. I watched him go into the house. Then Vanya arrived. A little later, Derek stepped out on the front porch, tried to set the property on fire.

"It was so strange because I was suddenly frozen in place; I could only watch what was happening, couldn't speak or move. I saw Vanya compel Derek to her as if he was in a trance. And they kissed. I was shocked since I knew how much he loved Edith. Then, Vanya simply took what she wanted from him. It was horrible, I could only stand there. I witnessed it, *all of it*, that evil consummation on the Fox property. When she was finished, the flames surrounded Derek. I still couldn't move, couldn't help him. Vanya just wandered away. Then I blacked out, have no idea what happened next..."

Sheila told him Vanya's version of the story, how she claimed Derek had attacked her.

Warren said bitterly, "It's all about lies with this thing! In Derek's notes, he wrote that he believed Katie, Maggie and Leah had actually been buried in the cellar of their home, not what history reports actually happened to them. He thought *that* was why they were 'haunting' him, begging him to dig up their bones, set them free so they could go to the light and all that nonsense. They wanted justice. He was convinced that their father, John Fox, had buried them and their mother alive. For months the sisters teased and lured Derek on, used their skills to trick him, get him to return to the house, go down into the cellar, unearth 'their bodies'. It was all a sham. He thought he was doing a good thing, never knowing it was a trap and Vanya was waiting for him..."

A hush settled over the candlelit room as they mulled over all that Warren had told them that evening. Sheila yawned, then Kevin did. Warren stretched, said it was time for bed. They each took a blue-flamed candle, started up the stairs.

CHAPTER 52.

The next morning, Sheila woke first.

Her eyes took in the unfamiliar room. Through the tattered drapes over the window she saw gray sky, the ever-present threat of rain. She sighed. For a moment, she had hoped she was awakening from an awful dream, but her memory was intact; she remembered all that had happened the day before: The library, the old photographs, Maggie and Katie Fox touching her, Roland summoning Leah, her parents' death reported in the newspaper and the mention of the mysterious third woman in the car, meeting Warren (her uncle!) after all these years, the terrible strange tale he had told them by the blue candlelight in the kitchen, their need to battle this strange entity…

She turned over slowly so as not to awaken Kevin. She needn't have bothered. He wasn't there, probably taking his morning pee.

Nestling deeper into the bed, she thought, *Sheila Irving awakes alone while her husband, successful real estate broker Kevin Jackson, prepares breakfast in bed for her. Soon, they plan to start their family, which will consist of 2.5 children. They already have a cat, Hendrick, are thinking of getting a dog. They will divide their time between their West End Avenue apartment and their weekend home in Bridgehampton. Sheila, now a weekend editor at the* New York Times, *writes of—*

"You going to sleep all day?"

Startled, she opened her eyes, looked in the direction of Kevin's voice. He was in the doorway, holding a cup of coffee. She smiled. "You brought me coffee."

"No, there's coffee downstairs." His tone was flat, gruff. Mean.

Was he kidding? He took another sip from his cup. Nope, he really wasn't joking. She put her annoyance aside, stretched, yawned. "I slept like a log. How 'bout you?"

"'Slept like a log'? Really? That's the best a journalist for the *Times* can come up with?" His back was to her now as he looked out the window.

"Ouch," she said, climbing out of the bed. The stress of the bizarre events had taken their toll; she'd give him a pass for now, give him some space. She pulled on her jeans and t-shirt. "I guess you didn't sleep well. Don't take it out on me." She waited for a response. He continued to stare out the window. She sighed, left the room, away from his bad mood, padded down the stairs, greeted Warren in the kitchen. "Morning. I hear there's coffee, but I can't smell it."

"Not in Hydesville you won't," he said cheerfully, poured her a cup.

She sniffed the contents of the mug. "Mmm. Smells like…nothing."

"Thank you. I made it fresh this morning. I also have flavorless toast, tasteless jam, and non-sweet sugar or bland milk for your coffee." They munched on the breakfast until Warren said, "I spoke to Kevin. He seems a little out of sorts. Anything happen last night?"

"Nope. We went to bed, fell asleep immediately. He was his usual pleasant Dr. Henry Jekyll last night, but this morning was the beastly Mr. Edward Hyde. Not sure what his problem is."

Warren didn't respond for a moment, finally said, "When I woke up …he was in my room. Just standing there, holding his steaming cup. I asked him if everything was all right. He said, 'No, nothing is right.' Then he walked out of the room. I got up, came down here. It was weird. The kitchen was as we left it last night; the coffee hadn't been made. Where'd he get his cup?"

"Maybe it wasn't coffee?" Sheila suggested.

"It was coffee," Kevin said flatly from the kitchen entry.

Sheila and Warren flinched in surprise.

Kevin said, "I woke early, came downstairs, made coffee, cleaned up, end of story."

"I guess I didn't see any coffee grinds or the coffee maker out, so…," Warren said sheepishly, his voice trailing off.

"You mean you checked?" Kevin asked bemused. "Over a cup of coffee? You think I'd lie about a cup of coffee, Warren? Really?"

"Kevin!" Sheila said. "Slow down! What's wrong with you?"

He turned to her. "You believe me, don't you?"

Kevin moved nearer. Sheila froze.

His once brown eyes were now green.

"Look, it doesn't matter," Warren said easily, trying to deflate the tension. "How about some breakfast, Kevin? You hungry for another Hydesville nothing-plate special?"

Sheila continued to stare at Kevin. After several seconds, she said, her voice tight, "Honey, I could use some…casting of characters."

He didn't respond.

"Kevin? Who are we?"

With his back to Warren, he finally said, "Okay, okay. I'm…Robert Mitchum, you're Polly Bergen."

"What movie?"

"*Cape Fear.* You know, the husband and wife, and the crazy bad guy."

"Gregory Peck was the husband," Sheila said evenly. "Robert Mitchum was the villain."

"You're right. Of course. Let me try again."

Puzzled, Warren watched this exchange, knew better than to interrupt to ask what was going on.

"John Gavin," Kevin said after a few seconds. "You're his sister, Janet Leigh."

Sheila didn't respond. Warren said, "You're talking about the movie, *Psycho*, right? Janet Leigh was his girlfriend, not his sister. What are—"

"Help me out, then, Warren," Kevin said, his eyes still locked on Sheila. "Who was Gavin's sister?"

"He didn't have one in the movie," Warren said. "Janet Leigh had a sister."

"Vera Miles," Sheila said quietly, her heart ramping up.

Kevin snapped his fingers. "Of course!" His bright green eyes were glowing with excitement.

"That's right! I'll be Gavin, you be Vera!" He turned to Warren. "We'll figure out a role for you, Warren."

"My God, Kevin! Your eyes!" Warren said, backing away.

"What do you mean? What's wrong with you two? First the coffee, and then—" Kevin stomped out of the kitchen without finishing his statement. They heard him pound his way up the stairs.

"What was that all about? You okay?" Warren asked, moving closer to Sheila.

She shook her head; he saw she was near tears. "No, I'm not. Kevin knows old movies, he started that little casting game years ago, choosing roles for us, putting us in romantic situations or selecting comedies for us to star in when things got difficult between us…to lighten the mood."

Warren said, "I get it. But why—"

"He'd *never* choose roles that put us in jeopardy or danger. Not even as a joke. And he's never confused roles that way. Never." She took a moment to catch her breath. "And his *eyes*! His eye color is brown, not that horrible, glittering green…"

Warren said, "If he was fine last night but was different this morning, I know from my past experience with Vanya and from Derek's notes that she can visit us in our dreams, when our guard is down. Makes reality unreality, switches it back and forth. More deception. At least, that's when she had the most power over Derek. She had tried on many occasions to seduce him, but he always told me that he woke up or broke the spell in time."

"You think Vanya seduced Kevin while he was asleep? But why? He's not part of the Fox bloodline."

"No, but she can use him to create a union child, remember? Human and inhuman? Maybe we were wrong, maybe she is a union child. How else do you explain the change in his behavior, the color of his eyes? It means she's begun to seduce him…"

Sheila couldn't respond, her mind now filled with offensive images of Kevin and Vanya together, their bodies twisting, thrusting together in passion. *How could he do such a thing*? she wondered. How would it feel to be with…one of them? She imagined herself penetrated by one of the inhumans, the pleasure of the experience blocking out any images of Vanya and Kevin. Moist, she wanted to touch herself, wanted the feeling again and again. It felt so good, feels so good. Did it happen? Was it happening?

She shuddered, put her hands over her face, felt Warren's comforting touch on her shoulder. She looked at him. "Do you think he would remember, if I asked, would he tell me?"

"Tell you what?"

Startled, they turned to see Kevin standing there. She noticed he had lazy bedhead hair, his eyes had a dopey, just-woke-up look.

She stared at his brown eyes.

Sheila was on her feet in an instant. "Cast us in a movie! Right now, quick!"

"Um, okay. Ah, David Niven and…Loretta Young in *Eternally Yours*."

Warren said casually, "Never saw that. What roles did they play?"

"He was a magician, she was his love interest."

Sheila said, "Do another." She couldn't help peering closely at his brown eyes.

"Okay…Glenn Ford, Geraldine Page in *Dear Heart*. What's this—"

Sheila smiled at Warren, said, "Glenn Ford was a greeting card salesman engaged to a shew." She asked Kevin, "Who played that role?"

"Angela Lansbury," Kevin said immediately. "Now, tell me what is going on!"

Sheila felt ridiculously like crying, she was so relived.

"What?" Kevin asked again, looking back and forth between Sheila and Warren.

"Did you have any dreams last night?" Warren asked.

"I…don't remember. Why?"

"Do you remember coming to my room this morning?"

Confused, Kevin said, "No." Then, "Did I?"

Warren and Sheila told Kevin about their morning encounters with him, his unpleasant attitude, the odd movie roles he chose, his inability to get the casting right, and his changed eye color. By the time they finished, all three of them were seated at the kitchen table, drinking the flavorless coffee.

"Wow," was Kevin's response. "Wow, wow, wow."

Sheila stroked his arm. "But no dreams you remember, and you don't recall anything we just told you about?"

"No, and it's the creepiest feeling to have no memory of any of this. I just woke up a whole ago, came down here, and then…all of this was told to me."

"But somehow, Vanya…got into you. We saw the change in behavior, the eye color," Warren said.

"But if I have no memory of it, then I'm helpless to control it, right?"

"I guess all we can do is monitor your behavior," Sheila said. "And your eyes."

"So now what? We can't just sit around waiting for her to change me again or for Leah or Roland or the Fox sisters to show up."

"No, we can't," Warren said. "We should find Derek, get him out of here. That's why I came here in the first place." He hesitated. "Then we need to deal with Vanya and Edith and the union children."

"When you say deal with…I mean, we can't just…," Kevin said slowly. "What do you mean when you say deal with?"

After they finished breakfast, they gathered on the front porch. The street was littered with leaves; the tree branches were now thin, bare, resembling dozens of hands reaching up in dire supplication to the gray sky.

"I still can't get over it," Sheila said in wonder. "It looks like fall arrived overnight."

Kevin looked around the area. "So, where to?"

Warren said, "I think we should go to the one place I've never been to yet, the Fox Woods. If Derek is anywhere in Hydesville, I think they probably have him there."

Fifteen minutes later, they stood in front of the brooding home of the Fox sisters.

"Should we burn it down?" Kevin asked. "Finish what Derek started?"

"No, I don't think it would impact anything, now," Warren said somberly. "This house was just a birthing place, to be used with the Fox blood. Vanya got what she wanted from Derek and this place. We need to find him, and then we can do battle with the others, face to face."

"And now that we have a better idea of what we're up against, we should be very careful in what we say," Sheila said, looking around.

Kevin looked at her questioningly.

"Remember, '*It can see as well as hear,*'" she said.

"And see doesn't just mean visually," Warren cautioned. "The Vanya thing is capable of looking into your mind and thoughts, so be careful what you think about, too."

Their footfalls crunched over the weeds as they walked around the side of the property toward the back yard and the path and fields beyond. Soon it was just the sound of their labored breathing as they made their way over the grassy area. Eventually, the clearing ran up against a massive wall of trees shrouded in a dark tapestry of shadows.

"The Fox Woods," Warren announced.

Sheila took Kevin's hand into her own.

"Like I said, in my time here, I never had the guts to go in there by myself," Warren admitted. "Now, with you here, I have the courage. No idea where we're headed, but I sense that somehow Derek will lead us to him. Kevin, perhaps you should suggest some characters for us to be?"

"Sure. The Three Stooges come to mind."

"Or the Three Musketeers?" Sheila suggested.

"Wait! I have the perfect idea," Warren said, chuckling to himself. "Bob Hope, Bing Crosby, and Dorothy Lamour! Know what that's from?"

"Sure do, and it's perfect!" Kevin agreed. "A *Road To* movie, a light comedy."

"Anything for a laugh," Sheila agreed. "We can call it *'The Road to the Fox Woods.'*"

For a few minutes, they talked about the series of popular 1940s road movies they'd seen, recalled favorite parts and bits of dialogue. Once the conversation had died out, Warren waited a beat, then asked, "So, are we ready to do this?"

Their brief, jovial spirit vanished.

They started forward.

487

VI:
The Woods

488

CHAPTER 53.

U nder the canopy of trees, the sounds of their shoes crunching on the dead leaves and overgrowth was magnified. Their panting was strenuous, hard. They didn't speak much, had to concentrate their efforts on making it through the difficult and obstructive undergrowth.

The deeper they progressed into the woods, the more the terrain transformed itself. At times, rocks seemed to burst out of the ground, edges sharp, dangerous, like fangs. Trees that soared fifty and one hundred feet above them had branches that appeared to lock arms, blocking out most of the ashen gray sky. Whatever bleak light the pale sun had provided in Hydesville was now diminished by the tightly packed forest.

The ground arched and dipped; they scrambled for footholds, the leaves were slick. Sheila fell hard after tripping over a fallen branch. She cursed herself; where had that come from? It was as if it had reached up, grabbed her. Behind her, she heard a sharp *Crack!* She turned just in time to see a thick, heavy limb crash with a huge *Whomp!*

She'd been at that exact spot seconds earlier.

"You okay?" Kevin asked. He was a few feet in front of her; they were both following Warren.

"Yeah," she answered, breathlessly. "It just seemed like it was aiming for me."

Kevin moved closer to her, lifted her chin. "Don't start thinking crazy thoughts now. Trees and rocks and leaves don't move about on their own."

"In the Fox Woods they do."

"You okay back there?" Warren called out.

They pressed on even as the woods gave no quarter. Like a living organism sensing it was being invaded by an unknown and possibly dangerous enemy, it closed ranks, tightened in on itself. At times, it seemed to aggressively oppose them making any progress. Rocks rolled ahead of them, causing them to abruptly stop, or small boulders tumbled down, painfully smacking into their ankles. More branches dropped, leaves shifted underfoot. It kept them under a constant state of nervous apprehension since they felt they were being pursued by an unseen enemy, had no choice but to continue.

Sheila thought, *It can see as well as hear.*

Minutes later, Warren called out, "I think there's a clearing up ahead." About fifty feet in front of them was an open area where three trees stood, attentive warriors on guard.

"Strange, isn't it?" Kevin said, gesturing with his head toward what they were all looking at. "All this forest around us, then this clearing, and just three trees in the center." He started toward them, compelled to discover why they were there. The nearer he got, the more he hurried.

Behind him, from far away, he heard Sheila and Warren calling.

The three trees were only ten yards away. He saw a familiar shape. He'd seen it in photos and movies all his life but had never actually touched one before. There was another one in the second tree, and also in the third.

"Kevin!" He heard Sheila, couldn't respond, was busy.

He stepped closer, looked up. A cold finger of awareness inched its way slowly down his back, bumping over each bone of his spine. His mouth opened to shout out a warning. Warren was already yelling at him to get back, get back, get back, but Kevin was planted deep, like the roots of the terribly ancient trees that surround him.

He looked up at the nooses that dangled, waiting, from the branches. Three coiled ropes, one for each of them. He could only stare at them.

When Sheila and Warren finally reached him, they followed Kevin's gaze to the nooses swaying and twisting gently in the breeze. A thick wind soon shouldered its way through the woods, crept across the fields, set the coiled ropes swinging like pendulums.

"This…is too much," Kevin managed to say. He watched, transfixed, at what he considered to be his noose. It dangled there lazily. The arc of the motion remained constant, reminding him of a child on a swing pumping his or her legs to keep it going.

"These are meant for us," Sheila murmured weakly, "right?" She recalled the stories about the unexplained hangings in the Fox Woods. Was this the very place where Derek's brother, Oswald, had died, and John Fox before him? *But how'd he get up on that branch?* "I'm not climbing a tree to hang myself!" she said, just to hear her own voice.

Warren said quietly, "You couldn't if you tried. None of us could. Look. It's a good fifty feet to the branch the rope is tied to."

"And it's a sleek tree," Kevin added, "no foot holds."

"We couldn't do this on our own, alone," Warren said. Then he had an idea. "We're going to need to help each other."

Although her neck was stiffening from gazing up, Sheila couldn't look away, was for some reason intent on counting the traditional thirteen loops that ended in the sliding knot. Hangman's Noose. Thirteen, an unlucky number, a foreboding sign for those about to die. Where had she read that, why had she remembered it?

Kevin's throat was tight, it was difficult to swallow, as if his noose was already at work; he wished he could lower his head. *How will I get up there?* he wondered. *If there's no ladder available...*

Warren's neck ached from gazing at the coiled rope. His eyes followed it back and forth as it swayed. "*Slack your rope, hangman, slack it for a while...*" he mumbled. He shook his head, trying to clear his thoughts, but his focus remained on the circle the noose formed. Looking through it, he thought he saw—

He blinked several times, squared his shoulders, devised a plan, a way to accomplish the task before them. *We're going to need to help each other.* He reasoned he'd have to assist Sheila and Kevin first. He'd trained all his life as a manservant, he could never go before anyone else, never be first in line. He supposed he could climb on Kevin's back, then

Sheila could scramble over both of them, a human ladder. She'd be first.

Yes, she'd hang first.

Warren sang the words to the old folk song: "'*Slack your rope hangman, slack it for a while, I think I see my true love comin', riding many a mile.*'" He cried out eagerly, "Well, shall we begin?" He rubbed his hands together enthusiastically.

"Begin what?" Sheila asked, sleepy, in a daze. Her thoughts were ones of desire, of recollections of being caressed by one of the inhumans, to be mounted, to feel it swell inside of her. Then, alarmed, awake, she said, "Warren?!"

"I was thinking that if Kevin embraced the trunk for support and I got on his shoulders, then perhaps you could climb over both of us, then perch on my shoulders?" He stepped backwards as he spoke, pointing at the smallest of the three trees. "I think this one must be yours, Sheila. You'll go first." Eyebrows raised with pleasant expectancy, he looked over at them.

They watched him in horror, their eyes wide with shock.

Warren felt his chest tighten with anxiety. He had solved the problem; why weren't they responding? "We can make a human ladder! We can *do* this! Don't you see? This is what we came here for, this is why we've come all this way."

Kevin said, "Warren, listen to me: It's messing with your mind. Fight it!"

Sheila went over to her uncle, touched his arm. His face was glistening, he looked pale and sickly to her. She wondered if he had overexerted himself as they had hiked through the woods. She wished they had some water. He looked at her; his eyes were dilated, seemed a bit wild, darting around her, not looking at her directly.

Overhead, a rustling from the branches. Snake-like, the ropes were squirming about as they were being lowered by a concealed presence. To Kevin, the jerky movements might as well have been three pairs of invisible hands letting down the nooses, hand over hand. Each loop now dangled at eye level while the other end remained firmly knotted to something more than fifty feet above. There was now no need for a ladder, human or otherwise.

Fascinated by what had just occurred, Kevin wanted to touch his rope, feel the rough fibers, the tight coils, the warmth. He knew it would be warm. Had he ever held a noose in his hands?

Sheila watched her rope as it swung back and forth hypnotically. "*'Slack your rope, hangman,'*" she said, smiling at the unfamiliar words. Was it a song or an old nursery rhyme?

In return, Warren called out happily, "*'Oh, slack it for a while, I think I see my true love'*"—

"*'—coming many a mile!'*" Sheila finished, laughing.

Kevin realized that the answers they had been seeking were at last right there, right in front of them. He eagerly reached out for his rope. At the same instant, the noose lurched toward him, meeting him halfway as if shaking hands in a greeting or agreement. There *was* a warmth within the thick coils as he suspected. The individual strands, entwined together, were thicker than he expected, about the width of one of his fingers. He reasoned they had to be strong, couldn't have the rope breaking…

Cheerfully, Warren said, "Maybe I should go first after all." He placed the noose around his neck. "See how easy it is?" He looked over at Sheila and Kevin. "This is what She wants me to do, this is the *real* reason why I am here! I thought it was to rescue Derek, but no, I just realized. *'I think I see my true love...'"*

For an instant, Sheila saw his face go slack with realization.

Then, he called out, *"Do as I do!"* Abruptly, the rope squeezed closed. Warren gasped. Then he was yanked upward twenty feet. There was a sharp crack in the stillness when his neck broke. His head tilted to the side as his legs kicked about trying to find footing in midair. His upper plate edged from his mouth as he gagged; it fell to the ground. His tongue jutted out as if he was mocking them from above. Then the rope jerked harshly again, lifted him higher into the trees. Kevin and Sheila heard the branch creak as it strained to support his weight. They watched Warren's fingers fluttering as if he was playing an invisible flute, then he clenched and unclenched his fists.

The rope jerked a third time.

Gazing up into the tree, Sheila screamed.

The sound shook Kevin out of his stupor.

Seventy feet above them on the thick branch, they saw three women in long black dresses gathering in the rope. For an instant, Kevin could see their determined grimaces as they struggled to haul Warren nearer. It reminded him of an insect hauling in a stunned victim, one that it was prepared to devour.

Helplessly, he and Sheila watched as Warren disappeared into the tree branches.

CHAPTER 54.

The two remaining nooses swayed like cobras mesmerizing their prey.

Sheila looked up to where she had last seen Warren's body. Kevin grabbed her hand. "Come on, we have to get out of here!"

They hurried over the rocks, heading to the right of the clearing, leaving the circle of three trees behind them, along with the town of Hydesville and the Fox home. Just as they left the field and re-entered the woods, there was a loud snap. They turned. From the distance, they could see Warren's body had been dropped back into sight; he swung back and forth a few times, then was still, only twisting slowly on the taunt rope. It finally turned, then held its position so that his broken, distorted face stared directly at them.

"Let's go," Kevin said. They fled back into the Fox Woods.

###

After twenty minutes, they stopped to rest. Sheila thought about Warren, found herself slipping into renewed grief. She had only just met her uncle. He had such a loyalty to Derek David, had been so determined to find and rescue the man. It had led him to his death. "Come on," she said once they had rested. "We have to finish what Warren started. We have got to find Derek."

###

They walked on through the afternoon. The Fox Woods continued to spread out before and around them, never thinning out. All they knew to do was forge ahead, one foot in front of the other. Neither spoke much, each a captive audience to his or her own thoughts.

Kevin was used to the bare-bones logic of real estate and financing. Houses had square footage that never changed, there were factual comps you could consult when setting a price for a sale, people's financial history and incomes determined whether or not they could qualify for a loan and for how much. Questions without answers were foreign to him; he was trained to deal with problems such as poor credit, failed inspections, complicated financing, the assertive effort required to secure second and third mortgages. He knew that when he worked hard, he would eventually solve the problem, find the buyer, make the sale.

But that was all before he encountered the entity known as Vanya Avery, the union children Roland and Margaret, the Fox sisters, the village of

Hydesville, and all the madness that had invaded his life. Now, all he had after all this time was crazy answers that made no sense.

Sweat stung his eyes. He wiped it away, watched Sheila stumbling on ahead of him. She moved purposely, like a machine that was plowing ever onward, stomping over the hilly terrain. She was tough, secure, dedicated to herself, to Kevin, to their relationship. He would marry her when this was all over, whatever *this* was. And they would go through life, sharing all their hopes and dreams…

Well, *almost* all their dreams. The memory of the one dream he had never told Sheila about surfaced languidly, like a flower slowly opening. His crotch grew tight and heavy as he recalled the erotic dream he'd had about Vanya.

He couldn't wait to see her again.

With each step, Kevin was more aroused as he thought about her. It made walking awkward, uncomfortable; he didn't want to stop thinking about her, which only made him swell up harder. It was so pleasant to succumb to thoughts of her; ever since he had the dream—had it only been last night?—the images kept replaying themselves. It was like trying to hold a flotation device underwater; it would always bob back to the surface. It was impossible to restrain or contain his thoughts of her. That morning he had masturbated three times, but still wasn't satisfied, still lusted for her, wouldn't be fulfilled until he had another chance with her. *I'll give you what you want*, he thought. But not in a dream, he wanted to touch her when he was fully awake…

He thought he heard Sheila saying something up ahead, but it sounded more like whispering. Who was speaking? The voice, or voices, hissed breathlessly but he couldn't make out the words over the crackling sound of a fire, the rapid smacking of moist lips. He tried to discern what was being spoken, but it was like static through a radio or a hive of insects…

Sheila had stopped, was facing him. He tilted his head to empty out all the buzzy noise, but everything just swarmed louder.

Sheila screamed at him.

"Your eyes!"

She backed away from him, turned, fled.

He was right behind her.

Sheila's shoes thudded madly over the ground, scattering pebbles and rocks, slashing past foliage, pushing aside tree branches. Her heart was pounding painfully but fear pumped in adrenaline and energy; she kept up her pace. She had to keep running, had to get away from Kevin and whatever he had become.

Behind her, she heard him as he crashed his way in pursuit. His eyes! Bright green, and the maniacal look. Why had he changed, just like earlier that morning? If he caught her, what would he do to her?

Within minutes, her legs were tired, getting heavier, her lungs were beginning to tighten, burn. Her side ached, a cramp was embracing her right calve. She couldn't catch her breath, she could hear Kevin's labored gasps closing in on her.

Dear God, help me!

Like a car running out of gas, her pace slackened, she started to limp, felt she was breaking down. Behind her, Kevin seemed to be having troubles of his own; the space between them had started to widen a bit. Then he stumbled, cursed, crashed to the ground. Sheila took a moment to glance back, make certain he had fallen. She could hear him thrashing about, wondered if he was injured, wondered what color his eyes were.

She risked stopping for a moment, frantically massaged her leg, poked at her side, tried to break up the painful knot that was there. She winced, wanted a drink, wanted food, a bed, a rest with Kevin—the real Kevin—not whatever the thing was behind her. She had to get going before he recovered. There was an incline directly in front of her. She groaned inwardly, charged ahead. Grunting with effort, she staggered up the hill, glad she would be able to let gravity help her down the other side.

At the top, she saw a deserted compound below. Four buildings, all in various states of ruin. They reminded her of a small army barracks. Each was alike with a sloping roof, uniformed line of windows, all painted industrial tan, which was peeling. The sidewalks that crisscrossed between the units were cracked, weeds between the squares. The landscaping throughout the area was either dead or wildly overgrown.

The buildings provided a place to hide and that's what she needed. She slid, ran, stumbled down the hill. Her feet met the sidewalk with a sharp *Plop!*

Where was Kevin?

She probably only had a few seconds before he'd appear, spot her, attack her. Sheila darted between two buildings on the left. A sign lay scratched and battered in the overgrowth. A fleeting glance at the faded lettering made her stop, look closer. She knelt down, brushed away some of the dirt and grime to be certain she was reading it correctly:

Keilgarden Colony. Established 1948.

"Warren questioned if it even existed," she whispered as she touched the sign to be certain it was real, read the words aloud: "Keilgarden Colony. Established 1948." Confused, she could only stare at it, repeating the information over and over, not wanting to believe what was right in front of her. She knew precious seconds were being lost, but she needed to take a moment, let the facts before her fully register.

She finally stood. With one last puzzled glance at the sign, she ran to the closest building. The rusted door had twisted off its hinges, so it was easy gaining entry. She stepped gingerly inside, apprehensive about disturbing any wild animals that may have made a home there, but then remembered she had never seen or heard any birds, animals or insects in the area. Most likely, she was alone.

Peering deep into the gloom, she could make out several short, battered tables for young children. Up front, a teacher's desk had been broken in half from the portion of the roof that had collapsed on it. She walked around the room, crunching over broken glass from the windows and other bits of debris. She needed a place to hide and a weapon. In a closet, she found a metal pipe about two feet long. She slapped it against her palm a few times; it would do fine.

She ventured further into the barrack searching for a place where she could take cover. She glanced nervously out the shattered, filthy windows. No sign of Kevin yet; where was he? Had he really injured himself, needed her help? Were his eyes still green? The heavy silence was disturbing, kept her on the edge of anxiety.

Overhead, something thumped.

She almost screamed, clamped her hand over her mouth, gripped the pipe tighter.

Was it Kevin? Had he somehow gotten into the building and upstairs without her knowing? In the room above, an item slid across the floor. She tried to discern the sound. Her hands had gone slick with perspiration; the metal bar could easily slide from her grasp if she wasn't careful. She rubbed her hand on her pant leg, re-gripped the pipe.

What or who was upstairs, what were the sounds she was hearing? She strained to listen; the room itself seemed to tighten with tension. It was as if something was gathering itself together, preparing to lash out.

Suddenly, she knew she was not alone, felt the pull of something as it studied her. Sheila spun around. In the back of the classroom, the opened double doors revealed a hallway, several more rooms.

At the far end of the corridor, a good fifty feet away, stood Katie, Maggie and Leah Fox. In the dim shadows, the sister's long, thick black dresses seeped into the blackness around them. Maggie was on the left, Leah on the right, and between them was Katie, the youngest. She had her arms around her sisters as if she was holding them all together. Their pale faces seemed suspended in air. They gazed mournfully at Sheila as they had in the photograph she and Kevin had seen on the wall in the Fox home and in the library.

"What do you want?" she managed to ask, speaking loud enough for her voice to carry. The women didn't respond. Sheila thought she saw a slight movement. Did Katie adjust her arm, the one that rested on Leah's shoulder? Did Maggie tilt her head a bit? Had Leah pursed her lips—was she going to speak or was she making an effort to hold her tongue? She was the oldest, most powerful sister, the one who had managed her sibling's careers as mediums, the one Roland had summoned.

Outside, a rushed clump of footsteps on the sidewalk.

Was it Kevin? Sheila wondered. *If so, which one? Brown eyes or green eyes?*

The Fox sisters heard the noise, too. They, as one, turned to the right where the sound had come from. Sheila followed their gaze. Through the large broken window, Kevin was staggering about, calling for her. He sounded normal, like he was looking for her, not hunting her. She glanced back down the gloomy hallway to see what the sisters were doing. Only thick shadows remained.

Had they really been there? Sheila asked herself. *Was I only seeing what Vanya wanted me to?*

Overhead, a sharp thump, followed by another, and a third. Whatever was up there had roused itself, seemed to be on the move, perhaps was heading down the stairs. Metal pipe in hand, Sheila hurried outside to check on Kevin before the thing from upstairs found her.

She came up behind him. "Turn around. Slowly."

Startled, he did as she said. When he faced her, he asked, "Are you okay? What happened? What is this place?"

"Don't come any closer! I want to see your eyes."

"My eyes?"

She kept the pipe raised to show him she wasn't kidding, took a step forward, leaned in, examined his face. The awful, intensely green hue to his eyes was gone.

"Choose us some characters," she demanded.

"No, I'm not in the mood. Not with you brandishing a metal pipe at me."

They embraced, then settled on the weedy grass, their backs against the building.

She explained that they were in the ruins of the Colony—"I guess Warren was wrong and it *does* exist"—told him about his strange behavior, why she ran from him, and the Fox sisters appearing to her.

"I don't remember...*anything* about chasing you," he said, baffled.

"Somehow, Vanya has gotten into you, takes over whenever she wants."

Kevin went still, closed his eyes, then, in a miserable rush of words, confessed to Sheila the dream he had had about Vanya, admitted how aroused he became at the recollections. When he was done, a wracking sob broke out of him. "God, help me, Sheila! You're right, she's *in* me, somehow." He grabbed his head as if he was in pain, hid his face.

Sheila tried to comfort him, but drew back, was disgusted to see he had an erection. It was as if he had cheated on her, *was* cheating on her at that very moment. It repulsed her. Disturbed, angry, confused at all she was feeling, she could only watch as he continued to weep, his voice muffled. Then she thought about what Warren had said, finally asked him, "In your dream…did you…satisfy her?"

He looked at her, his face red, blotchy. She could see the agony in his eyes, but she had to know.

"What? Why would you ask that?" he said.

"Because of what Warren told us, remember? Derek's brother Oswald wasn't able to satisfy her, so Vanya killed him, moved on to Derek, didn't let up until she was pregnant. So, tell me, what happened in your dream?"

He opened his mouth, closed it, slumped against the building. "I…don't remember."

"I do," Vanya said, stepping out from the side of the building. Before they could react, Vanya snatched the pipe from Sheila's hand, threw it into the overgrowth. The three of them watched it spin end over end until it vanished.

Sheila and Kevin scrambled up, stood before Vanya.

"I very much remember what happened between me and Kevin." Vanya wiped her hands clean, then said to Kevin in a mocking, dismissive tone, "Believe me, you start quickly enough, but you certainly don't provide a satisfying finish. But we will try again." She turned to Sheila. "Some people just need time to warm up to me."

The two women scrutinized one another for a moment. Neither broke the face-off. As Sheila stared into Vanya's bright green eyes, the revelation struck her hard in the gut. Infuriated, she cried out, "It was *you* who was in the car with my parents!"

"No, it wasn't me," Vanya said calmly, her gaze steady on Sheila. "It was your Aunt Letty."

"That's impossible," Sheila said, barely able to get the words out. "Aunt Letty wasn't with them. She was at home, caring for me that night."

"No," Vanya said, "the *television set* was with you, remember? You were watching TV for a few hours, Letty had made you dinner, then she set you off into the other room while she cleaned up. You didn't really know where she was, did you?"

Confused, Sheila said, "But how—"

"She became an apparition," Vanya said simply. "Something I taught her. She went into a deep trance, sent a specter of herself to you parent's car. It terrified them, your father was startled and distracted so he lost control of the car. That was all there was to it."

Astonished, Sheila and Kevin could only stand there, stunned by all that Vanya began to explain to them. "The shock of the accident disoriented Letty, causing her apparition to linger at the car wreck when it should have returned to her body. It took several minutes for it to withdraw from the area. That's why the papers picked up the story from eyewitnesses about a 'third woman' in the car. By the time the police and ambulance arrived, the manifestation of your aunt had vanished."

Kevin asked, "Why would Letty allow herself to be used to cause the car accident? It was her sister and brother-in-law."

"She had no choice," Vanya said, surprised at Kevin's question. She looked at both of them with renewed curiosity. "It was a waste of my time having you live with your parents. They only *watched* you, I needed to guide and *instruct* you. Teach you. It was much more convenient to have Letty care for you, it gave me much easier access."

They didn't respond, only looked at her.

"You really don't seem to understand, do you?" she said. "*'Do as I do.'* It's a command. Warren had no choice back there in the trees. Neither did Oswald. Or Derek. Or Letty. None of them have a choice in what occurs. I tell them what to do, and they do it."

"'Do as I do'," Sheila murmured.

"Yes, exactly."

"But why?" was all Sheila could think to ask. "Why would my aunt spend any time with you or want to learn anything from you?"

"Because she owed me," Vanya said. "I introduced her to the love of her life. She'd do anything for him, or me."

Sheila couldn't figure it out, had to know.

"My father," Vanya finally said, smiling. "I introduced your aunt to my father, and they had a child together…"

"No!" Sheila shook her head. "No! I know that's not true! I would have known if she had a child."

"Know *thyself*, child," Vanya said softly, waited for Sheila to comprehend what she was saying.

"What are you implying?" Sheila went pale, a lost look on her face, her eyes vacant, her thoughts murky. "My parents—"

"Your *adoptive* parents. Don't you remember?"

CHAPTER 55.

Kevin had been watching the encounter between the two women, shaken by all that had been said. He moved closer to Sheila, put his arm around her. She was trembling so violently, he thought she might become sick.

"Do you remember your sessions with me?" Vanya asked Sheila. "Or the time afterward, with the doctor? The one your parents sent you to, Dr. Lewis? He was trying to help you, Sheila, help you remember. Did you block your time with him out of your memories, too? Like you tried to shut me out?"

Sheila looked helplessly at Kevin. "I…it's not true. I don't know what she's saying. I don't remember, I…"

Vanya said, "You were already seeing a doctor at the time, trying to make sense of your abilities. And I can just imagine what would have happened if you had been told your gifts *weren't* from your Mom and Dad at all, but were from—"

"Stop it!" Kevin shouted. Sheila was sobbing, her body shaking in convulsions.

"You're lying!" Sheila screamed, her voice ragged with pain. "I don't remember *any* of this!"

"Really? You don't remember me visiting you? Our times together as teacher and pupil? It was the same thing that I did with Ann and her son, and the Fox sisters. Unsealing the box and following the bouncing ball was your favorite game."

Sheila felt Vanya had opened her up, was reaching inside of her like she was a doll house, rearranging her life, taking out what mattered most, replacing it with a foreign object, a different life. But the more Vanya spoke, the greater clarity came, along with a fuzzy disorientation. Images began to surface. Sheila could recall visits with a beautiful blonde woman with radiant green eyes, a lady who always brought several sealed wooden boxes, requested that Sheila attempt to open them. When she succeeded, there was a child's ball inside for the two of them to play with. Sheila enjoyed their times together but had been told they were a secret, not to be spoken of to anyone, only to be forgotten unless told otherwise.

Kevin squeezed Sheila's shoulder. "You okay?"

"She's fine," Vanya said. "She's just now recalling who she belongs to, who her family really is."

Sheila shook her head slowly. "No, I don't belong to you, I'm not part of your family…"

"Aren't you?" Vanya asked, bemused. "Remember what I just said. I introduced Letty to the love of her life, my father. Together, they had a child. But your aunt was a good Catholic, couldn't admit to being an unmarried mother having a baby.

Her sister Rachel couldn't seem to have a child. So, it was a perfect solution for Sam and Rachel to adopt you."

Sheila fell silent, crushed, overwhelmed, buried by all Vanya was saying. She wanted to fight off each new piece of information that was presented to her, slap it away, stomp on it until it no longer existed. But she knew it was true; in the most hateful way possible, the facts as laid out by Vanya tore at the very core of who she was, who she thought she was, but it was all true.

One question rose from where so many were clamoring. She wasn't certain she wanted the answer. Still, she had to ask. "If Letty is my biological mother, then Roland is—"

"—your half-brother," Vanya nodded, smiling. "You and he share the same father, my father."

Sheila felt numb inside, scrapped clean, a shell with no identity, nothing to hold on to. She was in freefall. Dizzy, she felt Kevin hold her so she wouldn't collapse.

Vanya broke into the moment. "You need to take especially good care of yourself now."

Warily, Sheila asked why.

Vanya looked at her. "Come now, don't be coy. Know thyself."

Kevin looked curiously at Sheila, who said, "I don't know what she's talking about!"

"Father recently manifested himself to you in a dream-union, just like I did with Kevin," Vanya said calmly. "However, unlike my coupling with Kevin, Father was successful. He always is. He satisfied himself, and you. Remember, I can see as well as hear…"

"No! No!" Sheila said, her eyes wide. "No! I don't remember any dream!"

"But it doesn't mean it didn't happen, right? Do you think it matters if you remember or not?"

"I'm *not* pregnant! And if I was, do you think I'd *keep* whatever union child monstrosity your father planted in me?"

"You *will* have a son," Vanya said firmly, "and not a union child but the very first *pure* union child. Think of it: The first offspring to inherit the gifts of my father and your own abilities. Finally…"

From behind them, a sound from the second story of the building. The three of them turned. A window squeaked painfully as it was opened.

Roland David pushed aside a rotten window blind, looked down at them. His emerald eyes glowed in the mid-afternoon gloom. Sheila assumed he had been the one upstairs the entire time she had been in the barracks. He leaned out the window, grinned at them, waved. It was astonishing to see him; he was no longer a five-year-old, he looked to be a teenager. Vanya returned his greeting, calling to him fondly.

Kevin used the distraction to grab Sheila's hand, nearly pulled her off her feet as they fled the area. They dashed past the second building, not bothering to look back to see if they were being pursued. After rounding the corner of the third structure, they slowed, then stopped, listened carefully. No pounding footfalls were hastening after them.

Sheila held Kevin's arm. "If what she said was true and I'm adopted, then that means Warren was right, I *am* a union child! And if I'm pregnant by her father—"

"No!" Kevin said. "Don't let her get in your head! Remember, all she does is lie."

He yanked at the door to the barracks. The handle broke off in his hand, but the door swung open. Inside, the air was stale, musty. Kevin pulled the door behind them. Cracks and breaks in the ceiling and walls let in slivers of light. Gradually, their eyes adjusted to the dim interior. They saw file cabinets, sealed crates, stacked office furniture, piles of papers and boxes; just an old storage area.

Then, out of the strained, black silence.

Hiss. Clink. Hiss. Clink. Hiss. Clink.

"It's Derek!" Sheila whispered excitedly. "He's here, he's *alive!*"

They fumbled about in the dark, trying to locate where the noise of Derek's respirator was coming from. They smacked their shins against boxes, banged their elbows against filing cabinets, stirred up mounds of dust, yet they were not able to find him.

Hiss. Clink.

They held their breaths. The sound seemed to be coming from above them.

Hiss. Clink.

"No, wait, it's in front of us," Kevin said.

They tried to isolate the location of the noise, but it swirled about, at times overhead, then behind them or off to the right. It gradually settled so they were able to inch their way forward to where it was originating from. There was a dim shaft of light providing them a feeble beacon to follow.

"There!" Sheila said. She hurried forward.

Hiss. Clink.

They felt around, touched the respirator apparatus. There was no wheelchair attached.

"Where's Derek?" she asked. "Why isn't it connected to him?"

"And…what's making the machine breathe?" Kevin said, a tremor in his voice.

Hiss. Clink.

"He can't survive without it," Sheila said, frantic now. They moved as quickly as they could through the storage room, found the back door which led into a long hallway. The tall, filthy windows on either side of the corridor allowed in dusty streams of light. They tried each closed door as they maneuvered down the hall, but they were all locked.

Kevin said, "There's no reason these old doors should be secured; it's like they knew we were coming."

From the opposite end, a floorboard creaked. Then, the *thud, thud, thud* of a bouncing ball, a child's delighted giggle. From out of the shadows, they saw a short figure emerge, awkwardly bouncing a rubber ball. As the youngster approached, they saw it was a girl about three years of age; dark blue dress, white socks, Mary Jane shoes that clicked on the tiled floor.

Sheila whispered, "It's Vanya's daughter, Margaret."

"And she's got one of those egg things, probably about ready to hatch," Kevin said.

"Then let's get it!" Sheila rushed forward, grabbed the ball between bounces. The child shrieked in surprise. Kevin and Sheila ran off with it while Margaret immediately started screaming with rage, calling out for her mother. At the far end of the hallway, the three Fox sisters materialized out of the shadows. Their thick, heavy dresses began to rustle loudly as they began to move forward. Behind Kevin and Sheila, the outraged cries of Margaret continued.

"I've had…enough of this," Sheila said suddenly, her tone hard.

"What are you going to do?" Kevin asked anxiously. "What *can* you do?"

"I'm going to get a little closer to my family!" She started down the hallway toward Katie, Maggie and Leah, ignoring Kevin's pleas for her to stay with him. She held Margaret's ball out like a weapon. She sensed Kevin had fallen in close behind her, took comfort in that, a unified front.

The Fox sisters stopped advancing, seemed leery that Sheila was aggressively moving toward them. At the same time, little Margaret went silent. Without turning around, Sheila sensed Vanya had arrived at the opposite end of the hallway to comfort her daughter. She didn't care; all her attention was on the three sisters in front of her. Sheila continued forward, her hand gripping the ball tightly. The Fox sisters glared warily at her.

Up close, Sheila saw that Katie had a rather pinched, sharp nose, a high, wide forehead, a rather bland face. Maggie had dark, expressionless eyes, a round, flat nose. Leah had a matronly, unlined face; her eyes were wide, full, defiant, dared you to look away. A faint, coy smile cured her lips. She was clearly the authority figure in the family, the disciplinary, the one whom the sisters deferred to in all matters, the most dominant of the three.

Sheila spoke harshly to the Leah apparition. "You *used* your sisters, exploited their deception for your own gain, never realizing that the entire time, Vanya was tricking *you* to achieve her goals. She played you! And now she brings you back to use all the power she gave you to destroy our world."

Kevin watched as Katie and Maggie stepped closer to Leah. The three of them held hands, united. The younger sisters gazed with adoration at Leah, then all three of them broke out into delighted smiles and laughter. They were laughing at what Sheila had said. It was obvious: They had known all along what Vanya was up to, had yielded happily to her. There was no revelation here, nothing and no one to call out. They had been willing participants to the entity's plan from the beginning.

Leah's countenance shifted from mirth to a triumphant calm. Maggie and Katie tittered for a moment longer, then went silent as they watched Sheila. A gentle awareness settled over Sheila, the realization that a child was growing inside of her. A boy. The phrase, *An heir and a spare* took root in Sheila's thoughts. *What does that mean?* she wondered.

Abruptly, the burning taste of whiskey filled her mouth. She coughed, spat it out, held the ball up higher. "Who is this?"

"Another family member," Vanya called out from the opposite end of the hallway. Sheila and Kevin turned. The woman was holding Margaret's hand; the child was whimpering, rubbing her eyes.

Margaret started to murmur, "Mar. Ea. Mar. Ea." Kept repeating the words like a chant; the sounds echoed around the corridor. *She's saying the name Maria, wants to summon her,* Sheila realized, remembering John and Margaret had other children. Warren had warned them that Vanya wanted all of the Fox children restored.

Sheila turned, began to pound the ball against the wall as hard as she could. Enraged, Margaret stopped speaking, screamed, yanked her hand from her mother's, charged Sheila. Kevin kept his eyes on the Fox sisters, who also were agitated yet remained in place. Margaret reached Sheila, began kicking at her, pulling at her arm. Sheila turned to the little girl, smashed the rubber ball as hard as she could across her face. Margaret fell to the ground; her cries shrill as she rolled in a furious tantrum on the filthy floor. Vanya hurried down the hallway to her daughter while the Fox sisters retreated deeper into the shadows.

Kevin grabbed Sheila's hand. They ran past Vanya and Margaret, burst through the double doors at the end of the corridor, continued past the third barrack. Once they were on the far side of the wall, they raced around the building, came up short, gasped in horror.

An enormous tree had arisen out of the earth. It took only an instant for Sheila to see what it contained; she groaned, staggered backward into Kevin's arms. He was silent, his mouth opened in shock, his eyes locked on the dreadfulness before them.

A rope had been thrown over a high branch of the tree. One end of the rope was anchored to the earth by the deep weight of a smashed wheelchair that had been dropped from a great height.

The other end finished off with a noose from which swung the horribly scarred torso of Derek David.

CHAPTER 56.

From behind the tree, Roland appeared. Now a teenager, his face had broadened, his shoulders and chest had filled out, there was a knowing, sullen demeanor about him. He was dressed in a stained, faded blue work shirt covered by a ragged black vest. Torn jeans, filthy work boots completed his attire.

He gazed up at Derek's torso which was twisting in the breeze. "Don't need him anymore, he was being kept around just in case after Vanya got what she wanted out of him. These last few weeks, he was just bait. Derek is the reason Warren showed up here and stayed here. And we only kept Warren around to help reel in you two." He stepped forward, spun the exposed wheel of the upside down wheelchair. It revolved unsteadily for a moment, then shuddered to a stop. He suggestively rubbed his hand in a circular motion over his crotch. His adolescent voice cracked as he said, "By tomorrow evening, Margaret should be ripe enough for me."

He stopped touching himself, looked at them. "Give me the ball."

"Fuck you," Sheila said. "Besides, I think I killed whatever is in it. Why do you want it so badly?"

"Vanya needs *all* the Fox family back. You know that. That's Maria you're holding."

"If Vanya's so powerful and mighty, why can't she just call them forth, why does she need union children to do it?"

He shrugged. "Rules are rules."

Kevin asked, "Then who called Maggie and Katie forth? You and Margaret weren't around."

Roland looked at Sheila. "Ask your girlfriend."

"What?" Sheila said, taking a step back as if pushed.

"There's so much you don't remember," Roland sighed. "Vanya's already had to remind you that your favorite game was 'open the box, follow the bouncing ball.' Only you were able to unseal the boxes, call forth what was inside. Maybe you just conveniently forgot that many, many years ago you were the one who summoned Maggie and Katie Fox."

Kevin watched Sheila's reaction.

"No," she said, shaking her head. "No, I didn't. That's not true, it's a mistake—"

Roland grimaced. "Oh, you made a huge mistake all right! That one time you were by yourself you opened the *wrong* box, fucked this up royally, summoned John Fox instead of one of the children! Once he was able, he took Leah's box away, hid it back in the cottage. We could have accomplished all of this *decades* ago if it wasn't for you screwing everything up!"

Sheila couldn't process all that he was saying. She noticed that even as he stood there, he was changing; his green eyes were more luminous, his body was shifting or shimmering in some unnatural way. *He's aging, growing right in front of me,* she thought. *If we don't hurry...*

"Where's Edith?" she asked.

Roland glanced back up at the tree as if that's where the answer was. "She went for a walk in the Fox Woods. Haven't seen her since."

Sheila thought of Warren, assumed Edith had met the same end. She recalled the phrase *Slave, not servant,* had come to mind when she had first met Edith. She was never really a part of this, never wanted to be. In her hand, the ball was warm, becoming warmer, didn't seem damaged. *This is Maria,* she thought, marveling at the realization. *I'm holding Maria Fox.* Buzzy sounds filled her head, wavered, faded.

"You can both leave now," Roland said. "Vanya doesn't need you here anymore." He pointed. "There's your car. All gassed up, road map in the glove compartment since I hear the GPS doesn't work well up here. Two checks on the dashboard, too, one for each of you. Not bad for three months' work."

"Give me the car keys," Kevin said. He swallowed nervously, grimaced at the sudden, burning taste in his mouth.

"They're already in the car."

"I don't believe you. Get them, bring them to me," Kevin said. "Then you can have the ball."

Roland sighed, sauntered off to the car.

While he was away, Kevin found a heavy rock the size of his fist that he palmed.

He whispered a plan to Sheila, then said, "Don't think about it. Remember, it can see as well as hear." She nodded, located a short, thick branch with a sharp edge that she jammed into her back pocket. They both filled their minds with images of stars from old movies—Spencer Tracy and Katherine Hepburn, Humphrey Bogart and Lauren Bacall, Rock Hudson and Doris Day, each couple laughing, crying, kissing in scenes from their films—and positioned themselves so their backs were to the tree, their weapons concealed.

Roland returned, jingling the keys in front of him. "Drive carefully, now that you're with child and all. Vanya wants you to get home safely."

Sheila stepped forward, extended the ball in front of her. The bait. She concentrated on Paul Newman and Joanne Woodward in *Rally Round the Flag, Boys!*

The rock was substantial in Kevin's hand. He moved deftly behind Roland, conjuring up images of Richard Carlson and Julie Adams in *Creature from the Black Lagoon.*

At the prospect of possessing the ball, Roland's eyes opened wide. He reached for it. Kevin crushed his skull with the rock. Sheila finished him off with the branch, using it as a knife. By the time they were through with Roland, his head had been separated from what little remained of his body.

Once they were in the Volvo, and the engine roared to life, they couldn't help shouting out with glee. Exhilarated, Kevin floored it. The car shot out of the ruins of the Keilgarden Colony.

Roland hadn't lied; the tank was full, there were two checks for them on the dash, the map was in the glove compartment along with a readable printout of their email directions. After Sheila figured out where they were, she said. "Okay, this side road… stay on it until we see the broken fence post…"

###

Fifteen minutes later, they were speeding through the deserted town of Hydesville. They passed the Fox house on their right. Neither of them bothered to give it a second glance, although Sheila thought she felt the ball grow warmer for an instant.

"What we did to Roland…" Sheila started to say.

"What about it? Remember what Warren said, he wasn't even human."

"I know. But his screams…" She paused. "Thinking about it—"

"Then don't think about it," Kevin cautioned her. "Ever again. It had to be done, right?" Then: "I wish we could have done the same with Vanya and Margaret."

"No! I couldn't have done that to a little girl…"

"I could have."

Sheila didn't know how to respond to such a cold statement. She gazed out the window as the landscape fled past. Hours from now, they'd be home. Then, in a few months, she'd be a mother. Would she marry Kevin? Did it even matter anymore? She had other plans now. She rested her hands on her lap, on her stomach.

An heir and a spare.

It only took her a few seconds before it dawned on her: *Of course! With Roland gone, Margaret will need someone to mate with. After all, Margaret was*

Derek David's daughter, the last of the Fox bloodline.

"Why so quiet?" Kevin asked.

"Just thinking."

Kevin left her to her distractions, didn't want to push her. It *had* been a brutal event with Roland, but with him destroyed, little Margaret—Vanya and Derek David's daughter—would have no one to reproduce with. And since the Fox bloodline was now wiped out, Vanya's plan was finished, there was no way she could proceed with it. He wondered what would happen to the entity? Would it vanish, seek some other world to corrupt, or just wait for another opportunity like the Fox sisters had presented? *She's patient*, Warren had said. *Ultimately, that is her greatest power, along with using supernatural phenomena to distract from her true intentions.*

The Volvo kicked up a cloud of dust on the backroads. Kevin looked forward to getting on I-90 and the smooth parkway. He glanced over at Sheila; she looked exhausted, her face drawn. "Hey, why don't you rest? Get some sleep."

She stretched, smiled sleepily at him, murmured, "Thanks, good idea." She reached into the back seat, dragged her pillow out from her bag. Soon she was fast asleep, head cushioned against the jostling car window.

###

Four hours later she woke. Kevin had the radio on. Sheila yawned, rubbed her eyes.

Kevin glanced over. "Hey, sleepyhead. Thanks for the company and sharing the drive with me."

"Sorry, I was so tired all of a sudden. Where are we?"

"About forty-five minutes north of the city."

The sign for Valhalla flashed by the car. Kevin glanced in the rearview mirror. A few times in the past hour, the pile of luggage had shifted, he thought he had seen… shapes. It had startled him until he had looked again, realized it was only his duffle bag with a tennis shoe escaping through the opening.

Sheila was bent over, digging through her purse for some gum or breath mints, asking about traffic, had there been much, why hadn't he awakened her if he wanted a break from driving.

He checked the mirror again, couldn't help himself. *Just in case.* But all he saw was the Taconic State Parkway rushing behind them, no movement from the back seat.

Sheila had pulled down the visor mirror, was brushing her hair, still chatting.

He thought he heard something behind him. He glanced quickly. Nothing. Of course there's nothing there. Just our jumbled bags shifting.

Sheila asked him something.

"What?"

She repeated herself, he didn't respond, couldn't.

Into his mouth, a harsh, grainy liquid had swelled until he gagged on it, coughed the brown stuff up all over the windshield. It dripped down his chin. More of it flooded his mouth. He started to choke on the amber alcohol. He wondered why Sheila didn't seem to be aware of what was happening to him, the whisky that was flowing from his mouth.

In the backseat, the Amish man rose up, reached out to them.

Kevin turned around, started to scream.

"Watch the road!" Sheila cried as she instinctively shielded her baby with her hands. Her eyes, bright green and terrified at what was happening, locked in with Kevin's as the car smashed through the guardrail.

CAR ACCIDENT KILLS TIMES' REPORTER, HER BOYFRIEND; UNIDENTIFIED MALE MISSING

New York Times' reporter Sheila Irving, 35, and her 33-year-old boyfriend, Kevin Jackson, were killed Tuesday afternoon when their car, driven by Jackson, broke through the guardrail at Route 22 near Valhalla and plunged 100 feet into the reservoir. Witnesses at the scene claim that a third person, a man with shoulder-length hair who appeared to be "Amish in appearance" was also seen at the wreckage, although his whereabouts are not known.

Irving, a features writer, had been employed by the *Times* for eight years. Jackson was a broker with Cochran Realty.

At the time of her death, Irving was working on a book about the Spiritualist movement which was scheduled to be published next year. Modern Spiritualism began in the village of Hydesville, New York in 1848 when Maggie and Katie Fox supposedly heard ghostly "rappings" in their farmhouse. The Fox sisters later admitted that they caused the sounds themselves.

Irving and Jackson were returning from Hydesville when their car went off the road.

Visibility was good that afternoon, the roads were clear of debris and there was little traffic. An investigation into the cause of the accident and efforts to locate the unidentified Amish man are underway.

END

EDITOR'S AFTERWORD

A Spooky Concurrence

Truth really is stranger than fiction.

I regularly work as an editor for HellBound Books, an up and coming small press publisher. A few days ago, I received a new editing assignment; a book called *The Children of Hydesville* by Jeff C. Stevenson. I have never met Jeff. I had not even heard of this author before, which is not so unusual in my line of work.

I immediately recognized the name Hydesville, where his story is set, and the memory of the Fox sisters' house sprang to mind. It couldn't be the *same* Hydesville. I mean, what are the odds? There must be a number of towns across America sharing the same name. Writers frequently write about fictitious towns, right? So, I started reading, which quickly resulted in a cold chill running down my spine. Right in the first paragraph he wrote: *"The Fox sisters and their family, however, were very real, as is most—but not all—of what I've included in this story about what occurred in Hydesville in 1848."*

This goes way beyond a freakish coincidence. It borders on the paranormal. If anyone knows a word which describes such a weird turn of events, I would love to hear from you. If serendipity has a dark, twisted and disturbing relative, that is probably the word I am after.

Here is a little family history:

Before I was born, my parents lived in a tiny little cottage in the small town of Hydesville, on the outskirts of Newark in upstate New York. Directly across the street from their cottage stood a house with—to say the very least—an interesting past. In the mid-1800's, a family with three sisters lived in the house, and even back then it had a reputation for being haunted. The family was often frightened by unexplained sounds. The three sisters began claiming to be mediums and were apparently responsible for the creation of Modern Spiritualism. Spiritualism is a religious practice based on supposed communication through a medium with the spirits of the dead. A medium is a person who uses their psychic or intuitive abilities to see the past, present, and future by tuning into the spirit energy surrounding them. In the late 1800s, the Fox sisters confessed to having orchestrated the weird happenings in Hydesville, but the Modern Spiritualism movement continued to grow nonetheless.

In April of 1916 the original Fox house was moved to Lily Dale, New York. On September 12, 1955 that house burned to the ground. In 1948, when the original cellar was dug up, some human hair and bones were found. Examination revealed that some of the bones were from a human skull. Later, an exact replica of the original Fox house would be built on the original stone foundation by a man named John.

All of this is documented.

According to my mother, who was newly married at nineteen years of age, John was a recluse. He was also rumored to be a Satanist. She talked of him traveling to another country to bring the body of his late wife back to the house, and having the grounds declared a cemetery so that he could have her buried in his backyard. She talked of visiting his house a few times, and of all the books on the occult she found there. One day, John showed up on her doorstep bearing a cookbook and a jar of honey. He told her to use the recipes in the book and to cook with the honey, or her child would be born with bad blood. My mother was taken aback. Although she *was* pregnant, she had told no one, not even my father. Still, she paid little mind to the ramblings of an old, very odd man and ignored his advice. I was born prematurely and with jaundice, which required me to have a complete blood transfusion shortly after birth.

So that was how I got my start in life.

The house burned beyond repair in 1983, and John was in the process of rebuilding when he passed on. The house stood—sorta—vacant. It was the talk of late night slumber parties where we would try to scare each other. We would each in turn tell stories about seeing flickering lights in the windows and hearing noises we couldn't explain. When I was about fifteen, a friend and I got up the nerve to go into the house. I remember my heart beating out of my chest, as we giggled like we were insane. Everywhere around us, there were books strewn all over the floor. Books on the occult and Satanism. They were charred. I remember picking one up and how it had smudged my fingers with black soot. I remember how thick and heavy the atmosphere was. And I remember hearing noises from deeper inside the house. Noises that made my friend and I run frantically for the door, and not stop until we were far enough away where we felt safe. I remember looking back at the house and thinking that I saw flickering lights in the window.

Close to thirty years later, I have children of my own. From time to time, the Fox sisters' house would come to mind, and I would wonder just exactly what it was I felt in that place, and what exactly I had heard and seen.

So what type of "coincidence" is required for Jeff C. Stevenson's book to arrive on Xtina Marie's desk? There are at least 10,000 horror writers trying to land a publishing deal in any given year. The US has more than fifty book publishers that publish books in the horror genre. There are several editors who work for HellBound and yet this story managed to find its way to me.

Weird, right?

ABOUT YOUR AUTHOR

Jeff C. Stevenson is a professional member of Pen America, an active member of the Horror Writers Association, and a finalist for the Best Published Midsouth Science Fiction and Fantasy Darrell Award. Jeff has published more than two dozen dark fiction stories and has been included in anthologies alongside Clive Barker, Ramsey Campbell, Richard Chizmar, Jack Ketchum, Brian Lumley, Adam Nevill, Graham Masterton, Edgar Allan Poe and Algernon Blackwood. Jeff is the author of the Amazon #1 bestselling *FORTNEY ROAD*: The True Story of Life, Death, and Deception in a Christian Cult. Hellbound Books will publish his suspense thriller, *I'LL COME BACK TO GET YOU* in late 2018. Jeff also writes mainstream fiction under the pen name of Mary Saliger.

Author profile: http://goo.gl/dWEA8N

Twitter:
https://twitter.com/JeffCStevenson

<u>Other HellBound Books Titles</u>
<u>Available at:</u>
<u>www.hellboundbookspublishing.com</u>

The Southern House

There are some places that lie where the barrier between worlds is thin and growing thinner. These corridors are as old as the Earth itself, hidden in dark and forgotten places, waiting to be found. There is a being who stalks these places and travels between those worlds. He was given the name Mr. Shift by generations of children and madmen.

Just as Hickory Grimble hits rock bottom, he inherits his grandparents' farm and believes his luck is changing. He soon finds he inherited more than money and land.

Haunted by his own inner demons, now he has new problems. He begins to see strange creatures on the dark, sprawling acreage, animals that have no business living in middle Tennessee. He also discovers a decrepit, abandoned house in the forest that never seems to be in the same place twice.

Balanced on a razor's edge between, addiction and fate, Hick is now face to face with an ancient evil that has returned once more to claim more of the town's children.

Them

Ray Sanders returns home from Florida to bury his mother.

Soon, the supernatural evidence behind his mother's demise begins to surface in the form of dreams and mysterious happenings.

During all of the madness, Sanders must face his destiny and vanquish the generations-old evil that has plagued his family since the 1800's...

In 1854, Louis Sanders, with the help of Elias Atkins, dug a well to provide water to the family farm. What they did not anticipate was the water to be infested with Odomulites - ancient sins. These malevolent beings - were trapped in our world on their way to the spirit world - formed a pact of protection with both Sanders and Atkins; the families would serve as guardians of the Odomulite nests and in return, a blind eye would be cast when the Odomulites took host bodies to inhabit and feed upon. It was this pact, which in 2016 would propel Sanders and Julie Fontaine - a young woman with a special connection to the Spirit World - into the heart of the last active nest to rid the town of its insidious Odomulite population.

Blood in The Woods

Based upon true events...

For Jody, growing up in the late eighties and early nineties in the small Louisiana town of Hammond with his best friend Jack was filled with wonderful childhood memories.

Time spent playing in the woods, shooting pellet guns, blowing up mailboxes, fighting at school and upon the dawning of interest in the fairer sex, their carefree lives typical of children with few responsibilities and no worries beyond the next pop-quiz or getting to second base. As they grow older together and experience the joys and pains of life, love, family and friendship, they uncover a grim secret that their home town has kept, and through little more than an innocent, idle curiosity, Jody and Jack stumble upon something horrific in the woods and their lives quickly take a most sinister and dangerous turn as they find themselves hunted by an unspeakable evil...

No Rest For The Wicked

From beyond the grave, a murderous wife seeks to complete her revenge on those who betrayed her in life; a powerless domestic still fears for her immortal soul while trying to scare off anyone who comes too close; and the former plantation master - a sadistic doctor who puts more faith in the teachings of de Sade than the Bible - battle amongst themselves and with the living to reveal or keep hidden the dark secrets that prevent any of them from resting in peace.

When Eric and Grace McLaughlin purchase Greenbrier Plantation, their dreams are just as big as those who have tried to tame the place before them. But, the doctor has learned a thing or two over his many years in the afterlife, is putting those new skills to the test, and will go to great lengths in order to gain the upper hand. While Grace digs into the death-filled history of her new home, Eric soon becomes a pawn of the doctor's unsavory desires and rapidly growing power, and is hell-bent on stopping her.

"If you're looking for a chilling ghost story filled with mystery and escalating tension, look no further. No Rest for the Wicked is the real deal - an expansive, unfolding riddle between the living and the dead." Hunter Shea - author of *"Tortures of the Damned"* & *"We Are Always Watching"*

Worship Me

Something is listening to the prayers of St. Paul's United Church, but it's not the god they asked for; it's something much, much older.

A quiet Sunday service turns into a living hell when this ancient entity descends upon the house of worship and claims the congregation for its own.

The terrified churchgoers must now prove their loyalty to their new god by giving it one of their children or in two days time it will return and destroy them all.

As fear rips the congregation apart, it becomes clear that if they're to survive this untold horror, the faithful must become the faithless and enter into a battle against God itself.

But as time runs out, they discover that true monsters come not from heaven or hell…
…they come from within.

Demons, Devils and Denizens of Hell: Vol, 2

The second volume in HellBound Books' outstanding horror anthology fair teems with tales of Hades' finest citizens – both resident and vacationing in our earthly realm…

Compiled by the inimitable P. Mattern and featuring: Savannah Morgan, Andrew MacKay, Jaap Boekestein, James H Longmore, Stephanie Kelley, Ryan Woods, James Nichols, P. Mattern, Marcus Mattern, Gerri R Gray, and legion more…

Shopping List 2: Another Horror Anthology

Once again, HellBound Books brings you an outstanding collection of horror, dark, slippery things, and supernatural terror - all from the very best up and coming minds in the genre.

We have given each and every one of our authors the opportunity to have their shopping lists read by you, the most wonderful reading public, and have the darkest corners of their creative psyche laid bare for all to see...

In all, 21 stories to chill the soul, tingle the spine and keep you awake in the cold, murky hours of the night from: Erin Lee, The Truth Artist, John Barackman, Serena Daniels, M.R. Wallace, Isobel Blackthorn, Alex Laybourne, Jason J. Nugent, Josh Darling, Jovan Jones, Nick Swain, Douglas Ford, Craig Bullock, Craig Bullock, Jeff C. Stevenson, PC3, David F Gray, Sergio Palumbo, Donna Maria McCarthy, David Clark & Megan E. Morales

Jeff C. Stevenson

A HellBound Books LLC
Publication

http://www.hellboundbookspublishing.com

Printed in the United States of America

www.ingramcontent.com/pod-product-compliance
Lightning Source LLC
Chambersburg PA
CBHW050600170726
48283CB00001B/40